THE BODIES
IN THE
LIBRARY

THE BODIES
IN THE
LIBRARY

MARTY WINGATE

BERKLEY PRIME CRIME
NEW YORK

BERKLEY PRIME CRIME
Published by Berkley
An imprint of Penguin Random House LLC
1745 Broadway, New York, NY 10019

Library of Congress Cataloging-in-Publication Data
Names: Wingate, Marty, author.
Title: The bodies in the library / Marty Wingate.
Description: New York: Berkley Prime Crime, 2019. | Series: A first edition library mystery; 1
Identifiers: LCCN 2019009818 | ISBN 9781984804105 (hardback) |
ISBN 9781984804129 (ebook)
Subjects: | BISAC: FICTION / Mystery & Detective / Women Sleuths. | FICTION /
Mystery & Detective / Traditional British. | GSAFD: Mystery fiction.
Classification: LCC PS3623.I66225 B63 2019 | DDC 813/.6—dc23
LC record available at https://lccn.loc.gov/2019009818

First Edition: October 2019

Printed in Canada
1   3   5   7   9   10   8   6   4   2

Cover art by Josee Bisaillin
Cover design by Rita Frangie
Book design by Laura K. Corless

To Leighton

ACKNOWLEDGMENTS

Many thanks to my agent, Christina Hogrebe, of the Jane Rotrosen Agency, for her support and sharp insight, and to editor Michelle Vega at Berkley, whose enthusiasm makes all the difference. Thanks to my writing group—Kara Pomeroy, Louise Creighton, and Joan Shott—for their spot-on feedback. I'm grateful to fellow author and Anglophile Alice K. Boatwright for teatime talks about books, publishing, and scones.

About Bath. If you've never been, you should visit—and when you do, you may realize I took a bit of literary license. I moved Gravel Walk to suit my own purposes, placing it behind the terrace in which Middlebank House resides. And where is that terrace? Let's just say it's in the vicinity of Lansdown Road. Also, there really is a small pub in Northumberland Place—but I have changed its name to the Minerva, just to remind us of the city's Roman past. I've left the Jane Austen Centre right where it should be on Gay Street—a must-see and great fun for any Regency fan.

Dear readers, I hope you enjoy *The Bodies in the Library* and your introduction to Hayley Burke and the First Edition Library—Lady Fowling's wonderful collection from the Golden Age of Mystery writers. I chose to highlight Agatha Christie for this first book—Miss Marple, how could I not?—but there are many wonderful women authors from that time to celebrate. I look forward to Hayley's next adventure—I hope you will, too.

THE BODIES
IN THE
LIBRARY

1

❧

I 'll be leaving now, Ms. Burke."

I leapt up from the desk at this announcement—knocking my phone on the floor in the process—and hurried out of my office.

"Yes, Mrs. Woolgar," I said, tugging on my jacket. "Have a lovely evening."

The secretary stood in the flagstone entry and reached for her coat off the hall stand. The open front door framed a twilight sky behind her, as a cool October breeze swirled round our ankles. Bunter, a tortoiseshell cat, sauntered down the staircase, his tail straight as a soldier apart from the question-mark curl at its tip. He settled on the bottom step.

"You will have a word with them, won't you?"

"I certainly will," I replied. "But"—I added with as much authority as I could muster under her steely gaze—"as I've explained, I don't feel we can ask them to move along just yet. And, I believe this connection to the local writing community will be a boon—helping us to build a base of support that will ensure the Society's future."

Mrs. Woolgar took a lace-edged hankie from her sleeve and polished the brass plate mounted at the door that read *The First Edition Society.*

"And the furniture?"

"I haven't forgotten the furniture," I assured her. "I'm terribly sorry they left the chairs in such disarray last week." And the week before. "It's only that Trist had shifted things round to act out a scene he'd written with the zombies."

Mrs. Woolgar's eyes were veiled as she snapped her handbag closed and brushed an imaginary speck off the lapel of her dress. "Yes, well, it's only that we have a great responsibility to maintain a certain caliber and excellent quality here at Middlebank House. Not only because this was Lady Fowling's own residence and she was held in high esteem here in Bath and greatly mourned three years ago when she died, but also because it sets the standard for her grand endeavor, the Society, which she began herself with . . ."

I stopped listening but kept the polite smile plastered on my face as Mrs. Woolgar continued to tell me my job. I was new to my position as curator at The First Edition Society, an organization founded and funded by the late Lady Georgiana Fowling. She had turned Middlebank House, her home, into the repository for her lifetime passion—acquiring first editions of the women authors from the Golden Age of Mystery. Her library comprised a vast collection not only from Agatha Christie, Dorothy L. Sayers, and the others— many of the books personally autographed—but also works from suspense author Daphne du Maurier, added to the list for the sole reason that she was one of Lady Fowling's favorites.

It may have appeared that I'd made quite an extraordinary leap from my former post—assistant to the assistant curator at the Jane Austen Centre—to my current position of sole curator at the Society, especially as my university degree was in nineteenth-century literature. Never having read a detective story in my life, I knew I needed to prove my worth—if not to the board, then to myself and Glynis Woolgar, a dear friend and personal assistant to Lady Fowling for donkey's years, and who now held the post of Society secretary *in perpetuum.*

Mrs. Woolgar was on one side or the other of sixty—closer than that I could not guess. It was because of her clothes. She dressed as if it were 1935—that great age of mystery writing. The narrow frocks with wide lapels and cinched waists suited her pencil-like physique. Perhaps some women might've added a whimsical flare at the hemline, but not Mrs. Woolgar. Lady Fowling—ninety-four when she died—had dressed in the same era, if the portrait on the stairs was anything to go by.

"This is a chance for growth," I said when the secretary had finally run out of steam. "And if we do not grow, we stagnate."

"The Society is not in need of funds," Mrs. Woolgar stated, and not for the first time.

Lady Fowling's vast fortune notwithstanding, I knew that money was finite. It could be used up or taken away, and then where would we be? I wasn't thinking only of my own financial history—what about her ladyship's lout of a nephew? I'd heard the whole story. He'd received a bequest—a shocking amount of money that I could've lived on for the rest of my life—yet he continued to look for ways to challenge his aunt's will. Apparently, he wanted the house, too— The First Edition Society be damned.

"That may be true," I replied, "but we mustn't forget Lady Fowling's admonition that we are 'dedicated to the enjoyment, education, and furtherance of both readers and writers of mysteries, by connecting the public to our collection.'"

"I doubt she meant your lot," Mrs. Woolgar muttered as she left.

My lot. It had been my idea to invite the fan-fiction writers group to hold its sessions at Middlebank. I had offered it free of charge, believing this was a first step in making the Society not a diminishing, albeit elite, group of elderly book lovers who were scattered across the globe, but a viable and growing concern.

Each writer in the group had chosen to create his or her own homage to Agatha Christie—the doyenne of the detective novel. Their ages were mixed, ensuring the word got out that the Society appealed not only to university researchers and rare-book collectors, but also to a lively assortment of arty types from twenty-somethings to pensioners. Apart from the fact I knew nothing about Christie's writings, how could this be a bad idea?

I checked the time, went to the small kitchenette behind the stairs, and made myself a sandwich. Middlebank, as was the case with terraced houses, stretched upward instead of outward, with four floors and a basement. The ground floor—street level—held our separate offices, Mrs. Woolgar's and mine, plus the kitchenette and a loo. Up one flight of stairs lay the library, with floor-to-ceiling shelves, a large table, fireplace, and cozy nooks, as well as a powder room. My flat was up one more flight—accommodations had been included in the job, and I was ever so grateful—and at the top, an attic.

The basement was never referred to as such—instead, it was called the lower ground floor, and that's where Mrs. Woolgar lived. Middlebank sat midway along a well-kept Georgian terrace made of golden Bath stone. The terrace had been built on a slope and the land fell away at the back, which meant her flat had plenty of light and access to the back garden. It was lovely—the brief glimpse I'd had.

My flat had windows that took in a sweeping expanse of the town and into the Somerset countryside, as well as having a bird's-eye view of both the back garden and the street in front. I had moved here from a dreary, cramped flat out on the Wells Road, and I counted myself more than lucky, although I needed a reminder of this each morning when Mrs. Woolgar and I held our briefing.

On Wednesday evenings, I remained on the ground floor and in my office while the writers group met upstairs in the library. Furniture moving wasn't the only black mark they'd received during their short tenure. Mrs. Woolgar had posted herself in a far corner of the library on the first evening the group met—she wanted to make sure no one touched any of the books. The group's discussion had become so heated it had spilled out onto the first-floor landing, where they'd knocked a Chippendale walnut chair against the frame of Lady Fowling's portrait. I heard shouts of "Poirot always had superpowers. I'm just bringing them to the forefront!" and "Vice in St. Mary Mead? I don't think so!" After that scene, Mrs. Woolgar began taking herself off the premises.

My second thoughts on inviting the group to meet at Middlebank had turned into third and fourth thoughts, and after only a few weeks, I was considering how I might turf them out and save face. I had yet to come up with a solution.

Bunter, who had accompanied me to the kitchen to receive his own repast, finished his meal before I'd finished mine, and so spent the remainder of the time watching me with golden eyes. Every minute or so, he would shift slightly and rewrap his tail round his toes just to let me know he was still there. I saved out a tiny bit of cheese and offered it to him on a fingertip. He sniffed politely before taking it in one lick and spending the next ten minutes washing up. When the front-door buzzer sounded, he scampered off.

A young woman stood clutching a laptop to her chest and wriggling with excitement. "Hiya, Hayley," she greeted me. Her pale blond hair—frizzy and chin length—fought with enthusiasm against the hair band that held it.

"Hello, Harry, ready for your session?" I asked.

She nodded frantically. "I've had a breakthrough in my plot—Miss Marple gave up a baby for adoption, and the baby's grown into a woman and has come to St. Mary Mead to track down the mother who deserted her."

"Goodness."

"You must be joking, Harry," said a voice behind the door as I started to close it.

"Sorry, Peter." I pulled the door open, and Peter—gray hair slicked back—slouched in, a worn canvas satchel thrown over his rounded shoulders. He was followed by Mariella, in her late thirties with pixie-cut black hair, creamy complexion, and dark circles under her eyes. They both wrote books with Hercule Poirot as protagonist, with the outstanding difference that Mariella imbued her character with superpowers.

"Who's going to believe an old thing like Miss Marple ever had a baby?" Mariella asked. She dropped her bag on the flagstone, and it landed like a sack of rocks. A sippy cup and a packet of rusks spilled out. Mariella, who looked perpetually exhausted, had a ten-month-old she left at home with her husband on Wednesdays.

"That's the point," Harry said. "It's the juxtaposition of the past and the present that leads to the murder."

"It'll be a hard sell," Peter commented as he breezed past me.

The three continued to bicker as they headed up the stairs while I stepped out onto the pavement. The streetlights had flared, and I spotted the last two writers hurrying along—Trist, leader of the group, and Amanda, who was dedicated but indecisive and continued to rewrite the first ten pages of her story, which starred Tommy and Tuppence, Christie's married sleuths.

"They aren't lightweights," Amanda complained, flipping a long, thick, blond braid over her shoulder and unbuttoning a coat that looked three sizes too big for her.

"She was having a lark when she penned those stories," Trist replied. "They aren't truly serious works of detective fiction."

Trist, who wrote like the wind, was not one to talk about serious fiction. But he turned a deaf ear when anyone told him that the Agatha Christie people would never let his book—*Miss Marple and*

Zombies—see the light of day. Not that the others could ever hope for official sanction of their books either.

"You think you're better than the rest of us," Amanda said, "just because you're fast, but you'll see—it's one of us who'll be published long before you. No one cares about zombies anymore, Miss Marple or no. Oh, thanks, Hayley," she added as I held the door for her. She hitched her worn canvas satchel higher on her shoulder and walked in.

"Trist—" I stopped him before he stepped inside. I needed to have a word, and I liked having the extra inch or two that the doorstep provided. It wasn't that I was short, but, although thin, he was well over six feet. He sported sparse hair in need of a trim and a scar that cut through his right eyebrow, giving him a perpetual look of scorn. "You will remember to put the furniture back, won't you? Mrs. Woolgar said that—"

"We put the place to rights before we left last week," Trist argued, taking a handkerchief from the outside pocket of his leather case and wiping his brow. "And anyway, I don't know what she's complaining about, she doesn't own the place."

"Both Mrs. Woolgar and I are responsible for what goes on inside Middlebank House," I reminded him. I was on the verge of slamming the door in the face of his insolence, but how would I get the rest of them out? "And when you were invited to hold the group here, you took on part of that responsibility. If that is more than you're willing to assume, we'll have to discuss—"

"Maybe it's her ladyship feeling restless," he cut in with a sly grin. "She's starting to rearrange the furniture."

I put a finger in his face. "Don't you start that again about a ghost. Lady Fowling has not returned to haunt Middlebank."

Trist grunted.

"Are you coming up this evening, Hayley?" Amanda asked.

I had monitored the group the second week they met at

Middlebank—just to assuage Mrs. Woolgar's worry—but I had no wish to hear those first ten pages again. "No, thanks. I've a project proposal to catch up on. I'm sure you all work better without an extra pair of ears."

Had I given Trist enough of a warning? Perhaps not—I would catch him on his way out. Momentarily defeated, I retreated to my office and a proposal I was writing to the board. The Society would offer a series of literary salons—intimate evening lectures on the local culture, entertainment, and writing of the 1930s. We'd serve wine and have a fire blazing. We would charge, of course—and members would receive a deep discount when they bought a ticket to the full series.

Mrs. Woolgar had raised an eyebrow at my idea, as I expected. But she would think differently when I roused the interest of the board of trustees. All five of them, not just my friend Adele Babbage. I was not required to get the board's permission, but as the salons would be the first big project I'd taken on, I wanted to show them just how forward-thinking and thorough I could be. I knew Adele would love the idea—she had my back as far as the Society was concerned. It was the remaining four I needed to win over—three of Lady Fowling's dear friends, now in their eighties, plus the daughter of another. I had the impression Mrs. Woolgar had the ear of at least one of them.

It had taken the board—working with Lady Fowling's solicitor—the entire three years after her death to get the Society up and running and to hire the first curator. During that time, Middlebank—busy during her ladyship's life with researchers, rare-book enthusiasts, and lovers of mysteries who came to admire the first editions—fell off the radar, so to speak, leaving the first curator wondering just what she was supposed to be doing. That sense of ennui, coupled with Lady Fowling's nephew mounting an assault on the estate and the Society in an attempt to break the will, was too much for her, and after four months of constant hounding, she'd had enough and retired to Torquay.

The event threw the board into crisis. This was not what they'd signed on for—they had expected an easy time of it, holding quarterly meetings in the library with the sherry decanter close to hand. The other board members, that is—not Adele. She didn't care for sherry, and besides, she believed Lady Fowling would want the Society to do and be more.

Their fear that the nephew might take advantage of the Society's instability coincided with a particularly low point in my year, when no matter how I did my sums, I could not seem to cover my expenses. Adele had looked at my nadir as the stars aligning and had talked me into applying for the post of curator, skating over my lack of knowledge about the mystery genre. "You've a university degree in literature," she reminded me. "Books are books." The other board members did not see a problem either, and at their next quarterly meeting, they welcomed me with raised glasses.

Not yet halfway through the evening, and all was quiet from the library upstairs. I'd been twirling the end of my ponytail and staring at the blank document on my computer screen for nearly an hour before I gave up and reached for my phone. My call went unanswered just as I expected, and so I left my usual message.

"Dinah, sweetie—it's Mum," I said, chipper in the face of dead silence. "Just ringing to see how you are—I transferred the money on Monday, so it should've landed in your account. Ring me when you can, sweetie. Cheers, bye!"

Where would a twenty-two-year-old woman be on a Wednesday evening? My darling daughter—in her second year at Sheffield studying the history of everyday life—was probably at the library. No, wait—maybe she'd found herself a part-time job. A pub, perhaps, or a café? There's something to hope for.

I noticed Mariella come down the stairs and pass by my office. I got to work, and had written a heading and a one-sentence précis of my proposal by the time she returned, mug in one hand, plate of biscuits in the other.

"Cuppa?"

"Thanks, I'd love one."

"I brought my own tea along this evening," she said. "I didn't touch the other."

Good thing. Two weeks before, when Mariella had made tea in the kitchenette, she'd used Mrs. Woolgar's Fortnum & Mason Assam Superb. Another black mark.

"It was good of you to remember."

Mariella hovered just inside my office, tugging on the stretched-out sleeves of her sweater and glancing round the room at my mahogany desk, the Palladian-style mantel, and the Queen Anne wingback chair near the door where Bunter now slept amid the warm glow thrown by the lamps.

"This house is gorgeous. All the dark wood and such—like out of some old film." She sighed. "We aren't too noisy for you?"

I took that to mean there had been a fair few arguments already this evening, but at least they had been behind closed doors. "No, I haven't heard a thing—that's what you get from good, solid, Georgian construction, you know. Along with Lady Fowling's refurbishments before she died. So, how's it going? Everyone come with something fresh?"

"Oh yes, we've made great progress," Mariella said, glancing behind her and up the stairs. "Apart from Amanda, of course."

Of course.

"Have you read all those books in the library?"

I opened my bottom desk drawer and bent over it to hide my blush lest she cotton on to the fact that I had yet to crack a cover of those first editions and collectible volumes of the Golden Age of Mystery authors.

"The ones her ladyship wrote, I mean," Mariella added, innocently giving me a way out.

"I haven't as yet, but I intend to."

Lady Fowling, as it happened, was a mystery writer, too, each of her many titles gloriously produced in tooled leather binding with gold lettering. She had known the publisher. Twelve books starred her own detective, but the rest had, as protagonist, one of the famous detectives from her favorite authors. Yes—fan fiction. It was as I had told Mrs. Woolgar when I booked the writers group in—if Lady Fowling had been alive today, she'd've joined them in the library on Wednesdays.

By ten o'clock, I had made considerable progress on my proposal, but when Bunter raised his head and yawned, so did I. Perhaps another cup of tea. I stood and stretched, and my phone rang. One glance told me it wasn't Dinah returning her mum's call.

"Hello, you," I answered.

"Why aren't you here in London with me? Why?"

"And why isn't Bath the perfect place for your business, not London?" I responded, sitting again. We both sighed.

My boyfriend, Wyn Rundle, was a brilliant inventor and businessman whose fully funded start-up—Eat Here, Eat Now—promised to deliver meals by robot to any address in Greater London, whether that was an office on the twenty-seventh floor of the Shard or a semidetached in Ealing. Initially, of course, they would concentrate on lunchtime in the one-mile City proper, but as Wyn and his best mate, Tommy, pointed out, the financial district alone would be a gold mine.

We'd met two years earlier here in Bath when Wyn had attended a business expo—one of those happy coincidences when we had both reached for the same flat white order at the Costa Coffee on Southgate. We'd laughed and got to chatting and . . . well, fueled by caffeine, things moved along fairly quickly after that, and by the time he'd returned to London two days later, we were smitten.

And yet we remained living separately. Was it our age—both of us midforties—that kept us from making that last leap and moving cities? We'd grown rather tired of the topic—apart from our requisite greeting on the phone—and had decided to enjoy our long-distance relationship to its fullest, supplementing widely spaced weekends together with phone calls and texts.

"We need a new navigation system for Myrtle," he said glumly. "She can't tell left from right. I'd just as soon throw the bloody thing off Tower Bridge at the moment."

Myrtle, the robot. Why did these things always have women's names?

I heard voices on the stairs. The writers must've reconciled their differences for the evening, because as they trooped down quietly, Peter asked, "Pub?" and the others murmured assents.

"Hang on a tick," I whispered to Wyn. "The group's leaving—I should probably have a quick word and then we can talk." I jumped up and hurried out to the entry.

"Sorry," Wyn replied in a rush. "Here's Tommy. We've got to get to work. Love you." And he was gone.

"Trist?" I called as the group filed out the door.

Already on the pavement, he replied, "See ya, Hayley."

"Library's all in order," Harry promised.

"Night, Hayley," came from the others.

"But I—"

I withdrew my objection when Mrs. Woolgar appeared—I got the idea she carried out surveillance from across the road and returned only when she saw the writers leaving.

"Turned a bit chilly," I commented to her as she marched past me.

"It'll do that in October. And tonight's damage?" she asked, shrugging off her coat and hanging it on a peg.

"I'm sure they took care—I'll check on my way up."

"Good night, then," she replied, and made straight for the stairs that led down to her flat.

I locked the door and set the alarm. I heard Mrs. Woolgar's door close, and I stood in the entry, listening to the silent house. The cat emerged from my office, stretched, and made his way into the next room to his bed behind Mrs. Woolgar's desk.

"Well then—good night, Bunter."

2

U p the stairs, I paused for a quick glance in the library—it certainly passed my muster—and then continued to my own flat, pulling the key out of my pocket. Yes, even within the house, Mrs. Woolgar and I had our accommodations secured—it was a good way to separate life from work. I walked in, switching on a lamp as I did so, and unbuttoned my jacket. Breathing a sigh of relief, I took a moment to be grateful, as I had done at the end of almost every day since I'd moved in two months earlier.

My flat occupied the second floor and consisted of a sitting room that segued into a small dining area next to a cozy kitchen, with bedroom and bathroom through the far door. It was the same area as the library on the floor below me, but—for someone who had moved from a place where I could knock into a wall if I spread my arms too wide—this was a palace. And it had come furnished with bits and bobs that may not have been antiques but could certainly be called vintage. Lady Fowling had probably bought them new. In addition to my flat, I had use of the attic, and that's where I'd stacked all of my daughter's boxes—everything from little-girl mementos to a young woman's passions. Dinah hadn't wanted to take any of it to Sheffield, but it's a mother's duty to hold on to the past.

I contemplated a cup of tea or a glass of wine as I glanced at the stacks of paperback books gleaned from charity shops in town—my self-assigned reading, the Golden Age authors themselves. Who would it be—Agatha Christie? Josephine Tey? Dorothy L. Sayers and her sleuth, Lord Peter Wimsey? Or that outlier, Daphne du Maurier?

I yawned. Perhaps tomorrow.

Misty rain made for a gray dawn, but that did not daunt me—I threw on my waterproof gear, pulled up the hood, closed the front door of Middlebank behind me, and set off for my early-morning two-mile walk. I had instituted this exercise program a week ago, when I noticed the button on my jacket becoming a bit snug, and although the button hadn't loosened, I felt all the better for the air and the unspoken camaraderie among those strangers I passed on my way—all of us dedicated to exercise.

I took a route that led me behind the Royal Crescent and down and through Royal Victoria Park, hooking round the Circus as if I were in orbit before breaking away onto Gravel Walk—a wide path that ran behind the entire terrace. This allowed me to avoid the steep climb up to our front door. I pulled up halfway along and huffed with satisfaction.

Middlebank's back gate didn't squeak, yet still I took care—Mrs. Woolgar's windows looked out onto the garden, and I didn't want to give her something else to complain about at our morning briefing. I crept up the stone stairs, through the back door, and into the ground-floor kitchenette. I was headed for the entry and the two flights up to my flat when the front door opened to our cleaner.

Spiky bits of her short blond hair stuck out from a bandanna embroi-
dered with *Cleaned by Pauline* along the edge. Her arms were full of
cleaning supplies and a vacuum, and she struggled to get her key out
of the lock.

"Morning, Pauline—here, let me help."

"Cheers, Hayley," she said as I grabbed the buckets and held the
door. "Alarm's already off?"

"It is—I've been out and back. Shall I leave your things here?"

Middlebank House did have its own cleaning supplies, of course,
but Pauline had declined use of what she referred to as "the world's
oldest Hoover," saying she was afraid it would blow the electrics.
She also preferred her own nontoxic products to whatever might be
on someone's shelf, and so she—and the three women who worked
for her—lugged their accoutrements along to each job.

I left her to it. She always started on the ground floor and later cleaned both my flat and Mrs. Woolgar's. No one but me had
ever cleaned any place I'd lived in the whole of my adult life, and so
this had made me uncomfortable at first. But Pauline told me to
think of it as a well-deserved treat—like getting a manicure. There's
something else I'd never done.

After a quick shower, I drank my tea sitting on a stool at the
kitchen window, looking out across the trees, now turning autumnal
gold, and the tops of buildings and into the hills. Below me, the city
stirred to life. The tour buses would begin to disgorge people near
the abbey, and the mannequin in Regency clothes would be set on
the pavement outside the Jane Austen Centre—but here at Middlebank, we were above the fray. On one hand, this was a comfort, but
on the other, I knew we couldn't remain too far from the bustle of
Bath—the Society needed to secure its place in this historic city.
We needed to make a name for ourselves. First editions by mystery
writers who were still popular today were not for rare-book lovers

only, but for those around the globe who enjoyed a good story. I sighed—this was a pep talk I gave myself frequently.

Pulling my jacket on, I stepped over the threshold of my flat and walked into my job.

Where I found, one flight down, Mrs. Woolgar standing at the open library door.

"At it again, were they?" she asked.

The writers group? "No, I checked—they put the furniture back."

She gave a single, sharp nod to the far wall.

The oak ladder—Edwardian, if I remembered correctly—had three rungs and a top cap wide enough to sit on. It usually occupied the far corner of the library, but this morning, it was behind the table, up against the shelves of books. Last night, I had missed this egregious error.

"Is it damaged?" I asked, striding over to examine the bit of furniture. "Scuffs? Scrapes? Gouges in the wood?"

"That's hardly the point," Mrs. Woolgar replied.

"But it is the point. I'm sorry that the ladder wasn't put in its proper place, but after all, it is a library ladder and this is a library."

"And does that mean they were handling the books?" The secretary remained in the doorway, squinting across the table and up to the top shelf.

"Possibly. Is there one missing?" I asked, following her gaze.

"Lady Fowling would never have left furniture in the middle of the room. Things have their proper place. There was a time when . . ."

I turned away from her and rolled my eyes. It's the same lecture she'd given me when I left the tin of shortbread on the counter in the kitchenette instead of on top of the fridge.

I assumed an air of nonchalance. "We should be well accustomed to the public handling the books by the time the exhibition rolls round."

My comment produced the expected result—a look from Mrs. Woolgar that said, *Over my dead body.*

It had been my first idea as curator—putting on an exhibition of those most-prized books owned by The First Edition Society. The library at Middlebank housed the majority of Lady Fowling's vast collection, but the rarest volumes—worth a fair amount—were locked away at the bank. Mounting an exhibition would mean letting the most important part of the collection see the light of day. Mrs. Woolgar had gone apoplectic at the idea.

I didn't need her approval for the venture, but I did want her support, and as it wasn't in my remit to give the secretary a heart attack, I tabled the idea for the time being. When I came back about the arrangement for the writers group, Mrs. Woolgar most likely saw it as the lesser of two evils, and we reached détente. Still, it didn't keep me from the occasional mention.

Now the secretary wittered on about our responsibilities as I moved the library ladder back to the corner, where I spied a small, worn notebook—a school exercise book, the kind with the marbled cover—on the floor. In one smooth movement, I set the ladder down and picked the notebook up, keeping it behind my back when I turned round so that I wouldn't next get a lecture about littering.

By late afternoon, I had written the upcoming newsletter for the Society, finished a rough draft of my proposal for the board, and received a sniff from Mrs. Woolgar when I told her. What would she say when I brought up my plan to raise the membership fees? I'd meet that obstacle when I came to it, because I had another "first" to tackle—at long last, I would enter the cellar.

In addition to Middlebank itself, Lady Fowling had left the contents of the house to the Society. And yet, no one could tell me quite *what* these "contents" were—only *where* they were. They resided in the locked cellar, the key to which was in a safety deposit box at the bank.

When I stated my intention of studying her ladyship's personal effects, members of the board had reacted as if I'd said I was turning grave robber. They murmured vague comments about how inconsequential these possessions must be—diaries and clothing and inexpensive jewelry. But Adele had encouraged me to continue my campaign, and so I had brought the subject up at several morning briefings with Mrs. Woolgar. Each time, I received a stiff reply that the solicitor had a complete list of contents and she did not see how a few personal items could be of any use to me—as if she worried that I'd ring the television program *Cash in the Attic* as soon as her back was turned.

But the contents of the house that I could see—the furniture and books—these told only a part of her ladyship's story. I needed to know the woman herself in order to convey her spirit and élan to the world—and keep the Society on its proper track. Of course, I could march down to the bank and get the key to the cellar all on my own—I was the curator, after all. But again, did I want to make a permanent enemy of Mrs. Woolgar? What sort of working life would I have then?

And so instead, I made a vague comment about discussing the cellar with the Society's solicitor, Duncan Rennie. Mr. Rennie, poor man, had learned early on he was to be referee between us, but this time, the threat alone was enough to send Mrs. Woolgar herself scurrying to the bank, and the following day she magically produced the key to the cellar.

Access at last. But, as my foray meant going to the lower ground floor and walking past the door to Mrs. Woolgar's flat, she naturally accompanied me, because God knows what I could get up to left to my own devices.

The key was stiff in the Yale lock, telling me that the secretary did not spend her evenings like Mrs. Danvers, rearranging Lady Fowling's hairbrushes and laying out her nightdress. There, you see, I was familiar with one of our Golden Age of Mystery authors— although the odd one out, du Maurier. And it was the film version of *Rebecca*, not the book.

The cellar door opened fully, but beyond its three-foot clearance, my entry was blocked by what looked like a floor-to-ceiling three-dimensional jigsaw puzzle made of wooden pieces. Stacked any which way they fit were side chairs, occasional tables, standing lamps with cloth-covered cords, an ancient rocking horse—Lady Fowling and her husband had had no children—broken hat stands, a dressing table with a cracked mirror, and other furniture accumulated from several lifetimes. Farther into the room—it ran about fifteen feet wide and deeper still—I could see columns of crates and cardboard boxes.

"Well, Ms. Burke." Mrs. Woolgar smirked. "Shall I leave you to it?"

"Yes, thanks." I saw her eyeing the key in the door. I reached over, extracted it, and dropped it into my jacket pocket. "This will be a fine project to tackle during my spare moments."

Mrs. Woolgar returned to her office, and I remained in the doorway, studying the stockpile before me. I sighed, and told myself, *Stiff upper, Hayley. Who else would get paid this well to do a clear-out?*

I began at the top, carefully removing lighter pieces, hoping I wouldn't be buried under an avalanche of furniture. Shifting a few side chairs, two hat stands, a nightstand, and a side table into the corridor outside the cellar door allowed me to reach a dresser and a highboy. I checked the drawers—they were empty apart from a loose button and a card of straight pins—and so I moved them out, too, their legs screeching across the stone floor. When I reviewed my progress, I saw I'd barely made a dent in the wall of furniture. I could do with a cup of tea.

When I heard footsteps, I thought Mrs. Woolgar might've read my mind, but although it was the secretary, she arrived with her hands empty and clasped at her waist.

"One of that group is at the door," she announced.

Was it the harsh light from the three naked bulbs hanging from the ceiling, or had Mrs. Woolgar's complexion taken on a blotchy scarlet tone? Was she ill?

I would never know—I'd dare not make such a personal enquiry. "Who is it?"

"The man—the tall one."

"Trist," I said, brushing myself off. "You asked him in—you didn't leave him on the doorstep?"

"I will not have him in this house unattended," Mrs. Woolgar retorted, and I was too stunned to reply before she turned on her heels and left.

I hurried after, but she'd already closed herself up in her office by the time I made it upstairs. When I opened the door to the street, a heavy mist was falling. Trist, who wore a thin jacket, had his leather case tucked under his arm, the unprotected corners covered in water spots.

"Hello, Trist. Please, come in. I was in the cellar and didn't hear the buzzer."

He stalked in and shook his head and arms, flinging droplets in a wide arc, which then landed on me.

"Fan fiction is a legitimate form of literature," he said. "But this treatment isn't unexpected—writers through time have been disparaged for their craft."

I brushed the water off my wool jacket and cut my eyes toward the secretary's door. "I'm sorry Mrs. Woolgar left you outside, but I have to say I don't believe it has anything to do with your writing. It's only that Middlebank has been her home for many years, and the opening up of the Society is taking some getting used to for her."

The thought just expressed—by me—gave me pause. I hadn't actually considered it that way before, but I suppose it was true. I should cut Mrs. Woolgar some slack.

"So," I said with a pleasant but businesslike manner, "what can I do for you today?"

"You should know that there've been complaints."

"Complaints about what?"

"About me and the way I run things—" He took a handkerchief out of his jacket pocket and wiped the rain off his forehead. "But I'm standing up for the quality of fan fiction—you just remember that. And I don't believe anyone should have a special advantage. So, if you hear talk . . ."

"Yes, if I hear talk, what am I supposed to do?"

"Be fair. I'm only trying to make everyone accountable for his or her own work."

"I'm not an arbiter for your or anyone else's writing, Trist. We provide space for your group, and that's all. And at this point, I must tell you, I am reconsidering that offer."

There. I exhaled with relief. I'd said it—he'd had his warning.

He took a step toward me, and more moisture cascaded off his thinning hair, splattering my face. I took a step back.

"I'm sure you realize"—he glanced up the stairs and back at me—"Lady Fowling wants us to be accommodated."

The ghost card, was it? See if I'd take that bait.

"Well, if that's all, Trist, I must get back to my work." Cleaning out the cellar.

I shut the door on him, knocked on Mrs. Woolgar's, and was given permission to enter.

"I want you to know I've warned Trist that the group may not be able to continue to meet here. I won't stop them next week, but I will suggest they look for another place."

"What did he say to you?" she demanded.

"I don't know what he was talking about, really—squabbles within the group, I think. He isn't the most pleasant person."

"You've a knack for understatement, Ms. Burke."

I returned to the cellar without a cup of tea and shifted a few more pieces of furniture halfheartedly before looking down at myself. Streaks of dust made my black wool jacket look like herringbone, and so I decided to hold off on further exploration until another time when I would wear my laundry-day togs. But I didn't fancy attempting to put back the furniture I'd pulled out into the corridor. It didn't look as if it would fit, but then, I was always bad at puzzles. Instead, I lined the pieces up along the wall in the corridor, locked the cellar, and went upstairs to explain.

"And so the pieces are nowhere near the door to your flat—they won't be in your way at all," I said to Mrs. Woolgar, who pressed her lips together as if to say she didn't believe a word of it. "That's a lovely highboy," I added.

"Queen Anne," the secretary replied. "It was Sir John's—when he was alive. I'm not sure her ladyship would approve of anyone else's using her husband's furniture."

"I didn't mean that I wanted—" Oh, forget it.

At last, the end of the day. I dashed upstairs and changed into denims, a light sweater, and trainers, rinsed my face, and washed my hands. I grabbed a jacket on my way out the door—I needed to clear my head of dust and do a bit of shopping. Perhaps I'd get the ingredients for an enormous salad for my evening meal.

I'd slacked off cooking over the last couple of years. Since Dinah moved away, I didn't really see the point—but I knew I should stop living off ready-made meals from Waitrose. But I loved Waitrose—it had everything I ever needed. In addition to the usual grocery supplies, the place included a café, a bakery, a fish market and a butcher, and an array of fine dinners that someone else had prepared.

Cars clogged the streets of Bath at this time of day—everyone on the way home—and so I avoided traffic and took the long route, walking by the Assembly Rooms with their Georgian columns and spacious rooms. I'd attended a Jane Austen event there, and had a grand time—although it meant I had to wear Regency clothes. I don't care for those high waists—the dresses always make me feel rather lumpy. Mrs. Woolgar, on the other hand—with a figure straight as a rail—would look lovely in them.

I had just crossed George Street when I spotted Adele—easy to do with her mass of red hair like a Celtic goddess and her penchant for wearing purple.

"All right for some," I said. "Wandering the streets of Bath in the late afternoon—schoolteachers have it easy, don't they?"

"Who was it let the curator loose?"

We laughed and, without voicing the decision, turned and headed down Old King Street to the Raven, where neither of us could resist the chicken-and-mushroom pie. Just at the corner of Quiet Street, we almost collided with a sleek runner who wore a skintight outfit of swirling colors, and if it hadn't been for the long blond braid, I never would have recognized her.

"Amanda!"

"Hayley, God, I'm sorry. Are you all right?" She ran in place as she asked.

"Yeah, fine."

"Good," she replied. "See ya next week."

"Bye," I said to her disappearing figure.

"Who's that, then?" Adele asked, also watching Amanda's figure.

"She's a writer—one of the fan-fiction group. Want me to introduce you?"

"No," Adele said as we climbed the stairs in the pub and took the corner table by the windows. "I've no great luck with being set up for a first date—that friend-of-a-friend thing. It's awkward when it doesn't work out."

"Yeah, better to meet like Wyn and I did—by accident."

"And how is the Inventor of Fleet Street?" Adele asked. "Has he been down to see you lately?"

"No"—I pulled a face—"not since I started the new job."

"Have you been up to London?"

"Haven't quite had the opportunity."

"Mmm. The usual?" she asked. I nodded, and she headed for the bar to get our drinks and order our pies. When she returned, we changed the subject.

Adele and I had met at my previous job at the Jane Austen Centre, where my greatest perk was that I worked behind the scenes, saving me from wearing a Regency-era dress every day and selling T-shirts splashed with *I'm the real Mr. Darcy!*

This was seven years ago, when Adele had a more militant way of letting her views be known. She had secured a job in the café solely to make a statement—this had been obvious the moment she'd arrived in her Regency gear, with shaved head, tattooed scalp, and ear riveted with silver studs, and proceeded to pass out leaflets that read *Was Jane Austen a lesbian?*

Needless to say, her tenure at the Centre had been short-lived. I had been assigned to escort her off the premises, and the two of us had snickered our way down the stairs and met for a drink later. We had become the sort of friends who always sat down for a chat on the rare occasions we happened to meet on the street. Since that event, Adele had toned down her protests, grown out her hair, lost a few studs, and taught school locally.

"I wish you could've known Georgiana," Adele said, shaking her head after I reported the latest indiscretion by the fan-fiction group. "She'd've loved what you're doing. Glynis is trying to cast her in stone, but she was truly a forward-thinking woman. And backward, too, I suppose—given her favorite writers."

"I wish I could've known the two of you as friends," I replied.

On the surface, Adele may have seemed an odd choice for board member of the Society—even Adele admitted that. She had met Lady Fowling at Topping & Company, both perusing a new release of Agatha Christie's secret notebooks. This triggered a lively conversation on detection and resulted in a warm friendship. They were, in a word, simpatico. Adele—never the wistful sort—had once told me it was too bad her own mother hadn't been more like Lady Fowling. In return, her ladyship had deemed the young woman "full of the spirit of our role models"—and had promptly appointed her to the board.

Over our pies and mash, Adele caught me up with stories about her school, a local academy where she had been voted best teacher two years in a row by both students and parents. In exchange, I told her about my recent triumph—starting on the cellar.

"I didn't get far—deconstructing the wall of furniture will take a while."

"God knows how long some of that stuff has been down there," Adele said.

I knew that Middlebank had seen the Fowlings through at least a century, and her ladyship had been the tail end of their occupation. A long tail, as she'd been only twenty years old when she married the seventy-year-old Sir John.

"I'm not sure how I'd feel about marrying someone fifty years my senior," I thought aloud.

"I doubt if you could find anyone that old at this point." Adele shot me a grin as she lifted her glass. "Georgiana said they were quite happy."

"But that makes it so tragic—they had only ten years before he died, and then she was a widow at thirty and alone for the next sixty-four years."

"She didn't let that hold her back—she found her passion and shared it with the world."

"And that's what I will get the Society back to." I jabbed a finger on the table for emphasis. "Lady Fowling's dream." And with that, I shared my latest idea—literary salons to be held at Middlebank.

"Brilliant," Adele said. She became thoughtful, tapping her fork on the edge of her plate. "Yes, quite good. What if you found a co-sponsor? Not necessarily to share costs, but to help get the word out to a wider audience. Bath College has that adult learning program, you know. They do writing classes."

"Yes, perfect. I'll have a look at their faculty and find a likely person to contact." I stared at our empty plates and glasses. "Another pint?"

"Go on, then," Adele replied.

3

Friday's highlight—at least for Mrs. Woolgar—was that she caught me out during our morning briefing when she mentioned Margery Allingham, one of the Golden Age of Mystery writers, and her protagonist, Albert Campion. I made the life-shattering mistake of referring to him as "inspector" when he was really an amateur sleuth. Score one for Team Woolgar.

Never mind—I had the weekend. On Saturday morning, I was at the station and on a train by seven o'clock, off to see my mum in Liverpool. It was a four-hour journey with two changes, but I didn't mind—it gave me time to read and think and drink tea as I stared out the window. It wouldn't take any less time if I drove, and besides—I didn't have a car.

Once I'd made my second change at Birmingham New Street, I secured a slice of lemon drizzle from the tea trolley when it came past and had just ripped it open when my phone lit up and I saw Dinah's name.

"Morning, Mum," she said with cheer, although the greeting was followed by a yawn. "Are you on the train?"

"I am. Are you in bed?"

"I'm not—but I am standing next to it. How's the job? Full of mysteries?"

"Good, it's quite good. You'll love my flat—although, I don't suppose you'll see it before Christmas, will you?"

"Yeah." It was a distracted answer. "Listen, about the money you sent."

"Yes, sweetie—what about it?"

"Thanks very much for it. It's only that . . . Dad came for a visit yesterday."

Those few words were enough to chill my blood.

"Did he?" I asked. "How lovely he could spend the time with you." I wanted to say *spare the time*, but I knew the rules—don't bad-mouth the ex in front of the child, even an adult child. No matter what went on between the parents, father and daughter had a right to their own relationship.

"And his car had something wrong with it, but he's a bit skint right now and couldn't pay for the repairs."

My head swam with the vilest names imaginable for this so-called father, this ingrate, this mooch, this— I swallowed hard and choked out, "Oh?"

"And so, you know, I lent him the money. He said he'll pay it back soon. He asked me not to tell you about it, but I knew you wouldn't mind."

I held the phone at arm's length and clapped my other hand over my mouth as I whimpered. The older gentleman across the aisle cut his eyes at me and went back to his newspaper.

"That was money for your share of the house," I reminded her. Dinah rented a large and mostly dilapidated Victorian pile of bricks with another young woman. The monthly rent was outrageous, but they loved the place. "Well, we can't have you turfed out, now, can we?" I laughed lightheartedly through clenched teeth. Believe me, it's possible, I've had plenty of practice.

"Thanks, Mum. I'm sorry about Dad. It's just he gets so pitiful—like a little boy. He hasn't really ever grown up, has he?"

Arrived in Liverpool, I walked up from Lime Street station to Mum's flat in a sheltered housing arrangement for pensioners. I greeted her nurse—slipping her an envelope with her pay as she left—and leaned over Mum's wheelchair to give her a kiss. After a quick coffee, the two of us were away for a day of shopping, lunch, a wander through a museum, tea, and then back to her flat for a much-needed nap. I got my two miles in and more, as I counted double when I pushed her chair up even the slightest incline.

Mum, although sound of mind and sharp of wit, had a game leg, the result of a car crash two years earlier in which she'd been a passenger. She'd got off better than her friend Edna, who had died after driving into a postbox on the side of the road when she'd suffered a heart attack. Mum had been left needing a walking frame for short distances and a wheelchair otherwise, but both her spirit and her insight were undaunted.

"But are you happy with Wyn in London and you in Bath?" she asked during our tea and cake and after I told her the latest on Myrtle.

"Of course. It's just the way it has to be right now—with his new company and my new job."

"Well"—she gave my hand a pat—"if you're happy, then I'm happy. As long as you're happy."

* * *

I took a midday train home on Sunday. Bunter greeted me at the door of Middlebank, and I dangled a catnip mouse in front of his nose, until he batted it out of my fingers and across the entry. He made quite a show of chasing it round the legs of the hall stand before clamping it in his mouth and trotting up the stairs to the library landing. I followed, and paused as the cat continued his play under the Chippendale chair that sat beside Lady Fowling's portrait. I gave her a nod.

No, I do not believe our benefactor had returned from the grave to her former home, as Trist proclaimed. It was the painting, you see—one of those vast, full-length works of art that occupied most of the wall and seemed so alive. Lady Fowling had been painted in a gorgeous 1930s-style burgundy satin evening gown. A halter bodice with a high neck, and cut on the bias, it draped elegantly to the floor. She was turned ever so slightly so you could see her bare back. Unlike Mrs. Woolgar's pencil-thin physique, her ladyship had a curve or two, and she and the dress suited each other perfectly. In the back of my mind was the weak hope that I'd come across this dress in the cellar and could try it on.

In the portrait, Lady Fowling stood next to a late-Regency upholstered armchair. It was empty, and her hand rested on its back—a symbol, no doubt, of her late husband. She looked in her forties to me—although it's possible I was projecting—and the artist had captured a playful gleam in her eye. Each Sunday evening upon my return we took a moment to regard each other.

At last, Bunter caught his latest prey, and—leather strip of a tail dangling from his mouth—took it off. I'd brought him back a new mouse each of the weekends since I'd moved to Middlebank, and since then had come across them stashed in the most unlikely places. I continued up to my flat, pausing only a moment for a last look over my shoulder at the portrait.

"Good night, Lady Fowling."

* * *

By Wednesday, the entire sum of my accomplishments for the week had been to serve tea to the board. Two of the members were to embark on a cruise to the Caribbean in eight days' time, and Mrs. Woolgar wanted to send them off in style. I agreed to help and spent all day Monday polishing silver and arranging Lady Fowling's nineteenth-century Minton tea set while the secretary set off to the Bertinet, a French bakery in town.

But was this all I was good for—serving tea? I felt myself being sucked into the same vortex of doubt as I had been each week, and faced with the same dilemma. The difficulty was that I had no shape to my workdays, apart from the morning briefings with Mrs. Woolgar, which usually took the form of the secretary reminding me of the sacred trust we held and must ensure to—blah, blah, blah.

If my days were without form, what of Glynis Woolgar, former personal assistant to Lady Fowling and now Society secretary? Early on, when it had occurred to me I had no idea what she did every day in front of her computer, I had asked point-blank. Not rudely, but in a "Just how do you stay busy these days?" sort of way. With shining eyes and head held high, Mrs. Woolgar explained that she felt it her duty to correspond with the Society's members across the globe. Yes, that's right—every single member personally. That may sound like an incredible feat, but I had seen the rolls and knew it couldn't be too taxing.

It wasn't as if I could brag about my own activities. I had read through two years' worth of old newsletters, and studied a stack of magazines—all at least five years old—that occasionally mentioned Lady Fowling. I often went upstairs to the library and stood staring at the shelves, overwhelmed by what I did not know. I discovered that the less I had to do, the more lethargic I became.

The truth of the matter was that nothing really went on with the Society. What was I curator of—a load of nothing? The thought frightened me—what if others noticed I had no real work to do? Would the Society cease to exist? If so, where would that leave me?

The most exciting thing I'd done by midweek was to e-mail Bath College and ask to be referred to someone who might like to discuss a collaborative literature program. I'd heard nothing back.

Right, time to take action. I cleared my desk, pulled out a clean notebook, and began to scribble ideas as I envisioned a long-term plan with concrete goals.

We would increase membership by 10 percent next year. Was that too much or not enough? *Consider twenty percent,* I added.

We would sponsor a lecture series and bring in scholars of the genre. That could be in addition to our literary salons, of course, and set apart by the fact that morning lectures included coffee and cake, whereas at evening activities, such as the salons, a glass of wine was essential.

Right, salons, lectures—what was next? Perhaps the board would approve a small scholarship to be given to a woman in the creative-writing field. Or an award for best first mystery by a woman?

Yes, that's the ticket—the Georgiana Fowling First Edition Society award. "There, you see," I said to no one in particular. An award would fulfill our mission statement and ensure that the Society leads into the future while . . . I ran out of steam at that point, but, as it was the end of the day, at least I finished with some satisfaction in knowing I had a point to my life.

The front-door buzzer sounded, and I checked the time. Far too early for the writers group. I went to answer, noticing out of the corner of my eye that Mrs. Woolgar had remained at her desk, the glow of the computer screen reflected in her glasses.

My hand hovered above the latch for a moment. We rarely had

surprise visitors at Middlebank, and a brief sensation of possibility—a scent of anticipation—put a welcoming smile on my face.

A man stood on the doorstep. He had chestnut hair threaded with silver and a closely trimmed beard. His green eyes matched the green of his corduroy jacket—dark, like the color of oak leaves in summer. He smiled, and his eyes crinkled at the corners in a rather charming way.

"Mrs. Woolgar?" he asked.

He lost his charm at that remark—did I really look like Mrs. Woolgar?

"I have an appointment," he added.

"She's just in her office." What sort of fellow was this, and what sort of an appointment did he have? "Come in, and I'll let her know you're here. What is your name?"

He glanced about the entry as he said, "Val Moffatt."

Mrs. Woolgar emerged from her office. "Mr. Moffatt? How do you do?" She extended her hand as she said to me, "Mr. Moffatt has an appointment with *you*, Ms. Burke."

"Does he?"

"I'm sorry," Moffatt said, looking from one of us to the other. "Have I come at the wrong time?"

"Mr. Moffatt is from Bath College. His appointment is in your diary," Mrs. Woolgar added, as if instructing a young child.

And she had said nothing, not even at our morning briefing. The cow. She'd made the appointment, written it in my diary, and didn't tell me about it—all on purpose. To what end other than to make me look a fool? An unpleasant idea crept out of my subconscious and settled itself front and center. It wasn't only that Mrs. Woolgar mourned the loss of Lady Fowling or thought I didn't know what I was doing—her primary motive was that she didn't want to share. She wanted to make me miserable enough to leave—scarper, just as the first curator had. She and others had pointed a finger at the nephew, saying he was responsible for that, but perhaps it was really Mrs. Woolgar who wanted Middlebank all to herself.

I put my hand out to the visitor. "Hello, I'm Hayley Burke, curator here at The First Edition Society. Mrs. Woolgar keeps my diary for me—" I flashed her an icy smile. "And what would I do without her? Well, Mr. Moffatt, let's go to my office, shall we?" I marched off.

"If you'd prefer I come back at another time . . ."

I turned round abruptly, not realizing how close he was, and found we were face-to-face.

"No," I said, backing off, "this is a perfect time—but, I do apologize, I'm not quite as prepared as I'd like to be." Well, that made no sense. Needless to say, this wouldn't happen again. From now on, I would examine my diary in detail each morning and evening—and perhaps over lunch as well, lest she try to slip something else in. "Here now, Bunter, make way."

Bunter, in the wingback chair, raised his head, his eyes dilating at the sight of a new human. Moffatt sat on his heels, put a hand out for the cat to sniff, and was given permission for a pet.

"Bunter, now, is it? He's yours?"

"He belongs to the house. Lady Fowling always had a tortoise-shell cat, and it was always named Bunter—this fellow came on board just before she died, and he was a great comfort to her, I'm told." I sat on the edge of my desk. "I'm happy for his company, too. We always had a cat at home—first Dougal, then Ermintrude, and then Zebedee."

He laughed as he stood up. "*The Magic Roundabout?* My girls loved that."

"It was my daughter's favorite television program—well, mine, too, when I was growing up."

"How old is your daughter?"

"Twenty-two—but still nine years old in my eyes. Yours?"

"Twenty-four. They're twins."

"Two at once—don't know that I could've managed that."

"My wife did most of the managing—for as long as she could. She died when the girls were quite young."

"Oh, I'm sorry."

He shrugged a shoulder and smiled an acceptance—probably well inured to such comments. "And you . . ."

"Divorced."

"I'm—"

I put a hand up to stop him. "I'll accept sympathy for the marriage, but not for the divorce." We both smiled and drifted into an oddly comfortable silence.

All at once I didn't know where I was. How had we arrived at such a personal place?

When Bunter jumped down from the wingback and wandered out the door, I gestured to the chair. "Please." I sat behind my desk, clasped my hands across the blotter, and regained my position.

"It's very good of you to come to us—when I sent the e-mail to the college, I expected a bit of to-and-fro before anyone would meet in person."

Moffatt settled in the chair and tugged on the cuffs of his jacket, which I now noticed were worn smooth of their corduroy. "Your e-mail went to the department head, of course, but a friend mentioned the Society to me, and so I said I would take this on."

"You're a lecturer?"

"Yes, in creative writing and genre fiction. Most of my courses are taught through the adult-learning division."

"That's excellent." And it was—here I had successfully located the right person from Bath College who knew about the Society and worked with adults. What more could I ask?

We talked over the idea of the literary salons. Moffatt wasn't able to commit—that would take the approval of the college—but we discussed topics, timing, promotion. It was all terribly useful, and even better, here I was having an intelligent conversation with a colleague about my work. Things were looking up.

"I doubt we could offer the speakers a fee," I admitted.

"Apart from a glass of wine," he said.

"You know, if we ever wanted to expand the salons and include the nineteenth century, I could get someone from the Jane Austen Centre—it's where I worked before this."

"Was it?" he asked, looking me over with both a frown and a smile. "I'm not sure I can see that."

"I was behind the scenes, not in the public eye."

"Your knowledge about the mystery genre must be quite extensive to have landed this post."

"There is always more to learn," I replied vaguely.

"Crime, suspense—you're the expert, I'm sure."

I felt myself being pushed out onto thin ice. "Popular literature, no matter the genre or era, contains many of the same elements, don't you think?"

"So, what do you think—if we put Inspector Grant up against Chief Inspector Alleyn, who do you believe would solve the crime first?"

"I . . . I . . ." I had no idea. Those names rang distant bells, but I couldn't tell you which Golden Age authors they belonged to, even though the library shelves were lined with their books. "It isn't fair for me to put them in a competition."

"It's a question I often ask my students," Moffatt replied. "It focuses them on the elements of the story." He glanced round the office. "And you live on the premises?"

"I'm not sure this has any bearing on the work we will carry out—"

"Well, you've certainly done well for yourself here." He rubbed his hands on the leather armchair. "A far cry from what a college lecturer can afford, I'll tell you that."

"My accommodations," I said, my face blazing, "are part of the compensation as curator. You can be sure, Mr. Moffatt, that my pay package reflects that fact. And just because I have rooms upstairs at Middlebank, it doesn't mean I am waited on hand and foot by servants."

"Tea?" Mrs. Woolgar asked, standing in the doorway with tray in hand.

4

❦

And I'll be sure to e-mail you with those details," I said coolly to
Val Moffatt. My cup of tea had sat untouched as we worked.
Although conversation had been stilted, I felt it was my duty to finish the meeting on a professional note, regardless of the cheek of the
man. "Thank you for coming today."

He interpreted my meaning correctly and rose to leave. "This is
a good idea," he said, "and I'm glad you thought of us."

Contacting Bath College had been Adele's idea, but I had no in-
clination to wander into personal details again. As we walked out to
the entry, I responded, "I certainly hope it will benefit both the college and the Society."

Moffatt frowned. "Ms. Burke, I hope you don't—"

The front-door buzzer sounded, followed by Mrs. Woolgar
emerging from her office, which reminded me it was Wednesday
evening. I opened the door and all five writers tumbled in as if they'd
been leaning against it.

"Mr. Moffatt!"

"Hello, Amanda," Moffatt replied.

"Ms. Burke." The secretary stood behind me as if I were her shield against the group. She began edging her way to freedom. "I do hope you will—"

"Yes, Mrs. Woolgar, I'll have a word. Wait—on second thought, why don't you relay your concern about—"

But she was gone.

"Hayley, could I talk with you?" Harry clutched her laptop to her chest, the corners of her mouth drooping. "It's a matter of respect, you see. I believe we should each of us—"

"Oh, lighten up, Harry," Peter said. "He didn't mean anything by it."

"He's that way with all of us," Mariella said, turning to Trist. "Aren't you?"

Harry put her nose in the air. "The curator of the Society should be made aware of how people are treated."

Trist clicked his tongue. "I thought you were tougher than that, Harry—going begging to our host. Don't look for any comfort there."

"Shut it, Trist," Amanda said. "Look, Harry, it isn't Hayley's place to solve our problems for us. We don't need a mediator—we're adults and should be able to talk things through on our own."

Or otherwise you'll be out on your bums. But I'd save that for later— I wasn't about to get in the middle of this now, and I could only hope Harry would take Amanda's advice.

"I understand the difference between critique and criticism," Harry said to me, walking backward as the group moved to the stairs like a single-celled organism. "And I don't think that line should be crossed."

That seemed to put an end to the complaint—for the moment. They continued up to the library, and I heaved a sigh, pushed the door closed, and turned round to find Val Moffatt still inside, hands in the pockets of his jacket as he watched the group and then returned his gaze to me. I opened the door again.

"You'll be hearing from me, Mr. Moffatt."

"Good evening, then, Ms. Burke."

While the writers worked quietly in the library above me, I exchanged texts with Wyn—Myrtle the robot's navigation system now sorted, the next step would be finding better wheels for her—and then settled down to finishing the proposal for the literary salons. Mrs. Woolgar made her timely appearance immediately after the group departed, and paused before descending to her flat.

"I hope your meeting with Mr. Moffatt went well."

"Perfect," I replied with enthusiasm. "We've only to work out the details. Our collaboration with Bath College is just the beginning."

I'd like to say she looked disappointed that her attempt to discombobulate me had not succeeded, but she had a knack for throwing me off balance, and instead she smiled and said, "Lovely. Good night."

It was twelve thirty before I could sit back, satisfied with the proposal. But I had enough sense to refrain from sending an e-mail off at that early an hour. No, I would wait for the morning, and with rested eyes, take one more look before I dispatched the document to Bath College—and then we would be on our way to establishing The First Edition Society as a cultural and educational hub for twentieth-century popular fiction. I hadn't thought of that last line until I was upstairs and in bed with the light off, so I'd turned it back on and written myself a note.

The result of my late night was that morning came a bit too soon for me, and a seven o'clock two-mile walk didn't really appeal. It had gone seven thirty by the time I rolled out of bed. But I asked myself how I would feel when it came time for a coffee and perhaps a shortbread finger at eleven o'clock if I hadn't walked first, and that got me moving. At last, when I was out the door and the sun hit the terrace, turning it to gold, I could see a bright day ahead. I inhaled deeply—the air chill and invigorating—and set off in a different direction to see where my feet would lead.

They led me into the shopping district, just waking for the new day. I took to the lanes, walking along narrow Northumberland Place and past the Minerva—a cozy pub framed by hanging baskets and window boxes now planted with autumnal shades of pansies and tiny yellow flowers that dripped over the edges of their containers. A signboard hung above the door with a painted rendition of the gilt bronze head of the goddess Minerva, which had been uncovered in the city's Roman baths in the eighteenth century. The goddess notwithstanding, it was a good little pub where our cleaner, Pauline, worked—it was run by her brother, I thought.

I basked in my accomplishments as I slowed down to admire the window displays of shops not yet open. I'd had enough money this month to transfer a second round to Dinah's account—that in itself was cause for celebration. When it came to discussing my ex with my daughter, I'd taken the high ground. I'd written a thorough proposal on the literary salons of The First Edition Society.

And it was Thursday—in two days I'd be off to Liverpool for my mini-holiday with Mum. Perhaps on Sunday I would take an early train from Liverpool to London. Wyn and I could have almost the entire day together, which we desperately needed.

That thought put an extra spring in my step. I showered and took my tea and toast while dreaming of a lazy Sunday afternoon with my boyfriend. Only when I checked the time did I remember about my late start. Grabbing for my jacket, I tore out the door, intent on sending the literary salon proposal before our morning briefing so the secretary would have no room to object. Not that that would stop her.

The library door was closed. Mrs. Woolgar must've already searched for damage from last night's group and, having found none, given up and gone to her office. I continued to the ground floor, paused at her doorway, and said, "Good morning."

But instead of Mrs. Woolgar, there was Pauline with a lambswool duster on an extension pole, working the corner cornices of the twelve-foot ceiling.

"Morning, Hayley," she replied.

"Mrs. Woolgar?" I asked.

"Haven't seen her—just as well, really. I'm running a bit late this morning. I gave the kitchenette a once-over and washed the mugs from last evening and thought myself lucky to get in here and finish her office before she came up. I'd a shift at the pub last night, you see, and then I couldn't find—oh well, you don't want to hear about that, do you?"

"Well, I'd better get stuck in—I'm a bit late myself," I told her. I walked back to my own office, but glanced down the stairs to the lower ground floor. Mrs. Woolgar late? Unheard of, as far as I knew. Was she ill? Should I check? But Pauline and I had been late—perhaps as the autumn days grew shorter, we all preferred to hibernate. I'd give her a few more minutes before I worried.

At my desk, I studied the proposal one last time, tweaking words and shifting phrases—then shifting them back again. Lastly, I filled in the e-mail address and then sat, frozen, with my finger hovering a fraction of an inch above the mouse as I began to second-guess myself. Had I taken the right tone? *A collaboration to benefit both the college and the Society*—should it sound as if we'd be on equal footing or would the college want more credit? Would Val Moffatt, envious of my job, sink the whole idea before it saw the light of day?

In the entry, Pauline dropped a vacuum attachment and I jumped, causing my finger to land on the mouse and click send. I gasped, and she looked in, catching me wringing my hands.

"Sorry, Hayley. All right there?"

"Mmm. Great."

"I'll go on up to the library, shall I?" Pauline asked. "Then I'll finish this floor after." She looked over her shoulder. "No sign of Mrs. Woolgar yet?"

I checked the time—ten minutes past our usual briefing—and alarm bells went off in my head. Leaping out of my chair, I hurried past Pauline.

"Yes, you go on upstairs. I'll just nip down to her flat and make sure everything's . . . That she isn't . . ."

Not bothering to finish, I grabbed hold of the handrail to swing myself round and head down to the lower ground floor, but the closer I got to her door, the slower my steps became. It seemed forever until I landed at the bottom. To my left, the corridor was lined with the furniture I'd dragged out of the cellar—I had yet to return to that project—and to my right, the door to Mrs. Woolgar's flat. A fan-shaped, art deco sconce kept the area dimly lit.

A light tap on her door brought no results. I put my ear against the solid oak and heard not a sound. My heart in my throat, I raised my hand again just as the door flew open.

"Ah!" I cried, reeling and my heart pounding.

"What are you doing?" Mrs. Woolgar demanded.

"I thought I'd better see that you were all right . . . I didn't know if . . ." I'd done nothing and yet here I was wrong-footed. I drew myself up. "It's only that . . . it's past your usual time."

Mrs. Woolgar studied her watch, shook her wrist, and peered at it again. "Dear me," she muttered. "I don't know how that happened. Well, Ms. Burke, you can be assured that I will—"

Her excuse was cut off by a shriek from above.

"Pauline?" I turned and ran up the stairs at a clip. Over my shoulder, I explained, "She went to start on the library."

"You don't think"—Mrs. Woolgar followed at my heels—"that a shelf of books fell on her?"

A shelf of books? Short of an earthquake, I couldn't see how that could happen. But as we got to the ground floor, made a hundred-eighty-degree turn, and ran to the next flight of stairs, I heard a heavy *thunk*.

"Pauline!" I shouted.

We found her on the landing between Lady Fowling's portrait and the overturned Chippendale side chair. She had flattened herself against the wall and held the duster in front of her as if warding off a vampire.

"He's in there! I didn't know," she stammered, pointing a shaky finger at the open library door and waving the duster in my face. "I thought you might've had someone in . . . for a meeting and he . . ."

I grabbed hold of her hands—they were icy. Had someone broken in and attacked her? The library appeared empty, but best to be on one's guard. "Mrs. Woolgar, shut the library door, put that chair in front of it, and ring for the police. Pauline, look at me. Are you all right? What did he do to you? Is he still in there? Did you fight back?"

The secretary went for the door, but Pauline cried out, "An ambulance—ring for an ambulance!"

"It's all right, Pauline," I said. "You've every right to defend yourself."

"*No*, you don't understand. I didn't do that to him—I *found* him like that."

Mrs. Woolgar and I exchanged looks. "Stay with her," I said. "I'll go in."

I edged my way over to the open door, my back to the wall. Silence from within the library. When close enough, I craned my neck round and peered in. On the far side of the table, the chairs were askew, and I could see the still form of a man on the floor. But I couldn't see well enough, and so I crept forward until I could take in the full scene.

He lay on his side, his face turned toward the wall with arms stretched above his head as if he'd been reaching up for something and had collapsed. I could see a wide round red mark on the back of his head and blood matted into his thin hair. Did I know him?

"Hello?" My voice trembled. "Are you all right? Sir?"

I leaned over and gave him a light shake. His entire body shifted, as if frozen. I pulled my hand back, but then took a deep breath and felt his cheek—a second's touch was enough to tell me he was stone cold. Only then did I roll the body over and see the scar that cut through his right eyebrow, giving him a perpetual look of scorn.

It was Trist.

5

Is he . . . ?" Mrs. Woolgar asked when I stumbled out of the library and closed the door.

"Dead. It's Trist," I said, my voice more air than sound. It was difficult to swallow.

"That writer?" Mrs. Woolgar put her hand to her chest.

"Then you know him?" Pauline asked.

The secretary frowned. "And he's been there all night?"

"No—they left," I said firmly. "I saw them all leave." And yet here he was.

The three of us stood in a tight group on the landing as a creeping dread came over me. Could someone else be in the house with us? When I noticed Mrs. Woolgar glance down the stairs, I knew the same thought had occurred to her. My eyes darted up toward my flat and the attic above it.

I tugged on my jacket, coughed, and said, "We need to phone the police." My voice was loud and reverberated in the space.

"An ambulance!" Pauline protested.

"That won't help now," I told her, using my mum voice and trying to keep my mind on autopilot. "It's the police we need." I took Pauline's arm as if to reassure her—but I didn't mind the extra support myself. "Mrs. Woolgar?"

"Yes, coming."

We turned our backs on the library and the three of us made our way carefully down the stairs, Pauline still clinging to her duster. At the bottom, we paused.

"Why don't we all go into my office?" I suggested. A part of me knew how ridiculous this was—surely we didn't need to hide. Hadn't Pauline and I walked all round the ground floor earlier? Hadn't Mrs. Woolgar and I both been in our flats? It wasn't possible for anyone to elude us.

Still, as we made our way, we paused at the secretary's office—empty—and the kitchenette—also empty. I closed us in my office. Pauline crossed the room and stood by the fireplace. Mrs. Woolgar took up a post behind the wingback chair. I rang 999.

O nce I'd reported the death, we had only to wait, but that wasn't as easy as it might seem, because when I sat at my desk, it was as if I could feel the weight of Trist's body above our heads in the library. I couldn't bear it and immediately sprang up.

"I'll go stand on the pavement—how will they find us otherwise?" It was an excuse that you could knock over with a feather, but they took no notice.

I flung open my office door to find an indignant tortoiseshell cat on the other side.

"Bunter!" I swept him up in my arms. "I'm sorry. Mrs. Woolgar—"

I turned, and she took him from me, saying, "Come here to me, boy."

Right, at least the cat was safe. I went outdoors. The sun shone, but the chilly air cut through my suit jacket, and I shivered. I felt odd and empty and wrapped my arms round myself, wishing for a cup of tea and then feeling guilty for wanting it.

The terrace had seen nothing like this before. When two police cars with their checkerboard blue-and-yellow side panels pulled up in front of Middlebank, and four uniformed officers—two men, two women—emerged, heads popped out of doors up and down the road. I led the police inside and up the stairs, talking over my shoulder along the way.

"I'm Hayley Burke, curator here at The First Edition Society. I know the man who died—he was part of a writers group that meets here on Wednesday evenings. But he left last evening when they finished—I saw all of them leave." We arrived at the library door, and I kept talking. "I don't know how he got back in—it's all quite confusing and—"

"Thank you, ma'am." A female police constable stopped me with a light touch on my shoulder. She looked about Dinah's age, and it made me feel so old. "Would you wait downstairs, please? Other officers will be on their way."

Behind her, in the library, the uniforms bent over the body while one spoke into a radio attached to her shoulder. I followed orders—gentle though they were—and went back to my office. Pauline and Mrs. Woolgar remained in place and Bunter had hopped up to the mantel, where he impersonated a ceramic cat figurine.

"We're to wait," I explained.

And we did—another fifteen minutes of silence that felt like hours until the front-door buzzer went off and we all jumped. I hurried out and let in several more people wearing plain clothes. "Hello," I said, not sure of which one to address, "I'm Hayley Burke, curator here at The First Edition Society. I—we—found the body. Upstairs—the other officers are there. I know the man, and I don't understand how he could've—"

"SOCO," a man replied, holding out his identification. "Scene-of-crime officers, ma'am. And the ME—medical examiner," he added, nodding to a woman as they all suited up in paper coveralls and slipped on paper booties over their shoes. "We'll take it from here, thanks."

They spread out, two going back toward the kitchenette, another looking in Mrs. Woolgar's office, several heading upstairs.

"Don't you want to know—"

"Police," a voice behind me said.

I turned back to the front door to find two more men. One looked about fifty, with mostly gray hair and a thick, bushy mustache like a push broom. His raised eyebrows seemed to question everything. The other, younger, had dark skin and shiny black hair—he had a notebook and pencil in hand. They both wore dark suits—I suppose they could be mistaken for door-to-door missionaries, if it weren't for the fact that there was a dead body upstairs.

The older man introduced himself as he held out a warrant card. I dutifully leaned in to read what I could. Detective Sergeant Ronald Hopgood.

". . . and this is Detective Constable Kenny Pye," he continued. "I see the uniforms arrived and SOCO. And you are?"

"I'm Hayley Burke—I'm curator here. I knew the deceased, but I don't understand how he came to be in the library." I rushed through my explanation, afraid he, too, would cut me off. "I saw him only last evening, but he and the rest of the group had left by half-past ten."

"And you found the body this morning?"

For a moment I couldn't go on, too overcome with emotion that at last someone was listening to me. I nodded and inhaled deeply. "I don't know how he died, and I don't know how he could've come back in. We've a security system, and the doors were locked—it really doesn't make any sense to me."

"And you are curator of . . . ?" Hopgood asked.

"Boss." DC Pye tapped his pencil against the brass plate beside the door, directing the sergeant's gaze to read *The First Edition Society*.

"We specialize in the Golden Age of Mystery authors," I added.

Hopgood's brows rose. "And where did you say the deceased was found?"

"In the library," I replied.

"Well, Ms. Burke, as it isn't April Fools', I will believe you," DS Hopgood said. "So what we've got is a body in the library at a society that specializes in murder mysteries. Doesn't that just take the biscuit?"

M rs. Woolgar and Pauline had their heads stuck out the door of my office, and so I managed quick introductions before DS Hopgood and DC Pye went to the library. I started up after them, but the sergeant held up and suggested I wait on the ground floor with "the others." And so, I returned to my office. Pauline had gone back to the fireplace and was absentmindedly dusting the screen when I walked in.

"We're to wait," I explained, dropping into my desk chair.

"Again," Mrs. Woolgar added. She took the wingback.

"Yes—but I'm sure the detective sergeant will want to talk with us. Why don't you sit down, Pauline?"

She sank into a corner chair and twirled the lambswool duster in her own face.

"I'm sorry—are you meant to be somewhere else by now?" I asked.

Pauline shook her head. "This is my only house today—the other three each have two cleanings. Thursdays are popular—getting ready for the weekend, you know. And I don't have a shift at the pub until tomorrow."

"We'll need to inform the board members," Mrs. Woolgar said.

"No!" Panic rose in me and caught in my throat. "That is, I mean, perhaps we should wait until the police have finished here. What could we tell the board members now?"

"That a dead man was found in the library—a man who was part of the writers group you invited to meet here at Middlebank."

True, all of it—although I didn't care for her accusatory tone. "Yes, Mrs. Woolgar—those are the facts, but other than that, we know nothing, and I feel it would be better to have answers to their inevitable questions. How did Trist get back into the house? Why was he here? He may've had an accident, perhaps he was ill, and fainted and hit his head in a fall."

We fell silent and watched the steady stream of traffic flow past my office door. At last, DC Pye stopped and put his head in.

"What's behind the locked doors—above and below?"

"Our flats," I explained. "Mrs. Woolgar and I live on the premises. We usually keep our doors locked—we wouldn't want any visitors thinking our flats were part of the Society." Not that we ever had any actual members of the public ask to come in—not since I'd been on staff. "But we leave them unlocked on Thursday mornings for Pauline."

"Are you the basement flat?" Pye asked me.

"Lower ground floor," Mrs. Woolgar corrected him. "That is mine."

"Mine's on the second floor—above the library."

"And you heard nothing during the night?" the DC asked.

"Not a sound. Good Georgian construction," I replied.

"With sympathetic updating by Lady Fowling in the 1980s," Mrs. Woolgar added. "Middlebank is, after all, Grade II listed."

The DC didn't seem interested in architectural standards. "And neither of you found anything disturbed in your flats?"

We shook our heads.

"The French doors in my flat that open onto the back garden are always locked and bolted," Mrs. Woolgar said.

"And the other door," Pye continued. "In the . . . lower ground floor?"

"The cellar," the secretary said. "It's used for storage—furniture mostly. Her ladyship's."

"And that leaves the top floor. Attic?" the detective constable asked.

"Yes," I said. "I've some cartons up there, but that's about all. Do you want me to get the attic key for you?"

"I'll leave that for the boss to decide."

"Could I make a pot of tea?" Pauline asked.

DC Pye glanced over his shoulder and said, "Yeah, you're all right."

Set free, Pauline dashed into the kitchenette, but returned to whisper a complaint that police had left dust everywhere.

"They're looking for fingerprints," the detective constable said from behind her. Pauline flinched. "We'll need to eliminate the three of yours from any we find. Sorry—that'll mean a trip down to the station. This afternoon, if you can."

Mrs. Woolgar's office was conscripted for what DC Pye called the "interview room" and DS Hopgood referred to as "a place to sit down and have a chat." Pauline supplied tea and a plate of Marie biscuits. I went in first. As DC Pye escorted Mrs. Woolgar upstairs, I heard him say, "Boss—no sign of forced entry."

Hopgood followed me into the office and settled into Mrs. Woolgar's chair, and I walked him through last evening and this morning, ending with a hopeful, "Was it an accident?"

"No, Ms. Burke," the sergeant replied. "Not an accident."

"He was . . . murdered?" My voice squeaked like a rusty gate.

Hopgood ignored my question and asked his own. "You had no idea that he—or anyone else—knew how to get back in?"

"How could he know? Was he a professional cat burglar? When did he get in? We left no windows open. After the group had left and Mrs. Woolgar returned, I switched on the alarm system, and this morning I switched it off when I left for my walk. And the doors were always locked."

"Security systems and locks are playthings in the hands of some, Ms. Burke. So—it looks as if this is one of your locked-room mysteries."

"Those are books, Sergeant Hopgood—stories."

Stories I hadn't read. I hoped he didn't start questioning me about plot lines.

"And speaking of those books"—the DS sat forward in Mrs. Woolgar's desk chair—"are they worth a great deal?"

"Lady Fowling had three hundred and fourteen first editions by the various authors—many by Agatha Christie—that were each worth about two thousand pounds." Hopgood's eyebrows shot up and I understood the question. "Those books are safely in storage at the bank. Not forever, you understand—they'll be coming out of the vault for an exhibition the Society will be mounting on the Golden Age of Mystery, so that the public can see the extent and deep interest the genre can engender." I glanced over my shoulder to make sure Mrs. Woolgar didn't hear and, just to be on the safe side, added, "We're still in the planning stages, of course."

"But you have a library brimming with old detective books," Hopgood pointed out.

"Yes, but the total worth of the library upstairs might be two hundred thousand pounds on a good day—so much depends on the whims of the collectible book market."

The DS gave a low whistle. "For a few books?"

"For five thousand twenty-seven books, and that includes Lady Fowling's own novels. Among the collection in the library, there are a great many second and third editions—reprints. A new dust jacket or a freshly written preface can be quite appealing to the collector. Foreign language editions, too. Several shelves are books signed by the authors to Lady Fowling personally—a lovely gesture, but it can decrease the value. That means each book is worth less than fifty quid, so unless Trist had decided to nick the entire library one book at a time and didn't think we'd notice, he wasn't going to be a wealthy man."

"Pye has taken Mrs. Woolgar upstairs to do a once-over. She would know if any were missing just by looking?"

"Oh, indeed she would," I replied. "And she'd be able to tell if they had been misshelved or were a quarter inch out of alignment."

"So you're saying no one could take a book away—even with permission?"

"Middlebank is the home of the collection—we are not a lending library. Fans of books and mysteries come to us." At least, that was the intention. What would this death do to my chances of revitalizing the Society?

"Is there anything else of value in the house?" Hopgood asked.

I shook my head. "Even our tea service is silver plate. Good quality, of course. Sergeant," I continued, breaking my Marie biscuit into pieces too tiny to dunk, "apart from how he got in, how did he die? I saw the—" I gestured to the back of my own head. "Did someone hit him?"

"It's early days yet, Ms. Burke, and the medical examiner will have more information for us once she's got him—"

He seemed to swallow his next words, and I was glad of it. My eyes fell to my cup of tea, sitting in the saucer, surrounded by biscuit crumbs.

"How well did you know the deceased?" Hopgood asked.

"I didn't know him—well. Just after I began my job here, I saw a notice that the writers group needed to find a new place to meet—their previous location was no longer available." Actually, I

was unclear on that point—I had a feeling they'd been booted
out of a coffee shop or something. "And as their focus is writing
Agatha Christie fan fiction, I felt they would be a good match for the
Society."

"And were they?"

"I . . . they . . . of course, I'm in no way able to . . ."

A commotion at the front door caught our attention.

"Where is Hayley?" I heard a familiar voice ask.

DS Hopgood strolled out of the office, but one of his team
stopped him with a question. I continued to the door. A uniform
blocked entry to Harry, who stood on the threshold, clutching her
laptop to her chest.

"Harry, what are you doing here?"

"You've got the police," she replied, trying to see over my shoulder.

"Yes, but how did you know that?"

"Amanda," she stated. "Amanda runs."

I waited for her to finish the sentence, and then realized she had.

"Yes, that's right. I saw her late one afternoon—running."

"And she ran past here earlier and saw the police cars. She texted
the group to say did we know what was up, and no one did."

"She texted you? And everyone answered?" Beads of cold sweat
broke out on my forehead.

"Yeah—no. Mariella, Peter—" She counted them off on her fingers. "But nothing from Trist yet. He's probably at work. Was it a
break-in?" She caught sight of a member of the coverall brigade
coming down the stairs. "Cor—SOCO. What's happened, Hayley?"

Her answer came from the DS. "I'm Detective Sergeant Hopgood." He held his warrant card over my shoulder, and I took a step
away from the door. "And you are . . . ?"

"Harry Tanner, sir. What's happened?"

"Harry, is it?" he asked.

"Harriet, if you must," she replied. "Although I prefer Harry. You've no idea the prejudice that still exists when it comes to a woman writing crime. Look how many of us still must resort to hiding our identity in order to be accepted—using initials and the like."

"Harry is a member of the writers group," I explained.

"Ah, in that case, Ms. Tanner, I'd like to have a word with you. One of your fellow writers, Tristram Cummins, was found dead in the library, and we have yet to sort out the circumstances."

Harry's eyes grew as big as full moons. "My God, Trist?" she whispered.

"Come with me, please." DS Hopgood led the way to Mrs. Woolgar's office.

Harry lagged behind as she pulled her phone out of a pocket. Her thumbs flew over the screen, and before she'd reached the office door, the phone had been put away again.

6

One by one they appeared at Middlebank's door. Not ten minutes after Harry went into the interview room, Mariella ignored the uniform's request to wait on the pavement and used the pushchair—with baby inside—to barrel her way into the entry. When Harry emerged from her interview, Mariella left the baby with her and went in next. Before Mariella had finished, Peter arrived, running his hand over his slicked-back hair as he ignored me, but questioned the PC about what happened. He received no answers. At last, here came Amanda—changed out of her sleek running togs and back into her shapeless coat.

After each member of the fan-fiction group cycled through the interview room and gave their statements, they—along with the baby in its pushchair—hung about in the entry, forcing police officers to navigate around them to get up or down the stairs. As the writers watched everything that went on, I stayed nearby, watching them.

At last, DS Hopgood finished with the group, and the interview tables were turned.

"Swept the scene, have they, Sergeant?" Peter asked.

Mariella bounced the pushchair as the baby fussed. "Are you sending them on a door-to-door?"

"What do you think, Sergeant—was he after the first editions?" Amanda speculated.

"He didn't care about the collection," Peter scoffed. "'An elitist's hobby,' he called it."

"You'll be reviewing the closest CCTV," Harry said, "but I doubt you'll find anything nearer than the bus stop on the other side of Guinea Lane."

"You know who Trist would blame, don't you?" Amanda asked her fellow writers.

"Will you be willing to share the forensics report, Sergeant?" Peter asked.

"Ms. Burke!" DS Hopgood shot me a look. "A word, please."

We stepped back into Mrs. Woolgar's office, leaving the writers in the entry discussing what time they would meet at the station the following morning to have their fingerprints taken and sign statements.

"This is not one of Mrs. Christie's stories," the DS hissed at me.

"Yes, Sergeant." I'd said the same thing to him, but I didn't think now was a good time to point that out, not with his face turned this deep shade of beetroot.

"They were asking me as many questions as I was asking them," he complained. "So, I would like your assurance that these people"— was I grateful he didn't call them *my lot?*—"will in no way hamper my investigation."

"I'll do what I can, but I am not responsible for—"

"Well, I'm making you responsible." His raised eyebrows drew up into a bristly peak. "And tell me—what did that one mean by who the victim would blame?"

"It was a joke, I'm afraid—Trist had made a few comments about Lady Fowling's ghost moving the furniture."

"Ghosts!" he sputtered. He gave the cluster of writers in the entry a hard look, which none of them noticed. "Keep them out of my way."

"Yes, sir."

My head hurt and I was hungry. I'd never seen such a crowd at Middlebank, and for a moment I thought, *Well, there you are—The First Edition Society can really pull them in, can't it?* I took two deep breaths before approaching the group.

"As you can see, the police have everything here in hand," I said. "Now, I realize you're all quite upset about Trist"—although, if that were true, they hid it well—"but it would be better for the investigation if you'd clear out and let Sergeant Hopgood and Constable . . ."

"Pye," the four of them filled in.

"Yes, Constable Pye. Let them do their jobs, all right?"

In mutinous fashion, they remained where they were until I said, "So, move along," as if they were yobs loitering on the pavement. They oozed toward the door like treacle, giving me plenty of time to add, "And I'm not sure about next week. I'll let you know. Wait, I only had Trist's number—could I have one of yours?" Once we had that sorted, I herded them out the door.

"Ronnie?"

The ME in her paper outfit padded out from the kitchenette, shaking what looked like an empty, clear plastic bag at Hopgood. He took it and held it up to the light while she stripped off her coveralls, and they had a brief and all-too-quiet conversation. The woman nodded behind her, and the two of them returned to the kitchenette—

I followed as they continued outdoors and down the stone steps and to the back gate, where DS Hopgood turned to me and said, "Would you wait here a moment, please?"

I watched as they entered Gravel Walk, a tree-lined public path behind the entire terrace. A wrought-iron railing ran along the back-garden side of the walk. It was painted black and punctuated by five-foot-high posts along the way—each post ornamented with a cannonball-sized topper. Now blue-and-white police tape stretched from the railing across the path, wrapped round a tree trunk, and back to the railing about fifteen feet down. The detective sergeant and medical examiner ducked under the tape, and she began a pantomime. Gesturing to one of the toppers, she spread her arms out and backed up toward the post. It took little imagination to understand her role-playing. Trist had hit his head on that particular cannonball topper.

A man with a Westie on a lead and two women with prams passed, taking the impromptu detour that spilled them out onto the grass before they could rejoin the path farther down. They glanced at the activity with mild interest but didn't stop. I scanned the area—so familiar and yet now so alien. On the other side of Gravel Walk a line of horse chestnut trees separated walkers from the road, and on the other side of the road was a car park for the tennis courts. This could be a busy area—at least during the day. If Trist got into Middlebank from the back and it was late at night, would anyone have seen?

When Hopgood and the ME returned, she continued into the house and he pulled up beside me.

"Well, here's the thing, Ms. Burke," he said. "It looks as if Mr. Cummins did indeed hit his head on something—on that rail topper down the way. Forensics has taken samples and will confirm that. And when he did, he must've collapsed onto the gravel—some of it is lodged in the wound. There doesn't seem to be a great deal of blood, which indicates he likely died immediately."

I stared at the gravel path and the railing. "How awful," I said. "But, if he died there, how did he get to the library?"

"A bit of a problem, isn't it?" Hopgood brushed his finger across his mustache thoughtfully. "Did the victim meet someone along Gravel Walk behind the terrace—or was it an unplanned encounter? Was he pushed into the railing or did he fall? If he died out here, why take him in there? He's a big man—tall, at least, although quite thin. Still, the body would've been unwieldy, and yet we find no indications that it was dragged off. The gravel tells no tales—it's been fairly dry and would be easy to scuff over. Still, the body would be quite a load for one person. Or did it require two?"

I didn't answer, as I was too taken up with the speculative way he was looking at me. At last, the penny dropped. "Seriously? Do you think Mrs. Woolgar and I moved a dead man from Gravel Walk into our back garden, up the stone steps, through the kitchenette, and up another flight of stairs to the library?"

"Doesn't make much sense, does it?" he agreed. "But someone did it."

During the morning, police had had what DS Hopgood called a "shufti" throughout the house. That apparently meant a nose round, although why he couldn't speak plain English was beyond me. Mrs. Woolgar had accompanied them for most of the tour while Pauline had remained in my office, except for forays into the kitchenette to make another pot of tea. The scene-of-crime officers had dusted doors for fingerprints, walked through our flats, stood in the doorway of the cellar—as far as they could get—and walked round my cartons in the attic.

Now, as they began to move out, I glanced up the stairs and panicked. What about Trist? Hopgood followed my gaze and said, "The hearse has collected the body. And we're finished with a sweep of the library, so you're welcome to go back inside."

Great, thanks.

"There's a solicitor involved with the Society, no doubt?" the sergeant asked.

"Mr. Duncan Rennie—I'll give you his details. The firm goes back a long way with the family—Mr. Rennie's grandfather started as Sir John's solicitor."

Both DS Hopgood and DC Pye handed out their cards to the three of us—Mrs. Woolgar, Pauline, and me—as we stood at the front door to bid them farewell, like good hosts.

"There'll be more questions," Hopgood warned us.

I had one. "Is it safe for us to stay here?"

"I'd say that's up to the two of you—Mrs. Woolgar's already asked about changing your outside door locks and the security code. Fine by us. You've got your own doors and you say nothing was disturbed in your flats, but you may want to get new locks there, too. And you may feel more comfortable—at least for a night or two—staying elsewhere. We'll keep an eye out—I'll have a patrol car drive by hourly and uniforms on foot along the path behind. We'll continue that as long as need be."

The door closed, and we were instantly wrapped in silence as if we'd been packed in cotton wool.

"Shall I come back another day to finish?" Pauline asked, the duster hanging lifelessly at her side. "I could do on Monday."

"No, next Thursday will be fine."

"You'll need a new key and code by then," Mrs. Woolgar said. "Shall I ring the locksmith now, Ms. Burke, and then look for the booklet on the security system?"

After Pauline left, Mrs. Woolgar and I retreated to our own flats, agreeing to meet at four o'clock to . . . to do what, I wasn't sure. But I had noticed the gray cast to her complexion that almost matched her steel-colored hair—and if Mrs. Woolgar felt half as drained as I did, we both needed a nap.

I locked myself in my flat and leaned on the door—grateful to escape into my sanctuary. But snippets of scenes from the day flitted across the screen of my mind like a poorly edited film—Trist's face with unseeing eyes, police tramping up and down the stairs—and a swell of emotion rose up in my chest.

"No!" I straightened up, banished any thoughts of murder, and went to the kitchen to cook an omelet for my lunch.

Food gave me a clearer head but did nothing for the ache in my heart. I needed to be comforted. I needed to talk to Wyn.

"Hello, you," he answered.

Upon hearing his chipper voice, I could barely speak, but at last eked out a feeble "Hello, you" in reply.

"Did you know it's quite important to keep a stable temperature in a cream sauce to keep it from breaking?"

Wyn had an interesting conversational style—he rarely introduced a topic before diving in. Although accustomed to it, I often had to gallop to keep up.

"Are you cooking?"

"No, only a bit of research. Tommy was looking into Italian for lunches, and I got worried about the alfredo sauce traveling all that way in Myrtle's food box. Temperature may be a bit of a problem, and also, the food is getting knocked round in there. Never mind—how's the world of mysteries?"

"I think I prefer them in a book to the real thing. You see . . ." and I dropped onto the sofa and told him of my day.

"My God, Hayley—right there, in your own house?"

Wyn was still a bit shaky about what constituted my living arrangements and thought I had the run of Middlebank, but I knew we'd sort that out when he came down for a visit. In the meantime, I heard the concern in his voice, and it made me a bit teary. I kept myself in check while I explained the various components of the house again.

"Well, you really shouldn't be there on your own until the police have sorted the whole thing."

"We're getting new locks, and we're changing the security code on the alarm—but I suppose I would feel better with someone else about." *Why not you? Wouldn't you come to Bath to comfort your girlfriend?*

"Say, why don't you stay with Adele? She'd have you for a night or two, wouldn't she?"

"Yeah, of course she would."

"And you'll be off to see your mum at the weekend?"

"I will."

"Look, here's Tommy now—I've got to go. We're going to walk a delivery route carrying the alfredo in the box—can't trust it to Myrtle yet—just to see how it fares. You sure you're all right?"

I made a noise that resembled an answer of sorts—all I could do as tears streamed down my cheeks.

"Love you," he said, and was gone.

"Love you"—I could only mouth the words as my face scrunched up and a howl escaped. I pulled a pillow to my chest as sobs racked my body, but in a few minutes, my misery eased to ragged breathing. After a hiccup or two, I panted as I regained my composure and wiped my face on my sleeve. This was not normal behavior for me—

it must be shock. I rested my head against the back of the sofa, and—
still clutching the pillow—fell asleep. I awoke confused, and it took me
a moment before I remembered it all. Yes, that's right—Trist, dead
in the library. And not by his own hand, it appeared. A murder.

I recoiled at my reflection in the bathroom mirror—blotchy face,
swollen eyes. I splashed cold water to no effect and tried to remember the puffy-eye remedies I'd read about in magazines. Slices of
cucumber? Didn't have time for that—didn't have the cucumber.
Used tea bags? I would need to drink a cup of tea first. I switched the
kettle on and checked the time. Just gone three—was Adele finished
with school yet? I dug my phone out from where it had slipped between sofa cushions.

Bit of bother here.

I stared at the words of the text I'd written. *Bother* made it sound
as if we had a leaky kitchen tap, not a murder. Problem? Fuss? Commotion? No, don't try to explain.

Give me a ring.

I'd finished my tea and worked my way into a package of chocolate hobnobs—eyeing the clock as the time edged toward four when
Adele rang.

"Sorry," she said, "I had the Young Suffragettes Club after school
today. Is something up?"

"Yeah, something is definitely up." I'd cried myself dry, and so I
was ready to give her a coherent rundown of events. "One of the
writers was murdered and left in the library for us to find."

"Bloody hell. Are you all right?"

"Yes—neither Mrs. Woolgar nor I heard a thing. It must've happened sometime during the night."

"And he was killed right there?"

"No, that's the thing. The writers had left. We were locked up—the alarm was set. But he died out on Gravel Walk—and apparently he was carried back in and up to the library."

"Who would . . . Listen, you don't want to stay there tonight, do you? Pack your bag—my sofa's free. I'll be home by six."

At four o'clock, I'd changed into denims and a sweater and tried more cold water on my face, but to no avail, and so I swore off mirrors for the time being. I carefully negotiated my way down the stairs and past the library door—closed and looking ever so innocent—and to the ground floor, where Mrs. Woolgar waited for me.

"The locksmith will be here tomorrow morning," she reported. "It's as early as I could get him. Perhaps the morning would also be a good time to sort out the security code change." The secretary kept her eyes on the floor. "I've decided not to stay here this evening, Ms. Burke—with what's happened, I'm not sure I would feel safe. I'm sorry to abandon you like this, but perhaps you could—"

"It's fine, Mrs. Woolgar, really." It was a relief, that's what it was—she was jumping ship first, and so I only needed to follow. "I've made other arrangements, too, but I'll be back well before nine o'clock tomorrow morning and ready to meet the locksmith." I glanced round the entry, so calm after the earlier congestion. "I wonder, will the police need to return?"

"I certainly hope not," she huffed. "Well, then—I'll be off." It was only then did I notice the small case just inside her office door and realized she was poised to flee.

"Before you go . . ." I began.

She paused and waited while I got up my nerve. I didn't want her to undermine my position and derail any plans for the Society, but I should tread carefully. "I'm sure you'll agree it's my place as curator to tell the board what has happened."

"They'll need to know soon," she replied.

"Of course they will. I will ring each one of them tomorrow morning and explain."

She conceded with a brief nod, and added, "Yes, all right."

But I had seen a flicker behind her eyes, and reminded myself that Mrs. Woolgar had a mole on the board. I knew then that I'd already lost my advantage.

7

❧❦❧

We left it at that. Tomorrow I would have to sort out whatever damage Mrs. Woolgar might have done to my position with the board of trustees. I flew up to my flat, crammed clean knickers and a toothbrush into my bag, and made it out the front door in three minutes. I set the alarm before leaving, although I wondered what good it would do.

Adele wouldn't be home for a while, but just as well, because I needed to have my fingerprints taken and sign my statement. I walked down to the police station amid the rest of the world—schoolchildren, autumn tourists at the Roman baths. They paid me no mind, but still I felt an alien among the throng, set apart by the discovery that morning of a corpse outside the door of my flat.

A sea of commuters swarmed up from the rail station, and I hurried to avoid them, taking a sharp right into the Avon and Somerset Constabulary. I stopped inside the lobby to get my bearings. A uniformed woman behind a desk greeted me, and when I told her why I was there, she didn't blink an eye, but directed me to a door where

I was met by another uniform, who took me to a counter where I proffered my hands. It was all so efficient and modern. No more inky fingers like in the old films—instead, I pressed my fingers onto a glass plate and my prints were scanned electronically. I signed my statement that Sergeant Hopgood—or, more likely, someone on his team—had typed up. After that, I was dismissed.

A mizzling rain had started up by the time I got to Adele's flat—a corner, one-bedroom place above a launderette. I was early, and since it hadn't occurred to me to bring a waterproof jacket, I ducked into the grocery across the road and shopped for a bottle of wine for the evening as I kept an eye out the window. I was at the till when I saw her arrive.

Dashing over as she unlocked the door at street level, I asked, "You think one bottle will be enough? I could nip back in for a second one."

Adele gave my cheek a pat. "You've had a dreadful day, haven't you? Never fear, I'm well stocked."

I followed her up the stairs, and once inside, I flumped onto the sofa while Adele dumped her school bag and keys and opened the wine as I recounted the events of the morning.

"I can't believe you'd been out for your walk and went up to your flat," she said, handing me a glass, "and all that time, he was in the library."

"Thanks. And I went to my office, and then downstairs to find out why Mrs. Woolgar was late—it wasn't until Pauline went into the library to clean that he was found. I've no idea how long he'd been there." I shuddered. "To see him stretched out like that on the floor, and to realize I'd known him, that I'd seen him alive only the evening before . . ."

"Well then." Adele held her own glass up. "Here's to him— here's to . . ."

"Trist."

We drank and I sighed and Adele asked, "What was he like?"

I could only shrug. "I don't know—I don't know any of them, actually. Although, I got the feeling he was a bit of a bully." Guilt washed over me for speaking ill of the dead.

"Do you think he could've fallen on Gravel Walk," Adele mused, "and received a mortal wound—but then didn't die immediately? Instead, he carried on—broke in, went up to the library, and collapsed. Haven't you heard of something like that happening?"

"I have to admit I prefer that idea—Trist dying on his own—to someone dragging him indoors and leaving him. Someone who got into Middlebank without any trouble. 'No sign of forced entry.' That's what they said."

"He could've been followed—I suppose the police swept the library for fingerprints and any signs of blood."

"Sergeant Hopgood said he died outdoors, and instantly. That's why there wasn't any blood. And anyway—ewww. How do you think of these things?"

"I read a lot of mysteries," Adele replied. "You should try it."

"All right, all right—I'll get to them." I fumed. "This won't be good for my efforts to increase the Society's standing in the world of genre fiction."

Adele laughed. "Hayley, listen to yourself. What detective writer or fan, upon hearing that a body was found at The First Edition Society in a library full of classic mysteries, wouldn't want to visit the spot? Or at the very least, get on your mailing list."

A thought struck me as hard as a slap. "You don't think the police will suspect I did it for the publicity, do you?"

"Don't be daft—how could you have dragged him up those stairs?"

"Sergeant Hopgood said it might've been two people. I believe his implication was that Mrs. Woolgar and I did it."

"I'd've bought a ticket to see that." Adele laughed again, and this time I joined her. "This is tough for you—and it can't be easy on Glynis either. How is she?"

"Staying off the premises, same as me." I took a drink of my rapidly disappearing wine and added, "I explained that I should be the one to tell the board members what's happened and that I would do it tomorrow morning. I didn't think it was wise to say anything before we had more information. But I think she's already been on the phone to them."

"I'm on the board, and you told me."

"Well, that's different—you're my friend."

"I daresay Glynis would use the same excuse—they're her friends." I reached for the bottle of wine as Adele reached for her phone. "Pizza?"

A nything on your literary salons?" Adele asked. "Did you hear back from Bath College?"

We'd moved away from the murder, and I was feeling much better—aided by food and the second bottle of wine. "Yes, a lecturer from the adult-learning program—Val Moffatt. We talked over the idea, and I think it'll work. Of course, first he'll have to get approval." My spirits took a nosedive. "But how will a murder help us there? The college will think we're a risky venture."

Adele bit her lip as she thought. "You might want to give the college a formal presentation. Be professional, stay focused. I don't see why you'd have to ask our board for permission, but if they want to know anything, remember to shift your emphasis—you know what I mean?"

Oh, I did indeed. She meant for our board, always make it about Lady Fowling—who would've been delighted at such a venture—

and not about tearing at the fabric of the quiet and complacent Society. For the college—"I'll need another meeting with Moffatt."

Adele turned away to reach for a slice of pizza. "And so this Moffatt—he's all right?"

"Actually, he's a bit of a tosser."

"Is he?"

"He had the nerve to point out my luxury accommodations, as if I'm some toff surrounded by the privileges of class and money."

"That's disappointing."

"Doesn't matter." I picked a shred of Parma ham off my pizza and dropped it in my mouth. "I don't need to like him, only to work with him."

I lay awake staring at the dark ceiling, thirsty, with visions of DS Hopgood clapping handcuffs on me and dragging me away as Mrs. Woolgar stood on the doorstep of Middlebank with a malicious grin. Adele was right—why would the police suspect me of having murdered him for the publicity? At three in the morning—Adele had a wall clock with hands that glowed purple—I got up, drank two glasses of water, and returned to the sofa to fall asleep at last. I awoke at half-past six, bloated and still thirsty.

"You can stay here and shower," Adele said as she buttoned her jacket and pulled her hair out from under the collar. "I've an early meeting."

I stabbed a spoon into a bowl of cornflakes. "No, thanks—I'll be off in a minute. I'll shower at home and get myself ready for the day. Must look my best for work, you know."

She gave me the once-over and said, "Good luck with that," as she backed out the door. Her grin, like the Cheshire cat's, was the last to leave.

I dragged myself to Middlebank and stood on the doorstep, over-whelmed by inertia and not a little uneasiness. Had Mrs. Woolgar returned? Had someone else come in during the night and left an-other body in the library? Could I get up the nerve and walk in alone? When a taxi flew down the street and honked at a wayward pedestrian, I jumped, my heart pounding. Shaking off my fears, I shoved the key in the door and entered.

Bunter trotted out of the secretary's office—his usual overnight accommodations—and chastised me for being late with his break-fast. I accompanied him to the kitchenette, topped up his dish—still half full—and cleaned out his litter pan, which resided in the adja-cent loo. Then I scurried upstairs, but stopped dead on the first-floor landing.

The library door was closed, as it had been when I left the after-noon before. I felt both drawn to look in and, at the same time, re-pelled by the thought—and that froze me to the spot. After a moment and with great effort, I crept closer, and with a shaking hand, opened the door. Nothing. The large table and chairs were perfectly composed. The shelves of books were undisturbed. The library ladder stood in its corner, and at the far end of the room near the fireplace, the wingback chairs and tea table looked not an inch out of place.

I laughed in relief. What did I think—that a murdered writer would be found in the same spot each morning? That the ghost of Lady Fowling would be waiting for me to begin my instruction in the ways of detecting?

A good, hot shower in my own flat brought me to my senses, and I arrived back on the ground floor in time to make myself a cup of tea before the door buzzed. I let the locksmith in.

Mrs. Woolgar surfaced from below to oversee the work. This took most of the morning, as it involved replacement locks for both the front and back doors as well as our flats—can't be too careful—and ended with each of us trying out the new keys to ensure everything was in working order. I took a set for Pauline, and the secretary said she would lock the other spare key in her desk as usual.

Spare key in her desk?

"I didn't realize you had a spare key." I had waited until the door closed on the locksmith before speaking. "Have you always kept it there?"

"Two spare sets, Ms. Burke—to the outside doors only," Mrs. Woolgar replied. "It is my policy to be prepared. And both were there yesterday morning when I checked. I explained that to the police."

But not to me—not until I asked.

After we sorted out programming a new code for the door, I tugged at my jacket and said, "I'm going to ring the board members now, Mrs. Woolgar. To let them know what has happened. I'll tell them the police are looking into Trist's death and there is no cause for concern."

"I daresay they may have got wind of it by now."

That was as good as a confession to me.

"Whatever they've heard, I need to assure them that there is nothing to worry about."

We retreated to our offices. First, I checked my e-mail, but there was nothing from Bath College or Val Moffatt. Perhaps no news was the best I could hope for on that front. I pulled out my list of board members, studied the five names, and put a small tick by Adele's before dialing the first number.

"Hello, Mrs. Arbuthnot? It's Hayley Burke."

"I've been expecting you to ring, dear." Jane Arbuthnot had a rather Eeyore-like tone of voice, full of doom and gloom, now topped with the heavy implication that she'd been waiting far too long for my call.

"Yes, well . . ." I breezed through my explanation of recent events, ending with a cheery, "And although it was a dreadful thing to happen, I want to assure you that everything is under control, and that we will carry on here at the Society while the police do their job."

"I suppose it's all one can expect from inviting a group of total strangers into Middlebank. I don't know what Georgiana would say."

"Lady Fowling herself wrote fan fiction, as I'm sure you know. I imagine she would've welcomed the group with open arms."

"Georgiana's little stories did not result in murder."

They did on the page—but was now the time to debate this?

Next up, Maureen Frost—the daughter of a friend of Lady Fowling's. The friend had died ages ago, and Ms. Frost herself must be near seventy.

"And so, Ms. Frost, I didn't want you to worry," I said after telling her what I was sure she already knew.

"I certainly hope this will put a stop to any other outrageous ideas," was her reply. "The Society is just fine as it is."

I could hear Mrs. Woolgar's influence in the words of both Mrs. Arbuthnot and Ms. Frost—but even if they were in the secretary's pocket, I still held a majority of support on the board with Adele and the last two names on my list.

"Hello, this is Hayley Burke at the Society," I said when my last phone call was answered. "Is this Mrs. Moon or Mrs. Moon?"

My attempt at a bit of lighthearted humor—Mrs. Sylvia Moon and Mrs. Audrey Moon—both dear friends of Lady Fowling—had married brothers. They had known each other for so long that, after their husbands died, Audrey had moved into Sylvia's town house, which they had refurbished so that the ladies' living quarters were on the ground floor and the first floor was let to a couple of architects.

"It's Hayley on the phone, Sylvia," Mrs. Audrey Moon called out. "Oh dear, Hayley, how awful for you that poor man dying like he did—practically under your nose."

"That's why I'm ringing—to let you know that the police have it all in hand. I didn't want you to worry, as I know you'll soon be off on your cruise." Time to change direction. "Have you started packing?" I asked brightly.

"Oh my, we've been packed for weeks—I've completely forgotten what I've put in my cases. Sylvia? Did you want to speak with Hayley?"

I heard a faint voice in the background. "Tell her bon voyage! Oh, wait, she's supposed to say that to us, isn't she?"

"Bon voyage!" I called.

"Hayley, dear," Mrs. Audrey Moon added with a note of high spirits in her voice, "while we're away—you won't get up to any more mischief, will you?"

8

❧◈❧

"That went quite well," I said to Bunter after I'd finished my calls to the board. "All things considered. My plan for the literary salons—they could never think that 'mischief,' could they? And it isn't as if I'll need the board's approval for the idea. I have powers as curator, and I can do these things." Bunter yawned.

The front-door buzzer went off, and I heard Mrs. Woolgar answer. After a brief exchange, she brought Amanda to my door and left without a word.

"Hi, Hayley." Amanda twisted the belt of her shapeless jacket round one finger. "I was hoping you had a minute."

"Yes, of course." I gestured to the wingback. "Bunter—could you . . ."

The cat hopped off and strolled over to the fireplace rug. Amanda took the vacated chair, perched on the edge of the seat, and looked at the floor. "I don't know what we're going to do without him."

"You mean about meeting here next Wednesday? I don't know yet if we can carry on the way we have."

"No, not that. Well, in a way, I did come about the group. It occurred to me that you don't know us well, and you may not be aware that some of us have . . . history with each other."

I had known next to nothing about the group before I had let them in the door—my mistake.

"Have you been meeting long?"

"About six months. Trist had posted a notice online about forming the group, so you'd think we'd've all been strangers coming together that way, but it wasn't the case. Turns out Trist and Harry had been previously . . . involved."

"Involved?"

"It's long over—two, three years ago, I think—and they had become friends, I suppose. But, I believe Harry still harbored a great deal of hurt. And you saw how Trist could be with people. Still, that's no excuse for—" A brief pause and then she hurried on. "It isn't that I suspect Harry of anything, it's only that the police should have every detail in an enquiry, but I'm not entirely sure she mentioned this to them. And so I thought you could let them know."

"But why don't *you* tell the police?"

"How would that look—a fellow writer grassing her up? And really, it would be better coming from a third party. I can't tell you the number of times Tommy and Tuppence were the ones to take evidence to police. Not that this is evidence, of course."

"And won't police want to know how this 'third party' got hold of the information?"

Amanda wrinkled her nose as she considered the problem. "Well, you've made friends with us in the group"—*Untrue*—"and so, of course you'd know a bit about our personal lives." *Also untrue.* "And maybe you could assume that the police are already aware of their past, and so you could mention it casually. Because, perhaps they do know. They would've searched Trist's flat and found his journal and read it."

"Would Trist have kept notes on a relationship from three years ago?"

"He's a writer—we keep notes on everything." Amanda popped up and flipped her blond braid over her shoulder. "Sorry, Hayley— I've got to dash."

She scooted out the door, leaving me trying to imagine a man pouring out his heart about a former relationship. Would he put his thoughts in a leather-bound diary with a tiny heart-shaped lock? No, I couldn't quite see it.

I sat back in my chair and considered the assignment Amanda had dropped in my lap. I didn't fancy the role of clearinghouse in this enquiry, but eventually, I dug out DS Hopgood's card and reached for my phone. Once again the buzzer went off, and Mrs. Woolgar answered. This time, she came to my door alone.

"It's two more of them."

I found Peter and Mariella on the doorstep—and the baby, wearing a blue Bath Rugby jersey, in his pushchair.

"I've been by the station and had my fingerprints taken," Mariella said in a pained voice. "The detective sergeant was quite short with me when I asked how the enquiry was going and if they'd found any untoward fibers on the rug in the library." She accompanied her complaint with jiggling the handle of the pushchair so that it bobbed up and down.

"I had been in just before Mariella and asked if the ME had finished the autopsy yet and received the same sort of response," Peter said. "We've a right to ask, but instead of answering, the sergeant only asked us more questions, and then referred us to you. Why?"

Because he's appointed me your minder, that's why.

I didn't invite them in. "I'm sorry, but no one's told me anything. I'd say we should let the police do their job, don't you think?"

"Early days yet, I suppose," Peter said.

"Did you two know Trist?" I asked, unable to stop myself. "Is that how you joined the group?"

They exchanged looks. Then Mariella said, "Trist fancied himself a book doctor. I had contacted him a couple of years ago about the format for my version of *Murder in Mesopotamia*."

At this comment, Peter sighed and dug his hands in his pockets. Mariella continued. "My Hercule Poirot's superpower is that he sees a suspect's thoughts as the person is speaking. The thoughts appear in a dialogue balloon like you see in old comics." She waved her arms in the air above our heads. "All the suspects' balloons are in green, except for the murderer—he sees *that* one in red. I'm considering publishing it as a graphic novel."

With a self-satisfied smile, she dropped her arms.

"That's quite . . . clever," I replied. "But then, wouldn't he—and the reader—know who the murderer was immediately and wouldn't that bring the end of the book rather too soon?"

Mariella's smile vanished. "I'm sorting out the problems—despite Trist's scathing comments."

"He didn't care for innovation," Peter said. "I'm rewriting *The Murder of Roger Ackroyd* and replacing all the characters with present-day celebrities. He told me I was mad as a box of frogs. And this from a man who wrote about zombies."

"But if he was in charge of the group and you didn't like his feedback, why did you stay in?" I asked.

Mariella shrugged. "He could come up with the occasional sharp insight into character."

"He understood pacing quite well," Peter added.

"And so, really," I continued, trying to get this straight, "you were all friends."

Peter snorted. "Yeah, right, best mates. Well, see you on Wednesday."

"What? No—that is, perhaps. I'm not sure. You'll hear from me about that."

After I offered the empty promise—to pass along anything I heard from the police—they left and I headed back to my office, pausing in Mrs. Woolgar's doorway.

"I don't know how they think I could know anything," I said.

"Perhaps they believe you've mounted your own enquiry," she replied.

When I was back sitting at my desk, I thought about what she had said and only then decided she'd meant it as an insult—suspecting, quite correctly, that I knew nothing about mysteries, murders, and detecting. I *harrumphed* loud enough to wake Bunter from his nap.

"Perhaps I should carry out my own investigation—that would show her," I whispered to him, knowing that I would do nothing of the kind.

When the buzzer sounded once more, I leapt to my feet and hurried to the door, calling, "I'll take care of it, Mrs. Woolgar."

I was not surprised to find Harry on the doorstep, laptop clutched to her chest.

"I've had my fingerprints taken," she stated.

"You took your computer along?"

She looked down at it. "I thought they might want to see my work in progress. Sort of prime the pump of their enquiry."

I sighed. "Come in, Harry." I led her to my office and the chairs by the fireplace. Bunter remained on the rug, and we were a threesome.

"Did they tell you anything?" I asked.

"I didn't see them—both DS Hopgood and DC Pye were otherwise engaged."

Or hiding. "Harry, did you know any of the other writers before you joined the group?"

It was an innocent-sounding question—at least I hoped that's how it came across. Harry didn't speak for a moment, but her eyes grew wide and filled with tears that threatened to overflow their banks.

"Trist and I . . . for about a year . . ." Her voice drifted off, weak and watery. "But it was ages ago. I ended it—I didn't feel it was a healthy relationship for me." She sniffed, blinked rapidly, and, miraculously, no tears fell.

"Still, his death must've come as quite a shock. You did tell the police about knowing him, didn't you?"

Harry cocked her head, as if listening to an echo of the question. After a moment, she said, "No, I didn't. There was no reason, really—it was over so long ago. And we remained friends, and so it was no bother to either of us to be in the group together."

"Isn't it the sort of thing police would prefer to know than not know? Even if it has no bearing on the enquiry?"

Harry stared at the cold fireplace for several seconds and then jumped up.

"Right, I'll go straight back to the station and tell them the entire story."

"And won't you feel better for it?" I asked, following her out.

Pausing at the open front door, Harry became wistful. "He had a keen ear for dialogue, did Trist—although we tried to joke with him that his Miss Marple could be switched out for Miss Silver and no one would ever know it."

I certainly wouldn't have—who was Miss Silver?

As I returned to my office, I recalled Harry and Trist's squabble on the last night of the group—something Trist had said edged too close to criticism for her. That must've been an old issue for them. But I hadn't long to think about it—I'd been back at my desk two minutes when the front door buzzed. For one second, I considered tearing it off the wall, but instead, I hurried out, noticing Mrs. Woolgar hadn't moved an inch from her desk, and flung open the door to Detective Sergeant Hopgood.

"Hello, good morning, Sergeant." I stepped aside to let him in.

"The end of a morning, Ms. Burke, which I have spent fielding questions from those writers."

I believe that *avoiding* those writers would be more correct, but it wasn't for me to say.

"Please come through."

As we passed her door, Mrs. Woolgar looked up and Hopgood nodded, and then stepped out of Bunter's way as the cat trotted up the stairs. He had several hiding places in Middlebank, and at that moment, I longed to follow him to one.

"I don't suppose you saw Harry Tanner outside?" I asked.

Hopgood stood in the doorway to my office, his eyes darting round as if expecting an ambush. "Ms. Tanner—was she here?"

"She dropped in. I believe she has something else to add to what she told you yesterday. We were all under a great deal of stress," I explained, not really sure why I felt the need to excuse Harry. "And that can make it difficult to remember everything one should say. Haven't you found that the case? Please, sit down, Sergeant. Would you like a cup of tea?"

"No, thank you." Hopgood settled in one of the fireplace chairs and I in the other. He pulled a small notebook and pencil out of his breast pocket. "Ms. Burke, who has access to your keys and the security code for your alarm system?"

I felt sure we'd been over this the day before. "No one—apart from me and Mrs. Woolgar. I don't think even the solicitor has a key. Oh, Pauline, our cleaner, has a key and the code."

"Ah, Ms. Lunn."

"But she's worked here since just after Lady Fowling died three years ago. She's completely trustworthy. Plus, I'm sure she knows the books in the library are not all that valuable. Did you ask her about the key yesterday?"

"And will continue to do so—police work is nothing if not repetitive. You can be sure Mrs. Woolgar will get the same question again before I leave." His mustache twitched. "Does Ms. Lunn have keys to your living quarters?"

"No, there didn't seem to be a need, as we were always here. We leave our flats unlocked for her on Thursdays. It's different getting her in the front door—I'm often out early in the morning, and Mrs. Woolgar hasn't come up from her flat yet when Pauline arrives."

"As you are in the same house, why do your flats have their own locks and keys?"

"Our flats are our homes," I explained, "and the rest of Middlebank is The First Edition Society. We didn't want to confuse Society members—or potential members—who come here to see the library and learn about Lady Fowling, as to which part of the house they had access to."

"And do you have many of these visitors?"

Just a routine question, I told myself, but still my face burned. "Not at present, but we have great plans."

He jotted something down, and then asked, "Now, Ms. Burke, your relationship to this writers group."

"I have no relationship to them—it was an arrangement. Have they been able to tell you anything?"

"Nothing useful as yet. What they most want to do is advise me." Hopgood drummed his fingertips on his knees. "I spoke too soon yesterday—about how the body was moved. It's been pointed out to me that it's entirely within the realm of possibility that one person— woman or man—could've picked the victim up and carried him in a fireman's lift with little problem." His eyebrows rose. "Do you know what that is?"

Did it make me a suspect if I did?

"With the person horizontal across both shoulders, is that right?"

"Mmm. The arrangement for the group to meet here—was it to continue?"

I squirmed. "I had started to reconsider the offer—I'm not sure they were a good fit for the Society. But I would hardly murder one of them to accomplish that—I only needed to tell them."

"Did they get along?"

"They had their differences of opinion, but at the end of an evening, they usually headed off to the pub together."

"Yes, so they tell me. We've got the CCTV from the pub and can see who left when and which way they went."

"Do you know what time Trist died?"

"Between two and four in the morning. I don't like having such a wide window. The temperature in the house is fairly stable, but if he lay outdoors for any length of time, the cold would've delayed the normal process the body goes through when—"

The DS held up, mid-thought, and I appreciated it, suspecting that he was nearing details I might not like to hear. But I did wish he would have caught himself just a wee bit earlier.

"So, Ms. Burke. A person such as yourself—curator of a society dedicated to first-edition mysteries and, I'm sure, a fan of Mrs. Christie and her detectives—you can't tell me you haven't come up with a few ideas of your own."

Here's the sum total of what I knew about Agatha Christie's sleuths—Miss Marple was a little old lady and Hercule Poirot a finicky Belgian. I'd never heard of Tommy and Tuppence until the writers group arrived.

"I don't know how you could think that."

"Oh, come now—all those detectives in books. You must've picked up a few pointers."

I shifted in my seat, unable to keep still as I sought a plausible excuse. "I'll have you know, Sergeant, that I understand the difference between my responsibilities and yours. It is not for me to dig into people's lives and ask a lot of unpleasant questions. I would not *presume* to do the job of the police. Why would I even *want* to?"

Hopgood held up his open hands in surrender. "All right, all right—keep your hat on. But you must see it's a bit odd that the mystery expert in our midst is the only one not trying to horn in on my enquiry."

"It isn't my place," I said, nose in the air. But as he had brought it up, I added, "Is it possible that it could be one of those accidents where Trist hit his head, but got up and came inside Middlebank and up to the library, and only then collapsed and died?"

"Aha!" Hopgood stabbed a victorious finger in the air. "I knew you would come up with something."

"It's only a thought," I said weakly. And not my own—it was Adele's.

"Sadly, no," the sergeant said. "You saw the wound at the back of his head, and you saw the topper on the railing—like a cannonball. Mr. Cummins would have had to be fair flying backward to crack his head that hard. It wasn't only an internal injury—his skin was broken. If he'd lived for even a few minutes, he would've bled profusely. No, he was shoved against that railing—and shoved with a great deal of force. Died instantly."

I sighed. Trist dead outside on Gravel Walk, then transported upstairs to the library—along with his . . .

"Sergeant, what about Trist's leather case? He always carried it."

"No sign of a case, Ms. Burke. Had you ever seen its contents?"

I shook my head. "So it was robbery?"

"The other writers—when I can get them away from advising me about the enquiry—say they had only ever seen printed pages of his book inside. And he had his wallet and identification with him, along with eighty-three pounds forty pence. The murderer didn't care one whit about that."

"Fingerprints anywhere?"

"Not a single dab," Hopgood said, then took note of my blank look. "That is, we found fingerprints around the library from you, Mrs. Woolgar, Ms. Lunn, and the writers. Except for the door—that had been wiped. A proper job of it, too."

Was that an oblique reference to the person who cleaned Middlebank? I made no comment.

"Well, I'll have that word with Mrs. Woolgar, and that'll be me away." The sergeant rose and I followed him out.

But Mrs. Woolgar was not in her office.

"She must be downstairs in her flat for lunch," I said, checking the time.

"Right, I'll catch her up later. Meanwhile, Ms. Burke, if you do think of anything, you will let us know."

It was high time for me to have a bite of lunch, too. I went to my flat, stood at the kitchen sink, and ate cheese and crackers and grapes, considering what sort of busywork I could assign myself for the afternoon. Ah, yes—the cellar. Changing into old denims and a sweater with a hole in the sleeve, I headed for the lower ground floor, looking into Mrs. Woolgar's office on my way, to find she had returned to her desk.

"Sergeant Hopgood wanted to have another word with you," I said.

"Did he say why?"

"It's about the keys, I think. He asked who would have access to the keys and the alarm code."

"I've told him already."

"Yes, well"—this was not my battle to fight—"I'll be below continuing with the cellar."

But my heart was not in it, and my work consisted only of shifting a few more bits of furniture, and then resting on a side chair. Chippendale—it matched the one on the library landing. I had reached the first carton and found it full of old copies of *Vogue*— really old—and settled down to peruse the June 1953 issue, brimming with stories and photos of the Queen's coronation. That's how Mrs. Woolgar found me when she appeared at the door.

"I'm staying elsewhere again tonight, Ms. Burke—I hope this won't be a problem."

"Thank you for telling me. I'll be perfectly fine here this evening, and I'll be off to Liverpool tomorrow morning as usual. I'll see you—"

"Monday morning." She didn't leave, but instead looked down at the key where I'd left it in the door.

"I will be sure to lock the cellar and keep the key in a safe place," I told her, and went back to my magazine.

But she'd broken the spell—my pretense that nothing was wrong and I always sat in cellars looking at decades-old magazines. I flipped a few more pages, but when I heard Mrs. Woolgar leave her flat and the front door upstairs close, it dawned on me that I was alone in Middlebank. I checked the time—just gone four o'clock. I needed to do a bit of shopping, and so closed up the cellar, retrieved my handbag from my flat, and was at the front door when Bunter reminded me about his dinner.

I fed him and left as he tucked into a dish of fish-in-gravy.

9

〜✧〜

At Waitrose, I stood in front of the refrigerated shelves of ready meals with a wire basket looped over an arm, perusing the offerings as if I were looking at frocks in the window at Jack Wills. While I pondered the macaroni cheese, another shopper came up beside me, and I shifted over a few inches to make room. But I realized I was being watched, and so I took a quick peek to size up the situation.

"Hello," he said.

It was Val Moffatt, wearing scruffy brown trousers, a sweater, and that same green jacket he'd worn the first time I'd seen him. His own shopping basket was half full. I noticed a tiny hole in the neck of his sweater, and then remembered the hole in the sleeve of my own. I put my hand over it.

"Oh, hello, Mr. Moffatt," I said airily.

Neither of us moved as a woman reached round me in a hurry to nab a chicken tikka masala and get on with it.

Moffatt peered in my basket. "You took the last cottage pie, did you?" he asked.

"Sorry?" I looked down at my hoard. "Oh, yes, I suppose I did."

"I'll trade you a lemon pepper chicken for it." He held the container out to me, his face full of hope.

I glanced into his basket. "Can't you do better than that?"

With what appeared to be great reluctance, he pulled out a different dinner. "I do have this four-cheese ravioli I might be willing to let go."

"Done."

We exchanged dinners and smiles, and his eyes crinkled at the corners.

"You wouldn't be interested in another swap?" he asked. "For example, what would you give me for this fine tub of organic strawberry yogurt?"

I wrinkled my nose. "I much prefer mango yogurt."

"Do you, now?" he murmured. "I'll have to keep that in mind."

Jostled from the back, I remembered where we were and said, "Well, I should get on with my shopping." But I found myself disinclined to move.

"I don't suppose—" He hesitated and looked at his shoes. "Did you happen to check your e-mail this afternoon?"

And with that, my spirits dropped to the floor and shattered. "Oh God, they know, don't they? Your people at Bath College have found out what happened at Middlebank. Did they say no to the project? Did they give up just because of a—" An elbow appeared in my vision as a woman reached in for beef stroganoff. I swallowed my next words. "You know, too, don't you—you know about the . . . incident?"

"Yes, I heard."

"So, that's it? We're written off as unreliable and attracting the wrong sort and being the scene of a crime—is that it? Is it over?" My voice trembled, and an edge of hysteria crept in until I ended in little more than a warble.

"Hang on," Moffatt said, and took my elbow, guiding me to the middle of the aisle and out of people's way. "I don't believe it's the end." He glanced at our surroundings—Waitrose on a Friday at five o'clock was a melee. "Look, do you fancy a coffee? I mean, we could go over a few issues before we decide how to approach them."

With great effort I regulated my breathing until I could reply. "Yes, all right—how about the café?"

We went through the basket till to pay and then lugged our bags up the stairs to the Waitrose café, where we joined the queue. I stood on tiptoe to look over the shoulders of the people in front of me and saw one fruit scone left. *Please let no one else take it.* Once I'd had a cup of tea, I'd be better able to assess the situation, as bleak as it seemed. My first big idea for the Society shot down because of a murder—doesn't it just figure?

At the café till, Moffatt asked for a dish of blackberry crumble and a little pitcher of custard with his coffee, and he paid for both our trays. When I protested, he said, "Doing my part in hopes that you won't shoot the messenger." I gave in, and we found a table by the windows that overlooked the bottom of Walcot Street and sat on plastic chairs under fluorescent lights.

Moffatt looked admiringly at our surroundings. "I could live at Waitrose," he said, tucking into his crumble.

"You what?"

"I'm serious. I'm thinking of slipping a cot into that back corner, near the beer aisle. They'd never get rid of me."

I giggled and he smiled. "There now, that's better."

"What is?"

"You were looking a bit glum back there."

"Yes, and with good reason." I buttered my scone and spread strawberry jam over half. "Go on, tell me what they said."

"Oh, various worries about being seen to condone violence and the instability of an organization that has yet to prove itself after the death of its founder. One of our more cynical faculty wondered if this wasn't a publicity stunt on the part of the Society."

"Publicity stunt? I'm sure the victim—Trist—would disagree. And if they'd care for a firsthand account, I'd be happy to describe how horrible it is to look down on the corpse of someone you knew." I sloshed milk into my tea. "Publicity stunt, my—"

"He was talking through his hat," Moffatt cut in.

"Well, there's nothing for it but to meet this head-on. I'll go and talk with them in person. Answer their questions, ease their worries."

Moffatt nodded, his mouth full. When he'd swallowed, he said, "It's just what I thought. Look, we've a faculty meeting on Monday afternoon, three o'clock. I'll put us on the agenda—we'll show them a solid front."

"Yes, that's good. And your friend Amanda can put in a good word for us."

"Amanda? What does she have to do with this?"

"You said it was a friend told you about the idea of a joint venture between the college and the Society. Last Wednesday, I saw that you and Amanda knew each other, so I thought she was the friend who told you about us."

Moffatt laughed. "Amanda's not my friend—she's my student."

"But then, who is your friend?"

"Adele."

I felt as if I'd been bopped on the head. "Adele Babbage?"

"Didn't she mention it?"

No, Adele had been surprisingly mum with this piece of information—even after I'd told her Moffatt was the one who'd been in touch.

"Probably slipped her mind," I offered, not believing my own excuse. A thought niggled at me, but I set it aside to be examined later. "Right, Monday afternoon. But I'll be away all weekend and won't have time to work up anything new. Can we sort out our approach now?"

We did, deciding who would take which talking points. By the time he'd finished his crumble and I'd taken the last bite of my scone, we had our plan—and I had another worry. Would the committee ask me a pointed question about one of those famous detectives in books that I knew nothing about? Would I at last be flushed out for the fraud I was? I shoved that problem into an empty wardrobe in my mind and slammed the door.

"So, you're away," Moffatt said. "It's probably for the best."

"I'm away every weekend. On Saturdays, I go up to see my mum in Liverpool. And this Sunday, I'll spend all day with my boyfriend in London—that's where he lives." I hadn't mentioned that to Wyn, but I knew there would be no problem.

Moffatt drained his cup. "Your mum is in Liverpool? Is that where you're from?"

"No, Herefordshire. When my mum remarried, she moved to Liverpool with her husband. Then he moved to Scotland. They're divorced now."

Toying with his coffee spoon, Moffatt said, "And has your boyfriend not come down here to Bath? You know, considering what you're going through."

"He's quite tied up with his work."

Moffatt lifted his eyebrows. "Where does he work?"

"He works for himself."

I heard my own words, and added quickly, "He's an inventor and at a crucial stage of a new project."

"What does he . . . invent?"

I launched into a vivid and detailed description of Eat Here, Eat Now. "And so, you see, it's difficult for him to get away at the moment, what with the delicate nature of . . . He and his business partner are sorting out the intricacies of . . ." I floundered and grabbed for the nearest life buoy. "It's a fully funded start-up."

Moffatt listened politely without asking questions.

"But I'll return Sunday evening, so there's no problem with the Monday-afternoon meeting."

"But in the meantime, you and Mrs. Woolgar aren't staying in your flats, are you?"

I arched an eyebrow, half waiting for another reference to how good I had it, but nothing else followed. Perhaps I'd taken his remark about my accommodations the wrong way and he'd only been admiring his surroundings. I certainly admired them on a daily basis.

"Mrs. Woolgar is staying elsewhere tonight."

"And you?"

"I stayed at Adele's last night."

"And you will tonight as well?" Moffatt asked with an insistent tone.

"No. I'm perfectly safe at Middlebank. We've changed the locks and the security code. I refuse to be frightened out of my own home."

Moffatt leaned in and whispered fiercely, "Yesterday morning you found a man murdered in the library. There's no point in trying to be brave about it."

"I don't need to be brave," I retorted. "This doesn't have anything to do with—"

"You should stay with Adele!"

"I want to sleep in my own bed!"

My voice echoed off the walls of the café as silence fell round us. I dropped my eyes to the table, wishing I could slide beneath it and hide.

"Do you think anyone heard that?" I asked quietly.

"Oh, I'd say everyone heard it."

I cut my eyes up at him and saw the smile he tried to hide. I returned the smile and then giggled. Without warning, the giggles exploded into shrieks of laughter. I clamped a hand over my mouth, but it did no good, and only resulted in a series of snorts. Tears streamed down my face, and when I took a gasping breath, it began all over again.

Moffatt's grin vanished, replaced by a look of concern. I knew I should stop, but I couldn't figure out how until he put a firm hand on my arm, forming a bridge back to reality. I began to calm down, and at last, panting, I wiped my eyes and blew my nose on one of the tiny paper café napkins. It disintegrated under the strain.

"I'm all right now," I assured him and myself. "Really I am. It's all just . . . you know."

Moffatt held out a clean paper napkin. "Sorry, I don't carry a handkerchief. Look, you're allowed a bit of a breakdown—this is a terrible business. And you can shout at me again if you like, but I still say you should—"

I held up a finger. "Wait—I have a solution. The police are sending a patrol car down the street every hour, and uniforms on foot along Gravel Walk behind. I'll ring and ask if they would meet me at the door."

His face lit up. "There now—that's good thinking. Let them look round indoors before you go in."

Sergeant Hopgood answered his mobile promptly and commended me for my forethought. I was so proud. It was only after I ended the call and said, "Sorted—officers will meet me at Middle-bank within thirty minutes," that reality struck.

I leapt up from the table. "I've got to go! It'll take me at least that long to walk back."

Moffatt leapt up, too. "I've my car—I'll drive you."

We dashed off, almost forgetting our shopping under the table, and then legging it to the car park, where he stopped at a dark red Renault that looked as if it had been through the wars. Our shopping safely stowed in the boot, we were off, pulling up to Middlebank only ten minutes later to find a police car at the curb and two uni-forms milling about on the pavement.

"Hello," I called, "here I am, thank you so much for waiting."

When I'd unlocked the door and turned off the alarm, the officers took over. "You stay here," the woman PC said, "and we'll have a shufti."

And so I waited in the entry as they took the key to my flat and searched Middlebank from top to bottom for any untoward visitors. Bunter sat in the doorway to my office, his radar ears going berserk, and Moffatt took my sacks of groceries from his car, handed them over, and then waited outside.

It didn't take the police long. "Right, Ms. Burke," the PC said as she handed back my key. "No one else here . . . Your friend who lives downstairs is out for the evening?"

My friend—I'm sure Mrs. Woolgar would love to hear that one. "Yes, she's away. Thanks so much for checking." They walked out, and as I pushed the door closed, I added my thanks to Moffatt.

"You'll ring if you need anything," he said.

"Yes, I will."

I closed the door, threw the lock, set the alarm, and skipped up the stairs to my flat, where I locked myself in. Kneeling on a chair, I unlatched and pushed open the front window and leaned out to look down at the street. Moffatt stood on the pavement and, when he saw me, gave a nod of satisfaction. It was silly, but I felt a tiny bit like Rapunzel, as if I should let down my ponytail and . . . *Get a grip, Hayley.*

"Good night, Mr. Moffatt."

A smile. "Good night, Ms. Burke."

10

‧๑෴๑‧

"Do they know what time he died?" Mum asked me as we sat over coffee in her flat.

"The police aren't certain. Sometime after midnight, I think."

"You should find that out—it'll give you a better picture of what happened. But if he was cold when you touched him, it would've been several hours before."

Everyone's a detective—everyone but me, that is.

"You feel safe at Middlebank, do you?"

Dinah had asked the same when I phoned her that morning. I assured her I did, and my daughter and I spent the rest of the conversation talking about whether she and her housemate should find a less expensive place to live.

Now I slid the plate of digestive biscuits closer to my mum and said, "Well, I can't imagine the person who killed Trist would then have a reason to come after me or Mrs. Woolgar. It isn't as if we have anything in common with the victim."

"True." Mum tapped a finger on the rim of her saucer. "You should ask a few questions about those writers, you know—find out more of their background."

"Mum, can't I leave that to the police? It's their job, after all."

She didn't answer, but she did give me that squinty glance of hers that meant she knew whereof she spoke.

"How is your Wyn?" she asked, pulling on her jacket as we readied for our outing under cloudy skies.

"He's super!" I exclaimed. "And he's working so hard. It's incredible the many things he needs to do—his work really takes up almost every day. He's constantly thinking of how he can make Eat Here, Eat Now the best business it possibly can be. For example, here's something they really had to think through—when to take Myrtle out for a test run. As it turns out, Sunday afternoon in London is the perfect time, because there are far fewer people walking about, and so no one will be in her way."

This was how Wyn had explained it to me when I rang him from the train on the way to Liverpool that morning and broached the subject of a Sunday visit. "If you came, I'd have to ignore you," he'd said in a sad voice. "I'd feel a right proper prat for doing it, too, and you'd end up miserable."

It was a perfectly reasonable excuse. There was no point in allowing my spirits to sink as low as they had just because my dreamy plans for Sunday with my boyfriend had been dashed. Even so, I had spent the rest of my journey staring glumly out the window and had brightened only when I'd reached Mum's flat.

Now she thrust her unopened brolly into the pocket on the side of her wheelchair as though it were a sword going into its scabbard, and faced the door. "Where are we off to today?"

* * *

This Val Moffatt," Mum said over our late breakfast the next morning. "How lucky it is for you to find someone to work with on your project. What's his story?"

"His story?" I asked. "I don't know anything about the man. He teaches classes at Bath College. Mostly in the adult-learning department. Oh, he has twin daughters who are twenty-four—his wife died when the girls were young." I reached for another slice of toast. "He likes *The Magic Roundabout*," I added, remembering he'd recognized the names of cats we'd had, who had been called after characters on the program. "And he's quite fond of Waitrose—that's funny, isn't it?"

"Funny as in funny or funny as in a coincidence that you're quite fond of Waitrose yourself?" Mum asked. "What does Adele think of him?"

My mum and Adele had met twice when my friend had taken the train up to Liverpool with me—once when she was to teach a short course at the university during her August summer holidays, and once when she continued to York to visit cousins. Mum and Adele had hit it off immediately.

Instead of waiting for an answer—could she guess Adele approved of him?—Mum took a battered paperback book from her lap and said, "Here—this is for you."

The Body in the Library.

"Really, Mum?"

"It seemed appropriate."

"I *am* going to read all the Agatha Christies," I said. "It's only that I haven't had the time yet."

"Well, you've a four-hour journey on the train today—there's your time."

I grumbled a reply but slid the book into my handbag and took myself off to the station. Low, dripping skies made for a gray view

from my window on the train, and with the heavy sigh of one greatly
put upon, I opened the paperback, and found myself in the middle
of a situation that was eerily familiar to my own.

H uddling at the far end of a bench on the platform at Bristol
Temple Meads, I glanced up to see the second train I'd missed
closing its doors. No matter—I was near the end of my journey and
the trains to Bath ran frequently. I had better things to do—Miss
Marple had just put the pieces together, but she had to make sure
she was right. I had to make sure, too. How was it that she could see
so clearly what the police could not?

I reached the last page, closed the book, and held it to my chest,
my heart rate tripping along as if I'd run a race. Only then did I
glance at my surroundings and was startled to see that the other
people on the platform went about their ordinary business, unaware
that I had just reached an epiphany.

Miss Marple, an unassuming little old lady, had solved the murder when the police had needed help. The clues had been right there
under everyone's nose, but she was the only one who saw them. At
last I understood. The detective story was a tale of subtlety and
deviousness and characters and cups of tea, and—in the end—order
out of chaos. I was astounded, and longed to shout my conversion to
all and sundry.

And would look barking mad if I did so. Instead, I stuffed the book
in my bag and boarded the next train. Fifteen minutes later, I hopped
off and, under murky skies, hurried up Manvers Street toward home.

Upon arrival at the door to Middlebank, I paused, remembering
my circumstances. Mrs. Woolgar might not have returned yet. But I
reminded myself that was no matter, because the house was secure
and I was safe. The new key slid in the lock without trouble, and I
walked in.

Bunter waited at the bottom of the stairs, and once I'd dealt with the alarm, he trotted over to weave a figure eight round my legs. After presentation of the catnip mouse, he monitored the cleaning of the litter pan and watched as I piled his dish high with food. But instead of tucking in, he returned with me to the entry, where he became possessed by one of those demons that caused him to race up and down the stairs several times. On his final return to the ground floor, he stopped abruptly and flopped over onto his new toy.

"Well done, cat," I said. "Good show."

I started up the stairs, but Bunter overtook me—mouse in mouth—and gave me a look over his shoulder. On the first-floor landing, he padded to the door of the library, dropped the mouse, and scrabbled at the threshold while he made low, throaty sounds.

"We aren't going in the library—not tonight," I said firmly. Bunter stood on his back legs and stretched his lithe body high, batting the door handle with a paw and meowing.

"There's nothing in there," I told him—and myself—but he was insistent and kept at it until I thought I'd better prove the point to both of us. I marched over, grabbed hold of the handle, and opened the door before I could think twice. When I hit the light switch, the cat seized his toy and trotted in while I remained in the doorway, scanning the room.

"You see, silly, there's no one."

Bunter made straight for the copper coal bucket at the fireplace, deposited the mouse, and returned to sit in front of me.

"Finished, are you?" I asked.

He blinked calmly, and then his gaze shifted ever so slightly, so that he was looking over my shoulder and out onto the landing. His eyes grew large and dark, and his whiskers stood at attention.

I broke out in a cold sweat. "Don't you try that with me, cat—you will not make me believe—" But I couldn't help myself. I whirled round, saw a larger-than-life form looming at the top of the stairs, and squealed. My heart pounded in my chest as the form took on detail, revealing itself to be Lady Fowling's portrait. I collapsed against the doorpost.

"Bunter!"

I turned to find the cat washing the back of a paw.

I spent the evening going back over the pages of *The Body in the Library*, looking for clues and marking particular passages in the tattered paperback with notes to myself. I ate my dinner—the four-cheese ravioli—with the book in one hand. When a text came in, I tore myself away from Miss Marple.

Safe home?

From Val Moffatt. I desperately needed to talk with someone about the new world I'd discovered. Would he think me daft for declaring myself a novice when it came to mysteries? My finger twitched over my phone screen, but I pulled it back in time. I'd already had a breakdown in front of him, and so I couldn't start rabbiting on about Miss Marple and have him believe I was totally unhinged. With great care, I replied:

All is well. See you tomorrow.

Later, when I heard another text come in, I scrambled for my phone, ready to abandon my caution and tell Val Moffatt everything. But instead, I found a photo of Wyn—sandy-colored hair curling round his forehead and a boyish grin on his face. He stood on the pavement with one arm round what looked to be a large metal box perched atop small pram wheels. The box wore kitchen attire—a red-checkered pinny. Myrtle. I replied with a string of hearts, and went to bed.

* * *

I approached Monday morning's briefing the way anyone would tackle an obstacle—with a compliment.

"That's a lovely dress, Mrs. Woolgar." And it was—that thirties narrow look that suited her so well. "And the color—sky blue?"

"Dresden," Mrs. Woolgar replied, opening the Society's membership ledger.

"Dresden," I echoed, wondering how we'd got on the subject of china. Then the penny dropped. "Yes, of course, Dresden blue."

After that stunning opener, we exchanged the obligatory "How was your weekend?" enquiries. I toyed with the idea of asking the secretary what she thought of Christie's ability to make a character look guilty or not, depending on the scene. Would the secretary and I enter into a lively and friendly discussion on the merits and pitfalls of detective fiction? I couldn't quite see it.

Instead, I told her about my meeting with Bath College that afternoon, and then I escaped—retreating to my office, where I wrote a news release about the literary salons as if they were already a reality.

The front-door buzzer sounded at half-past eleven. It was Amanda, her face pinched with worry. One hand played with her thick blond braid, and the other she had plunged into the pocket of her coat—not the baggy one she usually wore, but a smart red slicker with a hood. Behind her, a steady rain fell.

"Look, Hayley, I'm so very sorry to bother you like this."

"No, it's all right," I replied with little enthusiasm but an inkling of why she had stopped by. "Come through."

I sat at my desk, hoping the more businesslike position would let her know I had little time to spare.

Amanda didn't sit, but paced.

"The thing is," she said, "we find ourselves a bit lost. Who knew we relied on Trist so much to lead the group? His murder has rather thrown us for a loop—well, actually not all of us, but still . . ."

She'd stopped pacing and examined the end of her braid. "The police won't talk. Sergeant Hopgood keeps saying we should come to you."

I suspected Amanda's interpretation to be off the mark—it wasn't that the police wouldn't talk, it's that they were weary of the writers asking questions about the enquiry without offering any useful details, and the detective sergeant steered them my way as one would try to shoo a pesky fly out the window.

"I'm not privy to details of their investigation."

"Yes, yes, I understand, but the others don't. I didn't think there was any point in all of us badgering you, so I told them I would come alone. Peter's getting a bit aggressive, you see, and he'll just get himself in trouble again if he continues to . . ." She whirled round to face me. "I don't want to beg, but I think we all realize it would help us process what's happened if the group could carry on meeting here."

Just as I thought.

"Yes, all right—you can meet here this Wednesday. But really, I'm not sure if we can keep it up, and so you should look into other venues. A pub—the Minerva, perhaps. I think it has a tiny back room. Do you know it?"

"The Minerva." She nodded, as if filing away the suggestion. "Thanks for letting us return this week. And you know, it would be fine if you want to sit in on the session. You could bring DS Hopgood along, too."

I tried to imagine the sergeant joining the group round the table in the library. "Yes, well, we'll have to see about that. Until Wednesday, then."

With Amanda gone, I banished the writers group from my mind, wrenched my thoughts from Miss Marple, and concentrated on the afternoon's meeting. I should change clothes.

My foot had barely touched the bottom step on my way up when the buzzer went off.

Peter greeted me with, "They aren't taking us seriously. Police."

"Is Mariella with you?" I asked, leaning over to look behind him.

"What? No, why should she be?"

I had no answer to that, except that they seemed to travel as a pair. Wait—was that a clue? Should I make a note of it and mention it to the police?

"Would you like to come through?" I asked.

"Look"—Peter adjusted the shoulder strap on his satchel, but didn't move—"I know Trist had come whining to you about our complaints. I hope you didn't pay him any mind—he could be a bit touchy."

Peter stood at the door with the rain beaded up on his head and shoulders, and that—along with his belligerent attitude—reminded me of Trist's visit the afternoon I'd first been down in the cellar. What had he said? Something like "There have been complaints" and he, too, had grumbled about not being taken seriously. After he left, I'd dismissed it from my mind, not wanting to get in the middle of the group's politics. And then I'd forgotten to mention it to the police.

What sort of an amateur sleuth does that? Wouldn't Miss Marple at least have followed up on what he'd said? I wasn't sure what Hercule Poirot's next move would be—I'd yet to crack one of those books. Or Tommy and Tuppence, for that matter. But on the strength of reading one book, I now had Jane Marple sitting on my shoulder and, little old lady or no, I felt the weight of her.

Yet here was Peter telling me to ignore what looked very much like an important clue.

* * *

Peter left, and I hurried upstairs to my flat, where I popped a few grapes into my mouth as I tried on various outfits. I needed to make a good impression with the committee.

At last, I chose a burgundy dress with a square neck, nipped in at the waist, and with a flared skirt. I could breathe—just. Pulling the band from my ponytail, I brushed my hair and twisted it up high on the back of my head, and secured it with a spring clip.

"Too much?" I asked my mirror image. But I had no time to answer, as the front-door buzzer sounded. I grabbed my black wool blazer and hurried to the door, fearing I was doomed to be visited by each member of the writers group every single day until Trist's murder was solved. I would put shed to that right now.

I heaved open the door, talking as I did so. "Yes, you can meet here on Wednesday, but there's no point in complaining to me about the police, because—"

Val Moffatt stood on the doorstep peering at me from under the hood of his duffel coat.

"Wasn't I supposed to meet you there?"

"When I left home, I saw it was raining," he replied. "I thought I'd give you a lift."

"Thanks. But wasn't I out of your way?"

"No, not at all."

"Where do you live?" Because, you know, I might as well ask.

He cocked his head south. "Just off the Bristol Road—Oakhill."

"That's the other side of the college, Mr. Moffatt, and so I *was* out of your way."

He shrugged and grinned. "Didn't seem like it."

I reached for an umbrella, and when I turned back, I caught him trying not to stare at me.

"What?" I said, looking down at my dress. "I wanted to look my best. Is it all right, do you think?"

"Yeah," he answered, nodding quickly and turning pink. "It's . . . You're . . ." He laughed and shook his head. "You look lovely."

I tugged on my jacket and smoothed my skirt and blushed.

A black estate car pulled up to the curb, and DS Hopgood emerged, straightening his sleeves and his mustache. I watched as he came up behind Moffatt and nodded a greeting.

"Sergeant." I sighed. "I'm sorry, but I'm just on my way out. Is this urgent? Could we talk later?"

"I wouldn't want to keep you, Ms. Burke," he replied, the rain already glistening on his black mackintosh. "As it happens, I'm here for Mrs. Woolgar."

I turned to see the secretary emerge from her office, coat already buttoned. She had her handbag over an arm and gripped an umbrella so tightly her knuckles were white—which matched the color of her face, apart from the two red spots on her cheeks.

"I'm ready," she said.

My gaze darted from secretary to DS and back.

"Why have the police come for you?" I asked. "Sergeant, if there's something you need to know about the Society, I'll be happy to—"

"Mrs. Woolgar is accompanying me to the station. She's helping us with our enquiry," Hopgood said in a gentle voice. "No need for you to worry."

"If you'll excuse me, Ms. Burke," Mrs. Woolgar said as she edged past me.

I stood at the door and watched them get into the car and drive off.

"I don't understand," I said to Moffatt. "Why does Mrs. Woolgar have to go off with Sergeant Hopgood? And what does that mean—'helping them with their enquiry'?"

"It means she's a suspect."

11

I whirled round on Moffatt. "Mrs. Woolgar—a suspect? You're say-ing the police believe she killed Trist? That's mad! How could she—she would never . . . Why?" I demanded. "Why would the po-lice believe she—"

I shot out to the pavement as if I could take hold of Hopgood's car and stop its forward journey.

"Hayley!" Moffatt caught my hand and pulled me back into the entry.

"It might not be that bad," he said. "Maybe she's remem-bered something and she thinks it's important. Did she know him—Trist?"

I shook my head violently. "No. At least, she never said." I racked my brain for a clue to this recent turn of events.

"Look, do you want to follow them?" he asked. "I could take you to the station, and then I'll go on to the meeting at the college."

That brought me to my senses. "Certainly not. You and I must both be there so that the committee sees this is a cooperative effort.

I'm sure it's nothing serious with Mrs. Woolgar—and she's quite capable of taking care of herself." I looked down the empty street, then shrugged off my worry and threw back my shoulders. "Right, Mr. Moffatt. Val." He grinned. "We'd best be off."

During the short journey, I focused my thoughts on convincing the committee that a collaboration on a program of literary salons would raise both our profiles—in the best possible way. I must avoid the topic of murder, and yet I longed to weave my newly found mentor into the conversation.

"How would Miss Marple handle this?" I asked, under my breath.

"Sorry," Val said, leaning in, "did you say something about Jane Marple?"

We'd pulled into the car park at the college, and he switched off the engine and turned to me. It was time for a full confession.

I looked him in the eye and said, "I read *The Body in the Library* on the train yesterday. I'd never read anything like it before."

He pulled his chin back and gave me a quizzical look. "Are you saying you've never read Christie?"

"I've never read any of them—Sayers, Marsh. None."

"You're curator of an impressive collection of first editions from the Golden Age of Mystery," he reminded me.

I nodded miserably. "I'm a fraud. I studied nineteenth-century literature at uni. I read Trollope."

He chuckled, and I pursed my lips.

"Oh, come on, now," he said. "It isn't a crime."

"Ha-ha," I replied.

He continued in good humor. "And it isn't as if you can't catch up to the rest of us. It's your new beginning." He nudged me gently with his elbow. "Isn't it?"

I smiled in spite of myself.

* * *

H ow do you think it went?"
     We stood outside the building under clear but fading skies, and I looked back as if I could see through walls to where, at this very moment, the committee was deciding our fate.

"You were brilliant," Val said. "Especially the idea about putting on an evening hosted by Jane Marple. Where did you pull that from?"

"Thin air," I replied. "I don't know anyone who could impersonate Miss Marple, and I'm not sure we could actually get the Christie people to agree to it. Ah, well, cross that bridge . . ." I exhaled in a huff. "And so, now we wait."

"Shouldn't be long," he said, checking the time. "Another hour or so and they'll give me a ring."

"Well, we can't stand out on the pavement the entire time. Fancy a drink?" I asked, and glanced across the road. "What about there—the Black Fox?"

Val shook his head. "Full of students, and I'd end up fielding questions about grades."

"Do you know the Minerva? We aren't too far."

"The Minerva it is."

We walked to Northumberland Place while Val quizzed me about Lady Fowling.

"But Adele has told you all about her, surely," I said.

"Before Adele knew her—how did her husband make all his money?"

"Tins."

"Tin? He owned a mine?"

"No, he manufactured tins for food. Tomato soup. Beans. It was early in the twentieth century, and he captured the market."

"There was quite a spread in age between them," Val observed. "She became a widow awfully young, but never remarried."

"Yes, but she wasn't a recluse. She went out and about in society, and became known for her generosity—and also for her collection of first editions, of course."

"And never moved away from Middlebank."

"I believe she did leave briefly, not long after Sir John died, but returned and never left again. Who would want to?"

"Is there no other family?"

"Not on Sir John's side. Lady Fowling has her nephew, much to everyone's dismay. I've never met him—he lives abroad, I believe, for at least part of the year, but swept in after her ladyship died and tried to break her will. Apparently, he thought what she'd left him wasn't enough."

When I told Val what the nephew had received from the estate, he whistled.

Inside the Minerva, we spotted one of its six tables free, and Val threw his coat over a chair. Now, in the late afternoon, when the sun hit the stained-glass windows along the front and threw broken colors across the floor, it was as if we were trapped inside a kaleidoscope.

Pauline was working the bar. "Hiya," I said. "This is Val Moffatt." I turned to him. "Pauline Lunn—owner of Cleaned by Pauline." They exchanged greetings, and I added, "She comes to us every Thursday morning."

She shot me a look, reminding me it had been only the previous Thursday she'd found Trist's body.

"How are you, Pauline?" I asked, because she didn't look good—although, it could be the green light on her face that made her appear nauseous.

She shrugged halfheartedly. "All right, I suppose. It's terribly unsettling, though, isn't it, Hayley? Sorry"—she glanced at Val—"should I not talk about it?"

It didn't matter to me, but she had no chance as a customer came

up for another round. Val and I got our drinks and placed an order
for chips and took our table. At first, we hashed over the meeting
details, but that talk petered out, and we sat quietly until he gave his
stubbly beard a scratch in that way men do when they're about to
say something important and want to make it look casual.

And here came Pauline with our chips. Good thing, too—I was
halfway through my wine and needed ballast.

After I'd taken the edge off my hunger, I licked the grease from a
finger and asked, "So, Val Moffatt, where do you come from? Have
you always lived in Bath?"

He took a long drink of his pint before answering. "I grew up in
Margate."

"The seaside?"

"Well, close on."

"We used to go to Clacton-on-Sea or Southend every summer—
drive straight east from Hereford. I remember it taking us all day."
The walls of the Minerva faded away, and I saw a stretch of sand and
rock pools begging to be explored. "My dad would hire a caravan
and he and Mum would read under an enormous umbrella, and I
would spend my days as a pirate searching for booty or a scientist
counting the arms on starfish or I would build an enormous sand
castle. And I'd eat an ice cream every day." I sighed heavily. "I love
the seaside."

"Do you still go back?" Val asked.

My sand castle melted under the strong current of more recent
memories. "No, not for many years." I stole a glance at him. He
didn't speak, only waited as if he knew I had more. I dropped my
gaze to the table and told him the story I'd told few others. "The last
time was when we—Roger and I—took our daughter, Dinah, to
Brighton. She was ten. One afternoon, she and I were to go to a
magic show, but the day turned out fine, and so we went back to our
cottage to get her pail and shovel. I opened the door and interrupted

Roger and the young woman from the fish-and-chips stand. Right there, in our own—" I gestured into air, my voice thick. "Dinah didn't see—she was behind me. I pulled the door to as quickly as I could and told her Daddy wasn't feeling well and I'd take her to buy a new pail and shovel."

I laid my hands flat on the table to keep them from trembling, hating that after twelve years I still could be so angry. "It was her *birthday*. Dinah's, that is, not the . . ." I shook my head. "Since then, I haven't had much time for the seaside."

I chanced a look at Val and saw a spasm of pain cross his face.

"It doesn't go away, does it?" he asked. "The anger and the hurt— no matter how much time goes by. And you ask yourself, 'What did I do wrong?'"

My anger gave way to confusion. His wife had died—he'd told me so. What was this about?

Before I could ask for clarification, his phone rang.

Hearing half an important conversation is worse than hearing nothing at all. I listened to Val—"Yes, good. Well, I'm sure we can get—" and I took in every nod, shake of his head, eyebrow twitch, and gesture, trying to form it all into some coherent message. Was the Bath College committee saying yes or no?

"Of course—I'll make sure you have it in hand." Val ended the call and studied me for a moment.

"Please—put me out of my misery," I begged. "Am I a curator who can actually do her job or have they declined the offer, marking the beginning of the end of my short career?"

"They're ready to commit," he said. There was a *but* coming—I could feel it hanging in the air—and so I held back from a celebratory shout. "But they want the commitment to be strong on both sides. They want to know your board of trustees is one hundred percent behind the idea—every one of them. They'd like a signed statement."

"The board loves the idea," I said. "Will love . . . the idea. You know, I don't actually need their permission for every move I make as curator."

"Well, this time you do."

I began assessing my position. "All right, let me think. Certainly I have Adele's approval, and Mrs. Moon and Mrs. Moon would love the salons. But the other two—Mrs. Arbuthnot and Ms. Frost—they have a tendency to say no first and think second." I dropped my head in my hands and covered my face. "Oh no."

"What? What is it?"

"The Moons—they leave on Wednesday for a cruise, and they'll be gone two months."

Val frowned. "That'll put off approval until the new year."

"We can't wait that long—the literary salons should begin in January, it's the perfect winter activity. And the Society could use a boost in its image. No, we'll have to sort something out." I shifted my mind into top gear. "I'll invite the board to tea—an emergency meeting tomorrow afternoon. That'll catch the Moons before they're gone. Adele will be at school, and that's too bad, because I could really use her support—but she could be on the phone."

"I'll be there, too," Val said.

A flood of relief caused me to feel a bit giddy. "Yes, thanks—that will help." I began to talk to myself. "I'll have the acceptance already printed on letterhead, and all they'll need to do is sign it. First thing tomorrow, I'll need to dash off to the bakery, and then we can—"

"Let me sort out the food."

"Good, good. They're quite particular and really only prefer cakes and things from that French place." I looked at our empty glasses. "Shall I get us another round, and we'll plan it out?"

I waited at the end of the short bar as Pauline engaged in a quiet, but heated, discussion with a young woman who wore a *Cleaned by Pauline* bandanna over curly black hair.

"This is unfair harassment," the woman protested.

Pauline, a full head taller, towered over her. "You knew the job when you took it, and if you won't do it, you can just move along."

This appeared to be work-related, and I hesitated to intrude, but they broke off their exchange when they saw me.

"I don't mean to interrupt," I offered meekly. "Shall I come back?"

"No, it's fine." Pauline took the empties. "Same again?"

"Yeah, and oh, listen, I have the new key and code for you, so—"

"*Later.*" Pauline's voice cut like a knife. "Sorry, Hayley, it's only that—"

The pub door opened and clear light flooded in behind an influx of customers.

"It's only that it's a busy time," she finished.

Pauline began taking orders while the young woman stood at the end of the bar and watched. I felt a hand on my arm and turned to find Val had come up beside me.

"Sorry, Hayley, I got a bit carried away," he said. "I forgot I have a class in a half hour. Good thing I saw Amanda come in—it jogged my memory."

Both Pauline and the young woman shot glances at the pub door, and I looked past the new customers to see it swing shut.

"Where'd she go?" I asked.

Val looked, too. "I don't know. She probably saw me and remembered the same thing—it's the class she's in."

12

I declined Val's offer of a lift to Middlebank and spent the walk back on the phone. Adele quickly agreed to persuade Mrs. Arbuthnot and Ms. Frost to attend an emergency board meeting the next day.

"I'll ring them this minute."

"Hang on," I said. "Why didn't you tell me you knew Val Moffatt and that you were the one who told him about the salons?"

"Did I forget that?" Adele asked in a high, sweet, and completely fake-innocent voice. "Sorry—well, it hardly matters. All right, I'll tackle the recalcitrant board members—you take the pushovers."

I rang the Moons.

"No, Sylvia," Mrs. Audrey Moon explained to her sister-in-law across the phone's receiver, "our bon voyage tea was last week. Hayley has an idea to tell us about." She came back on the line. "But there will be tea, won't there?"

Now to explain it to Mrs. Woolgar.

That stopped me in my tracks. I stood on the corner of George

Street as cars crawled up Lansdown Road, and I remembered what I'd chosen to forget—Mrs. Woolgar had gone off with DS Hopgood to "help with their enquiries."

I hurried—propelled by an image of the secretary locked up in a cell, her hands gripping the bars as tightly as she had gripped her umbrella. No, surely not. Of course, as it was well after five o'clock, if they had let her go and she'd returned to Middlebank, she'd be in her flat. Would I dare knock on the door and ask her what the hell was going on? I doubted it.

But I needn't dare, because Mrs. Woolgar's office light was on and her door open. When I looked in, I saw that she sat bolt upright in her chair staring at a dark computer screen. I knocked lightly and broke her trance. She rose and smoothed the front of her dress.

"Ms. Burke, I owe you an explanation."

She didn't look good—her face was drained, and I could see her hands shaking.

"Shall I pop the kettle on first?"

I received a nod of agreement. The effort seemed to exhaust her, and she sank back into her chair. I retreated to the kitchenette, trying to keep my mind a blank as I dropped a bag of her Assam Superb in one mug and a bag of everyday builder's tea in another, and then waited for the kettle to boil. A few minutes later, I returned to her office, set her mug down, and perched on the edge of a chair with my tea in hand.

"Thank you," she said quietly. She shifted the mug a few inches to the right and then brought it to her mouth and paused as steam, curling like ribbons, drifted up and away. She took a sip, set it down, and put her hands in her lap.

"I knew who he was, you see—Trist Cummins. I knew of him before your group came here to Middlebank."

As that statement sank in, I searched for a reply or question or anything to cover my shock while Mrs. Woolgar calmly took another sip of tea and said, "Five years ago, I watched him every day during his trial. He stood in the dock accused of a violent attack against an elderly woman, a person who had no means to defend herself."

"He attacked you?"

"Not *me*," Mrs. Woolgar said with heat, and then regained her composure. "It happened to a friend. She was knocked down in her own home, and while she lay there injured, he helped himself to anything he could grab—silver, jewelry, a gold snuffbox that had belonged to her grandfather. Greedy, insolent, violent—"

"He went to prison for it?"

Mrs. Woolgar raised an eyebrow. "He was found not guilty on insufficient evidence—they questioned her ability to identify him. That's what a barrister with no morals can do for you."

"How dreadful for your friend." Now I counted three of us who had kept something back from the police—Harry's unmentioned relationship with Trist, my own encounter with him, and now Mrs. Woolgar's memory. "I can see how you could've forgotten to tell DS Hopgood last week. But I'm sure he understood, and was grateful that you rang him as soon as you remembered."

"It was the sergeant who contacted me. It was brought to his attention that there had been an incident outside the court the day that man was released. I was standing with my friend, and we watched him go by."

"And he attacked again?"

"No—I hit him with my handbag."

I sputtered into my tea, but Mrs. Woolgar took no notice and continued.

"He actually tried to bring charges against me, but Lady Fowling rang Mr. Rennie, and he took care of things. And so, you can understand how shocked I was when I saw him here that first time. Not that he took any notice of me—I spent the entire evening in the library with the group, and he acted as if I were a stranger. Too full of himself. I'm sorry, Ms. Burke. I realize I should've mentioned it to you from the moment I knew, but I never thought they would last this long . . ." She looked into her tea.

And that's the real reason you take yourself off the premises each Wednesday evening. I had thought she didn't like my idea of a fan-fiction writers group meeting at Middlebank, but really, it was because she had feared for her safety. Another thought occurred to me—at the end of a writers group evening and with impeccable timing, Mrs. Woolgar appeared. I had thought she might've been spying, waiting for the group—or me—to misbehave, but now I realized she had kept an eye on Middlebank in case there had been an incident involving Trist.

"The writers describe Trist as argumentative," I said, "but no one has mentioned to me that he was violent. I don't want you to think you did anything amiss."

But, if only she had said something, I would've had more reason to ask the group to move elsewhere, and we could've avoided this entire predicament. There would be no body in the library, no murder at Middlebank. Although, it would be no use for me to mention that now.

"And how is your friend?"

"She died a year later, and I can say unequivocally that man's actions precipitated her decline." Mrs. Woolgar took up her tea. "But regardless of his sordid history, I can assure you as I assured Detective Sergeant Hopgood, I had nothing to do with Trist Cummins's death."

"Of course you didn't." Yet now that thought had lodged in my brain.

"Well, it has been an exhausting day, and if you'll excuse me, I believe I'll retire."

"Just one more thing, Mrs. Woolgar"—this would either be an

easy sell or put her over the edge—"I need to tell you that the board will be here tomorrow afternoon for a special meeting." I gave her a clear and concise description of the event and the approval necessary to get our literary salons off the ground.

The secretary sniffed. "It could be seen as a bad time to embark on such a venture. We wouldn't want to call even more negative attention to Lady Fowling's memory."

I had to admire the woman's resilience—finished with her confession, she'd regained control of not only herself but also Middlebank and her precious ladyship's memory.

"I believe the literary salons will bring The First Edition Society back into people's minds in a good way," I insisted. "The way it was when Lady Fowling was alive and people actually came to view the collection. But you knew her, Mrs. Woolgar—tell me what you think. Would her ladyship have approved?"

Why hadn't it occurred to me before to put her on the spot like this? A bit of color returned to the secretary's face, and after a moment, she gave a single nod.

"I must admit her ladyship did have a bit of the risk taker about her."

On my way upstairs, I paused at Lady Fowling's portrait. "They will like it, won't they?" I asked. "You do think it's a good idea?"

I told myself I saw approval in that enigmatic gaze of hers. I gave her a nod of thanks and continued to my flat.

Thank God the silver didn't need polishing again. I spent half of Tuesday perfecting the one-paragraph letter of approval the board members would sign. *We agree to cosponsor the events with Bath*

College and look forward to the series of literary salons. We know that in com-
mitting to this partnership, we will be fulfilling our founder's wish to . . .

Several cups of tea and a few shortbread fingers later, I printed
out the final version and went up to my flat with two hours to
spare—plenty of time to worry. Then I remembered I still hadn't set
out the silver tea service. I dashed off, stopping in the library to
switch on the lamps, giving the room a warm, inviting glow. I moved
the sherry decanter and glasses off the drinks trolley and onto the
large table.

Downstairs in the kitchenette, I stood on tiptoe to reach the teapot, cream pitcher, and sugar bowl. I had just grabbed a large oval
platter when the buzzer sounded, and so I tucked it under my arm,
went out, and opened the front door to Val Moffatt in a suit and no
beard.

He had shaved. And now it was quite evident he had cheekbones.
And a chin—who knew he had a chin?

"I thought I'd try to look my best," he said sheepishly.

Only then did I realize I'd been staring.

"Yes. Of course—that is, I mean . . ." My hand stretched out to
smooth the lapel of his dark blue suit, but common sense saved me,
and instead I made a decisive grab for the two bakery boxes he held.
"They can't resist a well-laid tea."

Four board members in the flesh and one on a video conference
call—Adele's massive red locks filled the screen. The Moons
were delighted with her electronic presence and, every once in a
while, leaned over the table to wave at the computer, and then giggled when Adele waved back.

As expected, two board members dug their heels in. Mrs. Arbuthnot couldn't for the life of her see what good literary salons
would do. And the very mention of someone dressing up as a fic-

tional detective riled Ms. Frost, who said it sounded more panto than literature.

"Hang on, Maureen," Adele said with an exaggerated offhand air, "have you forgotten the years Georgiana held the Middlebank fancy dress ball? I seem to recall hearing that you once came as Rebecca de Winter and gave everyone an exceptionally dramatic reading from the book."

Maureen Frost's face flushed scarlet, actually a rather becoming contrast to her steel-gray pageboy. "Adele, I don't think it's necessary to dredge up old tales."

"I'm only pointing out that you all know, deep in your hearts, that Georgiana would love this idea. And regardless of what's happened—or perhaps because of it—we need to seize the opportunity that Hayley and Val have dropped in our laps."

Val leaned forward and smiled at Maureen, his eyes crinkling up at the corners. "I'm sorry I missed you as Rebecca de Winter. You know, in my courses, we occasionally do readings of mystery and suspense classics—it really brings them to life for the students. I don't suppose I could persuade you to take part?"

The deep shade of red on her face faded to a cherry-blossom pink. Maureen Frost smiled back at him. "Oh well, an educational setting makes all the difference, doesn't it? Have I mentioned I was quite active in the local theater for many years?"

We had four signatures—I would keep the letter until Adele had a chance to sign, and then we would present it to Bath College. The board members had departed happy, full of sweet and savory delicacies, tea, and, of course, sherry. Now Val and I were left alone, sitting across the library table from each other. We idly discussed the salons as we worked on the remaining treats. I took a bite-sized flaky pinwheel pastry while eyeing two small meringues filled with lemon curd.

"You chose well," I said, "although I doubt they would've noticed if we'd served them packets of custard cream biscuits, so charmed were they by your very presence."

Val acknowledged this with a dismissive nod. "Yes, I'm a big hit with women over seventy."

I laughed at him. "You shortchange yourself."

We fell silent. I ran my finger along the rim of the silver tray, and as I did so, Val reached his hand out, drawing nearer and nearer until it hovered only an inch away from mine. He hesitated, and then picked up the last little flaky bite.

A scrabbling sound drew our attention away—Bunter had a paw in the coal bucket, toying with his collection of catnip mice. I checked the time.

"Gone seven," I said with incredulity. "I don't know how that happened."

"Right, I'd best be on my way," Val said.

"No, don't—that is, I mean . . . look, would you like to stay to dinner? I could cook. In my flat."

"Oh well, I wouldn't want to put you out." It was a weak protest.

"No trouble—you can save your Waitrose ready meal for another evening." My mind frantically took stock of the cupboards and fridge in my flat. What did I have to offer apart from fish fingers?

"I could nip out to the shops for a bottle of wine," he offered.

"No need—I've wine and all." I nodded to the table. "We'd better clear these things away first."

I took the silver tray with cups and saucers, and Val the tea service and platter. At the top of the landing, as we were about to descend, I murmured, "Well done, Lady Fowling."

Val cut his eyes at the portrait and then at me, but didn't comment.

In the kitchenette, we fell into washing and drying with ease while we talked murder.

"Poirot sometimes had a personal reporter, you see," Val said. "Hastings. It was a handy way to see the Belgian as others saw him."

"Should I read all the Marples first or mix the two detectives in?"

Val leaned against the sink with the tea towel thrown over a shoulder. "If you want to keep with Jane Marple, you could go back to the first one—*The Murder at the Vicarage.*"

"The group's fan fiction consists of two Poirots, two Marples, and a Tommy and Tuppence. Perhaps I could ask them their favorites."

"You're letting them back in?" Val asked.

"Yes, at least for this week."

"I'll come round tomorrow evening, if that's all right," he said. "So you have some company."

"Will you?" Perhaps one more week of the writers wouldn't be so bad after all. "Thanks. You see, I want to get another look at each of them—examine their reactions to Trist's murder. Harry's quite affected. Why does Peter have such a combative attitude? Mariella—I don't really have a read on her yet."

"You aren't letting Miss Marple go to your head, are you?" he asked.

I ignored the comment. "Amanda has been appointed—or appointed herself—spokesperson for the group. She seems a bit jumpy."

Val nodded. "I can see what you mean there. At class yesterday evening, she was either unresponsive or interrupting. Grief works on us in different ways."

That reminded me of his wife. Did I have the nerve to ask him more?

Our eyes met, and I wondered if he could read my mind.

Glancing out the door that led to the back garden, he asked, "It happened out there? The *Chronicle* didn't give details, apart from his name. Adele told me a bit more."

So, he wanted to change the subject. I had done my best to avoid the news, which had reported the death briefly as "unexplained." I was caught between relief that the media ignored us and depression because The First Edition Society hadn't warranted more attention.

"The police say he hit his head on a post along Gravel Walk and someone carried him in here and up to the library." I leaned over the counter toward the window, peering out into the darkness. "Our library—there must be a reason for that."

Val put a hand on my arm, rubbing it lightly with his thumb. "And you're sure you feel safe here?"

I turned to look up at him and found myself closer than I'd realized. I didn't move except, perhaps, a wee bit closer.

The front-door buzzer went off, and we both froze, as if we expected a raid. He dropped his hand and I ran out to answer, but paused, a heaviness in my heart. *Please don't let it be DS Hopgood or one of the writers to spoil our evening.*

I pulled open the door and stared speechless at the person in front of me, his sandy-colored hair curling around his forehead and a boyish grin on his face.

"You!" I said to Wyn.

He pointed to himself. "Me."

13

I'd lost all sense of proper behavior, and for a moment, could only stare at Wyn, still standing on the doorstep.

"How did you . . . You never said you would . . ." Reality struck. "Come in."

He stepped in, and I was in his arms. It was the oddest sensation, almost unfamiliar. Of course it had been weeks and weeks since we'd seen each other and—

He kissed me long and hard, and I didn't mind that. Yes, now I knew where I was. My boyfriend had come to see me—to comfort me in this unstable, disconcerting time when a murder had taken place and I was desperately holding on to a job and . . .

I heard a throat being cleared.

I pulled myself away from Wyn, who pulled me back playfully, keeping one arm round my waist. Val had come out of the kitchenette, but stopped at the bottom of the stairs.

"Oh . . . um—" I couldn't catch my breath or my thoughts. "This is Wyn. Wyn, this is Val Moffatt—we're putting together the literary salons. I told you about them."

As the two men shook hands, I took a step away, crossing my arms tightly and looking at the floor.

Val circled round us, heading for the door. "Well-I'll-be-on-my-way-Hayley-I'll-let-you-know-if-there-are-any-other-concerns-from-the-college-Wyn-it-was-good-to-meet-you-Evening." And with that one run-on sentence, he vanished, and I could only stare at the closed door.

"My God, Hayley, look at this place." Wyn studied the ceiling and ran his hand over the mahogany hall stand. "Do I get a tour?"

"Yes, yes, of course you do," I gushed, grabbed his hand, and dragged him off, flinging my arm around as I described the layout. "Mrs. Woolgar's office is here, in the back is the kitchenette, and this is my office. Come in."

Wyn admired my desk, the paneling, and then he strolled over to the mantel, where Bunter had taken up his post as feline ceramic figurine. When the cat yawned, Wyn jumped back.

"Oh my God, it's real."

I laughed. "Of course he's real. Don't tell me you're afraid of a moggy."

He scooted closer to me. "I don't like the way they look at me."

"Silly," I said. "Come on—I'll introduce you to Lady Fowling."

I pulled him up the stairs, and on the landing, presented our founder's portrait. But Wyn barely glanced at her when he saw the library door standing open.

"Is that where it happened?" he whispered, creeping up and looking in. I followed and he turned on me suddenly. "Fascinating."

"Horrible," I corrected him.

"Yes, horrible," he agreed with a momentary sad look. "So, did they get away with any of those incredibly valuable first editions?"

"Those books are in the bank—remember I've explained that?" It had slipped my mind that Wyn could be cute, but exhausting.

He pulled me close with a sly grin. "So, I am allowed to see the rest of your house, aren't I? Including the bedroom?"

"Allowed? Don't be daft." After all, I told myself, he was my boyfriend and we'd been apart far too long. "Follow me."

M iddlebank isn't all mine," I explained—again. "Only the flat. The rest of the house is where I work—apart from Mrs. Woolgar's living quarters on the lower ground floor."

Wyn rolled over in bed, propped his head up on his hand, and grinned. "The cow."

"She isn't a cow—I never called her that." At least, not aloud. I had this new sympathy for Mrs. Woolgar, knowing her history with Trist. But her chat with the police had added a soupçon of suspicion to our relationship. It didn't mix well.

Wyn reached over my shoulder and grabbed his phone. "God, look at the time," he said.

He sat up, dragging the sheet off me. I grabbed it and pulled it up to my chin, and then blushed at acting so modest in front of him. Hadn't he just seen all of me—and not for the first time?

"Why don't I cook us a meal?" I asked. Instantly, a wave of guilt washed over me, a reminder I had made that same offer to another man not an hour earlier. Only, I couldn't identify from which direction the wave came.

"Can't," Wyn said as he hopped on one foot and pulled a sock on the other. I looked away. "I'm meeting a fellow this evening at the restaurant in the Bath Priory Hotel—out on the Weston Road. He's got an idea for a software program to log orders into Myrtle's system so that she can make the decision herself about which meal to collect and deliver next. It's far superior to anything else we've found. I'm hoping we can bring him on board."

I bolted upright. "You what? You came down to Bath for a business meeting?"

"Couldn't pass that up, could I? He's here just for this one day—otherwise, I'd've had to fly to Brussels to see him."

"I thought it might've been because of me," I said, angry at how pitiful I sounded.

"And you, of course." Wyn leaned over and kissed me. "I always want to be with you." He stuffed his shirt into his trousers and picked up his shoes.

"After your meeting, you'll come back here?"

"Sorry, Hayley—I've got to get the train back to London tonight. Eight o'clock meeting tomorrow morning with one of our investors—he's being a bit balky at recent costs. I'll let you know how it goes." He finished his excuse as he dashed from the bedroom. Just before he closed the door of my flat, he called out, "Love you."

For the longest time, I sat in bed, chin resting on a knee, alone in the silence and with my mind drifting like a fog across unsettled seas. Finally, I got up, dressed, and went downstairs, turning off lamps in the library on my way to the ground floor, where I set the alarm. In the kitchenette, I opened cupboards to put the silver service away, and noticed teardrops splashing onto the tray.

"Stop it," I muttered. I dried the tray with a tea towel, then wiped my eyes and blew my nose on it and crammed it in my pocket.

Upstairs, I pulled a paperback from my cache of used mysteries and set it on the table, then showered, and—dressed in a ragged pair of flannel pajamas—ate scrambled eggs as I began *The Murder at the Vicarage*. But my heart wasn't in it, and after only two chapters, I bid Miss Marple and St. Mary Mead a good night.

* * *

Our morning briefing was coolly cordial, if there is such a thing. Mrs. Woolgar had been out the previous afternoon and missed the board meeting, so I caught her up.

"We're thrilled that the salons will go ahead," I said, "although it will mean a great deal of work to get them up and running."

"The group returns this evening?" the secretary asked.

We couldn't be seen to dwell too long on success. "Yes, but I don't want you to be concerned—you carry on with your usual plans. Mr. Moffatt will be here, you see—I'm sure he and I will get stuck in on scheduling and planning the salons." He would still stop in, wouldn't he? He had said so.

I took a big breath. "I'm going to the police station to see Detective Sergeant Hopgood today." The secretary blanched and I rushed on. "Not about you—it's only I had a few other things to clear up."

More than that—I had to find out what was going on with the enquiry. Miss Marple always kept abreast of clues and suspects and the like—the police even consulted her on cases. Of course, I wasn't quite there yet, so I knew I had to raise my game. Until now, I'd been acting as if this investigation had nothing to do with me, but since my conversion on Sunday afternoon when I'd read my first Christie, *The Body in the Library*, I'd come to realize that Trist's murder was not something for other people to solve. I needed to sort this out. I needed to do this for the Society, so that we could move forward under clear skies. I was, after all, curator of one of the finest collections of first editions from the Golden Age of Mystery. Who better?

Assuming Mrs. Woolgar would think I'd lost my mind if I made this confession, I ended our briefing with, "I don't expect anyone while I'm out, but if you need me, you can reach me on my mobile."

She never had and never would, but it was only polite to make the offer.

* * *

A hint of woodsmoke drifted on the air, and the tops of the beeches looked frosted in gold. A fine October morning, and it inspired me to take the long way to the police station. I'd missed my walk earlier—after a restless night, I'd fallen into a heavy sleep that gave me barely enough time to dress and get to work. So now I walked—through the wrought-iron gates at Hedgemead Park. Yellow leaves from the plane trees drifted in front of my eyes, gently landing on the path where they'd soon be ground into leaf mold. I zigzagged down the hill and came out at the bottom and onto The Paragon. That road took me south and, conveniently, quite near to Waitrose. I cut across to Walcot Street and climbed the stairs to the café for a coffee and a raisin bun. I sat near the window and searched the shoppers scurrying in and out on the street below, half expecting to see Val. My feelings about this possibility sloshed back and forth between hope and worry. Eventually, I made it to the police station nearing eleven o'clock.

Five or six people milled about near the desk in the lobby, and four more sat in chairs against the wall. I didn't relish having an audience for my request, but, as the officer behind the desk didn't seem to remember me, I had to begin at the beginning.

I leaned over the counter and spoke quietly. "Hello, I'm Hayley Burke, curator at The First Edition Society. We had an incident there last week—"

"Do you need to fill out a complaint form?" the woman asked, reaching over to a stack of papers.

"No, I'm not complaining, it was . . . that is, the incident, you see . . ."

"Ms. Burke?"

Saved by Detective Constable Kenny Pye, who had emerged from a door behind the desk.

"Constable Pye, hello. I'm here to talk with Sergeant Hopgood."

He gave me a quizzical look. "Is he expecting you? Do you have something for us?"

I had little to give. I had hoped rather to solicit information, but I didn't care to be lumped with the writers. "There are a few things I need to go over with him."

"Right, well, come through."

Pye escorted me from the lobby to a room labeled *Interview #1.*

"I'll let him know you're here—would you like a cup of tea?"

I declined and waited. And waited, becoming convinced that these dark, sterile rooms were designed to make people nervous. I drummed my fingernails on the table and tapped my toes, and jumped an inch off my chair when the door opened.

"Ms. Burke." Sergeant Hopgood swept into the room. "I'm sorry to keep you waiting. Did you want tea?"

"No, thank you. I don't mean to take up your time, but I did want to clear a few things up."

The DS settled across the table and offered me a benign smile, as if he were a friendly uncle sat down for a chat. Although, I didn't think he could be that many years my senior.

"Well, then," he said. "Is this about Mrs. Woolgar?"

"No, no—" Although it could be if he wanted to tell me anything. "I'm sure you realize that an event like that so far in her past isn't relevant to Trist's murder."

"I'll say what's relevant and what isn't," Hopgood said, a sharp point poking through his soft demeanor.

"Yes, of course. Well, the thing is—I'm afraid I, too, have forgotten to tell you something." Hopgood's eyebrows shot up in anticipation. "The Friday afternoon before he was killed, Trist stopped by Middlebank. He told me there were complaints against him, but that they weren't warranted. He didn't go into detail, and at the time, I didn't think it was my place to pursue the matter, and so I let it slip from my mind. But then, just this past Monday, Peter stopped in to tell me that I should ignore any complaints Trist made about the . . . complaints."

The DS leaned back in his chair and studied me. "Power struggle or artistic argument? Perhaps a long-standing feud?"

I hurried on, zeal clouding my judgment. "The thing is, Sergeant, when you get right down to the heart of the matter—it's *The Body in the Library*, just as you first observed. It's Christie."

"Ah, Ms. Burke—you, too?"

"He wasn't killed in the library, someone put him there. Was it on purpose or for convenience? Although, in the book, a window was forced, and we found no evidence of a break-in. Did we?"

"*We*—that is, the police—are looking into every possibility." Duly chastised, I sat back and dropped my gaze to my lap. "And yes," the sergeant added, "the parallels have not escaped me."

Any second, he may tell me to mind my own business, but until then—"Did they all go home after the pub that night?"

Hopgood chewed his lip for a moment. "CCTV along Northumberland Place shows the five of them dispersing."

"Northumberland Place? They go to the Minerva?"

"You didn't know that? So now I'm sure you're aware of the connection—the person who works at the pub and also works for you?"

I had not known the writers frequented the Minerva, and so was unaware of the potential connection. And yet, what did I know about Pauline? She'd seemed friendly, kind. Although now I knew she had trouble with at least one of the women who worked for her—I'd seen them arguing at the pub, and Pauline had taken a hard line.

"Do you believe Pauline had something to do with Trist's murder?"

"Belief does not come into the matter."

"What about intuition? Don't you get 'feelings' about people?"

Hopgood grunted, and I took that to mean that perhaps police-man's intuition did exist. That could be good or bad, I suppose.

"Does Pauline know any of the writers? Do they know her?" I asked.

"She was working at the pub on Wednesday evening, and the next morning she found Mr. Cummins's body. And remember, she's the only other person with a key and the security code."

"You said keys and codes were playthings to some people," I re-minded him. "Do you know where they went after they left the pub?"

"CCTV across the lane shows Ms. Amanda Seabrook left on her own, Ms. Harry Tanner and the victim walked off together, as did Mr. Talbot and Ms. Vine. Right now, we are checking feed from an ever-broadening area, but I can spare only one PC for the job, and I fear the fellow's eyes are glazing over."

"Why are Peter and Mariella always together?"

"They're neighbors—Mr. Talbot works with Ms. Vine's husband at a local machine shop."

These were details I'd never asked the writers. I really needed to pay more attention to people.

"But why would any one of them kill Trist?"

"You're asking for motivation—now we are bordering on the philosophical. Something that may seem trivial to one person could mean the world to someone else. And here's a difference from your mysteries—in real life, murder changes people."

"And so," I said, "you are saying that no one has been eliminated from your enquiry. That means I'm on your list of suspects"—I had hoped for a denial, but he offered nothing—"as well as Mrs. Wool-gar, Pauline, and the entire group. But if the writers are suspects, why do you keep fobbing them off on me?"

"Because for every question I ask them, they ask me two—and they offer nothing useful. Therefore, Ms. Burke, as you are a curator by profession, you may look on this as curating the enquiry—at least as far as those four are concerned. It will let me alone to do my job."

Two raps at the door, and DC Pye put his head in.

"She's there again, boss."

Hopgood rubbed his face and sighed. Then, his eyebrows lifted. "Well now, Ms. Burke—here's your chance. It seems Ms. Tanner has adopted us."

"Harry?"

"She's given up coming into the station, but has, for the last three days, taken up a post sitting on that low wall across the road. My DC went out to chat with her, and she said she was waiting in case we needed her again."

"Did Harry tell you about her relationship with Trist?"

"She did, in rather sketchy and benign terms. Do you have further details? Do you believe he might've abused her?"

"No, I . . . well, it didn't seem so." When Harry told me about Trist, it was with sadness, not anger. "Would you like me to talk with her?"

"Indeed I would."

I rose to leave but stopped at the door, snagged by a thought.

"Sergeant, that little incident with Mrs. Woolgar five years ago, when she hit Trist with her handbag. Charges were never brought against her, so who told you it happened?"

Hopgood chewed on the corner of his mustache for a moment, and then, instead of answering my question, he went off in a different direction.

"Ms. Burke, I think it wise to let you know that the victim had health problems—limited lung capacity. Weakened him, you see."

14

The low stone wall across the road from the police station ran along the front of a car park. Shade was creeping up the road—at the moment, Harry, clutching her laptop to her chest, sat on the sunny end, but that wouldn't last. I gave her a little wave as I waited for traffic to clear, and when I'd made it across and approached her, she looked up at me hopefully.

"Do they know something, Hayley? Have they caught the person who murdered Trist?"

Harry had changed. She looked dreadful, her eyes hollow, her usually exuberant frizzy blond hair hanging listlessly. I dropped down beside her on the wall. Sun or no, the stone was cold on my bottom. How could she sit here for hours?

"I have no news, but DS Hopgood is concerned about you being out here every day. Don't you want to go home? Or, should you be at . . . sorry, I don't know where it is you work."

"Avec Fleurs—the florist across from the rail station. But the

owner suggested I take a few days off. She could see I was"—she
gave a weak laugh—"well, I think I was frightening the customers."

"And you've no one at home?"

Harry shook her head. "Lost my flatmate last month. She moved
to Bristol."

We sat quietly for a moment as I planned my next move.

"The group has been together for a while now," I said. "You must
know a fair bit about each other, and I know so little. Amanda, for
example."

"Amanda's taken over managing the group, and as it turns
out, she's just as bossy as Trist was. I told her someone needed
to mourn him, and that's part of the reason I wait out here every
day—to show him respect. Her only response was to tell me to be
careful or I'd look guilty."

"Do you know much about Peter and Mariella?"

"Mariella's all right. She reads a lot of fantasy, though—comes
through in her writing."

"Trist wrote about zombies."

"Zombies are a metaphor for the disintegration of society," Harry
said, sounding as if she were repeating the company line. "Trist
looked at his writing as crossing genres—traditional mystery with
the dystopian. You can't deny it was an interesting concept."

"Mmm. Certainly a world apart from Amanda's story with Tommy
and Tuppence."

"It was an odd choice, wasn't it? I don't think those two detectives
suit her. That's probably why she has writer's block."

I ventured further. "You had some strong arguments in the
group."

"Strong? Oh, you're talking about Trist and Peter, aren't you?"

I threw the suspect spotlight on Peter. He was burly and could
easily have thrown Trist against that wrought-iron post and then

carried the body up to the library. But with the information DS Hop-good had just handed me—Trist was weak from lung problems—perhaps anyone could've done it. I gave Harry a sideways glance, sizing up her ability.

"I can't see Peter killing Trist," she said. "Although they have had their moments—that's why we were turfed out of the coffee shop. Lucky you invited us to Middlebank."

Yes, wasn't it?

Harry's eyes puddled with tears. "It was cruel—mocking him like that, by taking him up to the library."

"How did Trist treat you when you two were together? Was he . . . that is, did he . . ."

She swiped her cheek. "I know what you're asking. He never hit me. And although he could be sharp with his criticism, it's the way he was with everyone, not only me." She shrugged. "Sometimes you just have to accept a person for who he is, and make sure you're safe in yourself. You know what I mean?"

I congratulated myself on carrying out a successful interview. I'd learned more about each writer, and now I could begin to form a better picture of them and weigh the possibility of guilt. Still, where were those clues, the kind Jane Marple found—the fingernail clippings, the dress? I needed something concrete. Also, I needed to talk with Pauline.

But a man was pulling pints for the lunch crowd at the Minerva when I walked in. Was this her brother, the owner? I didn't think she'd ever mentioned his name.

Snaking between and around customers, I made my way to the bar and said, "Hello, I'm Hayley Burke, a friend of Pauline's. Is she working today?"

The fellow set an overflowing pint of bitter on the beer mat as he said, "No, she's scrubbing floors somewhere."

I had an instant and unpleasant reaction to his disparaging comment about Pauline's cleaning business, but I told myself that Miss Marple would remain calm and nonjudgmental.

"Are you her brother?" I asked.

"Yeah." He paused for a moment to take a good look at me. I could just see a resemblance to his sister, although his hair wasn't as blond, and his face not quite as open and friendly.

"That's right, I remember—you're Hayley. She's not on until this evening. Do you have her mobile?"

"Yes, thanks. But it's not important—I'll catch her up later."

"Can I get you something?"

Be a customer, Hayley, ingratiate yourself with the barman. "Yes, I'll have a packet of crisps, please—lightly salted. And an orange squash."

"Soda water or plain?"

"Soda water, please."

I watched as he added the fizz to my drink, aware that this was a bad time to strike up a conversation. So I moved to stand near the door, and set my glass on a narrow window ledge while I tore open my crisps and observed the crowd as any competent detective should. I spied a good-looking burger on the far table and wished I'd ordered one.

There was no returning to the bar when I finished—I'd never make it through the wall of bodies—so I left my glass on the ledge and walked out of the pub as my phone rang.

"Dinah, sweetie, how lovely to hear from you."

"Well, Mum, I thought I'd better check up on you and your murder enquiry. Is everything all right? Have the police caught the perp?"

Perp? Did my daughter spend her free time watching American television programs?

"No, sweetie, but I have no doubt they will. And how are you?"

"Mum, I've found a job."

"Dinah! That's fantastic."

"It's at the Sheffield Manor Lodge—working in the 1940s cottages."

"Well done, you."

"It doesn't actually pay anything—it's more volunteer work, plus lunch. And it's only one Sunday a month—but still, it fits with my course work in the history of everyday living. Don't you think?"

"And the contacts you'll make," said the mum inside me, always looking for the silver lining.

"Mum, did you keep that diorama I did when I was a little girl—the one we made in the shoe box?"

She had been eight years old, and we'd spent every evening for a week with nail scissors and paper, colored markers, and the wooden sticks left over from iced lollies as we built the model of a house—kitchen, sitting room, bath, and two bedrooms, replete with figures of mum, dad, and a little girl.

"Of course I did—it's in the attic." As I stood on Northumberland Place outside the Minerva, my mind wandered back in time to fond memories of Dinah as a little girl. "Do you remember you soaked cotton balls in cold tea to make Dougal the cat?"

"And we put me asleep in my bed and you in the kitchen, and we almost forgot to make the dad figure."

Roger never saw the diorama—he'd traveled a good bit for work at the time. At least, that was what he'd said, although revisionist history might tell a different tale. When Dinah and I had left Swindon for Bath, and I'd packed up the diorama, it was all I could do not to rip the father figure out of his easy chair.

"Could you get it out for me? We've got a *This Is My History* project in one of my courses, and I thought it would be fun to show them an antique."

Antique?

"When do you—"

I lost my train of thought as a young woman passed in front of me and headed into the pub. I'd seen her before—she was the one who'd been arguing with Pauline on Monday when Val and I had been here. What had that been about? Perhaps I should introduce myself under the pretense of . . . I'd think of something. I followed her in.

"Also, Mum," Dinah continued, "I thought I'd pop over and visit Gran tomorrow."

"Oh, sweetie, how lovely." I stepped from daylight into the darkened pub and kept near the door as I peered over shoulders, searching for the woman. "Gran will be thrilled—but give her a ring first to make sure it isn't her day with Working with Women Veterans or Cats Rescue People."

"Will do."

"Dinah, look, I must—"

"It's the rail fare, you know—a return to Liverpool and probably at peak time."

"Sweetie, let me get that for you—my treat. I'll do it this afternoon, all right? And e-mail the ticket to you."

My response was automatic, so accustomed was I to this. But a girl and her granny deserve to spend the day together.

"Thanks, Mum. You're the best."

The best at spoiling my daughter.

I located the woman at last—behind the bar talking with Pauline's brother, who towered over her, his face red, hers sullen. The noise level masked what they were saying, but perhaps if I crept closer, I could . . .

I began to push my way through the bodies. The barman's gaze darted between the woman and his customers, and for one second, his eyes fell on me. Then he turned back to her, said something, and jerked his head toward the kitchen. She disappeared within.

Had Pauline's brother warned the young woman off me? I ducked behind the throng to keep out of his line of sight and backed out of the pub—knocking into several people who were trying to get in—until I stumbled into the lane full of pedestrians. What would Jane Marple make of what I'd just seen?

Was Pauline the murderer? Had I missed a clue in her manner or words when she arrived at Middlebank the morning we found Trist? Was this a plot involving her brother and that other woman? Had they conspired to kill Trist, because . . .

I hit the irritatingly solid brick wall of motive. I tried wild speculation, but all I could come up with was that they were zombies and didn't like the way Trist had portrayed them.

Temporarily giving up on my enquiry, I stopped back by Waitrose and bought a roast chicken, a couple of prepared salads, and a loaf of granary bread. I'd just gone through the basket till, when a text came in from Mrs. Woolgar.

Will you return soon?

Was this a reprimand for staying away so long? No, it couldn't be that—she relished any time she had alone at Middlebank, able to pretend it was the way it had been before I arrived. I walked out of the shop with my bag, still staring at my phone. How odd. Her words carried no emotion, but the fact that she had sent them seemed a cry for help.

On my way.

My steps quickened the closer I came to my destination, puffing up the terrace until I reached our door at a trot and stopped, wheezing, to catch my breath.

Once composed, I located my key, walked into the entry, and

closed the door behind me. Approaching her office, I said, "Mrs. Woolgar. Sorry I've been out the entire morning, it's only that—" I stopped in the doorway.

The secretary stood behind her desk with her back against the wall. Facing her across the desk was a man wearing a brown plaid suit with leather elbow patches. He had one hand on the back of the chair and one in his jacket pocket. He turned his attention to me, and his lips slowly folded back into what might've been a grin.

He was short of stature but wide of girth, and the leer accentuated his toadlike appearance. He had black hair streaked with gray at the temples and pulled into a thick ponytail that shot straight out from the back of his head. I'd seen him only in photos, but I knew him in an instant.

"Ms. Burke," Mrs. Woolgar said, sounding as if there were a hand round her throat, "may I present Mr. Dill."

Yes, Charles Henry Dill . . . Lady Fowling's lout of a nephew.

15

Here he was—Charles Henry Dill, the man who hounded solicitor Duncan Rennie, Mrs. Woolgar, and indeed, even the memory of Lady Fowling. He'd broken the spirit of the original curator of The First Edition Society and sent her running—providing me with a job, I reminded myself. But it wouldn't be for long if he got his way. He was the man who wanted nothing more than to shut down the Society, sell off anything of worth, and claim Middlebank for his own.

I slapped a polite smile on my face and put my hand out. "Mr. Dill, pleased to meet you."

He took my hand, but instead of a shake, gave it a fleshy squeeze.

"Ms. Burke," he said in an oily bass voice, "a delight to meet you at last. So, you are the chosen one—the next chosen one, that is. Curator to Aunt Georgiana's vast and musty collection of has-been authors from a bygone era."

"I didn't realize you were in Bath," I said, not taking his bait.

"I've only just arrived this morning—I came at once when I

heard the dreadful news." He shook his head and clicked his tongue. "I am here to offer my condolences." He glanced at his surroundings with a possessive gleam in his eye, inhaled deeply, and then exhaled like a beach ball losing air. "How marvelous to be back at Middlebank again. Like a homecoming, really. I say, Ms. Burke, Woolley and I"—he threw a sly look at Mrs. Woolgar, and she cringed— "were just about to sit down for a cup of tea and have a right old chin-wag. Won't you join us?"

"How kind of you to invite me," I said. "And how unfortunate you've arrived at such an inconvenient time. You see, Mrs. Woolgar and I are extremely busy this afternoon. We'll have to postpone that tea to a later date." *Such as, when hell freezes over.*

I stepped aside to clear the doorway for him, and then I waited—as obvious a dismissal as I could give without the addition of a swift kick to his bum, which I had not completely ruled out. I saw a flicker of disappointment cross his face, followed by the return of the leer.

Clasping his hands across his stomach, he said, "No matter. But I did think it best to come to you immediately and offer my help in settling matters. I can't imagine the board of trustees is best pleased with how things are turning out. But I tell you what, you and Woolley get on with your work. I can fend for myself—perhaps I'll have a nose round the library."

"I'm sure you realize that isn't possible." Mrs. Woolgar had found her voice, and it held a threatening note. "Unless you would like to have a word with Mr. Rennie first?"

Charles Henry Dill paled, and I could see sweat break out on his upper lip.

"No need to bring Duncan into this, Woolley. Well then, I'll leave you ladies for now, but please do remember I'm at your disposal. You can reach me at the Royal Crescent."

I saw him out, closed the door, and leaned against it.

"What an odious man," I said. "I didn't think he could be as bad as you and Adele painted him, but he's worse. Why did the solicitor's name make him so nervous?"

Mrs. Woolgar stared at the closed door for a moment. "After her ladyship's funeral reception, a set of eighteenth-century silver basting spoons turned up missing. There was little doubt where they'd gone—into Charles Henry's pockets and out the door."

"He nicked his own aunt's silver?"

"Her ladyship knew Charles Henry for what he is—an opportunist—but she always retained a bit of family guilt. She'd given him a set of silver teaspoons for his birthday the year before, and he tried to say that she had also promised him the basting spoons."

"But how could he get off scot-free?"

"Mr. Rennie thought it easier to go along with the lie but left it quite clear there would be consequences if it happened again. After that, Charles Henry moved on to attempting to break her ladyship's will. I doubt we've seen the last of him—he'll certainly try to use this murder to his own advantage." Mrs. Woolgar sighed. "Thank you for returning so quickly, Ms. Burke—I didn't know if I could face him alone. And now, if you don't mind, I believe I'll rest in my flat before I go out for the evening."

I stowed my shopping in the kitchenette fridge, made myself a cup of tea, and went about my business—at least for an hour, then I ran up to my flat and took the band out of my hair, releasing my ponytail. I gave my hair a good brush before pulling it into the semblance of a French twist and securing it with every hairpin I could find—all three of them. I tucked a bottle of wine under my arm and had made it to the door when I held up, dithering. I dashed back to the mirror and took a good look at myself. *Why, Hayley?* I returned my hair to its normal ponytail and calmly walked down two sets of stairs to my office, where I first set the wine on the mantel, then on the small tea table, and finally stashed it in the kitchenette.

When Val Moffatt arrived, I was the picture of nonchalance. "Oh, hello. Come in."

"I'm not too early?" he asked, hesitating near the hall stand and glancing up the stairs.

He was here an hour before the group's time, but I followed his gaze, and thought he might not be looking for the writers. "Not too early. We have plenty of work to do—I have a few ideas about the salons."

We walked into my office just as my phone rang. I saw the caller and muttered, "Oh dear—I'm a bad mum. Sorry," I said to Val, and then answered. "Dinah, sweetie. I'm just getting your ticket now. You all set for tomorrow? That's grand—have a lovely day."

"She's going to see my mum tomorrow," I explained to Val. "This afternoon I told her I'd get her train ticket, but then it went clean out of my head. Do you mind?"

"No"—he nodded to my phone—"you go on."

Out of the corner of my eye as I bought and e-mailed the ticket, I saw Val lean over Bunter, who was curled up in the wingback, and give his head a scratch. The cat sat up and rubbed his face against Val's chin.

When finished, I set my phone down. "Right—done and done," I said, and added, "Starving student, you know."

"Oh, I do know," he said. "Times two. I'm happy those days are finished. How old did you say your daughter was?"

"Twenty-two. She took a gap year." I looked up, chagrined. "She took two, actually."

"It's difficult to say no to them, isn't it?" Val asked.

The tension in my shoulders eased as our lines of communication opened once again. I looked back on the apprehension that had been building inside me throughout the afternoon and thought how silly I'd been—we have a good working relationship, Val and I. We're colleagues. I glanced at Bunter and then gestured to the fireplace chairs. "I suppose we'd better sit over here."

We worked through the details of the literary salons. "I've classes Monday and Thursday evenings," Val said, "but I'm free Tuesdays. Although, I don't suppose it would be necessary for me to attend."

"Of course it's necessary," I said. "I'm not doing this without you." The words *by my side* tried to push their way out of my mouth, but I clamped my lips together until they retreated. "Should we come up with topics first or brainstorm a list of possible lecturers? I could contact the Christie people about a recommendation—they might give us a bit of publicity."

"Also, there's an author who's writing Dorothy L. Sayers's characters."

"You mean fan fiction?"

"I believe she got the nod from the estate. I'll tell you what," Val said. He leaned forward and I caught a twinkle in his green eyes. "If we want an expert on Lord Peter Wimsey, we could do no better than to ask his valet, Bunter. Or perhaps, his namesake." He turned to the cat. "What do you think, Bunter—will you give us a lecture about your life of mystery?" In the wingback, Bunter stretched out his front and back legs, becoming twice as long as normal, and then turned over onto his back and gazed at us upside down.

"Ladies and gentlemen," I announced in a smooth voice, "welcome to The First Edition Society's inaugural literary salon. This evening, in conversation with Bath College's own Val Moffatt, we have none other than Bunter the cat."

The buzzer interrupted, and I dragged myself off to answer. Val rose, too, but hung back while I greeted the group, clustered on the doorstep.

Peter had lost a bit of his normal arrogance, and now his slouch gave him a defeated look. Mariella, on the other hand, appeared perkier than usual—perhaps the baby was sleeping through the night—and greeted me with, "Thanks, Hayley. You're ace for letting us back in." Harry's brave smile set against her ashen face looked pitiful. And—who was that in the back?

Amanda—although I had needed a second look to identify her. She had cut off her braid, and now her thick blond hair was styled in a shingle, angled from just below her ear and to a point at her chin. It was a bit retro and suited her perfectly.

She blushed when I mentioned it, putting her hand up to run through her new 'do. "It had started getting in my way—time for a change. Hiya, Mr. Moffatt," she called, and then turned to the other three writers. "Come on, you lot, let's get to work."

I watched as they trooped up the stairs, and then said, "Well, that's them sorted."

"Shall we get back to it?" Val asked.

"We could do, yes—although, I've a cold supper if you're interested." I shrugged away any impression of importance. "Not much—just chicken and salad. From Waitrose."

"I would expect nothing less."

"Through here," I said, leading him to the kitchenette.

Val glanced at the table—already set—and then at me. "I knew I would have you at 'Waitrose,'" I said. "There's mustard down there"—I nodded to a square basket sitting on a low shelf—"and pickle. Whatever you need."

He perused the contents, and then reached in and drew out a catnip mouse by its tail.

"Bunter's contribution, I take it?"

We ate our meal and drank the wine at the tiny table and talked and talked. I quizzed him about growing up in Margate, and he enquired as to how my mum was doing.

"Have you always been a teacher?" I asked.

Val paused, glass in hand, and gave me half a nod. "I've been a teacher for as long as I can remember. And you?" he asked. "Always a curator?"

"Let's count the number of professions open to someone with a degree in nineteenth-century literature," I said. "My first job was in the reference library of the Great Western Railway Museum in Swindon—that's where we lived. About twelve years ago, Dinah and I moved here—she had just turned eleven—and I got on with the Jane Austen Centre."

With the story I'd told him in the pub, I believed that he could clearly put the pieces of my life in the right order—in Swindon, married with a daughter, followed by Bath, divorced with a daughter.

"What did you do at the Centre?"

"Assistant to the assistant curator—in other words, office worker. The people were lovely, but the pay wasn't quite enough for us to live on, so I took in student papers for proofreading. They wanted more than their grammar corrected, of course. 'Can't you just write it for me?' they'd ask. They didn't much care for my reply."

"Which was 'Write your own bloody paper'?" Val asked, and we both laughed. "And now you're running the show here at Middlebank."

"But for how long?" I told him the latest—the arrival of Charles Henry Dill. "He made everyone's life a misery after Lady Fowling died, and I'm going to have to keep my eye on him. If he tries to intimidate me, I'll report him—now that I have an in with the police, you know. Although, perhaps I'll start with Detective Constable Pye."

"Kenny Pye?" Val asked. "Is he in on the murder enquiry? He's in my Thursday-evening short-story course."

"DC Pye is taking a class from you?"

"And not the first. He writes stories set in 1920s London with a private investigator as his protagonist. Wait—that was his sergeant I saw here on Monday? What's his name?"

"Ronald Hopgood."

Val threw back his head and laughed. "His PI is called Alehouse."

I laughed, too, but asked, "Could he get in trouble for that?"

"I don't see how—historical fiction, after all. And Alehouse is a smart man—he can be friendly, but take care of that sharp edge."

"That's DS Hopgood all right. Constable Pye must keep busy with both police work and writing."

"You make time for what you love," Val said.

We fell quiet. Since the previous evening, I'd felt the need to explain myself, and throughout the afternoon I'd attempted to pull together a few thoughts, but they were muddled. Here now was the perfect moment to say something, but the right words eluded me.

"It was good of you to come round this evening," I said. "I wasn't sure you would."

"I wasn't sure I would be needed, what with Wyn here now."

I couldn't hold his gaze, and looked instead at my empty plate.

"As it turned out, he couldn't stay."

"Ah, back to the Big Smoke first thing this morning, was it?"

Val was fishing—he couldn't be more obvious—and I shouldn't answer.

"He had to leave last night, actually. He'd come down to Bath to see a fellow from Brussels who was here only for the one day—a software programmer. It was vital Wyn meet with him about . . . er . . . programming software for Myrtle."

"Who's Myrtle?"

"The robot that delivers the meals for Wyn's company."

"And so," Val said, his forehead furrowed, "he didn't actually come to Bath see you. Instead—"

"Of course he came to see me."

"Were you an afterthought?" Val persisted. "Even though some-one had broken in here and left a murder victim in the library below your flat? Is it always business first with him?"

Suddenly I was filled with righteous indignation, and ready to rail against anyone who believed Wyn would take me for granted. The fact that I was now a member of that group made not one whit of difference.

"Wyn's business"—I jabbed my finger on the table—"is at an extremely delicate stage with finances, and research and development and . . . the like. It's an enormous responsibility, and so, of course, he's quite focused and concerned."

"Shouldn't he be concerned about you?"

"What's that supposed to mean?"

"It means you make a lot of excuses for your boyfriend."

I leapt up from the table. "I do not make excuses for him—he makes his own excuses!"

Harry's wan face appeared at the door. "Sorry, Hayley," she whispered, "it's only . . . we wanted to let you know we'll be on our way now."

I gripped the back of the chair to steady myself. "Right, thanks, Harry. Let me show you out." I followed her to the door, where the others waited. "I'll be in touch about next Wednesday," I told them.

"You can give me a ring," Amanda said. "I'll let everyone know."

She walked out first, followed by Peter and Mariella. Harry stayed behind.

"Pub, Harry?" Mariella asked.

"Yeah, sure," she replied, backing up toward the kitchenette. "You go on, though, and I'll catch you up—I just need to nip into the loo."

The others left, and I closed the door and turned to find Val

Moffatt waiting, in a repeat of last Wednesday evening. Had that been only a week ago?

Opening the door again, I said, "Well, that's a start for the salons. You'll let me know if the dates suit the college?"

He didn't move, only watched me. I looked at the floor. Hadn't I made a big enough fool of myself for one evening?

"Hayley—" he began, but I was saved when Harry came out of the loo.

"Good evening," I said to him. He nodded to each of us and left.

I waited for Harry to walk out, too, but found she had sunk down onto the bottom step of the stairs and put her head against the railing.

"You all right, Harry? Was it a difficult session this evening?"

"My story has become quite sad," she said wistfully, "full of missed opportunities and regret. I wanted Miss Marple and the baby she had given up for adoption—who is now a member of Parliament—to be reconciled, but the characters won't do what I want."

"But aren't you in charge of what they do?" I asked. "Seems it would be easier to move characters around the page than make real people do what you want?"

"You would think," she agreed. "Hayley, are we allowed to look at the books in the library?"

"Allowed?" This is what comes of Mrs. Woolgar's treating the library as a shrine. "Of course you're allowed—that's the entire point of Lady Fowling's collection. Did you want to see any title in particular?"

Harry shook her head. "No, not me. Trist didn't think it was a good idea—he said no amount of wallowing in atmosphere could help some writing."

"That's a bit harsh."

"Well, I suppose I'd better catch them up. Mariella and Peter have run into difficulties with their manuscripts, but Amanda had twenty new pages this week. Although, they were a bit odd. Well, so, we're celebrating. Would you like to go along?"

"To the Minerva?" I glanced up the stairs—I really should do my nightly check on the condition of the library and then get to bed— where I could lie awake and feel miserable about arguing with Val.

"Yeah, sure, why not?"

16

What clues would Miss Marple have picked up from our drinks at the pub? I could detect none. Neither Pauline nor her brother was behind the bar, and the short woman was nowhere in sight. The writers lasted through only one round and held their conversation steady to the topic of a new television production of Christie's *Pocketful of Rye*.

When I attempted to edge the talk toward Trist by asking a leading question—"What do you think he meant by 'soaking up atmosphere won't help a bad manuscript'?"—no one replied, and Harry wouldn't meet my eye. Soon after that, they all swiftly reached the bottoms of their glasses, collectively yawned, and made to leave.

Defeated, discontented, and disillusioned, I followed them out. The others moved off, but I stopped with Harry and held her laptop as she struggled with her coat. She'd just taken her computer back when we heard the commotion.

"You keep your hands off it!" Amanda yelled. I whipped round to see

her in a tug-of-war with Peter over a canvas bag while passersby gave them barely a glance.

"I should've known I had the wrong one," he countered in a loud voice. "Yours is so jammed with paper it's a wonder you can find anything. Here, take it." He let go, causing Amanda to lurch backward. He reached for her. "Give me mine, then," he said.

Amanda shrieked—*"Don't you touch me!"*—and shoved him. He stumbled back, and Mariella caught his arm.

"Oi!" I called, and hurried over to put myself between them. "Amanda, are you all right?"

"Why are you asking her?" Mariella demanded. "What about Peter?"

"Well, that is"—I divided my attention to be fair—"Peter, are you all right?"

"Fine," he spat. "Can I have my own bag now?"

Amanda held two brown canvas satchels, one in each hand, both shoddy and overstuffed. I hadn't realized they were almost identical. She seemed to weigh them for a moment, and then handed one over.

"Right, well—night all," she said. "See you next week."

"Yeah, night," the others replied.

As they ambled off, I asked Harry, "What was that about?"

She shrugged. "Dunno. Just the usual."

We walked together to Union Passage, where I turned right and Harry left.

"Night, Hayley," she said.

The pubs were still open, so the narrow lane was quiet apart from a few clusters of smokers puffing away in the chill. I'd left the last of them behind and took a gulp of clean air as I passed a shadowy corner, when a hand shot out and gripped my arm.

"Ah!" I cried, and then saw who it was. "Oh God, Amanda, you frightened the wits out of me."

She let go of my arm. "Sorry, Hayley, I didn't mean to. It's only that I started home, but then thought I'd better find you and apologize for that." She nodded her head in the Minerva's direction.

"What happened?" I asked.

Amanda wrinkled her nose. "Nothing, really—I overreacted. I guess we're all a bit on edge. Police are being closemouthed about the enquiry, yet they keep coming back to each of us, and asking the same questions over and over. They're doing that to you as well?" She didn't wait for an answer but continued. "Still, I should know better than to annoy Peter after what happened between him and Trist."

I thought of the group's first evening at Middlebank and the scuffle on the landing. "When you began meeting in the library?"

"No, even before the group formed—this was yonks ago," she said dismissively. "The two of them were collaborating on a book with both Poirot and Miss Marple as dueling protagonists. I can't imagine writing with someone else, and it certainly didn't work out well for them. There was a big bust-up—I believe Peter broke Trist's nose."

In the moment of silence that ensued, I imagined Peter overtaking Trist on Gravel Walk behind Middlebank, shoving him hard, and then carrying his body up to the library. Immediately the same missing key points lined themselves out: What were they doing there, how did they get back in, and why in God's name did it happen?

"They patched things up after that," Amanda added. "But still, it comes down to the same thing—I just don't know what we're going to do without him."

Only the next morning did I remember that I hadn't checked on the state of the library after the group had departed. What if a chair had been left out of place? What if they'd been into the sherry?

What if there was another dead body?

I dressed for my walk, but stopped at the library door on my way down. My hand hovered over the door handle, and it annoyed me that the simple task of peeking into a room could cause my pulse to race. I looked back to the portrait of Lady Fowling for courage and found that she emitted a serene aura in the still morning. I took this as a good sign and pushed in.

All was not as it should've been. Books had gone astray from their proper places—a few were stacked on the table and several more pulled out and left lying on a shelf.

A stab of fear was followed close on by a giggle. What did we have here? It looked very much like a library—the sort where people actually made use of the books. Hadn't Harry mentioned this? I glanced at the volumes as I reshelved. Two Poirot stories and one Miss Marple. In fact, the latter was *The Murder at the Vicarage*—the one I had stayed up into the wee hours to finish.

As I left for my walk, I considered how Miss Marple solved crimes. In the story, everything had been laid out from the start— the suspects, the alibis. People lied, but no one cottoned on—except her, an unassuming little old lady who spent time in her garden and could see through deceit. Talk about a superpower.

My morning circuit of Bath helped to clear my head, and I returned up the back-garden path. For the past week, I'd come at the gate from the opposite end of Gravel Walk for the sole reason of avoiding the wrought-iron post into which Trist had been shoved.

I gave Bunter his breakfast and was about to go up to shower when I heard laughter outside on the front step. I opened the door to find Pauline, dressed for work in coveralls and bandanna. Next to her was Adele—her massive head of red curls loose, tumbling over her shoulders—holding one of the pails of cleaning supplies.

"I'm trying to talk Adele into a new career." Pauline shifted the vacuum from one arm to the other and stuck the folded-up extension duster in her back pocket.

Adele picked up the second pail. "I told Pauline if she saw my flat, she'd know cleaning wasn't my strong suit."

"That's me as well," Pauline commiserated. "The cobbler's children syndrome, I'm afraid. You wouldn't want to look in my drawers."

Adele grinned and looked ready to reply, but instead she walked past me and set the cleaning supplies down. "Morning, Hayley."

"Morning," I said. "Do you two know each other?"

Pauline deposited the vacuum and, over her shoulder, said, "We've only just met."

"I've come to sign the letter," Adele said. "Literary salons? I thought I'd better do it this morning, as I'm taking the Suffragette Club up to London on a school trip until tomorrow."

"Of course, yes. In here. You all right, Pauline?"

She'd already got to work on the baseboards. "Yeah, grand. Oh—do you have the new key for me? And the code?"

"Yes, I'll bring them out." In my office, Adele had perched on the arm of the wingback. "So, Pauline owns her own business?"

"She does." I retrieved the file with the board's letter of approval. "Plus, her brother runs the Minerva, and she takes a few shifts there every week."

"Does she? We should go there."

No detective was needed to pick up on the barely concealed interest in her voice. I verified this with a quick glance—Adele's cheeks were glowing.

"We should," I said, but with little enthusiasm. "Sometime."

"What?" Adele asked, narrowing her eyes at me. "What's wrong?"

"Nothing."

"Something," Adele said.

It was clear that I would need to resolve the issue of Pauline's guilt or innocence as soon as possible, but for the moment, I had an easy excuse to hand. "It's only that you don't want me involved. I've just this minute introduced you to a friend of mine—as far as you're concerned, that's the kiss of death for a relationship, isn't it?"

Adele frowned at my logic but changed topics—good thing it had already escaped her that I hadn't done any introducing, actually. "How are the literary salons progressing?" she asked. "Working together with Val all right?"

I laid the letter down and handed over a pen. "Speaking of such things—I know what you're up to, Ms. Babbage, even though you don't believe in setting people up. Need I remind you, I have a boyfriend?"

"Yes, so I've heard," she said under her breath as she signed. "And how is he?"

"Fine." I snatched the pen from her and—before she could see straight through my lie—said, "Have a good day at school."

When I stepped into the hall, Adele had gone, and Pauline was vacuuming the rug in Mrs. Woolgar's office. She switched off the vacuum when she saw me.

"Here you go." I held out the new key and the code written on a sticky note, but for one moment, I couldn't let go. Was I doing the right thing? "You don't . . . er . . ."

"I'll put them away safely, you can be sure of that. I won't let them out of my sight." As if to prove it, Pauline stared at the key and paper until I cleared my throat. "And oh, Hayley," she added in a nonchalant tone I'd heard only recently. "Adele. She seems nice."

Pauline was a suspect in a murder enquiry—she could even be the prime suspect. Did I want my friend to become involved with a murderer? Possible murderer. Was Pauline a murderer?

"Do you have time for a chat after you finish?" I asked.

"I'd love to, really I would, it's only that I'm chockablock today."

I heard the door of Mrs. Woolgar's flat closing downstairs. Pauline revved up the vacuum again, and added, "Better crack on."

Pauline had moved on to my flat by the time Mrs. Woolgar and I sat down for our morning briefing. It was our twice-monthly membership overview for The First Edition Society. Since I'd started my job, the reports had been dismal—always several names in the "have not renewed" category and rarely a new name. This week, however, the two lists evened out—four members dropped and four members added. Nothing to cause Mrs. Woolgar to leap on her desk and do a jig—there's a sight I'd like to see—but still, not as bleak as usual.

"They do know we don't offer a murder every month, don't they?" I asked, only half joking.

Mrs. Woolgar did not respond, and instead read out a new letter of welcome she wanted to send. I had difficulty concentrating, as suspects in the enquiry paraded through my mind—Pauline with the key and the code to Middlebank, as well as a dodgy-looking brother, and the others, the writers, who had neither key nor code. That group formed an oddly disconnected yet solid front. They didn't seem to like one another yet were quick to gloss over problems inside the group.

And still, did the police have any idea why Trist would be lurking along the path behind Middlebank in the middle of the night?

"And your activities for the day, Ms. Burke?" Mrs. Woolgar asked.

Yes, what would I do? Perhaps I would spend my day slumped in a chair at my desk, stewing in a vat of regret for how my evening with Val had turned out. That was just where I'd end up if I didn't find a well-defined task, a project that would engage my mind and keep it off other topics—murder and suspects and boyfriends. Fortunately, I didn't have to look far.

"I'm going to talk with Mr. Dill," I told Mrs. Woolgar.

I might've said I was going to throw myself off the top of St. Paul's Cathedral or swim the English Channel before lunch for the reaction I got—the secretary's eyes opened wide in shock and her face drained of color.

"You what?"

"I'm going to the Royal Crescent Hotel," I said firmly. "I will not cower and worry and obsess—I will come right out with it and ask his intentions."

"You can't do that," Mrs. Woolgar insisted. "You don't know what he's like. He takes what you say and twists it to his own advantage. He's up to no good. I promise you he's looking for a way this very minute to use the murder to further his own agenda. He's a disrupter—that's how he operates."

I was more impressed with Mrs. Woolgar's passion than I was with her warning.

"It's all right," I assured her. "I can take care of myself. I'll be reasonable and polite."

A clatter on the stairs brought me up short.

"Sorry, Mrs. Woolgar." I leapt up and backed out of her office as I explained. "It's only that I wanted to catch Pauline about something before she leaves."

The cleaner was on a call. She had her phone to her ear with one hand, and her head down as she shifted the vacuum and pails from the entry to the front step, propping open the door with her bum. The extension duster, folded up on itself, stuck out of her back pocket like a foxtail with a bad perm.

"I did this for you, Leonard," Pauline snapped. "Now look how it's turned out. If this keeps up, she'll find herself in the nick." She turned round for the last pail and jumped at the sight of me. "So, yeah," she said lightly, "I'll be there on time for my shift. See ya."

"Pauline," I began.

"Sorry, Hayley, I've got to run. I promised Leonard I'd take a shift at the Minerva this afternoon, and I've still another house to do." Safely outside, she paused. "Did you need me for something?"

I need to eliminate you from my suspect list and then vet you as a possible girlfriend for Adele. But it was looking worse for Pauline, not better.

"No, it's nothing really. Although, perhaps I'll stop round the pub later."

B ut first, the nephew. I went to my flat for my handbag, and when I returned to the entry, found Mrs. Woolgar waiting at the bottom of the stairs. She followed me to the door.

"It'll be fine," I assured her. "You'll see. Whatever his devious plans are, he needs to know that I am no pushover."

"There's something you should know," Mrs. Woolgar said, twisting her hands together.

Those were words no one welcomed. I stood at the open door, umbrella in hand, and waited for her to go on.

"One of the reasons Eileen Merton left"—Eileen Merton, the first curator, I reminded myself as I waited an excruciatingly long second before Mrs. Woolgar continued—"was because Charles Henry had come across a slightly embarrassing bit of scandal in her family's history, concerning birthright."

"An illegitimacy? Really, that isn't the sort of information anyone would consider a scandal these days."

"It would have devastated Eileen for the world to know her grandfather had not earned his title properly," the secretary said. "I've no idea how Charles Henry had sussed it out, but his threats of exposure were enough to push her into retirement. You see how he works."

"Well, let him just try to put the wind up me."

"Ms. Burke"—she put a hand on my arm—"mind how you go."

17

No one can walk up to and along the Royal Crescent without being impressed. A sweeping five-hundred-foot-long arc of tall Georgian town houses built from Bath stone in the Palladian style, it offered a panoramic view of Royal Victoria Park and had a deep connection with the Regency period and with Jane Austen. Although she never lived on the Crescent herself, a few of her characters had. That thought led me back to my previous job at the Jane Austen Centre, not a ten-minute walk away where I had spent my days filing and copying and making tea. Now look at me—I'd taken an enormous leap and was curator in my own right of The First Edition Society. I wasn't about to let anyone take that away from me without a fight.

"Hello, I'm Hayley Burke," I said to the young woman behind the reception desk at the Royal Crescent Hotel. "I'm curator of The First Edition Society at Middlebank House—we're only just round the corner from you."

The young woman kept the smile on her face, but I believe I saw

the tiniest flicker of recognition, quickly quashed by her good man-
ners. An older woman in a business suit, her silver hair in a neat
chignon, appeared in the doorway behind. She carried a tablet, and
her eyes darted to me and back to the screen. Were they both thinking, *Oh yes, that's the place where that fellow was found dead in the library?*

"Hello, good morning, Ms. Burke," the young woman said, "and
welcome to the Royal Crescent. How can I help you?"

"I believe Charles Henry Dill is staying with you, and I'd like to
speak with him. Do you know if he's in?"

"Mr. Dill," she replied, shifting a few papers round on the desk, as
if she'd mislaid Charles Henry. "Well, I'm not sure if I'm able to—"

The older woman looked up and said, "It's all right, Sandy, go on
and ring Mr. Dill's room."

"Yes, Ms. Carlisle," Sandy replied and did as she was told.

"Thank you." I beamed at her. "I'll just wait over here."

I stood next to a Chinese palm for a few minutes, until he
emerged from the lift. He wore the same brown plaid suit but had
lost the leer—apparently not a good look for a posh hotel lobby.

"How delightful to see you, Ms. Burke." He extended his hand
and I obliged in kind, barely containing a shudder as he gave me the
squeeze.

"Mr. Dill, I stopped in to have a chat."

"Oh, how disappointing," he said in an obsequious manner. "I'm
so sorry to say that you've wasted a journey. You see, I was just this
minute going out. Unavoidable appointment, I'm afraid. If it were
any other time, we could have coffee—"

Perhaps he hadn't prepared for such a quick return on his invitation. Perhaps he had a reason to try to avoid me. But Charles Henry
Dill had no idea with whom he dealt. If I could cut off the escape
route of a fifteen-year-old Dinah intent on meeting friends for an
evening of cider drinking, I could certainly stop him. I raised my
voice slightly so all could hear.

"Coffee? Yes, I'd love coffee. Thanks so much, Mr. Dill."

The older woman approached us with a welcoming smile. I glanced at her name tag—the word *Manager* stood out.

"Coffee for two, Mr. Dill?" she asked. "Let me ring the kitchen for you and have a tray sent into the drawing room. Would you like to go through?"

What choice did he have? "Yes, well," Dill conceded, "coffee, why not?"

I led the way. When I chanced a look over my shoulder to make sure Charles Henry followed, I saw the hotelier, behind him, with a smile. I smiled back—grateful for the assistance she unknowingly had offered.

The drawing room, with its ecru walls, ornate plasterwork ceiling, and decorative Greek-style cornices, oozed Georgian class. Tall windows ran along the front wall, and elegant tables, chairs, and sofas formed groupings round the room. I'd been here before—we'd had afternoon tea at the Royal Crescent for Dinah's twelfth birthday along with three of her friends. That had set me back, I can tell you.

I made for two chairs in the corner with a low table between them, and a young man with the coffee service arrived on our heels. I was delighted to see a plate of macarons—purple, pink, and a pale yellow that I hoped had buttercream filling. I slipped one onto my saucer and, as the young man poured, couldn't resist a bite.

The combination of crisp meringue and smooth buttercream bolstered my nerves. To begin in a civil manner, I took a sip of coffee and said, "Tell me, Mr. Dill, where do you call home?"

"You mean apart from Middlebank?"

Middlebank wasn't even in the equation, as far as I knew—he'd never lived there, spent only a few summers growing up. Adele told me Lady Fowling had thought it her duty, as Charles Henry's mother was her younger sister.

"I mean, where do you live?"

"Abroad for the most part, Ms. Burke," Dill said glibly. "I have international interests."

"And what brings you to Bath?"

He popped his second macaron into his mouth and took another before answering. I could tell this was going to be a fight to finish the last crumb on the plate.

"What else could I do, when I heard the news, but offer my deepest condolences for your loss."

"And what loss is that?"

"How odd it is"—Dill set down his half-empty coffee cup—"that a murder would be committed in the very house dedicated to enlightening the world about this more commercial side of literature. By the way, how is the enquiry progressing?"

"That is a matter for the police."

"The murder was a rather obvious nod to our Mrs. Christie, wasn't it?" Dill took another macaron and sat back.

Our Mrs. Christie—what was he playing at? What happened to the *musty collection of has-been authors from a bygone era?*

"I tell you truthfully, Ms. Burke, I'm desperately concerned about my dear aunt Georgiana's legacy. Throughout her life, she strove to create a place that crossed the boundaries of time and genre in the world of literature. To think that someone would use the very subject of her favorite books to tear down what she built."

The landscape was shifting, and I scurried to reposition myself.

"I'm not sure we can go as far as to say—" I began.

"It was *The Body in the Library*, of course, although, there were elements of other books, too—don't you think? What about the one with the house-and-garden tour—let me see, which one was that?"

He leaned closer and fixed me with an unwavering gaze, waiting for an answer. A house-and-garden tour? Was this Agatha Christie?

I cleared my throat. "It seems a bit farfetched to believe that someone would—"

"It's a remarkable world, detective fiction, isn't it?"

Dill rested his elbows on the arms of the chair, offering me a smile that was just short of his characteristic leer. I could feel my advantage slip away as he gained the high ground.

"I can't tell you what a pleasure it is to be able to discuss the mystery writers with an expert of your caliber," he said. "And tell me, what do you make of those New Zealand detective stories?"

Was he having me on? Surely Agatha Christie didn't write books set in New Zealand. It must be one of the other mystery writers— but which? I needed to stop this line of questioning immediately—I was not capable of engaging in a mystery-genre duel.

I straightened up in my chair and threw back my shoulders. "If you're concerned about the state of the Society, Mr. Dill, I can assure you that this unfortunate event will have no impact whatsoever. We are already in the midst of planning a variety of activities that will fulfill Lady Fowling's fondest wish that the world know and appreciate her favorite books."

He gave me a sly look. "That is just what I intend, too—to reestablish The First Edition Society to its rightful place in the literary sphere. And although it's true that I have only lately come to realize the brilliance of Aunt Georgiana's dedication to the mystery and suspense genre, I now know that the Society's very survival depends on the collection's continuation. As I see you are a reasonable woman, I'm sure you understand that because the Society is a family legacy, its guidance should remain within the family."

It was a punch to the stomach that took my breath away. Now I saw what he was up to—Charles Henry had carried out his own investigation on my background and knew me for a charlatan. Mrs. Woolgar was right, he would use anything he could find—he'd chased away the first curator with threats of exposing her grandfather as an illegitimate Edwardian earl. Now I was the target.

He would poke and prod until he created a fissure in my

competence—*First,* he would say, *she knows nothing about mystery, and second, a murder right under her nose!* Once I was compromised, he would dive in for the kill. He would delight in using Trist's murder as a way of undermining me, hoping I would scarper as had Eileen Merton. And when he had gained control of The First Edition Society—what then?

Dill stood and brushed the colorful snow of crumbs from his stomach. "I've so enjoyed our chat, Ms. Burke, but now you really will have to excuse me." He took my hand, bending over it as if to plant a kiss. I jerked it away in the nick of time. "Until we meet again," he added, and walked out.

18

The delights of macarons and the drawing room decor drained away, and I realized this was it—the end. If even Mrs. Woolgar was afraid of Charles Henry Dill, what hope did I have of fighting off a takeover? I stood but my legs wobbled, and I had to brace myself against the chair. As I waited to regain my strength and stop my head from spinning, the manager from reception looked in, saw the room empty but for me, and approached.

"Ms. Burke, I didn't introduce myself earlier. I'm Linda Carlisle, guest manager. I've been at the Royal Crescent for twenty years, and I wanted to tell you what fond memories I have of Lady Fowling. She and her friends would come to tea every month. It was an afternoon the entire staff enjoyed—we were always caught up in her élan and her far-reaching interests. She was such a lovely woman—and she's very much missed. But I'm so happy to know you are carrying on her vision."

I had been teetering on the precipice of despair, but her words took hold and pulled me back to safety. My eyes filled with tears.

"How kind of you, Ms. Carlisle." I could go no further, and searched my pockets for a tissue.

"Please, it's Linda."

"Yes, of course." I sniffed and daubed my eyes with an ancient crumpled specimen. "And call me Hayley. I took the job of curator only a few months ago, and I never actually met Lady Fowling. But I feel her spirit at Middlebank still."

"I'm sorry you're going through this difficult time," Linda said quietly. "How is Glynis holding up?"

"Oh, you know Mrs. Woolgar, too?"

"Indeed—she came along to the teas, as well as Mrs. Sylvia and Mrs. Audrey Moon, and sometimes Mrs. Arbuthnot."

It sounded like a board meeting. "Ms. Frost?"

"Maureen? Occasionally, with her mother—Maureen was always a headstrong woman and didn't really settle down until after her mother died. After that, she was a regular. And, the last few years, there was a lively young woman—quite striking in her appearance."

"That would be Adele Babbage," I said.

"Yes, that's it. Those were always such happy gatherings." Linda's reminiscence faded as her gaze drifted toward the door of the drawing room leading to the lobby.

I followed her eyes and then asked, "Had you met Mr. Dill before this visit of his?"

"No, although I was . . . aware of him."

That pause spoke volumes, and I sensed in Linda Carlisle an ally.

"I hadn't met him either," I said. "But both Adele and Mrs. Woolgar—and even the solicitor, Mr. Rennie—warned me—"

Linda's look sharpened, and I was seized with worry—had I said too much?

"That is—" I stammered, but she waved a hand as if to brush my words away.

"I've heard concerns from Glynis. Even Lady Fowling had the

occasion to mention him, and not in the most favorable light. But even if I hadn't already known the sort of man he is," Linda said, "I would've cottoned on since his arrival yesterday. He's taken every opportunity to make it known that he is Lady Fowling's nephew and it's 'only a matter of time' before he moves into Middlebank."

"The nerve!" My voice was shrill in my own ears, and I dropped it to a whisper. "What did he do—pull up in a taxi with all his belongings?"

"No, he walked in on his own, and then had the hotel's car and driver bring his things over."

I heaved a great sigh. It was one thing to hope for and possibly assist in a quick resolution to Trist's murder, but it was an entirely different matter to have to battle Charles Henry Dill at the same time. For a moment, I entertained the idea of escape. I could march straight down to the rail station and board a train to . . . where? I caught a whiff of briny air, and I could hear the sea crashing against rocks and feel the edge of a foamy wave roll over my toes. Fancies—I shook my head.

"Thank you, Linda." I extended my hand, and we exchanged a warm and firm shake. "I appreciate your telling me your memories of Lady Fowling. There's a large portrait of her on the first-floor landing at Middlebank, and I admit that sometimes I think she's watching over us. I suppose it's more a wish. Well, I'd best be on my way."

"Oh, look," Linda said, contemplating the remaining macarons. "Those will just have to be binned. I do hate the waste. The coffee service is on Mr. Dill's room, of course, but I don't suppose I could persuade you to take them away with you?"

Three macarons—one each, purple, pink, and buttercream— were my reward for facing up to Charles Henry Dill. I finished them off as I walked into the city center, not really seeing where my feet led as I tried to assess the viability of his threats. It was only when I stopped in front of the police station that I realized another part of my mind had planned the route. Yes, I would talk with Detective Sergeant Hopgood.

He came out to the lobby, and I looked at him in a new light—as inspiration for Kenny Pye's 1920s private detective. I'd quite like to read those stories—although I'd have to put them at the back of the queue, with dozens and dozens of mystery books ahead of them.

"Ms. Burke," Hopgood greeted me. "Come through." I followed him in and he opened the door of Interview #1—my home away from home. "Do you have something for us?" he asked.

I had built up a good head of steam on my walk down, but now I sputtered. "Yes, there is something I'd like to discuss with you, although I'm not sure you would consider it evidence."

"No matter," Hopgood replied. "I have something to show you. Will you wait?"

I took my usual chair and had ample time to put my thoughts into reasonable order. When I had done that, I realized I was in the wrong place—I shouldn't be at the police station, I should be in Duncan Rennie's office—our solicitor for the Society. He'd dealt with Charles Henry before, he could do it again.

Hopgood returned with a long roll of paper, which he unfurled across the table. It was a map of the city center lavishly decorated in five colors of felt markers. There were *X*s, large dots, arcs, and trails of dotted lines. Off to the side the writers' names were listed—each with his or her own color.

"A map of their movements that night," Hopgood explained, giving his mustache a quick brush with his fingers. "Here now, let me show you. You see Mariella Vine and Peter Talbot"—purple and brown, respectively—"and here, Amanda Seabrook on her own"—green—"and Harry Tanner leaving with the victim."

Harry, red, and Trist, black. The sergeant described each route, tapping the map and tracing the lines as if giving a battle plan to his army, as he indicated the various positions of the writers after they left the Minerva, where, that very evening, Pauline had been behind the bar.

But I couldn't concentrate on his details—my head was too full of a more immediate crisis, and only when the room had turned silent did I realize Hopgood was staring at me with expectation.

"Sorry, what was that?" I asked.

"As I said, we lose them here"—he pointed to dots on the map—"here, and here. But please note—not a one of them leaves the pub walking in the direction of their respective homes."

"Where were they going?"

"To the shop for milk or to avoid a roadworks closure or enjoying the fine night or—well, they seemed to have a multitude of destinations." The sergeant did not sound convinced by any of them. "And," he continued, "there's no CCTV at either end of Gravel Walk behind Middlebank. The car park across the road has it, but not pointed to our advantage. What I want to know from you, Ms. Burke, is this—if you were standing at each of these locations, which way would you take to arrive at the back-garden entrance of Middlebank?"

I stared at the map, forcing myself to consider the possibilities. "From here"—I pointed at Amanda's green line—"I'd be likely to take this corner and come round on the far end. And there"—my finger traced Harry's red path—"it's quite convenient to take this pass-through. Now, these two—" One by one I put myself on the pavement or in the lanes and walked to Middlebank. The DS made notes as I went along, and in the end seemed pleased enough.

"My PC who is viewing every working CCTV in the city will be grateful for this—narrows his search down a bit."

Good—see what a help I can be?

"Now, Sergeant, I'm sure you have a great deal yet to do on this investigation, but do you have any idea how long it will take to solve Trist's murder?" There went the eyebrows in the silent question *Are you mad?* I hurried on. "It's only that we find ourselves unable to move forward at The First Edition Society because of the enquiry, and now, on top of that, Charles Henry Dill has arrived to cause trouble."

"Who is Charles Henry Dill?"

For a moment, I was taken aback, but then it came to me that the DS had no reason to know him. "He is Lady Fowling's"—*lout of a*—"nephew."

"Did he know Trist Cummins?" Hopgood asked. "Is this about the murder? Does he live here in Bath?"

"He doesn't live here—he arrived yesterday and made straight for Middlebank. He's using this enquiry to try for a takeover—The First Edition Society, the house, Lady Fowling's estate—he's always thought he should've inherited everything."

"Why is this a matter for the police? Is he harassing you?"

He's trying to steal my job from me, and I want you to tell him to stop.

"He feeds off other people's misery," I said. "He creates chaos."

"Those are sharp words, Ms. Burke."

"Sergeant, how could you pull Mrs. Woolgar into the station and accuse her of murder based on a long-ago incident—when she hit Trist with her handbag?"

"Mrs. Woolgar preferred to answer our questions here—that was her idea," he replied, switching to his kindly police tone. "And she is not accused of murder. It was merely a chat."

But my questions had opened a door in my mind. Charles Henry Dill had applied himself to finding my weak spot—that my background had nothing to do with the Golden Age of Mystery—and sought to turn it to his own advantage. If he could do it to me, he could do it to others, and who better to target than the person who embodied the continuation of Lady Fowling's spirit—Mrs. Woolgar.

"Who told you about that incident?"

"A tip phoned into the station—it was anonymous."

"Anonymous my eye," I said. "I'll tell you who put that flea in your ear—and he did it only to make trouble. It was Charles Henry Dill."

M y accusation had made no impact on Sergeant Hopgood, and to avoid looking entirely useless, I had passed on the bit Amanda had told me about Peter and Trist's set-to when they had tried to collaborate. After that, I left, carrying my frustration along with me. I looked for Harry, but the low wall across the road from the station was empty, as it had been when I arrived. Perhaps she had returned to work, giving up on her Trist vigil.

Next on my agenda, Pauline. I checked my watch—lunch was not the best time to carry out an interview in the pub. I would try later in the afternoon. Instead, I stopped off at the Waitrose café and had a sandwich before returning to Middlebank, where, in an unprecedented turn of events, Mrs. Woolgar and I held our second briefing in less than twenty-four hours. I gave her a blow-by-blow account of my meeting with Dill.

"His plan is to get rid of me just as he got rid of the first curator," I said. "But he'll soon discover I won't budge. He has no ability to take over the Society—and no backing or support."

Mrs. Woolgar frowned.

"He doesn't—does he?" I asked.

"No, certainly not." She pressed her lips together. "Of course, I doubt if that would stop him from muddying the waters. Perhaps I'd better speak with Mr. Rennie."

"Yes, good idea. I'm back out again this afternoon to see Pauline—she's got a shift at the Minerva."

"Quite right. I don't believe Ms. Lunn has sufficiently explained her movements. She is the only other person, after all, with a way in."

My initial response was to ignore my doubts and defend Pauline. "But did she know Trist? What sort of an altercation would they have had? Why ever would she take him into the library?" I shook my head. "Nothing holds up."

Although I tried to make a good show of it, I wasn't entirely convinced of Pauline's innocence. I blamed this on her brother, Leonard, and that young woman—they were the ones who worried me. They looked shifty enough to be involved in something untoward, but *I don't like the look of them* didn't seem enough to take to the police. How could I find out if they knew Trist? If I learned something, I would take it straight to Sergeant Hopgood, regardless of whether it implicated Pauline. In an enquiry, all parties must be treated equally.

Gathering my notebook and pen, I rose, but paused at the office door and got up the courage to push out into uncharted waters.

"Charles Henry Dill thinks I'm vulnerable, because my background is not in twentieth-century literature." More to the point, commercial detective fiction. "And I know that has been a . . . concern of yours, too, Mrs. Woolgar. But I'm taking care of it. I've already read *The Murder at the Vicarage* and *The Body in the Library*. Last night, I started on *The Mysterious Affair at Styles*. I thought it would be good for me to understand Poirot, too." Val had recommended that one, and I'd hoped we could discuss it next time we met. If we ever met again.

"No one understands Poirot," the secretary commiserated. "He of the little gray cells."

I added, "Also, I'll skim a couple of Tommy and Tuppence stories. That way I'll have the writers group's detectives covered before I go on to another author."

"Would that we were all as sharp as Jane Marple."

Buoyed by what I perceived as her support, I edged dangerously toward emotion. "Mrs. Woolgar, I just wanted to say that . . . our recent briefings have been . . . quite . . ."

"Useful?" she offered. Yes, there's a term that would keep us at arm's length.

"Yes, that's it. We are, after all, both dedicated to carrying on Lady Fowling's vision."

The secretary gave a curt nod, indicating that was enough bonding for one day.

Pauline didn't seem best pleased to see me walk into the pub, and that made me sad. Did I already look like the enemy to her? I liked her and thought that she and Adele would get along well together. I wasn't altogether sure that Pauline was gay, but that was something the two women could work out on their own. They certainly seemed to hit it off, and I did so want Adele to find someone nice.

Just not a murderer.

Only one of the six tables at the Minerva was occupied and no one was at the bar, so I climbed up on a stool and smiled.

"Hiya," Pauline said, not meeting my eye as she loaded glasses into the tiny dishwasher under the counter. "You finished for the day?"

"Oh, well"—I exhaled in a gust and made a show of checking the time—"close enough. I'll have a glass of red wine, please. And a packet of crisps—lightly salted."

Pauline filled my order silently and then busied herself with straightening the lineup of bottles on the shelves against the mirror.

"Pauline, could I ask you something?"

She whipped round and put her hands on the counter behind, as if bracing for the worst.

"Look, Hayley, I know I've been distracted lately, but the thing is, I'm feeling a bit overwhelmed. I've had to double up on my cleaning schedule, because one of my workers doesn't. Work, that is. I'm this far from sacking her. I'm not supposed to be coming in here for Leonard this often, but he had someone quit, and so here I am. It's put me all at sixes and sevens. So, I'm really sorry about that man dying and all, but it has nothing to do with me."

"Of course it doesn't," I replied, wishing she hadn't sounded so defensive. "Sorry if I'm being a nosey parker, but—is it that young woman I saw you talking with on Monday—is she the one you're wanting to let go?"

Pauline jutted her chin out in a defiant reaction, but then her body slumped. "Lulu Ingleby," she said with a bitter tone. "A little slip of a thing, and yet she's doing a fine job of bollocksing up my life as well as Leonard's."

I took a sip of wine and leaned forward, pushing aside the packet of crisps for the moment. "She works for you—I saw her bandanna. And does she work here, too? Is that how your brother knows her?"

"Lulu is Leonard's girlfriend. He begged me to give her a job as one of my cleaners. She doesn't work here at the pub—says that she's allergic to the smell of beer. That doesn't keep her from swanning in and out of the place several times a day—usually in the process of skiving off an assignment I've given her. Or to complain about her flatmate."

"So, you're letting her go?"

"I threaten, but so far haven't had the nerve. Leonard's quite taken with her and, after all, he's my brother." Pauline picked up a bar towel, twisting it, as if to wring it dry.

As an only child, I found that a weak argument. "Is it that you don't trust her?" When I'd overheard Pauline on the phone earlier with her brother, she'd been accusing someone of stealing—had that someone been Lulu?

"I don't know what Leonard's even doing with her," Pauline complained.

Not the answer I was looking for—not really an answer at all. But still, as annoying as this situation was for her, I looked at this as good news for Pauline. Troubles with Lulu Ingleby—she wasn't a good cleaner, she wouldn't work in the pub—were troubles that were separate from the murder enquiry.

Now to sweep away the rest of my worries. "And on top of all that, you've got the police asking you questions." I saw the blinds go down in her eyes and hurried on. "It's happening to all of us. I've been in to see the police twice now, since the day you—we—found the body in the library. And so has Mrs. Woolgar. But of course, they have to be thorough—how else can they solve this crime?"

"They keep asking me about having a key and the code to Middlebank. Of course I have them—and for my other houses, too. I have to be able to go in and out without bothering anyone. But why would I jeopardize my business for a load of old books?"

I ignored her last remark. "And I'm sure that when you talked with them, they asked if you knew any of the group that meets at Middlebank. Didn't they?"

Pauline nodded. "I'm not entirely sure they believed me when I said I didn't, because it turns out they had all been in here the evening before—that fellow as well as the rest of the group. Your writers."

I opened my mouth to protest that they weren't my writers, but decided to let it slide.

"I never work here on a Wednesday," Pauline continued, "and I didn't remember if I'd seen any of them before that. I hate doing the last shift of the evening." She took a clean glass and absentmindedly dried it. "It means closing up and then cleaning—I do enough of that during the day. And I finish here so late—that's why I was a bit after my time the next morning."

I thought about DS Hopgood's map. Pauline's name had not been on it. Was that good or bad? "Isn't your flat out off the London Road?"

"Yeah, and I told police we have CCTV at the building. But they came back to me and said there was something wrong with the feed that night. That isn't my fault."

"All you can do is tell the truth," I said. From the closed look on Pauline's face, I'd say that was unwelcome advice. "What I mean is—"

Never try to have a serious conversation with a person working behind a bar, because just when you think you can get to the meat of the matter, in comes half a rugby team.

"I'm sorry, Pauline." I had one more item on my agenda and rushed on. "I know it's all a mess right now, and you don't need this on top of everything else. I don't see why you should have to worry about Lulu's flatmate. Flatmates can be difficult, can't they? You don't have a flatmate, do you—or, you know, a partner or . . . anyone significant?"

I winced at my clunky segue, but Pauline—in the midst of a barrage of orders—didn't seem to mind.

"No, I live alone. Right, lads, I'm coming."

19

Four o'clock Friday morning, my eyes popped open, and I stared into the darkness with a sudden revelation—I knew who had killed Trist Cummins. During the night while I slept, my mind had put the pieces together, and when the last clue had dropped into place, an alarm went off in my head louder than any windup clock.

Charles Henry Dill was the murderer.

It was as clear as day—a day that would not come for another three hours. Mrs. Woolgar and I had thought Dill was using Trist's murder to stir up discontent in hopes he could gain leverage and somehow get hold of Middlebank—but no. He wasn't using an incident he heard had taken place—he himself was the perpetrator.

I paced my flat until six, going over every detail we knew of the enquiry, and then I headed out in the early-morning darkness for my walk, pausing in Victoria Park to stare across the grassy expanse to the Royal Crescent Hotel. Sleep peacefully, Mr. Dill—while you can.

On my return to Middlebank, I did not avoid the spot where Trist died, as I had been doing. Instead, I came along Gravel Walk and stopped a few feet from the fatal wrought-iron post and considered the events leading up to the night of the murder. Charles Henry had studied us at Middlebank, searching for our weaknesses. He had uncovered information about Mrs. Woolgar's animosity toward Trist, and so decided to sacrifice the writer to his greedy desires— after which, he would lead police astray by pointing them in Mrs. Woolgar's direction.

The killing. Having learned Trist was physically weak, Dill trailed—or lured—him to this spot. It had taken little effort to shove his victim hard enough to crack his head against the cannonball-sized railing topper. Knowing Trist was dead, Dill slung the body across his shoulders. How smug and clever he must feel, staging the scene in the library at Middlebank in his quest to put us in the worst possible light.

And now I held the vital clue to prove his guilt. It was the sort of thing Miss Marple would've picked up on—the one piece of information that would crack the case. As I finished my morning routine—shower, tea, toast—I couldn't help giving myself a tiny pat on the back. *Well done, you.*

At nine o'clock, I hurried down the stairs and into Mrs. Woolgar's office for our morning briefing.

Without looking up, she began. "I've had a think about this latest turn of events, and believe that you are—" A glance at me stopped her. "Ms. Burke, are you all right?"

She probably had noticed my glow of excitement. I sat in the chair across from her, but immediately popped up again to make my announcement.

"I know who did it—I know who murdered Trist."

After an appropriately significant pause, Mrs. Woolgar asked, "Who?"

"Charles Henry Dill."

"Dear God," she breathed, putting a hand to her chest. Then she frowned. "But didn't he just arrive on Wednesday of this week?"

"So he says," I replied with great import, and dropped into my chair. "But during the night I remembered something. Linda Carlisle at the hotel told me when Charles Henry showed up on Wednesday—two days ago—he ordered the hotel's car to bring his bags *over.*" I tapped Mrs. Woolgar's desk for emphasis.

"But, from the rail station?" she asked.

"No." I shook my head. "You'd bring them *up* from the station, not *over. Over* means he was already in Bath but staying somewhere else."

The secretary's eyes widened, causing her glasses to slip down the bridge of her nose. "Already here. Of course—and for how long?"

"Long enough. And I'm afraid there's more. I'm almost certain he is the one who rang the police with the tale of you and Trist and your handbag. He's lied to us. It was all a setup—part of his takeover plan. And I'm going to prove it."

"That his greed would cause him to take a life—I can only be relieved Lady Fowling didn't live to see this day. And I suspect he's been busy elsewhere, too, in his diabolical effort to erode support for you and the Society." The secretary leaned over her desk as if Bunter—asleep in his bed in the corner—might overhear. "I believe he's approached some of the board members."

I took stock of The First Edition Society's board of trustees—all five of them. Two were aboard a cruise ship bound for the Caribbean, and one—Adele—would brook no shady threats from Dill. That left the other two.

"Are you talking about Mrs. Arbuthnot or Ms. Frost? Do you believe either one of them would give Charles Henry the time of day?"

Mrs. Woolgar sighed. "I can say no more at the moment. I will speak with them this afternoon—separately. Leave this to me, Ms. Burke."

Until only recently, I would assume Mrs. Woolgar had scheduled a meeting with her moles to discuss my overthrow—but as she was now faced with the fear of Charles Henry Dill taking everything, I was the least of her worries.

"Did you speak to Mr. Rennie?" I asked, only that moment remembering we might need our solicitor.

"I did," Mrs. Woolgar replied grimly. "That was my other news. Charles Henry has requested to see the governing documents for the Society. Mr. Rennie believes he may try to question our status as a charitable trust."

"How can one person be so evil?"

I entered the Royal Crescent from the far end, coming up behind a guided tour of the city and using it as a cover. The hotel sat mid-Crescent, and I didn't want to be seen by Charles Henry Dill before I could get into the lobby and talk with Linda Carlisle, with whom I could confirm my suspicions before going to the police.

As she walked backward, the tour leader—an out-of-work actor, no doubt—gave a dramatic reading of a scene from *Northanger Abbey* that takes place on the Crescent. I crept along at a respectable distance and kept an eye on the door of the hotel up ahead.

When at last we reached my goal, I broke away, plunged into the lobby, and stepped to the side, giving the place a quick scan. No Charles Henry in sight, but I must be cautious, and so I made straight for the large Chinese palm against the wall on the other side of the reception desk, taking refuge behind its tall, lush foliage.

"Hello, good morning." The young woman from my first visit

leaned over the desk and called to me. "Oh, it's Ms. Burke, isn't it?" Good to be recognized—I hoped. "Are you looking for Mr. Dill? Shall I ring his room?"

"Good morning." My stage whisper carried across the quiet lobby. "No need to bother Mr. Dill. I'm here to see Ms. Carlisle—is she available?"

"She's just popped in to see the general manager. Could I get you a coffee? Would you like to wait in the drawing room for her?"

Too exposed. "I'll stay here, if that's all right."

She went back to her business, but I saw her eyes dart toward me occasionally. When Linda Carlisle appeared, the young woman spoke quietly to her, nodding in my direction. The manager showed no signs of alarm—well practiced, I was sure, after decades of dealing with slightly daft hotel patrons. Instead, she came straight for me with a smile.

"Good morning, Hayley, it's good to see you again. Shall we go into my office? It's just here."

Thank God she had an office. I followed her through the door behind reception, and when we were safely closed off from anyone strolling through the lobby, Linda gestured to chairs and we sat.

Now, to prove I wasn't mental. "You must think me quite odd—hiding behind the palm."

"Not at all," Linda said. "You seem . . . mysterious. I rather feel as if I'm in the middle of one of Lady Fowling's own detective novels."

"You've read them?"

"Only a few—I've heard she wrote many."

"We have the complete set, of course—you're welcome to borrow them anytime." Now, to business. "I've stopped by this morning because I wanted to ask you about something you said yesterday concerning Charles Henry Dill. You mentioned that upon his arrival at the hotel, he asked to have his bags brought over."

"Yes—although 'ask' is too weak a word, as it implies some level of courtesy on his part."

"Did you mean his bags were brought up from the rail station?" I held my breath.

Linda looked off into the middle distance as if listening to Dill's request. "No," she said slowly. "He had not arrived by train. He walked in with nothing and sent the car off to an address where his bags, he said, were waiting."

"Do you know where?"

The manager sat back for a moment and studied me. Then, as if she'd come to a decision, she rose. "I don't, but I can easily find out." She went to the phone on her desk and made a call. "Davey, on Wednesday, you fetched bags for Mr. Dill . . . Yes, he's the one. Where did he send you? . . . Mmm, yes . . . Right, thanks." She turned to me. "A flat in Grove Street—at number forty-two."

Flushed with success, I explained. "He told us he'd only just arrived in Bath on Wednesday. That's obviously not the case. Why else would his bags be at someone's flat?"

"I understand if you can't answer," Linda said, "but does this have anything to do with your recent difficulties at Middlebank?"

"The body in the library?" I asked. "Charles Henry Dill's convenient appearance on the scene?" I sighed. "I can't quite say yet—I hope you understand."

"Of course. And if I can do more, please ask. I wish you all the best. And I hope you don't mind me saying that I rather feel Lady Fowling's hand in your selection as curator of The First Edition Society."

"It's kind of you to say so, but in truth, I was the board's only choice at a critical time."

"Still—" Linda opened her office door wide but threw an arm up to prevent me from leaving. "Wait," she whispered, pulling the door almost closed. "He's just there."

I squinted through a crack and watched as Charles Henry strode through the lobby and out onto the Crescent. I noticed he had a great fondness for brown plaid suits—or perhaps he had only one set of clothes to his name. On the pavement, he looked about him as if sniffing the air, and then turned left and walked off.

"Right, that's me away," I said. "Thanks ever so much."

Outside, I peered up the Crescent and spotted Dill almost to the corner. I followed, dodging behind one pedestrian then another, keeping my distance. I wasn't sure Miss Marple ever carried out her own investigation this way—as much as I had read, she seemed more likely to hear something over a cup of tea or send someone else off to Somerset House to look up records. But, I told myself, needs must, and if I have to sneak along after Charles Henry, then so be it.

He crossed the Pulteney Bridge, and I boldly followed. The bridge over the river Avon—Bath's own Ponte Vecchio—had shops lining both sides. These blocked views of the river and the weir but provided me with handy doorways in which to duck. When Dill turned up Grove Street, I knew I had him—he was going to the same address where he'd stayed.

He paused to answer his phone, and I leapt behind the corner of a building before he saw me. I waited until I hoped it was safe, and then, keeping my back to the wall, I slithered round the corner and parted the branches of a rangy rhododendron that hung over the pavement, only to be met by a postman pushing his red delivery trolley. I froze when he saw me.

"Hello," I said brightly. "I've . . . lost my cat. Have you seen him?"

"What does he look like?"

"He's . . . er . . . black and white."

The postman's eyes narrowed. "No, I haven't. And my name isn't Pat."

The lesson here was *Don't give the first excuse that comes into your mind*. Naturally, I had landed on Postman Pat and his black-and-white cat—Dinah had loved that old television program when she was a little girl. The postal carriers of Britain had probably tired of the joke long ago.

The postman went on his way, and I was met with an empty pavement. Charles Henry must've gone inside number forty-two—it was a new, purpose-built complex of flats, but at least it had only one door. I made my way to the entrance, walking as close to the shrubbery as I could. I needed to reach the door and read the residents' names next to the buzzers. I had only just begun to run my finger down the list when I saw movement inside the lobby and lost my nerve.

I quickly retreated down the road, continually glancing over my shoulder. I crossed and came back along, but stopped short of Charles Henry's building and did my best to stay out of the line of sight from its windows. Instead, I loitered near the corner of a former girls' school that had been refurbished into a block of flats—not nearly as posh as number forty-two. There were few cars at this time of day, and no one passing by took any notice of me.

After fifteen minutes, I came to the conclusion that this surveillance business could be quite boring. How do police do it? Charles Henry Dill was becoming less important by the minute as the need to dash off to the public toilets in Henrietta Park grew. And after that, I would really like a cup of tea and a sandwich.

I was in the middle of an enormous yawn when the door of number forty-two opened. I jumped back, plastering myself against the side of the building and then carefully putting one eye round the corner.

There he was, Charles Henry, pausing to tug on the cuffs of his shirt and stretch his neck as if his collar was too tight. He strolled off down the pavement, back toward Pulteney Bridge. When the road took a bend, he disappeared from sight, and I scampered across the street to stand in front of his building and stare after him.

What had he been up to in there—meeting with his accomplice, his partner in crime? Too bad I didn't catch which flat he went in. Still, I would take a snapshot of the residents' names.

I turned back toward the building entrance and stopped. Not ten feet ahead of me on the pavement, Lulu Ingleby approached.

20

I had seen Lulu Ingleby only twice and both times at the Minerva—
once when Pauline was giving her a talking-to and once when
Leonard appeared to warn her off me. Even so, there was no mis-
taking her—short, black hair with curls sticking out from around
the *Cleaned by Pauline* bandanna she wore.

"Hello," I said.

She gave me a quick look and flinched. She mumbled something
and hurried past me, but I pivoted on the spot and said, "I know who
you are."

Lulu stopped dead, and having obtained her attention, I contin-
ued. "We haven't actually met, but I've seen you at the Minerva.
I know Pauline, and you work for her." I stuck my hand out. "I'm
Hayley Burke. How do you do?"

Few people can refuse a proffered hand. She put hers—limp
and dry—in mine, and I did the shaking. I waited with a smile and
an expectant look until she coughed up the minimum amount of
civility.

"Hello. I'm Lulu." Her eyes shot over my shoulder back toward number forty-two, and with a jolt it came to me that she was looking for Charles Henry.

"Am I in your way? Were you trying to catch someone up?" I nodded over her shoulder. "He's gone down that way—did you need to speak with him?"

Her gaze darted round like a dragonfly until it landed on salvation.

"There's my bus—sorry!" She flew across the road, waving to the driver, who pulled up and waited for her to jump aboard.

I didn't watch her leave, but instead kept my gaze in the direction Charles Henry had gone as I tried to make the connections among him, Trist, and Lulu. Someone had to be guilty of something. But, no matter what Sergeant Hopgood said about the fireman's lift, surely Lulu couldn't've carried Trist's body up the stairs at Middlebank. That had to have been Dill. But Lulu was involved. She could've acquired the key and code from Pauline. But had Pauline handed them over, or had Lulu stolen them?

Heaving a great sigh, I set off on his trail, but heard a voice behind me.

"Hayley!"

Amanda. She must've come off the bus Lulu got on. She wore her tight running gear and hitched a gym holdall high on her shoulder.

"Who was that I saw you with?" she demanded.

"Mmm?" I was loath to tip my hand here—revealing I knew someone who might be a suspect. It had come to my attention that Amanda liked to talk.

"No one," I said. "No one I know—I was only asking did that bus run by the Waitrose. I need to do a bit of shopping."

She watched me, and I found I couldn't hold her gaze.

"Or maybe you were looking for me?" she asked. "Is there a problem with the group? Wait now." She frowned. "How did you know what street I lived on? Did someone tell you? Was it Harry?"

I had only that moment remembered DS Hopgood's map and Amanda's green spot here in Grove Street—but I didn't want her to think I had been spying, because I hadn't. At least, not on her.

"I don't remember," I replied. "Might've been—or didn't you mention it yourself?"

"Not me—no, it was probably Harry. She has a bit of the snitch about her, don't you think? Although, it's probably because she's feeling guilty after how she treated Trist. No telling what that led to. But then, you have to expect her to act out, don't you? You have to give her enough rope to"—she laughed—"no, that isn't what I meant. Give her some allowance, that's it."

I waited, but apparently Amanda's motor had finally run down. She looked at her nails and picked at a cuticle.

"Well," I said, "I'd best be off. Just out for a stroll on my lunch break. See you next Wednesday, right?"

"Right," she echoed.

So you see, Charles Henry Dill is not what he seems."

I sat across the table from Detective Sergeant Hopgood and Detective Constable Pye in Interview #1 and toyed with the cup of tea I had mistakenly accepted. I'd not had long to wait in the lobby of the station—not after I'd told the officer at the desk that I had a "significant piece of evidence" about the Trist Cummins murder case. DC Pye had appeared almost instantly, and before I knew it, I was telling my tale to both officers on the enquiry.

Sergeant Hopgood listened, but as I spoke, his eyebrows migrated until they met in the middle. "Ms. Burke," he said at last, his stern voice matching his expression. "You do realize that on the day we met and I made reference to you having your own ideas about the enquiry, I was not serious. And as I recall, your reply was that you are a curator, not a detective. Do I need to remind you of our respective roles?"

"As I recall, I warned you about Charles Henry Dill yesterday, and you brushed me off."

Hopgood's eyebrows broke apart and leapt to his hairline.

"That is," I said apologetically, "it's only because I recalled what Linda Carlisle at the hotel had said about where his bags had been collected."

"And I commend you for your fine memory," the sergeant replied. "But that is as far as you should've taken it. You are not expected to set up your own surveillance—that's for the police to manage."

"Yes, sir."

"Thank you for the information, and be assured we will take it from here."

"Of course."

I left the police station on autopilot and made my way to Waitrose. My story of Dill and how I'd followed him had not gone over well with DS Hopgood and DC Pye, and so I had thought it best not to mention my encounter with Lulu or my suspicion about her, Leonard, or, of course, Pauline. Why? I would examine my reasons later. For now, I told myself as I shopped the ready-meal aisle, I needed to be content with knowing the police would find out exactly where Charles Henry had been staying and for how long. And with whom. Where that led, Sergeant Hopgood had reminded me, was none of my business.

* * *

Mrs. Woolgar was gone by the time I returned to Middlebank—on her own investigative mission to learn what Dill had said to Mrs. Arbuthnot and Ms. Frost. Would she uncover anything significant? Would it get us in hot water with the police? Would I spend the rest of the day worrying about it?

No, I would not. I put away my groceries and changed into denims and a sweater, and headed down to the chilly cellar. I squeezed by the furniture I'd dragged out and left in the corridor, and when I unlocked the door, Bunter, like a tortiseshell shadow, slipped past me and disappeared into the mass of boxes and furniture.

"Well, cat—where shall I start today?" I asked with hands on hips. I glanced behind me into the dim corridor, the thought occurring to me that I was alone at Middlebank.

"That's silly, isn't it?" I asked the unseen Bunter. "There's nothing to feel nervous about." Still, no harm in securing my position. I took the key out of the lock, closed the door, reinserted it on the inside, and locked myself in.

I decided my goal for the rest of the afternoon would be to reach the stacked cartons along the far wall. It was slow going—I shifted furniture a few inches this way and that to create a path. Occasionally, I heard a scrabbling from deep within the room's contents. "Did you bring one of your catnip mice with you?" I asked. At least, I hoped it was of the catnip variety.

As I worked, I carried on a one-sided conversation with Bunter. Not about murder or clues or evidence or writers—instead, I tried to sort through the confusion that was or was not my love life. I found it comforting, and the cat made no objections.

"The thing is, when Wyn and I started up, I didn't mind that he lived in London and I lived here in Bath. It was fun and exciting, and we neither of us asked for more. I felt rather lucky to have an even occasional boyfriend. I don't mind telling you, Bunter—because I know it won't go any farther than this cellar—there had been a fairly long dry spell before I met Wyn. But now the idea has entered my head that the odd weekend or flying visit doesn't quite pass muster. I want more. And it is possible that . . . oh, I don't know, am I reading too much into Val's behavior? Am I imagining it? Bunter, what are you after?"

The cat had emerged from under a chair and leapt from floor to table to highboy to the top of a long-case clock, which shook, causing the chimes to sound faintly. He then hopped down to another table next to one of the stacks of cartons. The tape on the third box from the top had long since lost its stickiness, and now hung like a ringlet down the side, and Bunter had decided to attack. He batted the tape over and over and meowed—not a complaining yowl, but as if he were calling to me.

"Yes, yes, all right—I'll come and look." I squeezed past a walnut sideboard and removed the top two cartons. They were labeled in block letters: UNNECESSARY KITCHEN ITEMS and JOHN/BUSINESS ACCTS 1920–21. I had to turn the third one round to read its contents. NOTEBOOKS.

And so it was. When I opened the carton, I found it packed to the gills with ordinary school exercise notebooks, the sort with the marbled covers. I took out a handful. They appeared well used—worn corners and the occasional ring where a cup of tea or a glass had been set. In the upper-right-hand corner of each, spidery handwriting identified the owner: *Georgiana Fowling.*

I flipped through a few pages and found every one filled—not a line left blank—with all manner of thoughts, ideas, and opinions. Here was a heading of *My Favorite Poirot*—a numbered ranking of the stories starring the Belgian she liked best. She had apparently changed her mind several times, crossing out, renumbering, or drawing arrows to move a title up or down.

I turned the page and found a short essay she'd written titled "John and Georgiana Go for a Walk," centered on Sir John's forgetting his handkerchief and therefore being unable to clean off a park bench for them. There was a bit about a bossy blackbird that made me laugh.

That was followed by a schedule of window washing at Middlebank, and after that, a short story—two pages long—about a tortoiseshell cat. "Not you, I don't think," I said without looking up. "Must've been an earlier Bunter."

Her scrolly handwriting was quite legible, and she wrote in complete sentences, even for her shopping lists. I was amazed—here was a life in lined exercise books.

I picked up a handful of them and looked round for a place to sit, finally edging over and throwing a sheet off what looked to be a Victorian fainting sofa, upholstered in burgundy velvet with heavy ornate carvings of elephants marching along the ridge. "No wonder she covered it up." I stretched out and got stuck in, reading selections aloud to Bunter, who listened patiently.

I had not known these existed. Had I? I stared at a page on which Lady Fowling had assembled all Christie's murder methods and my eyes became unfocused. Perhaps I had seen one, but I couldn't quite remember where or when. It was one of those moments of déjà vu when you can't be sure if your memory is real or not.

But I knew one thing for certain—I beheld a cornucopia of material for the Society's newsletter. I could see the headlines now—LADY FOWLING'S FAVORITE PRIME SUSPECTS, LADY FOWLING ON THE WEAPON AT HAND—that sort of thing. I don't see why I couldn't also get a few scholarly articles out of them.

"Thank you, Bunter," I said to the cat, who had settled like a sphinx atop the highboy. "Thank you, Lady Fowling," I whispered.

I had struck gold. These notebooks were the way to bring the Society back to the wider audience of both authors and readers of mystery, and keep Georgiana Fowling's dream alive.

"Oh, I like that." I repeated the sentence aloud, and then called out, "Bunter, I need a pen—I want to write that phrase down and use it." I had no pen, of course. Why would I need a pen in the cellar? I hadn't even brought my phone—and so I repeated the phrase over and over, searing it into my brain.

"Never mind about the pen, Bunter," I said, reaching for another notebook. "But you wouldn't go and make us a cup of tea, would you? I'm gasping."

The cat watched me with golden eyes, and then yawned. I yawned back.

I pulled the band off my ponytail, rested my head against the sofa, and closed my eyes. I would show the notebooks to Val—he would be amazed, wouldn't he? We might write something together, perhaps a series of articles about Lady Fowling. Our literary salons would become famous. We might be interviewed by the book reviewer in *The Guardian*.

My mind let go of Lady Fowling but kept hold of Val as I drifted off into a lovely scene. We had escaped our busy lives and gone to the seaside, and now we stood on the sand, his arms enclosing me, shielding me from a chilly wind. We were quiet and content and I looked up at him, and his green eyes crinkled at the corners as he smiled at me.

"Did you ever think this would happen?" I asked him.

Voices answered me. Too many voices.

Bam bam bam

I bolted upright, and notebooks scattered across the floor. Bunter jumped off the highboy and disappeared.

Bam bam bam

"Hayley?"

My heart sang! I knew that voice—it was Val.

"Ms. Burke? Are you in there? Are you all right?"

I knew that voice, too—Detective Sergeant Hopgood.

"Yes, I'm here!" I called out, navigating furniture and boxes like a rat in a maze as I rushed to the door before they knocked it down. "Wait now, let me reach the key."

Flinging the door wide, I found a queue. The corridor, squeezed with furniture, was wide enough for only one abreast, and so they had lined themselves up. Hopgood stood at the head with Val behind him, followed by Adele, Detective Constable Kenny Pye, and—peering round the DC's shoulder—Mrs. Woolgar.

My hand went to my throat. "Oh no, what's happened?"

Their collective sigh nearly knocked me off my feet.

"You were suspected of being missing, Ms. Burke," Hopgood said. "No one could get in touch with you, and until Ms. Babbage contacted Mrs. Woolgar and she met us out front, I thought we might need to break the door of Middlebank down."

"But I was only here in the cellar," I offered weakly.

"Yes, well." The sergeant turned to Val. "It's all right, Mr. Moffatt—under the circumstances, it was a wise thing to contact us."

Mrs. Woolgar, at the back of the queue, said, "Well then, now that a crisis has been averted, I believe I'll retire to my flat. It's been a tiring day."

The end of the day meant I'd been holed up in the cellar for three or four hours.

"Mrs. Woolgar, wait." I pushed down the line of people, brushing Val's hand as I did so. "I'm sorry I caused such an uproar." On closer view, I noticed the hollow look round her eyes and her pinched face.

"No matter, Ms. Burke. It's only that I'm a bit weary."

"How was"—I glanced over my shoulder at the attentive queue and lowered my voice—"your afternoon?"

"Perhaps that's better left until our Monday briefing. You are away the weekend?"

"Yes—are you sure you'll be all right?"

The secretary bristled, replying with a snappy "Fine"—a sure sign she was no worse for her afternoon with Mrs. Arbuthnot and Ms. Frost.

The crowd dispersed. Mrs. Woolgar shut the door of her flat in our faces, and Adele followed the police upstairs, chatting with DS Hopgood about his daughter, who apparently went to the school where Adele taught. Only Val was left standing at the cellar door. I went back to him.

"I sent you a text and got no answer," he said, looking both relieved and vexed. "I rang and got no answer. So I came round here and no one answered the door. I didn't know what to think. I phoned Adele and she got hold of Mrs. Woolgar, and then . . . I rang the police, too. Because, after what happened—" He swallowed. "Well."

I smiled at him. "You saved me."

His frown deepened, and then he barked a short laugh. "You didn't need saving."

"That's hardly the point," I replied. Shreds of my dream lingered as if his arms were still round me. "You had my back. I can't tell you when I've ever felt that way." The voices upstairs faded. It was only the two of us. "I'm sorry," I said. "About how I acted the other evening."

"No." Val shook his head vehemently. "I'm sorry. What's between you and your boyfriend is your concern. It's none of my business."

He locked his eyes on me, and I heard his statement for what it was—a challenge, a plea. *Tell me I'm wrong. Tell me it is my business.*

It was, but I couldn't say the words aloud. Not yet.

Instead, I overcompensated, saying with manic cheer, "Wait till you see what I found here in the cellar—a carton full of Lady Fowling's notebooks!"

My words threw cold water over the moment, and Val took a step back.

"Will you stay?" I continued. "We'll take the box up to my flat and look through them. It's really quite exciting." I ran to the bottom of the stairs and called up. "Adele! Adele!"

She came halfway down and peered at us, her red curls tumbling over the railing.

"You've nothing on this evening," I said, praying that was true. "Stay, won't you? Val is staying—I have something I want to show you both. I'll order pizza!"

Adele's gaze went from me to Val and back.

"Do I look like a gooseberry?" she demanded.

Val crossed his arms tightly, his face like thunder. "We don't need a chaperone, Adele. We're going to look at scrapbooks."

"They aren't scrapbooks," I said, hurrying back into the cellar and scrambling to gather notebooks from the floor and repack the carton. "Here." I shoved the box in Val's arms. "Bunter, where are you?"

The cat scooted from under a dresser, out the door, and up the stairs. I locked the cellar and Val marched off without speaking.

I followed, pulling on Adele's arm and whispering, "Come along. Please. I don't want it to be awkward."

"Don't you mean 'more awkward'?"

I thanked the police and they left, after which the three of us continued to my flat. Inside, I switched the kettle on, ignored Val's pout and Adele's eye rolling, and revealed my find.

They were amazed, as I knew they would be. Even Val melted a bit as we dug out notebook after notebook, scanning the contents. Eventually, we began checking the dates, and putting the notebooks in chronological order.

"I wonder, did she know about Agatha Christie's notebooks?" Val asked. "Although, they only came to light a few years ago. Also, I don't think Christie's notebooks were nearly this legible."

Adele's eyes sparkled with tears as she ran her hand lightly over the pages. "Georgiana had lovely cursive writing—it's becoming a lost art."

"Do you think she would mind if we used them?" I asked.

"No, Hayley—she'd love it, I'm sure. It's like she's here again." Adele gave me a sly look. "You say Bunter showed you where they were—I have a feeling Georgiana wanted you to find them."

First Linda Carlisle and now Adele. I blushed and shrugged as a warm thrill ran through me. Although I wouldn't say so aloud, I had come away with the unaccountably pleasant feeling that Bunter and I had had company in the cellar.

21

We took turns reading out interesting pieces of Lady Fowling's writings. Val, particularly taken with her mock interview titled "Meet Jane Marple," thought we might reenact it for the salons. "One of the women on your board was an actress," he reminded me.

"Maureen Frost," Adele offered. "I saw her about ten years ago in a production of *She Stoops to Conquer* during a Restoration comedy summer. She was good."

I envisioned Ms. Frost—her gray pageboy swept back into a tidy bun. "Well, there's our Jane Marple," I said. "Unless she'd prefer to be Lady Fowling."

Adele looked up from one of the notebooks. "Here's something Georgiana wrote about her own detective, François Flambeaux."

"François Flambeaux? He wasn't French, by any chance?" I asked helpfully, and Val sputtered into his tea.

Adele threw us a look and replied, "He was from Dorset."

That set both of us off. Adele giggled, too, but added, "You should read some of her books—they're quite fun. Listen to this: *The detective held his breath and peered through a slit in the heavy velvet draperies sewn from a depressingly busy paisley print in heliotrope and trimmed in gaudy gold fringe with tassels as big as school bells. A movement in the room pulled his attention away from the window coverings to the nurse, attired in a crisp aquamarine blue uniform with snow-white starched apron and cap.*"

"But what color were her shoes?" I asked. Adele ignored me and continued.

"*She eyed her patient, who slept peacefully on a sateen pillow as green as a cricket lawn and edged in knotted lace said to have come from the nuns in Ireland. He lay unaware that the concoction being prepared for him would be the last thing to pass his lips. Flambeaux watched as the nurse filled a small glass halfway with water, then drew a chestnut-brown vial from her pocket, took the cork stopper between her teeth, and wrenched it out like a cowboy desperate for a slug from his bottle of whiskey. She raised the glass and vial and poured out*—hang on, now." Adele fumbled turning the page. Both Val and I leaned forward, waiting until she continued, "*—one tablespoon of Fairy washing-up liquid. Spray this on the roses every few days to get rid of green fly.*"

We snorted with laughter as Adele flipped through a few more pages in hopes of learning the fate of the sleeping victim, but to no avail.

"Did Flambeaux come to the rescue?" Val asked.

"Did he replace those awful draperies with a more modern print?" I wondered.

"What about Georgiana's battle with green fly?" Adele added over her shoulder as she took our tea things into the kitchen.

I rang in our pizza order, and Val opened a bottle of wine. He had warmed a bit while we'd read the notebooks, but now withdrew again—civil but businesslike. It would have to do, this reserved Val Moffatt. For now.

While Adele and I washed and dried, he said, "I'll go wait for the pizza, shall I?" We scrambled for our purses, but he waved us away. "We'll settle up later." And then he escaped, leaving the door of my flat ajar.

Tea dishes cleared away, Adele and I sat at the kitchen table with wine. I asked about her foray up to London with the Suffragette Club, and she described in colorful terms what it was like to be on a two-hour coach trip with thirty twelve-year-old girls, after which she leaned back in her chair and stuck her hands in the pockets of her purple trousers.

"So," she said. "Val."

I rose and stood at the counter, my back to her, and launched into an overly enthusiastic description of our strictly working relationship and the hopes for the literary salons.

"Lovely," she replied. "And now—you and Val. The two of you."

"There is no 'two of us.'"

"Well, it's clear there should be."

"Is it?" I whirled round, clasping my empty wineglass to my chest. "I mean, do you think? I don't know. I'm not sure I can tell, actually—I'm rather out of practice."

"He can't keep his eyes off you," Adele replied. "What's holding you up?"

"Isn't that obvious? I have a boyfriend."

"Do you? Hayley, whatever is between you and Wyn has never seemed to reach the status of boyfriend-girlfriend."

"Regardless"—righteous fervor shot through me—"I will not do to someone else what was done to me. And I don't believe Val would want that either." I toyed with the stem of my glass. "Has he told you about his wife?"

"Mmm," Adele said. "Not much. She died when his daughters were young?"

"Yes, well, I believe there's more to it than that. He got a funny look when I told him about Roger." I sighed. "But at the moment, that's beside the point. I've got to settle things before I will embark on a . . ."

"A new adventure?"

I walked out to the sitting room so she wouldn't see my smile, and at once I was enveloped in the warm scent of garlic and cheese and crust. The aroma of the pizza had arrived before the actual food. As the door to my flat stood half open, I knew that meant Val was just outside on the landing, and probably had been for a few minutes—perhaps long enough to hear my exchange with Adele.

I reached over and opened the door the rest of the way, and there he stood, boxes in hand.

"Oh," he said, his cheeks pink. "Pizza's arrived."

The three of us sat at the kitchen table and ate pizza and regaled each other with work stories.

Mine came from my days at the Jane Austen Centre. "There was a woman worked in the tearoom who knew *Pride and Prejudice* by heart. By heart! All you had to do was throw out a line and she would pick up the story, word for word."

"At least she didn't claim to have written it," Val said. "I had a student try to pass off the first chapter of *A Murder Is Announced* as her own. When called out, she said the ghost of Christie told her to write it."

"Sounds like one of the writers in my group. It wasn't Amanda, was it?" I asked as a joke.

"God, it was, now that you mention it," Val replied.

"Is that Tommy and Tuppence?" I asked. "They're her detectives now."

"No, Marple. This was two years ago—she's changed since then. And changed again, it seems."

"Do most of your students repeat courses?"

Val nodded. "Adult education is a process. There isn't necessarily an end product."

"Look, Hayley," Adele said, "is it all right with you if I take a few of the notebooks down to show Glynis? She seemed a bit fragile, you know, and if I have an excuse to check on her, she won't be so—"

"Truculent?" I asked. "Shall I come along?"

"No, stay." Her eyes barely flickered to Val. "You know how she can be—it'll be better on my own."

Adele collected several notebooks and left. Val and I remained on the sofa, both of us quiet. I felt a nervous tension in the air, broken at last when he took several quick breaths and said, "We were young when we married—Jill and I." He shook his head. "Too young—but when you're twenty, you don't listen to anyone, do you?"

So this was it—the story of his marriage. He looked at me. I thought he might be waiting for permission to continue, and so I answered with a small smile.

"The twins were born a year later," he went on. "It was a busy time, but we were happy. It seemed. Then, just after the girls turned five, Jill came to me and said she felt as if she were suffocating, losing herself in being mother and wife. She needed time off." Val looked away from me now. "I asked was there someone else and she said no, that she loved me and the girls and this wouldn't be forever. So I agreed, because what else was there?"

"She left you?"

"Not exactly. Not at first. She began going out with friends— weekends, then weeknights, too. We missed her—our daughters couldn't quite understand why their mum wasn't much at home. I took on extra work and my folks helped with the girls, and one afternoon, when I should've been at a teachers' meeting, I came home unexpectedly. At least, Jill hadn't expected me. Neither had the fellow she'd been having an affair with."

Ah, now the story sounded familiar.

"That was it. Without much discussion, she moved out, promising she'd keep in touch with the girls. She and the bloke moved to Norwich, and one day about four months later, the divorce papers came in the mail. Do you know"—a note of incredulity crept into his voice—"until they arrived, I half thought she'd come back. Did you ever think that?" he asked me.

"I did . . . God help me."

He nodded at my confirmation. "I let them lie for a week, and then I had a phone call from him . . . He told me Jill had contracted bacterial meningitis. There were complications and it was serious."

"Oh no."

"The doctors couldn't say how she caught it, but that it's rarely contagious. Her . . . he asked did I want to come up to see her." Val's faced flushed. "Was he mad? I don't care how small the possibility of catching or carrying it, there was no way I would put my daughters at risk. I thought she would pull through it, but she died three days later."

No matter how much I disliked Roger, I didn't want him to die. At least, not often.

Val rubbed his hands on his legs, his face drawn up into a puzzle of anger and guilt. "By not going to Norwich," he asked, "was I punishing her for leaving?"

"You were right to consider your daughters first," I said, probably the same thing he had told himself over and over for almost twenty years. "And have they done all right?"

At this, he smiled with relief. "They have—they're fine young women. What about your Dinah—how did she manage after the divorce?"

Happy to shift the attention away from his pain, I said, "Wonderfully—along with the tears and rebellion, of course. My mum helped." I went over to the side table and retrieved my phone.

"Dinah sent a photo of them from their visit on Wednesday. Here you are." Val came to my side and studied the photo of my daughter and my mum, cheek to cheek. Dinah had my hair color—brown with a gold tint, although my gold had faded a bit. Mum's had been the same, but now it was brown with silver highlights. "They're lovely," I said with a sigh, "both of them."

Val brushed a lock of my hair away from my face, tracing a line from my forehead to my chin. He looked from the image on the phone to me. "That's three of a kind, I'd say."

Neither of us moved. Time slowed, and I thought I could stand there forever with his hand cupping my cheek, before I needed anything else in the world.

"Right," I said, taking a quick breath to bring me to my senses. "I've shown you mine, now you show me yours."

Val grinned and dug in his pocket, pulling out his phone. He made a great show of flipping through photos until he said, "Here we are—last Christmas."

Dad standing between his two identical daughters—young women a bit older than Dinah. They had dark hair—perhaps that had been Jill's—but eyes that crinkled at the corners when they smiled.

"Now there's a happy family," I said. "What are their names?"

"Elizabeth and Rebecca."

"You didn't go in for the twin alliteration?" I asked, and then it dawned on me. "Oh, wait, perhaps you did. It's Becky and—"

"Bess," Val replied. He gave his girls one more look, stuck his phone back in his pocket, and slid his arm round my waist. He hadn't let his beard grow back, and it was all I could do not to reach up and run my finger down his smooth jawline. It was that most delicious moment of anticipation.

I swallowed hard. "Where is Adele?"

"Mmm?"

"I think we need that gooseberry after all."

He lifted one eyebrow. "So, I'm not imagining this, am I? Because, I have to admit, it's been a while."

"Imagining it? No, I don't suppose we are. It's only that . . . I have a few things to clear up before I can . . . er . . . move on."

"Yeah." He dropped his arm and caught my hand, and his fingertips stroked my palm so lightly it felt like butterfly wings.

"You do understand?" I whispered.

"Of course I do."

"Good, that's good." Still, he didn't pull away and neither did I—until heavy footsteps on the landing and a loud cough heralded the arrival of our gooseberry.

How is Mrs. Woolgar?" I asked Adele, who had taken so long to get to the door that I could've completely dressed before she walked in. Not that I had undressed, but . . . well, she took her time.

"Why didn't you tell me about Charles Henry turning up on your doorstep?" was her reply.

It was as if I was incapable of holding two things in my head at the same time. "Did she tell you everything?" I asked now, breathless for an entirely different reason than a few minutes earlier. I called to Val, who had gone into the kitchen to open another bottle of wine. "I think we've got him—the murderer. Do you remember I told you about Lady Fowling's nephew?"

With our glasses refilled, I began a rundown of my day.

"A tail!" Adele exclaimed. "Nice work, Hayley."

"You followed him?" Val asked. "A murderer?"

"I had to know," I explained. "I'd had a poor reception from Sergeant Hopgood, but now, with this latest, he can't deny Dill is involved."

"But from now on, you will let the police take care of it?" Val's question edged toward entreaty.

"Didn't Miss Marple ever tail anyone?" I answered, pleased with his concern. "I was in no danger—broad daylight and a normal road with normal people. I saw Amanda—she lives nearby. And look, now, I even know how he got in, because I ran into Lulu Ingleby. She must be his accomplice. Her boyfriend is Leonard—he manages the Minerva—and he's Pauline's brother. Remember you met Pauline," I said to Val. "She cleans for us, and so she has a key and the code for Middlebank."

I regretted the words as soon as they left my lips.

"Oh." Adele blinked at this. "Does that mean Pauline is a suspect?"

"Not necessarily," I rushed on. The police phrase, *no sign of forced entry,* echoed in my mind. "It could be that Lulu stole the key and code without Pauline knowing it and gave them to Charles Henry."

"Would Dill have his own copy of the key?" Val asked.

"Yes—yes, he could very well. Somehow. He's a sneak, and also quite good at research, apparently. He may have been planning this for ages."

Upon learning that Pauline could be involved, Adele had lost her spark. But there was nothing I could do about that—she would have to wait it out. Instead, I drew her attention elsewhere.

"Did Mrs. Woolgar say anything about her talk with Mrs. Arbuthnot and Ms. Frost?"

Adele shook her head. "But she said there would be more to tell the police next week, and implied she needed to talk with you first. Have you and Glynis become friends?"

"Friends?" I tried to imagine the two of us going shopping together or for a drink at the Minerva or sitting over coffee at the Waitrose café. I laughed. "I think it's only that at the moment, we have a common enemy."

* * *

As they readied to leave, Adele stood at my front window. "I love this view of the city," she said.

I joined her. South, beyond the sparkling lights of Bath, a dark ridge of countryside rose. "I do, too. I can see Alexandra Park in the day." Brought back as I was to the reality of my situation, a wave of melancholy rippled over me. "I suppose I'd better enjoy it while I can."

Val came up, and the three of us stood looking out. "You aren't thinking of leaving?" he asked. "Your work here has just begun."

"Has it? Or is it about to end—courtesy of Charles Henry Dill?"

"We will not allow that to happen," Adele said. "Right, you off to see your mum tomorrow? Give her my love."

"Yes, Liverpool. And on Sunday, I think I'll return by way of London."

I said it as casually as I could and kept my eyes on the skyline, but I knew my words had the ring of a Big Announcement.

"Sounds like a good plan," Adele replied as she gathered her bag.

I walked my guests to the front door of Middlebank. Adele made short work of leaving. "Night. Give me a ring Monday." We planted a quick kiss on each other's cheek, and off she dashed.

"Hold up, Adele," Val called. "I'll give you a lift."

He turned back to me, and I knew we'd better say a speedy good night or I'd end up in his arms.

"Thanks again for my rescue."

"Some rescue—but you're very welcome." He inched closer, and I leaned in and primly offered my cheek. Out of the corner of my eye, I saw him grin. He gave me a kiss, his lips lingering, and I could still feel them on my skin after he'd at last drawn away. "For the hostess," he murmured.

I closed the door, set the alarm, and danced up the stairs.

* * *

A day with my mum is like a tonic—and like a tonic, it is both invigorating and sometimes hard to swallow.

"You don't suspect Charles Henry Dill only because he's an unpleasant person, do you?" she asked over tea and scones on Saturday afternoon.

"He wants Middlebank—that gives him motive," I insisted, my fervor for Dill as murderer still at its zenith.

"Don't lose sight of your other suspects—don't be blinded to what could be right in front of you."

I relented, but only a bit. "Sergeant Hopgood is looking at the movements of the writers group that night, trying to locate Trist as he approached Gravel Walk—and see who followed him."

Mum tsked. "Killed and then dragged away and practically put on display like a prize turkey. Someone was showing off."

In the evening, we watched a television production of *Nemesis*— Miss Marple's stately-home-tour mystery, which Dill had made reference to. I moved the book to the top of my mental reading list. Before she went to bed, Mum commented that it would be lovely to go on such a holiday. Sans murder, of course.

I caught a late-afternoon train to London on Sunday and spent the first half of my journey on my phone researching deluxe, four-star coach tours of stately homes—after all, my mum deserved the best. I choked at the prices.

Next, heeding my mum's advice, I listed every single person I thought might have to do with Trist's murder case—not just Charles Henry Dill, but the writers, too. What sort of a run-in did Peter and Trist have? What did Amanda mean by referring to what Harry had done to Trist? I thought it had been the other way round. And where was Harry—back at work at the flower shop or returned to keep vigil outside the police station? That last question worried me, because, of all the writers, Harry seemed the most fragile. I would find out Monday.

Not until I was on the Tube from Euston Station to the Barbican and Wyn's flat did I finally force myself to consider what I was about to do. I had avoided the subject entirely at Mum's until she'd brought it up that morning.

"Are you breaking it off with Wyn today?" she had asked.

"And why do you say that, Jane Marple?"

"You are transparent to your mother," she had replied, "just as Dinah is transparent to you. You spent half of yesterday talking about Val Moffatt and then last night, right before bed, casually mentioned you might go home by way of London."

And here I was. I climbed the steps from the Barbican Tube station and, once on the pavement, took a deep breath, gathering my courage, before taking the short walk—too short—to Wyn's building on Britton Street. This shouldn't take long—Wyn wasn't one for lengthy conversations—and soon I'd be on my way home to Bath. In the lobby, I went past the lift and took the stairs up to the second floor—it helped to work off my nerves. Still, when I'd arrived at his door, I stood there, not pressing the bell. *Go on, Hayley.*

A second after it rang, the door flew open. "You!" he exclaimed, pulling me inside and kissing me. I felt like scum. He was such a cheerful fellow, and what was I about to do to him?

I stalled by looking round his corner flat, which had a view of the Gherkin, the Shard, the Cheesegrater—all the bizarre buildings that had gone up in London over the last couple of decades—now twinkling against the twilight sky. He'd bought the place with a modest inheritance, which he still lived off. The flat had been chosen not for its view, but because of the fantastic light that came in both sides. He was an artist in tinkering, and he had created a workshop in the sitting room where his creation, Myrtle, took pride of place.

"God, Hayley, I wish you'd told me you were coming. We're just off to Brussels. Remember the chap I told you about—the one with the software program that will let Myrtle make independent decisions about deliveries? Tommy and I and one of our local investors are heading over to spend a couple of days with him. You won't believe how far he's gone with the latest version. He thinks he can—"

"Wyn, I need to talk with you."

I moved my head back and forth in front of him like an owl, trying to get him to focus on my face.

"Of course, we'll talk"—he pulled me close, and his hand wandered down to my bottom—"but I'm damned sorry we won't have time for anything else."

"It's only that—Wyn?"

He'd gone over to his laptop, which was hooked up to Myrtle by a cable, and began tapping away. "Yes—listening. I only need to download our current program to show Philippe. He's got an idea about installing a weather station, because the outside temperature can so easily change the interior environment of Myrtle's box. We wouldn't want anyone's bouillabaisse to go off, now, would we?"

There was nothing for it but to stay the course. I followed him over. "Wyn, I've been thinking. About how we have such separate lives, you know? And, although the time we've had together has meant so much to me, and you are such a kind man, I'm not sure if this is really the way either of us wants to live."

He closed the laptop, disengaged the cord, and shoved both in the pocket of his computer bag, which he slung across his shoulder.

"Wyn—were you listening? Did you hear what I said?"

He straightened up and snapped his fingers.

"You're right, Hayley—of course, you're right. And I know what needs to happen."

"Oh, Wyn, I knew you would see—"

"Let's get married!"

22

*W*hat?"

"Let's get married!" Wyn said, full of glee. "You can leave Bath and move up here to London—no more of this Golden Age of whatever and your irritating housemate and those undesirables and people dropping dead. We'll be together all the time!"

I felt as if I'd been run over by a train. "No, Wyn, you see, that isn't what I meant, actually. I wanted to tell you—"

"It's perfect, isn't it?" He took me by the arms and kissed me again.

"Not perfect—"

"Oh, I know, but you'll learn to love London, you really will."

"Please, you aren't listening."

The door burst open and in walked Tommy, Wyn's business partner, and another man.

"Hayley!" Tommy greeted me. "It's been donkey's years! Don't tell me Wyn's got you minding Myrtle while we're away?"

Wyn flung his arms out. "We're getting married!"

"As much as you may like to," the other man said, "I don't think you can marry Myrtle."

"Good one, Bartie," Wyn said with a laugh. "No, Hayley and I are getting married."

"*Wyn!*" I shouted above their snappy repartee. "We need to talk."

"I know, I know," he said, "all the plans. After we're back from Brussels, we'll start the whole ball rolling. Gotta run, Hayley, our flight's from London City. Throw the latch on the door when you leave. Love you!"

And just like that, we were alone—Myrtle and me. I had no feeling in my fingertips or my toes, and the room was spinning. I sank onto the sofa with my head between my knees.

B unter made a point of ignoring me when I walked in. I was several hours past my usual arrival time on a Sunday evening, and he wanted to make sure I knew that he knew—although he was reluctant to disappear altogether, and instead kept to the other side of the hall stand, his tail flicking as he waited. I drew his newest catnip mouse out of my bag and dangled it above his nose. He accepted as if doing me a favor, and trotted up the stairs. I followed. My body was weary and my mind was numb—I had worn my spirit ragged on the train from London to Bath, replaying the scene in Wyn's flat, wondering what I should've done differently. Now it was all I could do to get myself to bed.

Where I didn't sleep. Instead, I stared at my blank phone, imagining Val staring at his, waiting for a text from me that would say *All clear!* Not all clear. Not by a long shot.

I trust you had a restful weekend and your mother is well?" Mrs. Woolgar asked.

I needn't go into detail about my sleepless night. I hadn't gone on my usual walk, instead choosing to fret in my flat until past eight o'clock, when I rang Wyn and got his voice mail. The only message I'd left had been *Please call me, we need to talk.*

"Thank you, Mrs. Woolgar, yes, it was fine. And yours?"

"I spent the weekend on the case," the secretary replied. "There was a great deal of research—times, dates, witness accounts."

"About Charles Henry? Why didn't you tell me—I would've stayed to help." Was she trying to out-Miss-Marple me?

"It was nothing you could attend to, Ms. Burke. Stories of the past, for the most part. But I've discovered how Charles Henry Dill hopes to undermine the Society . . . Blackmail."

"Blackmail," I echoed in a whisper. "You?"

"Certainly not. About eighteen years ago, Charles Henry had the wild notion of producing one of her ladyship's detective stories on the stage. He told her it would secure her name as a latter-day Golden Age of Mystery author, that her popularity would broaden the same as Christie's had with *The Mousetrap*—a load of his usual blag. He had already entangled a local actress in his dodgy scheme— and she was old enough to know better. Lady Fowling entertained his idea, but only briefly, before her common sense took over. She knew once she opened a tap of money for Charles Henry, it wouldn't be easy to shut off. Fortunately, the actress saw the error of her ways, too."

"She called the scam off?"

"Firstly, she hadn't looked at it as a scam—she looked at it as a chance at a leading role, something that doesn't come round that often for a woman of fifty. And secondly, no, not the theatrical production—what she called off was their . . ."

Mrs. Woolgar might have been reluctant to name it, but I leapt in. "She was having an affair with Charles Henry? Who was this actress? Is she local? What does this have to do with the Society?"

The secretary's lips were pressed together so tightly they looked as if they'd been glued. And then it came to me. At the emergency board meeting, Val and I had called to get approval for the literary salons, one of the Society's board members had boasted of her acting career in local theater. And only Friday, Val had asked if this board member might like to take part in a reading of *Meet Jane Marple*.

My jaw dropped. "Charles Henry Dill and Maureen Frost had an affair?"

"I'd rather not give details." Mrs. Woolgar put her nose in the air. "Our past indiscretions, once atoned for, should remain in the past."

That nonanswer screamed *YES*. "But, isn't she a widow?" I asked.

"She wasn't then."

"So, this is his blackmail—she sides with him in his fight to get hold of everything or he'll squeal?"

Mrs. Woolgar winced at my language—and really, where had I got that from?—but acknowledged my supposition with a nod. "This is not the sort of thing Maureen wants dragged into the light of day—she's quite proud and would be mortified if her actions reflected badly on her late husband. I believe Charles Henry is using that threat to coerce her. And where Maureen goes, Jane Arbuthnot is likely to follow. She's always been easily led."

But as unpleasant as the thought of this long-ago affair was, even I saw the problem. "It may be part of Dill's takeover plan, but it isn't about the murder, is it?" I asked. I dragged myself out of the chair. "Still, I need to see Detective Hopgood."

"Not about this." Mrs. Woolgar popped up. "Surely that isn't necessary."

"If Maureen Frost would file a complaint about harassment, that could help stop Charles Henry."

"I'm not sure she looks on his recent attention as harassment."

"You don't mean—" How would I ever get that notion out of my head? I changed the subject. "Mrs. Woolgar—Lady Fowling's notebooks."

The secretary smiled—a rare occurrence. I sat down again.

"What a delight when Ms. Babbage brought them down for me to see. And how lovely a surprise for you to come across that particular carton. I've not seen one of her ladyship's notebooks for so long, I'd almost forgotten they existed. I recall now she packed them away a year or so before she died. It was as if she were wrapping up her life, putting it safely in the cellar for others to find."

Lady Fowling had lived to a grand old age—ninety-four—and still the poignancy of that act brought tears to my eyes.

"The thing is," I said, sniffing, "are you sure there aren't a few notebooks lying about? It's only that I have the strangest feeling I've seen one before."

Mrs. Woolgar shook her head. "Not that I recall."

"She was quite prolific, wasn't she?" I commented. "Writing about everything from detectives to washing-up liquid?"

"Lady Fowling knew that in the everyday is hidden the seed of a good story."

I rather liked that phrase and wondered if Mrs. Woolgar would give me permission to use it—with proper attribution, of course. I would bring that up later.

"I may be out for most of the day—you don't mind?" I asked.

"That is fine, Ms. Burke. I plan to ring Mrs. Arbuthnot later this morning. She needs to be reminded of a few things."

"If Charles Henry drops in while I'm away—"

"Let him just try."

Our battle plans set, I gathered my handbag, donned my jacket, and took up an umbrella—my armor against the mizzling rain.

I strode down Manvers Street to the police station, where, across the road, no Harry kept watch. Given up or unwilling to spend the day sitting on a wet stone wall? I faced the police station. I wanted to know what Sergeant Hopgood had learned about Charles Henry's arrival in Bath, but I hesitated, afraid the DS had begun to consider me as much a pest as the writers. Perhaps I would save my visit for later—give them time to arrest Dill. First, I would find out if Harry had returned to work.

Avec Fleurs—a floral extravaganza crammed into a shopfront no more than ten feet wide—sat across the road from the entrance to the rail station just at the end of Manvers. Stacked on risers in front of the window were buckets brimming with rusty-red mums, speckled alstroemeria, and lilies still in bud, sitting cheek by jowl with pots of star jasmine and blue hydrangeas. Raindrops beaded on each leaf and petal and sprinkled my feet as I brushed by. The sign was turned to *Open*, but the door itself was locked. I rattled it, then peered through the window, where the floral jungle had colonized not only the walls, but also most of the floor space up to the counter. I saw no one, but a movement behind a beaded curtain caught my eye. I knocked to no avail.

Stepping back, I closed my umbrella and looked round. To the left was a pass-through, which should lead to the rear of the shop, and so I took it and found the back door to Avec Fleurs propped open by more buckets—empty or half filled with water, and a few carrying forlorn stems of unwanted daisies and airy fillers I couldn't identify.

I followed the bucket trail indoors. Harry had her back to me. She stood at a worktable lined with short, fat glass vases that held domes of roses in shades of coral and antique yellow. No wonder she hadn't heard me, she had earbuds in—I could see her gently rocking to an inaudible rhythm while she trimmed the roses to fit.

"Harry!" I called. *"Harry!"* I tapped her shoulder.

She spun round, and I saw the scissors in her hand heading straight for my face. I staggered back, collided with buckets, and lost my balance. My arms flapped, and I twisted and lurched and grabbed the edge of the door, which slowed my speed, thereby dropping me gently to the floor.

"Hayley! My God, I've killed you! Hayley—please, I'm sorry!"

Harry flung the scissors away, yanked out her earbuds, and dropped to her knees next to me, patting my head and my arms and then clasping her hands and rocking back and forth.

"I'm all right, Harry, I am." I had to keep repeating that, finally taking her hands in mine and giving them a shake. "Look at me—no harm done. I'm sorry I surprised you."

"But you're hurt," she wailed. "What have I done?"

"I'm not hurt," I said, moving my arms and legs to demonstrate. "But I wouldn't mind a hand."

I could've pulled her down easier than she pulled me up—I finally scrambled to my feet and caught a glimpse of both of us in a small round mirror mounted beside the beaded curtain. My ponytail had come loose, and I looked as if I'd been caught in a windstorm. Harry's frizzy blond hair formed a halo round her pale face, and her eyes were large and dark, reminding me of Bunter.

"Sorry." Her voice wobbled. "It's just I'm a bit on edge."

"Yes, I can tell."

That brought out a little smile. She rescued my hair band from the puddle and it dripped as she held it out to me.

A shadow appeared in the doorway.

"Gainsborough Hotel?" a man asked.

Harry jumped. "Oh yeah—half a mo." Wiping her nose on the back of her sleeve, she began loading the vases into two shallow boxes. The man tucked a clipboard under his arm, leaned against the doorpost, and watched. I went over and helped Harry.

"Thanks, Hayley—we do the table flowers for a couple of local hotels. I should've had these finished by now, but I got a bit of a late start after stopping to ask the police how the enquiry was progressing."

"How did that go over?" I asked.

Harry cut her eyes at me but said nothing—that was answer enough. We loaded the boxes into the man's delivery van and tidied the array of buckets. I combed my fingers through my hair and said, "There now, all better. I could just do with a coffee. How about you? I'll bring them over from next door if you're not too busy."

She brightened considerably. "Could I have a latte with chocolate and coconut and almond flavorings? I love that—tastes like a Bounty Bar."

"Done."

23

I hesitated outside the coffee shop for another call to Wyn and another message. *Please ring when you get this. I need to clear a few things up.* When I returned, Harry and I sat on high stools at the front counter with our drinks and buttery croissants, chatting between sales of mixed bouquets.

She held her coffee with both hands as if seeking comfort from its warmth. "Sergeant Hopgood says they can see me walking away from the pub with Trist, but there's no other CCTV of him and none of me for another two hours—until they catch me in the road here."

"Catch you?"

"My flat's just above."

I stuffed a wad of croissant in my mouth and chewed thoughtfully. "I know I surprised you, Harry, but your reaction seemed a bit . . . extreme. Also, why was the front door of the shop locked?"

She didn't answer right away, but instead kept her dark eyes on me. Then, a sip of coffee to fortify her, she said, "You're going to think I'm mad, but I've had the feeling someone has been watching me."

"Do you know who?"

Harry shrugged as she swept errant flakes of pastry along with shreds of leaves and stray petals into a pile on the countertop. "I never see anyone, that's the thing. And so, I've thought—what if it isn't a real person? What if it's Trist?"

Oh dear. Is this guilt or loss or grief or—is it Trist? More than once I have felt Lady Fowling's presence at Middlebank, so if believing Trist is watching her makes Harry mad, then so am I.

I covered her hand. "I don't think that at all. It's difficult to let go of someone we've lost. But, Harry, the thing is—did you think that locking the door would keep Trist out?"

Her eyes widened. "I hadn't thought of that." She snickered and covered her mouth as she broke out in a fit of giggles. "I guess I am a bit barmy."

"So, you and Trist left the pub together that night." I squirmed on my high stool, both from guilt—I had learned this piece of information from the police—and because I'd landed in a puddle in the back room, and now my wool trousers were soaked through. But would Jane Marple be deterred by a wet bottom? I didn't think so.

Harry nodded. "Trist wanted to talk with me about the group. He'd decided the chemistry wasn't right and he wanted to leave, maybe start a new one."

"He was planning to leave the group behind—even you?"

She shrugged.

"You told the police, didn't you—about this impending breakup?"

"It didn't seem relevant. And, if I had told the police, they might put me in the frame for Trist's murder, and I didn't do it, and so thought it best not to distract them from the enquiry."

In the frame. I continued to place Charles Henry Dill in the frame for Trist's murder, and so I tended to agree with Harry. Still, every bit of information should be handed over to the police. I blushed, remembering my omission—suspicions about Lulu and her connection to Pauline.

"Harry, the police do need to know everything."

"Yes, yes—" Harry squirmed and then heaved a sigh. "All right, I'll tell them. If they'll let me into the station again."

Now I only needed to persuade myself to come clean, too.

"Where did you leave Trist?" I asked. "Where did you go?"

"I had a great deal to think about, and Trist said he wanted to catch the others up and tell them, so he turned back. And I took a walk up through Bathwick Fields. You can see the lights of the city. I go there often—it's a good way to clear my head. Although I'm not sure the police believe me. Would I believe me? Would Miss Marple?"

"Is that safe—walking there late at night?"

"There are always dog walkers about both late and early—and also, I carry an air horn with me. Anyone tries anything, and I could burst his eardrums. Do you want to hear?"

"No thanks—you sound prepared, so good on you. After you left Trist"—there was no harm in asking, was there?—"did you see anyone else? Did you see a large man wearing a brown plaid suit?"

"A what?"

"Never mind."

"The thing is," Harry said, "Trist didn't think we could make it on our own. Wouldn't he be surprised?"

I don't know what we're going to do without him—that's what Amanda had said to me. More than once.

"But you have Amanda at the reins now. To guide you."

"It feels more like a choke hold. Do you know she e-mailed instructions to us for this week? Instructions! I'd never seen this side of her, but we're following along. I suppose it shows you we need someone to take charge—even Peter does. Amanda says someone's got to keep us writing and it might as well be her."

"Did Trist get to the others that night—to tell them about leaving the group?"

"I haven't asked," Harry said, her face reddening. "I didn't want to let on I knew in case he hadn't. Amanda thinks I've got loose lips. But I've not been grassing anyone up."

"By 'grassing up,' do you mean turning over information to the police that might be useful in their enquiry into Trist's murder?"

"Yeah, I suppose."

"And you told them about your relationship with Trist yourself."

"I did. But Amanda thinks I'm the one who let on about the set-to Trist and Peter had. And that I told them about Mariella."

"What about Mariella?"

"It was nothing really. Only that she's given her Poirot special powers. Trist called that a superficial plot device, and she told him she hoped he would meet his end at the hands of one of Miss Marple's zombies."

For a moment, we watched a woman outside fishing round in the buckets, pulling out stems to make her own arrangement. Harry swirled the dregs of her coffee and drank it down.

"Even though I'm back at work," she said, "the enquiry is always on my mind. And I've been wondering—I know you said the books in the library weren't the valuable ones, but was there anything else someone might've wanted?"

Had someone been searching the library for valuables? Now that she'd brought it up, it had occurred to me that if the murderer could get in once—when he carried Trist up to the library—he could've been in at other times, too. On Wednesday evenings, after the writers left, I would give the library a cursory inspection and think all was well, but the next morning, Mrs. Woolgar would spot chairs out of place and books taken off shelves. Had I not been paying close enough attention, or had someone come back into Middlebank later—wandering the house, having his way with the library, standing at the doors of our flats? I shuddered.

What if Trist had found out about this and had gone to confront him, and only then had the would-be thief turned into a murderer?

"Harry, remember you asked me if it was all right to take the books off the shelves, and I said it was fine? I have noticed that someone has handled them. Who was it?"

The door opened, and in came the woman with her arms full of flowers. Harry hopped off her stool.

"Oh ... er ... that was just a general question," she replied, and with that, having reminded herself of Amanda's comment about loose lips, Harry snapped hers shut.

T he woman at the coffee shop next door let me nip into their toilet, and I gave her a wave of thanks as I left. Stepping out onto the pavement, I saw two women approach—the older one in a wheelchair and the younger one pushing. I held the door open for them.

"Here you are."

The older woman patted my arm as they passed. "Bless," she said.

The younger one gave me a smile. "Thanks."

"You've very welcome," I replied. "Enjoy your coffees."

That could be my mum and me—and it reminded me of my mother's admonishment about keeping an open mind on the enquiry. Dill shouldn't be the only bird in my cage of suspects. Right, well, I would make straight for Detective Sergeant Hopgood and show him that I had an open mind and was able to pick up on clues and put them together and come to conclusions and not just be stuck in a rut. Also, I could find out if they'd arrested Charles Henry yet.

I turned the corner and marched up Manvers, the police station in sight and my resolve firm. I slid my hand along the top of the metal railing as I walked the concrete ramp, and reached the doors just as Charles Henry Dill burst out, nearly knocking me over. We stopped—the shock that went through me reflected on his face. But for only a second. Then his eyes narrowed, and he stuck a finger at my face. I couldn't help noticing the nail was filed and buffed, cuticle trimmed. Tosser—spending his inheritance on manicures?

"Do you think I don't know you're behind this?" he hissed. Every bit of his smarmy charm had been torn away, and what was left was not pretty. "Required to prove my whereabouts the past fortnight like a common criminal? You're lucky I don't press charges for harassment."

We had dropped into the middle of a battle that, up to that moment, had been fought only in my head.

"Harassment?" I snapped. "Pull the other one, why don't you. If anyone's doing the harassing, it's you. With your petty scheming, you are threatening the memory of Lady Fowling and her legacy. And you do it for your own gain."

"You did not know my aunt, Ms. Burke, and I'll thank you not to imagine her thoughts and feelings."

"I don't have to imagine—those closest to her know full well her views and her deepest desires."

He took a step closer and I wanted more than the world to shrink away, but I steeled myself and didn't move. "The police came to visit me." He spoke in a low, menacing voice. "At my hotel. They called me out to the lobby of the Royal Crescent in front of other guests. You can't tell me you and Woolley didn't have something to do with that."

"Did they clap you in irons and drag you out the door? Did they chain you to a pillar? Or did they have a quiet word to clear a few things up. The police are an entity unto themselves, Mr. Dill— neither I nor Mrs. Woolgar can order them around Bath and force them to talk with people even if those people may have information vital to an ongoing enquiry. And by the way, does Maureen Frost know you have another *friend* in town?"

His face went puce, and his eyes bugged out like a cartoon character. I would've laughed, except it frightened me.

"How does my personal life concern you?" he choked out.

"What concerns me is your motive, your desire, to destroy your aunt's lifelong work, the thing she loved above all else."

"There, you've said it—what she 'loved above all else.' Books—made-up stories about detectives. Not real people—not her own family."

"You ungrateful—" Before I knew it, I was advancing on him. His face went from purple to white as he stumbled backward, bumping into the railing. "Perhaps if you hadn't always come at her with your hand out, you'd've discovered what a lovely woman she was. You just keep this up, Mr. Dill—we know what you're really about. We know what you've done. And truth will out."

"What, Shakespeare?" He laughed as he straightened his jacket. "Shouldn't you be quoting Jane Marple—or are you that unfamiliar with her?"

The door to the station opened, and both of us jumped. DC Kenny Pye put his head out.

"Is everything all right here?" he asked, eyeing us.

"Yes, thank you for asking, Detective Constable Pye," I said. "As it happens, I've come to have a word with you and Sergeant Hopgood." I breezed past Dill into the station.

K enny Pye went in search of Hopgood as I waited near the front desk. The dark look on the sergeant's face when he appeared made me unsure of my welcome.

"I will take up as little of your time as possible," I said. "But it's occurred to me that the person who murdered Trist may have gained entry to Middlebank before that night—may have spent time in the library and even searched the house, for all I know. I mean, if he got in once, why couldn't he have—"

Constable Pye interrupted. "Sarge."

Hopgood looked from his DC to me, his eyebrows a solid horizontal line. He didn't speak, but it was as if I could see the gears turning in his mind. At last, he nodded. "Come through, Ms. Burke."

The officers dropped me off in Interview #1 and excused themselves. I tried to get comfortable in the hard chair—next time, I'd bring a pillow to sit on and my own cup of tea. I was alone long enough to let my thoughts wander away from the murder enquiry and down other roads. I knew why Wyn hadn't phoned back—I had seen him so absorbed in work that he heard or saw nothing else. He and his crew were holed up in a Brussels hotel room talking software programming and working up manufacturing quotes to build an army of Myrtles. I had wanted to end our relationship in person, but if I had to break it off over the phone, I would.

When Sergeant Hopgood swept into the room with DC Pye in his wake, my thoughts scattered in the wind.

"Now, about these earlier break-ins," Hopgood began.

"What earlier break-ins?" I asked, my eyes on the two thick files Kenny Pye had laid on the table. "Oh, wait, yes, I see. I can't say for certain, but looking back, it's possible things had been moved round the library, and it may have happened when no one was about."

"'May have'?" Hopgood repeated.

"Or not." The more I thought about it, the less sure I became. "On Wednesday evenings, after the writers group left, I almost always looked into the library before going up to my flat—to check that they'd left it tidy, you know. It would look fine to me at the time. And yet the next morning, Mrs. Woolgar always seemed to find a chair out of place or a book left unshelved."

Perhaps ignoring a chair out of place or a book down off the shelf

had been my way of protesting Mrs. Woolgar's rigid view of how the
Society and Middlebank should be run. I regretted that now.

"And so now you believe someone had been in the library before
the night of the murder?" Pye asked.

"I can't be sure, but what else could it be?"

Trist would've chalked it up to Lady Fowling's ghost—that had
always been his flippant remark when I brought it up. Had he been
covering for his own actions—or someone else's? Because I knew for
certain it had not been Lady Fowling's ghost—she would never play
cheap tricks like that.

"You're certain nothing was taken?" the sergeant asked.

Pye had opened one of the files. As he ran his finger down a half-
page list of numbers, I tried to read upside down. Were they dates?

"I will check the books against our catalog," I said, "but as I told
you before, the valuable part of the collection is at the bank. I suppose some of the paintings or furniture could be worth a bit, but I
feel certain I'd notice if someone had carried the mahogany hall
stand out the door." I couldn't hold my curiosity any longer. "This
isn't about Trist, is it?"

"Thank you for your time, Ms. Burke."

"I'm dismissed? But, Sergeant, what about Charles Henry Dill?"

"That was quite alert of you, picking up on the fact that Mr. Dill
did arrive in Bath earlier than he initially stated." Hopgood's tone
had eased, making me think he was relieved at this change of topic.
"Two days earlier, in fact. But still, that was well after the murder,
and there is no evidence that points to him."

My shoulders sagged.

"Picking a favorite too early in the race can lead us astray," the
sergeant said gently. "We must keep an open mind, even when faced
with unpleasant facts."

I must introduce Sergeant Hopgood to my mother one of these
days.

24

I walked out of the station and stood holding on to the railing for a moment, washed out and in need of lunch. No wonder—gone four o'clock. Waitrose was in one direction, but I headed the other way, opting for the café in Marks & Spencer instead. It was a good second, and closer to my next destination. I had an egg-and-cress sandwich and tea and felt much better for it, although I had to go in search of a Boots to buy dental floss before continuing to Bath College. All day, I had longed to see Val, and yet I had been filled with apprehension. At last, longing had won.

I took time for only one more chore. Standing on the pavement on Stall Street, I made another attempt at Wyn. Voice mail again. *I know your meetings in Brussels are important, but please ring. We need to talk.*

On the day Val and I had met with the committee about the literary salons, he had stopped by his office, and so, when I walked through the glass-front entry of the college, at least I knew where to look for him.

His door stood open, and he sat at a desk that was stacked with books in precarious columns. Any other open space had been filled with loose sheets of paper. At one corner lay an open laptop, and at another, I saw the backs of photo frames. He had his head down, reading a paperback, but I couldn't see the title and I didn't want to disturb. Instead, I took in the sight of him, wearing his slightly worn green corduroy jacket and a green plaid shirt with a dark wool tie that hung askew. I could straighten that for him. Only when two students passed behind me in the corridor, laughing, did he look up.

"Hello," I said.

"Hi." He rose with a smile and walked round the desk. "Come in."

"I'm disturbing you—you're preparing for class."

"No, I've nothing to prepare for this evening. It's the 'Unnamed Manuscript' night—students who want to submit a few pages of a new piece can do so, anonymously. I read them out and anyone can offer a first impression."

"Oh, that sounds interesting." I fiddled with the zipper on my bag and my gaze wandered round the room. I was at a loss as to how to begin.

Val's smile faded—my apprehension must be contagious. I needed to get this over with.

"Look—"

"Do you want to sit down?" He gestured to two chairs by a low table.

"Thanks." He closed the door before joining me. But as soon as I sat, I popped up again. He followed suit.

"I went to London yesterday. To see Wyn."

My throat was dry and I coughed, and Val lost a bit of color in his face, and his smile vanished altogether.

"Yeah," he said.

"I was going to tell him, explain to him, that he and I were . . . that it wasn't really working out . . . and so . . . but there was a problem."

"What problem?"

"He proposed."

Val cocked his head, as if he hadn't heard properly. "He proposed—marriage?"

I nodded, my misery complete.

"You didn't accept, did you?"

"Of course I didn't accept! It's only that I didn't have the opportunity to tell him no. Tommy walked in with some other bloke and they all breezed out the door, off to Brussels to talk with a fellow about bloody Myrtle and how to keep the bouillabaisse from going bad. I tried to stop him and tell him we needed to talk, but he paid me no mind. Off he went." I flung my arm out, and Val had to step back or be struck.

My outburst had drained me and I sank back into the chair, hugged my bag, and stared at the floor. "He doesn't listen," I muttered. "He never listens."

Val perched on the edge of his chair. I stole a look at him—his face gave nothing away.

I popped up again. "I've left three voice mails for him today. He gets so absorbed in this Eat Here, Eat Now business he pays no attention to anything else. I would rather talk with him and explain, but if I have to break up by voice mail, so be it." I frowned and my frown deepened—better that than let my chin quiver. "Am I being ridiculous? Insisting on stopping this with him before I . . . we . . . start something else?"

"No, you aren't ridiculous. You're cautious. You're considerate." Val stepped close and ran his hand down my arm. Then he pulled back and stuck his hands in his pockets, as if they couldn't be trusted.

"I will get this sorted," I said.

He nodded. His hands came out of his pockets, and he stuck them under his arms. "Will you have dinner with me? Not this evening, but—"

"Yes." His invitation caught me by surprise—a lovely, warm surprise—but I was quick and sure with my answer. "Dinner. Where will we go—the café at Waitrose?"

His smile returned. "I'll try to do a bit better than that. How about Friday?"

Oh, I see. He's giving me a deadline—and I could work with that. I nodded. "Friday."

We stood grinning at each other, and I decided that perhaps a kiss—just a small one—would be all right. But a knock came at the door along with a voice calling, "Mr. Moffatt?" and then my phone rang.

"Class," Val said.

"Dinah," I replied, looking at the screen.

"Stay here and take it," he offered. He chanced a light squeeze of my hand on his way out. "I'll talk to you soon."

And, Mum, when I said why couldn't we make the box room into a bedroom and then find another housemate, she said she'd been thinking the same, and so we advertised and just like that found this woman who's going through a divorce and she's moving in tomorrow. That's three of us, and just think, this will slash the amount of rent I owe."

"Dinah, sweetie, that's fantastic. Well done." I sat back in Val's desk chair and envisioned my bank account rising by a few precious quid every month.

"I'm going to start saving for a car!" Her enthusiasm bubbled over. "Then I'll only need to take driving lessons and I'll be set. I wonder, how much do they cost?"

Enough, I was sure. Plus, there would be insurance and petrol. The bank account dipped once again.

"Just think—when I have a car, it'll be no problem to pop over and take Gran for a day out. She'd like that."

She would indeed—I gave my daughter credit for spending time with her grandmother and for knowing what would persuade her mum to fork over the money.

"Right, sweetie, we'd better take this slowly, though—don't you think?"

"Oh yeah, sure," she said with great equanimity. "There's no hurry. Oh, Mum—have you dug out my diorama yet?"

A vague memory surfaced—I was to find the model of our home she'd built as a girl. She needed it for one of her courses at uni.

"It's only up in the attic—I can put my hands on it in a second. I expect it may need a bit of repair after all these years. Don't worry—I'm on it."

We rang off, and my eyes fell on a triptych of photos of Val's own girls amid the books and papers. The center snapshot showed them grown, but on each side was an identical twin at about age seven. The girls wore kilts in a blue-and-green tartan and flat black shoes, and each had one hand on her hip and one curved over her head. Scottish dancers—I would ask him about that over dinner on Friday. Dinner on Friday—it sounded like heaven.

I rang Wyn and left another message, then stepped out into the corridor, where I heard Val's voice coming out of a nearby classroom. I moved closer to its open door and listened to him read from a student's new work.

"I didn't do it, and nothing you can do will say I did."

"Nothing?" The detective smirked. "You forget I have your finger-prints on a glass, and it would be nothing to transfer your dabs to the key, the alarm pad, the door—all with only a bit of Sellotape."

"No one's going to believe that."

With a note of mock sadness, the detective said, "One wrong word, and this can all so easily go pear-shaped for you."

"Right, that's it. I don't care if they do nick me for those robberies, I'm going to the police and tell them everything."

Never turn your back on a murderer.

The knife slid into the victim with such ease—a long, thin blade with a double curved point and so sharp that it sliced through skin, tissue, and muscle like jelly—between the ribs it went and then up and into the heart. It took only a second. Death was instantaneous, the detective observed—otherwise there would've been blood, so much blood.

The story brought gooseflesh to my arms. Were any of the Golden Age of Mystery writers like this? Did we have books in The First Edition Society library that spoke of blood and gore? I hoped not.

No alarm was necessary on Tuesday morning—I was up and on my walk by seven o'clock, back in my flat before eight, showered and on my second cup of tea by nine. That's when I rang Wyn. Was I mad—doing the same thing over and over and expecting a different result?

Mrs. Woolgar looked grim when I stepped into her office for our morning briefing. "Do you read the local tabloids, Ms. Burke?"

"I pick up a *Chronicle* on Thursdays." Although, I'd been avoiding the news since we found the body in the library, afraid of what Bath might make of us. Me.

"The online rags. I was only searching for a weather forecast and saw this—it was posted today." She nodded to her computer monitor, and I walked behind her chair and bent over to read.

No Leads in Death of Local Man

Nearly a fortnight has passed since the death of local writer Tristram Cummins. He was killed at Middlebank, a Grade-II listed
Georgian terrace house designed by John Palmer, now the home
of The First Edition Society, an organization that describes itself
as a collection of "detective stories." A source who spoke to this
reporter on the condition of anonymity revealed that the upheaval
the murder has caused in the ranks of the Society is threatening
its very survival, and in a last-gasp effort, the board of trustees
may need to turn to founder Lady Georgiana Fowling's only living
relative, Charles Henry Dill, of Nottingham. Mr. Dill had no comment on the rumors, except to say that if called upon, he would,
of course, do everything in his power to save his aunt's vision of
sharing her favorite books with the world.

The words on the screen swam in front of my eyes, and I was
unable to breathe. At last I drew in a wheezy lungful of air and
choked out, "*Rubbish!* How can they print such lies? And do they
think we don't know who their anonymous source is?"

"Charles Henry has a knack for collecting secrets," Mrs. Woolgar
said, "and he must have one on this reporter. Blackmail. We should
pay these so-called news items no mind." She reached for her mouse
to click away, but something caught my eye.

"Wait—what's this about?" I pointed to another headline.

"An advert, no doubt," Mrs. Woolgar said. "These untrustworthy
online sites attempt to entice us to follow them down the rabbit hole.
I will not succumb."

"No—look at the headline. 'No Sign of Forced Entry.' That's
what the police said about us. Go on—let's have a look."

With a huff, Mrs. Woolgar clicked through to a short item about
a break-in in Bathhampton—an area just northeast of the city. It was

a fairly dry account compared with the piece about us, telling of a robbery at a house where no one was at home. Some jewelry and several small but valuable objects were taken. It was the third such crime in the area since the beginning of September.

"They take what is easy to carry and hide about their person," said Detective Sergeant Hopgood of the Avon and Somerset Constabulary. "They need to travel light—they aren't about to drag an antique hall stand out with them."

I tapped on the screen. "Those are *my* words. I told DS Hopgood that if a thief had been inside Middlebank looking for something to steal, they'd come up short and that we would've noticed if someone had tried to drag the mahogany hall stand out the door."

"I'm afraid I'm a bit lost here, Ms. Burke."

Mrs. Woolgar hadn't heard my idea about the murderer being in Middlebank before the night Trist died, and so I took the chair and explained.

"I don't want you to feel unsafe," I said, "but we must consider the possibility this has happened."

"I will not be frightened out of my own home," she snapped.

"Good—neither will I."

You see what he's doing," I said, pointing to the news item I'd brought up on my phone. I had declined a trip to Interview #1, and instead, DS Hopgood and I stood off to the side in the police station's lobby.

"It's poor journalism at best," he said. "I'd pay it no mind, if I were you. I've certainly learned to."

"It is his goal to make our lives miserable," I complained.

"He's full of hot air," the DS replied. "I've seen the sort before—he's all mouth and no trousers."

If he kept up this amiable demeanor, I'd soon be calling him Uncle Ronnie. But I thought I'd better take advantage while I could, so I next brought up the article on the break-ins. "And look here, Sergeant—about this series of robberies. No hall stands gone missing?"

One side of his mouth lifted, drawing up a corner of his mustache. "My apologies for borrowing your turn of phrase, but it was a fine example."

"Those robberies had 'no sign of forced entry'—just as ours did."

Hopgood nodded. "I tried to see a connection between the two enquiries, but the simple fact is that nothing was taken at Middlebank—and robbers are so seldom murderers. A thief wants to get in and get out without any fuss. Unlike at Middlebank, where someone took the effort to bring the victim into the house, thus creating a murder scene."

Defeated, I dropped my phone in my bag. "And Charles Henry Dill?" I asked without hope. "What was he doing in Grove Street? With whom had he stayed before he moved to the Royal Crescent Hotel?"

"The business of your Society, Ms. Burke, unless a law is broken, is not the business of the police."

Sergeant Hopgood's mention of the Society was as good as an answer—Charles Henry must have been staying with Maureen Frost in Grove Street. Why hadn't I thought of that before this moment? Because I'd jumped to conclusions, that's why. I'd seen Dill and then I'd seen Lulu Ingleby, and I had latched on to the idea that the two of them had carried out the break-in and the murder.

Evidence—or the lack thereof—was forcing me to look elsewhere for Trist's killer.

Lulu remained a suspect in my mind. I had seen her argue with Pauline, her employer, and there had been what looked to me like a suspicious exchange between Lulu and Leonard. But I had not a shred of evidence against her, and I felt Sergeant Hopgood, as kindly as he'd been about my suspicions of Charles Henry, was nearing his limit of patience. Surely I could carry out this one piece of investigation on my own in order to eliminate her from the enquiry. Or put her in the frame.

I rang Pauline.

"Hiya, Hayley." I could hear the clanking of metal behind her—must be a delivery of kegs to the Minerva.

"Sorry to bother you at work. I had a quick question about Lulu." I wasn't sure how I could ask this without making it sound important and mysterious, but I could only try.

"Hang on." Pauline turned away from the phone and I heard her say, "Did he ask you about the winter ale? Right, fine—yeah, I'm sure he'll let you know. No, here now, I can sign for him." When she came back to the phone, she sounded both distracted and annoyed. "You want to know about the little princess? Don't get me started. If she doesn't show up here in the next hour, I'm giving her the boot. What did you want to know?"

"Oh, nothing, really," I gushed, thrilled with my accidental success. "I remembered you were concerned, and only wondered how it was going. It sounds like you're busy, though—we'll talk on Thursday. See you."

There you are—I would head for the Minerva, snap a photo of Lulu, and show it around to the writers and Mrs. Woolgar. I might even stick it in Charles Henry's face to see if I got a reaction. If one of them recognized her, we could be onto something. That is, I would hand over the matter to the police.

I hurried up to Northumberland Place and to the café on the other side of the pub. I marched in, ordered and paid, and then installed myself at an outdoor table. When the server brought out my coffee and cinnamon bun, he made a comment about the heavy gray skies and chill in the air and said they wouldn't start up the outdoor heater until the lunch crowd arrived. Didn't I want an inside table? I'd brought only a light jacket along, not expecting to spend a late October morning staking out a pub, but I told him the temperature suited me fine, and he shrugged, probably thinking I was a smoker.

I pulled one of the old paperbacks out of my bag. *A Caribbean Mystery*—I had thought it might be fun to see Miss Marple on holiday. I opened it to a random page and kept one eye on the door of the pub while sipping my coffee and not even breaking my attention when I made a quick call to Wyn. Voice mail.

Lulu appeared just short of her hour deadline, wearing coveralls and her *Cleaned by Pauline* bandanna. The lane had filled with pedestrians, and the other café tables were occupied with people already ordering lunch—they sat clustered round the heater—and so she didn't notice me even though I was only twenty feet away. I fumbled for my phone—my fingers numb from the cold—and moved to the edge of my chair, ready and waiting. Lulu popped out of the pub in only a couple of minutes, looking flushed and flustered. She tore the bandanna off, ran her fingers through her black curls, and tossed the scarf in the nearest bin. When she looked round, I ducked behind my Miss Marple, and when I saw Lulu stomp away, I hurried after, wanting to get just close enough for a clear shot.

When she looked back over her shoulder, I hopped into a shop doorway and right onto the toe of an extremely high-heeled shoe. "So sorry. Are you all right?" I asked the woman wearing it. I didn't wait for an answer, but bounded away up to the next shop entry. Lulu had stopped—here it was, my chance. I stuck my arm out into the lane, only barely able to tell I was pointing at my subject, and snapped once, readjusted, and snapped again. I checked that it had worked.

It had—too well. My cold finger had lingered on the button, and instead of a couple of photos, I'd taken two "bursts" of about thirty each. Were any of them useful? I glanced at the first few—yes, I could recognize Lulu. But would anyone else?

After making certain she had disappeared, I stepped out into the lane and saw my phone screen rapidly spattered with heavy raindrops. I stuck it back in my bag, put my collar up, and hurried off.

25

What began as fat drops rapidly grew into sheets of unrelenting rain, and by the time I had climbed the terrace and reached Middlebank, I could barely see from the rain in my eyes, and my hand shook with cold when I put the key in the lock.

Inside, I dripped on the entry rug and peered at myself in the hall-stand mirror. My drenched ponytail drooped in a single sodden hank, rivulets of water ran down my neck, and the light jacket I'd put on for a cool October morning would need to be wrung out. As I kicked off my shoes and shivered, my phone rang.

"Dinah, sweetie, you've caught me just in from the rain. Can I ring you back?"

"No need, Mum—I only wanted to tell you this one thing. I mentioned to Dad about getting a car, and he said he would be willing to sell me his. He sort of acted as if it was already done and dusted. It's a cute car, I know, but I thought I'd find out from you if that would be the . . . you know, right sort of thing to do."

Anger flared in an instant, and I had to take another look at myself in the mirror to make sure I didn't look like a cartoon character with steam coming out of my ears.

"Listen, sweetie"—I pressed the heel of my hand against my forehead—"wouldn't you rather have a little Ford Fiesta? Something guaranteed to run?"

We both got a laugh out of that, mine sharp and caustic. Roger's ancient sports car spent more time with the mechanic than it did on the road. And here he was trying to foist it off on his own daughter. Of course, he knew who would be paying for it.

"Yeah," Dinah said in a rush, and I could hear the relief in her voice, "that's what I thought, too. But, you know how he is. I wonder if—"

"Let me have a word with him. And then we'll start looking for a proper car for you, all right?"

We rang off, and I squished my way over to Mrs. Woolgar's office. When the secretary caught sight of me, she hurried over before I could step in.

"Have you ever seen this woman?" I asked. Shivering, I held up a photo of Lulu.

Mrs. Woolgar adjusted her glasses and examined the image. "No," she said. "Who is she?"

"She works for Pauline. She looks . . . shifty."

Mrs. Woolgar didn't answer, but gave me a look.

"I don't know if it has anything to do with Pauline—it's just an idea I have."

I dropped the phone into my bag. "But for now, I need a hot shower. And then I think I'll spend the rest of the day in my flat reading Lady Fowling's notebooks, if you don't mind. I'm not going back out in that." I headed for the stairs, but stopped. "Mrs. Woolgar—what about Jane Arbuthnot?"

"Promising news on that front—she's distancing herself from

Maureen and this whole affair." The secretary blushed. "That is, the . . . well, regardless, she understands the danger Charles Henry represents. I'll have another word with Maureen, try to make her see sense."

A hot shower did wonders for me. I dried my hair and dressed in . . . I confess, I put on my flannel pajamas, literally giving up for the rest of the day. Bunter had followed me to my flat, no doubt sensing the possibility of a nap, and had settled at the end of the sofa.

I joined him. A bowl of grapes and the carton of notebooks within reach, I covered myself with a throw. I was asleep in seconds, and awoke two hours later when Bunter sat down on my chest. I got up and opened the door for him and he trotted away, full of purpose. I stretched, popped a few grapes, and thought how rare for me to have an afternoon to myself in my own flat. Also, I was quite hungry, but lunchtime was long over. An early dinner? While I considered my options, I had a cup of tea and two tiny Bakewell tarts, and, thus fortified, rang my ex.

I admit I was primed to give Roger the brunt of my bad mood—combining my growing frustration with the murder enquiry, my anger at Charles Henry Dill, and my annoyance at Wyn for not answering his phone. When I added those to my highly charged reaction to Roger's "offer" of selling that junk heap of a car to our daughter, it put me over the edge. It's possible he didn't deserve such a tongue-lashing—this time. But I certainly felt the better for it, and having put shed to his car idea, I allowed him to natter on about his new girlfriend for a good long while. Eventually, I knocked at my own door and then said, "Oh, here's the committee now—sorry, Roger, I must run. Best of luck with Leaf."

At least I think that's what he said her name was.

I enjoyed a fine dinner of fish fingers and mash and two glasses of wine. Well into my second glass, my phone rang, and my heart thumped against my chest. If it were Wyn, I must be kind, but firm. Kind, but firm.

It was Val.

"Just a quick call," he said. "I'm not phoning about . . . I don't want you to think I'm . . . Look, you've got the writers group tomorrow evening? I wonder if it would be all right for me to stop in beforehand so that we could have a talk. It isn't about . . . you know."

It could be about the man in the moon, and I'd still welcome him. "Of course, it's fine. If you can spare the time away from your lectures."

"Wednesdays are light," Val replied. "It's Thursday I'm booked up. That's the day I have a class in the morning, two in the afternoon, and one in the evening."

"Ah yes, Thursday evening is the one with DC Pye. Well, if you have all tomorrow evening free, would you like to sit in on the group? I've done it only once, but they're always inviting me. They might welcome an actual writing teacher."

"I would do, yeah, sure," Val said. "If they all agree."

"Good." We were quiet. There was really nothing else to say—or rather, there was far too much to say—and so I took my comfort in knowing he waited at the other end of the phone line.

"I could bring along a light supper," he offered. "Any requests?"

You. "Cheese and pickle, please."

He laughed and I giggled, and he exhaled and said, "See you tomorrow."

The second we ended our call, I made another.

Ring me, Wyn. Don't make me say this in a voice mail.

It was an early night.

* * *

I would save my walk until after our morning briefing, because I knew I'd be crisscrossing the city. We accomplished little sitting across the desk from each other. Mrs. Woolgar seemed distracted—or perhaps I was the one who couldn't keep her mind on a discussion about redesigning the newsletter—and so we wrapped up rather quickly.

"I am off to talk with the writers—one by one," I explained, shrugging on a coat and pulling my ponytail out from under the collar.

"Are you canceling this evening?" Mrs. Woolgar asked with a hopeful note in her voice.

"No, I don't think that's—it's only, if we. . . . If I have them still meet here, I may learn something. That I can pass along to police," I added.

"Do you suspect one of them?"

"I'm not sure any of them liked Trist." Realizing Mrs. Woolgar certainly hadn't had fond feelings for him, I hurried on. "Not that liking or disliking is a motive for murder. Each of them seemed to be annoyed by his attitude and cutting remarks, but at the same time, appreciated his feedback. It's an odd dynamic."

"Do you know where to find them?"

"I know where to begin."

My destination was Avec Fleurs, but before I even walked out the door of Middlebank, I sent Wyn a text. Yes, I broke up with him in the most unfeeling and inappropriate way imaginable. I wasn't happy about it, but I told myself if he had only phoned me, I could have made a proper job of it. But now I'd had my fill of the entire situation. In the text, I didn't even acknowledge his proposal—

such as it was—and instead told him we were "too different" and he was a good man who "deserved more."

I went on my way, my heart lighter—and yet a shadow of guilt lurked in the recesses of my mind. I should've talked with him. No, make that I *would've* talked with him. He had to know how serious this was, but instead of facing up to it, he was choosing to ignore me and how I felt. This wasn't my fault.

The sign in the door of the flower shop was turned to *Open*, and miraculously, the door was unlocked. Even better, Harry stood behind the counter, looking at her phone.

She glanced up and greeted me with, "I need to work every day for the next month to make up the time I took off. It's no bother, actually. I'm rather glad to keep busy—saves me from thinking too much." The corners of her mouth drooped. "You aren't coming to tell me you're turfing us out of Middlebank, are you?"

"Not a bit of it—I'll be ready and waiting for the group this evening. But what I do need, Harry, is to have a little chat with Peter and Mariella and Amanda. Let them know in person that we're still on. It's only that . . . I'm not quite sure where they live."

Harry happily cooperated. "Peter'll probably be at work, but he's only over on the Lower Bristol Road—do you know that garden machinery shop? And Mariella will be at home or in the park with the little one—here, now, I'll write this all down. Amanda lives the other way altogether, across the Pulteney Bridge."

"Yes, that's right—Grove Street. Would you write down the number? Of course, she could be at work, too."

Harry wrinkled her nose in thought. "I don't believe she's working at the moment. Hang on, I've got the number of the building." She flipped through screens on her phone, adding, "When the group first started, we had the idea to take turns meeting in our own homes or flats, but Amanda didn't like that idea."

"Thanks so much for this, Harry. And also, can you tell me

something?" I switched to photos on my phone as a customer walked in.

"My order ready?" he asked.

Two women followed on his heels.

"I'll be right with you," Harry called to the women. She turned to the man and said, "I'll just nip into the back for your order. Won't take me two ticks."

I followed her through the curtain of beads into the workroom and heard her curse under her breath. "He said an afternoon pickup—good thing I'm just about finished."

I gave the magnificent arrangement of late roses mixed with rose hips and berries barely a glance—"Lovely"—and put the phone in front of Harry. "Look, have you ever seen this woman?"

Harry took my phone and studied the photo of Lulu, squinting.

"I know it isn't the best shot, but do you recognize her? There are loads more photos—go on and flip through."

"Hello?" the man at the counter called. "Could I go ahead and write on this little card?"

"I'll take care of him," I whispered, and dashed out. "Yes, sir, of course—oh, I see you've chosen that lovely enclosure with the antique illustration. Gorgeous. Now, you go ahead and write your message—do you need a pen?"

I stood behind the counter as if I worked there every day and watched as the customer, pen in hand, seemed to be stuck for the right words. The women looked over at me and I smiled.

"Can you help us here?" one of them asked, holding up a pot of shockingly orange daisies. "Do you have these Gerberas in more of a coppery shade?"

"Oh, I . . . let me just check with—"

Harry arrived at the counter to save the day. She set down the vase of flowers and pulled my phone out of the pocket of her smock, handing it over. "I don't know her, Hayley. But—"

The woman gave the pot of daisies a shake at us and asked, "Or in blue?"

"They don't come in blue," Harry said. "But I've a fiery red that's perfect for autumn. It's in the back, let me fetch it. Sorry, Hayley," she added to me quietly. "Can we talk later?"

I found Peter in the back of the garden machinery workshop, wearing protective goggles and dismantling the engine on an enormous riding lawn mower. When he saw me, he turned off the noisy machine in front of him and stood.

"Hayley—is there something wrong?"

"No, not at all. I just happened to be coming out this direction"—a twenty-five-minute walk—"and Harry had mentioned where it was you worked."

"Any word on the enquiry?" Peter asked.

"I've heard nothing." Although, it wasn't for want of asking.

"They're wasting their time, coming to me again and again, asking me about the punch-up Trist and I had." Peter tapped the wrench he was holding against the edge of a bench. "I admit I wasn't best pleased when he tried to nick my ideas for his own work, but we got over it. It's ancient history." He gave the bench a heavy whack.

"The police have asked all of you your whereabouts that night, haven't they—after you left the pub? And, if you happened to see Trist again. Harry told me she went for a long walk, just to clear her head. And, I'm sure, think about her writing."

"Oh yes, the police have asked. And now you want to know, too."

How did Miss Marple question suspects without sounding as if she were interrogating them? I failed at coming up with an appropriately vague response for Peter.

He shrugged it off. "It doesn't matter," he said as he used the wrench like a drumstick. "It's the same every Wednesday after group and after the pub—Mariella takes a curry home to her husband from that Indian place near the Abbey. It's a bit out of the way, so it may look to someone who's tracking us on CCTV that we go off in the wrong direction."

Right, let's move along. "And speaking of Wednesdays, I wanted to remind you that the group's still welcome at Middlebank this evening. Oh, and also"—I took great care to sound as casual as possible—"I wonder, have you ever seen this woman?"

He pulled the goggles off but didn't look at my phone. "They're using you now? When we've volunteered to assist with the enquiry? That's not to say you aren't a great help to them, Hayley, but it's the four of us who understand the criminal mind."

Another worker had started up a drill, and its high-pitched whine pierced my eardrums. I winced and raised my voice. "I'm not sure they would consider what I'm doing 'help.'" I held up the photo. "So, have you seen her?"

Peter took his time studying the snap of Lulu, but I saw no recognition in his eyes. He shook his head. "Sorry. You don't want to tell me who she is?"

"I'm not sure myself, it's only that—say, doesn't Mariella's husband work here?"

Peter nodded to a tall young man wearing headphones on the far side of the workshop. "Look, if you talk with him, you won't ask him about Trist or mention the murder, will you? It's only that he's nervous enough about Mariella being a writer, and so she hasn't told him what's gone on."

"But it's been in the news."

"He isn't the sort to follow the news."

"Right, then—not a word."

Mariella's husband looked like an affable fellow. He told me his wife had taken the wee lad to his playgroup today and then to lunch and wouldn't be home until just before she left for the writers group.

"It's her evening out, you know, and she really enjoys herself, so I don't mind staying with the boy."

I would catch Mariella before the group started up that evening. In the meantime, I now traipsed back across the city to Grove Street. As it turned out, Amanda lived in the building that had been converted from a girls' school—only across the road from what I assumed was Maureen Frost's flat. That meant I could ask her if she'd ever seen Charles Henry Dill—although my real goal, I reminded myself, was to show her Lulu's photo. I found Amanda's name on the residents' list and buzzed her flat, but got no answer.

My morning had been for naught. I retraced my steps across the Pulteney Bridge but took a slight detour on my walk back to Middlebank and looped around to the Minerva in a last-ditch effort to find the tiniest useful clue. Instead, I found Leonard behind the bar and a lunch crowd blocking my path. I wriggled my way through and was greeted with a "What'll it be?"

"Orange squash, please."

He glowered at me and, without asking, topped up the mixer with fizzy water.

"And crisps."

He tossed a packet of lightly salted on the bar. He had a good memory for a customer's preferences, I'll say that for him.

"Will Lulu be stopping by soon?" I asked, handing over my coins.

He pulled a pint for another customer while over his shoulder he said to me, "She's got a cleaning job."

"Not for Pauline, though."

He leaned over the bar. "You leave my sister out of this."

My pulse raced. I could not identify the topic of our conversation— was it murder?

"Leave her out of what?" I asked, innocent and polite, my heart in my throat.

Leonard continued to serve his customers, setting two pints on the bar mat and then wiping his forehead on his shoulder. He smiled at me in a friendly and yet creepy way.

"It's only that Lulu and I have been having a few problems—you know the sort. Pauline's trying to help, but I blame Lulu's flatmate. She loves stirring up trouble."

"Who is her flatmate? Where does Lulu live?"

His face went blank, and his eyes looked dead. He turned away and didn't look at me again.

26

Who is her flatmate? Where does Lulu live? Those were important questions—that much was obvious from Leonard's reaction. I might not have an answer, but I could at least ask the questions again—and this time to the police. I hadn't finished my orange squash but had taken my packet of crisps and eaten as I walked. Tipping the last bits into my mouth as I reached the station door, I inhaled a crumb and spent the first five minutes at the desk in a coughing fit. A PC brought me a cup of water, and I sat down in the lobby until my eyes stopped watering and I could breathe without wheezing.

"I'm here to see Detective Sergeant Hopgood," I announced, the reediness of my voice belying the vital need of my request.

"Sergeant Hopgood is out."

"Detective Constable Pye?"

"Gone as well—just this minute."

"While I was coughing?"

"Well, I don't think they did it on purpose—they had a callout. Would you like to leave a message for either one?"

My appearance didn't even warrant an offer to wait in Interview #1—I got the idea the woman at the desk had me pegged as a pest. I would leave a message, but I had no words for my suspicions. First, I needed to introduce the DS to Lulu Ingleby—by way of my photos. Nothing would make any sense otherwise. Foiled in my latest attempt at being a detective, I left the station and retreated to Middlebank. I ate an omelet for my lunch and then sat at my desk the rest of the afternoon thinking about the literary salons and dreaming about the many planning sessions Val and I would need.

Bunter kept an eye on me from the wingback chair near the door, and when I opened my bottom desk drawer—looking for one of the many draft proposals for the salons—he hopped in and nearly sat on a half-empty packet of custard cream biscuits, which I snatched away just in time.

I bit into one as I studied the cat. "Bunter, it's just occurred to me that you might've seen everything that happened that night. If you could talk, you would tell us, wouldn't you? Who brought Trist's body back inside and up to the library?"

He gazed at me with golden eyes—as enigmatic as Lady Fowling's portrait.

Nearly five o'clock—Val would arrive any minute. I burst into top speed, rushing upstairs, brushing my hair and my teeth, and adding a bit of lipstick. Should I change clothes? No, I was meant to be working—dark wool trousers and jacket would have to do. This wasn't a social occasion, after all. Was it?

I heard my phone ringing as I descended the last set of stairs and dashed the rest of the way into my office. When I saw the caller, I started up the stairs again as I answered.

"Dinah, sweetie, are you phoning about your diorama? Because I'm just this minute going up into the attic." I don't usually do two sets of stairs down and immediately do them back up again. I arrived at my flat panting.

"Are you sure, Mum? Because I don't *have* to have it for my project."

"Of course you must have it." Inside my flat, I retrieved the attic key from the drawer of an occasional table covered in unwanted post—flyers and adverts—and set off up yet another flight of stairs, these narrower and steeper. "I know exactly where it is, and it won't take me two ticks to put my hands on it. I'll ring you back and let you know I've got it, all right?"

"Just a text, Mum, that'll do. Or phone me tomorrow. I'm about to pop out to the pub to meet this fellow."

"Fellow?" I wheezed as I reached the landing and made for the attic door. I attempted to mask my interest with an offhand manner. "That's lovely, sweetie. Who is he? What's his name? Is he a student?"

Dinah laughed. "Oh, Mum, really. I tell you what, I'll ask him to send you his CV. Cheers now—bye."

She was joking, but that would be no bad thing.

The few boxes of possessions I'd stored in the attic when I'd first arrived just over three months ago appeared to have multiplied fourfold—or possibly I'd forgotten how many I had. Beyond my stacks of cartons were chairs with broken legs, a sofa with horsehair stuffing spilling out of disintegrating chintz, tables with no tops, and a massive kitchen dresser that would never have fit in my flat or Mrs. Woolgar's. The attic was home to furniture not even fit for the cellar, apparently. I'd grouped my boxes in the middle of the floor, hoping whatever had gnawed at the upholstery and chair legs could see I had nothing to offer. I padded over to begin my search, and looked at my feet. The dust sifted down like snow here in the attic—a thick coat had accumulated on the bare wood floor, almost extinguishing the police footprints made during their search the morning we'd found Trist's body. I'd need to clean my shoes when I finished.

My own scribbled labels—so unlike Lady Fowling's careful writing—made vague references to places in the house or eras of my life. KIT—kitchen. BED—not the entire bed, but extra blankets and such. SPORT. This was a tall box and closed only by folded flaps, and so I took a peek. Oh yes, cricket paraphernalia from Dinah's short-lived and yet outrageously expensive schoolgirl passion. She'd been kitted out well, plus we bought her a good-quality girl's willow bat. I should donate the lot to a club.

Diorama—now where might that be? I spotted a box marked BABY. Dinah as a baby—no, certainly not there. That carton was filled with shiny black shoes that were never walked in and tiny dresses appliquéd with bunnies. And then I remembered something else the carton contained—a lovely china figurine Mum had given us when Dinah was born. It played "Edelweiss" as a dancer slowly twirled. For a while, it was the only thing that would put Dinah to sleep. Even now, I could see her liquid blue eyes watching in wonder as it played and turned, until her lids grew heavy and she drifted off. Tears filled my own eyes as I wondered where my baby girl had gone. I decided to unpack the carton and bring the china figurine back into the light of day, and had shifted two boxes when, in the distance, I heard the front-door buzzer.

I flew down three flights of stairs, shouting, "I'll get it, Mrs. Woolgar," and when I reached the ground floor, I had to put one hand against the door to catch my breath before I opened it.

Val held up an enormous shopping bag from Waitrose. "I'm working for their delivery service now."

"And have you moved your bed into the beer aisle?" I held the door open.

"Yet to be sorted."

In the kitchenette, he spread the food out on the table, and I admired his choices while I put the kettle on. "You've outdone yourself, chef. I'm sure any one of the salads would've been enough." He opened a bakery box, and I exclaimed, "Ooh, mini sausage rolls."

"How's the enquiry? Anything on the nephew?"

He seized that topic with great enthusiasm, and I thought it was to stay off the subject of Wyn.

"It's looking as if Charles Henry might be innocent—more's the pity. But . . . well, I might have found something out." I paused for dramatic effect.

Val waited and then said, "Right then, c'mon, don't hold back."

I retrieved my phone from my office and explained about Lulu. "She works for Pauline, but I don't think Pauline is involved—although, I know I shouldn't play favorites. I had hoped Lulu and Charles Henry were in it together, but that seems unlikely now. Still, she's a dodgy character."

Val hadn't responded. Instead, he was studying one of the photos of Lulu. "We saw her at the Minerva—after we presented to the committee about the salons."

"Yes, we did. Do you know her?"

"I've seen her around college," he said. "In the evenings. She must be a student. Do you want me to find out?"

"Yes, please—because the more we know, the more definite we become." I liked that phrase. "That sounds like something Miss Marple might say, doesn't it?"

I smiled, and Val, watching me, smiled back. He held out my

phone. "Why don't you send that photo to me, and I'll ask the other evening lecturers if they know her?"

"Will do. I meant to take only a couple, but instead got two of those 'bursts.' I don't know how to pull just one photo out, so you'll get about a million of them." I looked up when I finished. "Also, there's a chance that someone—the murderer—might've come into Middlebank even before that night."

I explained what I'd told the police and Val didn't take it well.

"You shouldn't stay here."

"It's been a fortnight since Trist was murdered—and we haven't noticed anything disturbed since then."

"Surely the police found something during the original search? Fingerprints?"

I shook my head. "Either they found our fingerprints or the writers'—all in the usual places—or they found nothing. Except, Trist's leather case was missing."

Val frowned and drummed his fingers on the table. "Still—how can it be safe for you?"

"Now, don't spoil our lovely meal with worry. Let's talk about something else. Notebooks—I have an idea about Lady Fowling's. A series of articles for the newsletter—we could call it *The Real Georgiana Fowling* or *The Mystery of the Woman Behind the Collection*. We could use photos of her handwritten pages. What do you think?"

"That's brilliant, that is."

I went as red as a beetroot.

"Every writer has his or her own way of keeping track of ideas," he said. "You could put out a call for guest pieces about other writers' methods. I'm sure your group would love to talk about theirs."

After that, we got stuck in to our meal, and exchanged stories about our daughters. That led me to Dinah's news that she wanted a car and of my ex hoping to unload his wreck onto her.

"What work does Roger do?" Val asked.

"Bridges," I said, and popped a mini sausage roll in my mouth.

"He builds bridges?"

My mouth full, I shook my head.

"He designs bridges?"

Another shake.

Val's eyes crinkled at the corners as he asked, "Are they dental bridges?"

I snorted into my napkin.

"Palladian bridges," I replied at last. "He's made a specialty for himself—the decorative elements of architecture, particularly bridges, and he consults on the conservation of all those pediments and scallop shells." I took another sausage roll, and added grimly, "It's spotty work."

"Isn't that a Palladian bridge at Prior Park?"

I nodded. Only a brief but exhaustingly uphill walk south of the rail station in Bath sat Prior Park with exquisite views and its own magnificent eighteenth-century bridge. "It was restored in the nineties and is currently in fine fettle. No consultation required."

"How are the writers taking Trist's murder?" Val asked.

We were back to murder, but away from my ex, and that suited me. "I don't know any of them well, but how could it not affect them? Harry and Trist had a relationship a couple of years ago, and that's probably made this harder on her than the others. Peter and Mariella seem all right. Amanda keeps moaning that she doesn't know what they'll do without Trist, yet she's the one who has taken charge."

"It's Amanda I wanted to talk about. These last two class meetings after the murder, her writing has veered away from traditional mystery into—well, I can't quite describe it. Her words are sharp, her characters have hardened, nothing quite makes sense in her stories, and her responses to comments are combative."

"I heard you reading a piece to your students on Monday—only a snatch, but it sounded as if the detective was the killer."

Val nodded. "That was Amanda's—you see what I mean."

"A far cry from Tommy and Tuppence. But Sergeant Hopgood says that murder changes people. Perhaps this evening, we'll get a better idea of how they are coping."

Val sat back in his chair. I rearranged the empty food containers and toyed with my fork, spilling a few grains of couscous onto the table. All at once I couldn't think of a thing to say.

"I sent Wyn a text this morning."

Oh, look, I did have something to say after all.

I gulped. "I broke it off with him in a text. That's awful, isn't it?" I covered my face with my hands, the reality of my actions hitting me full force. "I'm a terrible person."

Val leaned forward and pried my hands away. He kept hold of them, resting his elbows on the table. "You're not. It's normal to feel a bit guilty, isn't it? But how long were you supposed to wait for him to ring you? You did everything you could." I couldn't lift my head but looked up through my lashes and saw him blush. "It's just possible I'm biased, of course."

I smiled.

"Ms. Burke."

Mrs. Woolgar stood in the doorway. Val and I popped out of our chairs, as if we were teenagers caught snogging on the sitting room sofa.

"Hello, Mr. Moffatt," she continued, giving me a moment to compose myself. "Lovely to see you again."

"Mrs. Woolgar. How are you? I've come to keep Hayley company, as it's the evening for the writers group."

She smiled and nodded. "That's very good of you. I only wanted to say I'm off now. Good evening."

I followed her to the door, and Val stayed behind in the kitchenette. Mrs. Woolgar had excellent timing—as she walked away, Peter and Mariella came up from the other direction.

"Hello, good evening." I held the door for them. "I've a visitor this evening—Val Moffatt. He teaches writing at Bath College, and Amanda's taking a course from him. I wonder if you'd mind if we both sat in on the session?"

"Oh yeah," Mariella said, "I'd like that. It's difficult to be only four all of a sudden."

"Dynamics have changed," Peter agreed. "I'd welcome a new face."

"Right, well, I'll make sure it's all right with Harry and Amanda when they arrive. Before you go up, Mariella, I want to show you a photo."

I nipped back for my phone, and brought Val out with me, introducing him to Peter and Mariella plus Harry, who had arrived with her, laptop clutched to her chest.

"Are you coming up for the group, Mr. Moffatt?" she asked. "Amanda's said lovely things about your course."

Val said he would be there. We remained in the entry, and Harry took a keen interest when I showed Lulu's photo to Mariella.

"No, sorry, don't know her."

Harry asked me, "Can I have a word before we go up?"

"No time for idle talk," Amanda announced on the doorstep. "Up to the library with you, chop-chop."

"Val and Hayley are coming up this evening," Peter said, shooting a quick look at Mariella and Harry. "We think it's fine—all right with you?"

Amanda's left eyebrow jumped. She scanned the group, and then said, "Lovely—the more the merrier."

* * *

B efore you begin," I said when they were seated round the library table, "I want to say thanks for letting us sit in."

"You're always welcome, Hayley," Mariella said.

They'd always invited me, but once had been enough until now.

"Well, yes, I know that, but I don't want to be a bother—except I do want to tell you about an interesting find I've made here at Middlebank. Lady Fowling kept notebooks—I've come across an entire carton of them in storage. She wrote about everything, from detectives to cooking. And it got me to wondering, do all writers do that? I've noticed you have your works in progress on your computers and that you print pieces out—but do you have a place to jot down ideas and that sort of thing?"

Harry plunged her hand into her bag and brought out a small black notebook that had swelled with extra bits of paper folded up and inserted between pages. It might once have had an elastic band to keep it closed, but now it was wrapped several times over with a thick rubber band. She held it up proudly.

Peter looked deep into his canvas bag, rummaged round, and came up with a spiral-bound notepad, the metal pulled out of shape. "I go through about one a month," he said. "I've got them in order taking up an entire set of shelves."

"Well, that's grand," Amanda said. "Now, I suppose we'd better get started."

"Yes, sorry," I whispered. "I didn't mean to—"

"Not at all, Hayley," she replied briskly. "Lovely to have you here. Right, who's first?"

We were observers only. At least, I was—the proverbial bump on the log. But the writers sought out Val's opinion and I enjoyed watching him in action. He had the most amazing knack of offering both praise and criticism. No, make that critique. Val didn't voice disapproval over the writing but offered a balanced evaluation. He told Harry that her representation of Miss Marple as a single mother who had given up her child imbued the amateur detective with a humanity seldom seen. Harry's eyes had filled with tears. Peter hadn't cried, but he did look rather chuffed when Val commented that using current celebrities as the characters in *The Murder of Roger Ackroyd* brought to light the shallowness of their lives.

Mariella would read her piece next after the short break. Harry asked Val a question about point of view, and I took the opportunity to show Amanda the photo of Lulu. "It's nothing, really—she works for a friend. Have you ever seen her?"

"All right if I go downstairs to make the tea, Hayley?" Mariella asked.

"Oh, tea, that's right. No, I'll do it." I turned back to Amanda. "Take your time with the photos. There are loads of them—my fault—but you need to look at only the first few. Everyone else has seen them."

"Would you like help?" Val asked as I passed him.

"Oh, I don't think so," I murmured. "You're too much of a hit here."

In the kitchenette, I had filled the kettle, set it on the hob, and took out the large teapot. When the front door buzzed I paused, wondering if the woman at the desk in the police station had told Sergeant Hopgood of my earlier visit. Had he stopped by to find out what I had wanted? I would need to get my phone back from Amanda to show him the photos of Lulu.

Those were my thoughts as I opened the door, and so I wasn't prepared for what waited on the other side.

Wyn.

"What are you doing here?" I asked.

His computer bag was slung across his shoulder—the strap had caught the lapel of his jacket, turning it up, while his tie looped under and over, the end sticking straight out. His usually boyish face was pale, with the shadow of a frown across his brow.

"I mean"—I was already on the wrong foot—"come in. I didn't realize you were back from Brussels."

"When I saw your text, I changed my flight and came into Bristol, and got the train." He stepped in, but didn't move far.

The guilt that had flitted around in the corners of my mind throughout the day grew large and dark and difficult to see through. But then a tiny thought pierced the blackness—my text had been sent more than twelve hours ago and there must be dozens of flights from Brussels. The entire journey to Bath couldn't be much more than two hours.

"I'm sorry, Wyn, but you wouldn't answer your phone. It's what I tried to explain on Sunday."

"You caught me at a bad time on Sunday."

"Yes, and I'm sorry about that, too, but if we'd only had a chance to talk—"

"It's him, isn't it?"

My blood ran cold. "Who?"

Wyn's gaze darted round the entry. "That bloke I met last time I was here."

I threw back my shoulders and reminded myself I had nothing to feel guilty about. It helped, but not much.

"I introduced you to Val Moffatt from Bath College. As I've told you, the Society and the college are coordinating a series of literary salons beginning in January, and Val was kind enough to come here to Middlebank for a planning session."

"To your bedroom?"

"Don't be—" I took a calming breath. "To my office here on the ground floor. As I've mentioned before, the entirety of Middlebank is not my home."

The frown was no longer a shadow. Wyn stuck out his lower lip. "Hayley, I proposed to you."

"Proposed?" I choked out. "'Let's get married!' You call that a proposal? You could've been asking me out for fish and chips, for all I could tell." I heard voices from upstairs and remembered the library door stood wide open. A movement on the landing caught my eye, and I glanced up, trying to see who it was. When I turned back, the most awful sight met my eyes.

Wyn was down on one knee. He grabbed my hand, held it tight, and looked up at me.

"Hayley Burke, I love you. Will you marry me?"

27

I heard the library door click closed, shutting off the voices, and I knew, I was certain, that Val had been standing on the landing and had heard and seen everything.

"*Get up!*" I yanked on the strap of Wyn's computer bag and dragged him to his feet. "Have you heard nothing I've said? A marriage proposal will not fix this—we are too different. I will not move to London. Your business is your life, but it's not the sort of life I can share—there's no room for me in it. But it's what makes you happy, and I will not try to change that. So it's over, Wyn—you must see that."

He straightened his lapel and tie and adjusted the strap. "I thought that was what you wanted," he complained. "To be married. I thought I was giving you your heart's desire."

My heart's desire? Were those the choices in life, either marriage or occasional couplings? Surely there was something between. The anger drained away, leaving me empty and tired and in great need of talking with Val.

"No, Wyn, it isn't my heart's desire."

I heard the kettle, its whistle gaining force and rising in pitch. The library door opened and Harry called down, "Do you need help with the tea, Hayley?"

"No, thanks—I'll be right there." I nodded up the stairs and said to Wyn, "The writers are here, and I've got to get back to it. You all right? Can I get you something? Cup of tea?"

Wyn's head bobbed somewhere between a nod and a shake. "No, I . . ."

His phone rang. I motioned for him to answer and walked back to the kitchenette. I'd leave him to it, and when I came through with the tea, we'd have a properly sweet—but brief—goodbye. I would wish him best of luck with Myrtle and his entire business, and he would leave with no hard feelings.

I poured up the pot and put milk, sugar, and mugs on the tray alongside a packet of shortbread fingers. I returned to the entry to see Wyn walking out the door while on his phone.

"No, Tommy," he was saying, "drone delivery won't work in the City, the population's too dense. We can't deal with airspace problems now, we've got to stick to what we know—the pavement. Although, saying that, we must sort out Myrtle's ability to detect foot traffic, or we'll be buggered. What if she crashes into some rich American from California—we'd never get overseas investments. I'm on my way now, let's have another look at the details before we go any further."

He didn't even turn, but reached round behind and pulled the door closed.

I continued up to the library, where Mariella began reading as soon as the tea was distributed. She was followed by Amanda, her piece sounding innocuous, and familiar. The glances darting round the room told me she'd gone back to rewriting those ten pages.

Through the rest of the evening, Val wouldn't meet my eye.

What did he think had happened downstairs? Didn't he trust me? I spent the remainder of the time annoyed and hurt and scared, and wanting it all to be over as quickly as possible.

Peter took the tea tray downstairs and then left with Mariella. Amanda looked set to rush out but paused long enough to leave my phone on the hall stand and say, "Sorry, Hayley, I didn't recognize her." She leaned closer and added quietly, "I handed your phone to Mariella, too. Hope that was all right."

"She'd already seen the photos, but thanks." Amanda scooted out the door before I could wish her good evening.

That left Val and me alone in the entry. He stood at the bottom of the stairs while I kept near the door—a vast ocean of misunderstanding between us.

"I had only stepped out onto the landing to ask if you needed help," he said. "I didn't mean to overhear you and Wyn."

"It's all right—I'm glad you heard."

He shifted, looked down at his shoes, and put his hands in his jacket pockets. "I don't want to get between the two of you."

"That would be impossible to do, because Wyn and I are no longer together."

"I saw him propose—he must care for you. And if I have, in any way—"

I crossed my arms and stuck out my chin. "You should've stayed on the landing to hear the rest. The part where I told him no, I would not marry him, and he was so entirely heartbroken that when he got a call from his business partner, he walked out, wittering on about Myrtle's navigation system and trying to land an American investor. It was quite touching."

"Look, Hayley, maybe we should—" Val took one step toward me with his hand out, and Harry appeared from the kitchenette.

"Sorry," she whispered, lifting her shoulders and scrunching up her face. "I always seem to be interrupting, don't I? I stayed to tidy up the kitchen. The thing is, Hayley, could I have a quick word? And then I swear I'm gone."

"No need to hurry," Val said. "I'm just off. Good evening."

"Thank you for attending our group, Mr. Moffatt," Harry called after him. "Your comments were quite helpful." Val acknowledged her with a wave. Harry and I watched him walk down the pavement, the light from the streetlamps turning his green jacket gray.

"Do you think he'll come back?" she asked.

"I don't know."

I took my time closing the door, blinking like mad to empty my eyes of unwanted tears. I sniffed and faced Harry and smiled. "So, now, what did you want to tell me?"

"Well, so." Harry looked over her shoulder, although we were alone. "It's your photos of that woman."

"Lulu Ingleby."

"Lulu. There were a great many of them—"

"I did that by accident. But you could see her well enough in the first few."

"Did you show them to the others?"

"Yes. Peter saw them earlier today, and I showed Mariella before we went up. And Amanda just before I came down to make the tea. No one recognized her."

"The photos covered a few seconds of time," Harry said. "Did you look at all of them? Because—can I show you?"

I grabbed my phone off the hall stand, opened *photos*, and was met with a shot of Bunter I'd taken a week ago as he lay asleep on the bottom step. I flipped forward, but there was nothing. I flipped the other way and went further back in time.

"Where have they gone?" This was no time for a camera malfunction, but no amount of furious swiping brought up the bursts of Lulu.

Harry tried and I tried again.

"Maybe they were deleted," Harry suggested.

"No, that's not—wait, though. Even if they were, they'd still be in 'recently deleted'!" I zeroed in on that last-hope file and found it empty.

"They've vanished—all of them." My words echoed in my head. "What's happened?"

"When you gave your phone to Amanda, did she give it back?" Harry asked.

"She brought it downstairs at the end and set it there on the hall stand. She told me she had handed it to Mariella, but Mariella had already seen them."

"So the photos were there when you gave Amanda the phone, and now they're gone."

"Harry, are you saying Amanda deleted all those photos of Lulu Ingleby?"

"I'm saying that at the end of the second burst of photos, I saw one that showed Amanda and Lulu talking."

28

Harry peppered me with questions about Lulu Ingleby, but I replied only vaguely, and instead countered with my own queries. "Are you sure they were talking to each other? Could you tell their expressions? Friendly? Angry?"

"It was definitely an enounter of some kind. And I wouldn't say either of them looked happy. Why won't you tell me who she is? Is she involved in Trist's murder?"

"She works for Pauline, who cleans for us. If she is involved, the police will find out—I will ring them first thing in the morning. Better still, I'll go in to the station."

"I'll meet you there," Harry said quickly, and then just as fast she moaned. "No, I can't. We've a massive order for a wedding, and I won't have a minute to myself."

"Just as well—the police probably won't tell me what they know. Now, off you go. Will you be all right walking home? I mean, are you still nervous about being watched?"

She gave me a sad smile. "I'm not nervous, no. After I said it aloud—that I felt Trist was watching me—it sort of made me feel better. But, if I believe that, does it make me daft?"

I certainly hoped not.

M rs. Woolgar and I were like ships passing in the night—she returned and we nodded to each other as I took the stairs. Tomorrow, at our morning briefing, we would talk.

In my flat, I worked over and over this new evidence. Amanda knew—or at the very least had encountered—Lulu, but she had lied about it. Why? How well did they know each other? I drew up connections in my mind the way Sergeant Hopgood had drawn lines to show where the suspects had walked the night of Trist's murder.

Amanda lived in Grove Street.

I had seen Lulu in Grove Street. She must live there, too.

Amanda and Lulu knew each other. They could be flatmates.

After that initial connection, my suppositions drifted into wild ideas. Lulu had access to houses through Cleaned by Pauline—was she part of a gang that carried out those "no sign of forced entry" break-ins? Had she gained access to Middlebank by stealing the key and code from Pauline? Had she somehow involved her flatmate? Had Trist discovered this and confronted them—or was he part of the gang? After all, he had been accused of theft five years ago. And acquitted, I reminded myself—much to Mrs. Woolgar's dismay.

I pulled the online news site up on my phone—the "rag" that ran the brief about Trist's murder and where I'd seen the item about the break-ins. There might be more clues there than I'd first noticed.

More than a clue—there was an update. Another break-in had occurred only that afternoon—a quiet street, empty during daylight hours after everyone had left for work. But someone had noticed unusual activity and the police were notified. Sergeant Hopgood and Constable Pye had been on a callout this afternoon—and now a woman had been detained and was helping them with their enquiries.

"Detained"? "Helping"? Anyone could read between those lines—they'd got her, a suspect in the robberies.

But who was it? Lulu? Amanda? Pauline? No, wait—not Amanda, because she attended the writers group this evening. Did I have this completely wrong?

I could ask myself questions until my head burst, but none would be answered until tomorrow, so I took a bath, sinking up to my chin in hot water. Only when the bath cooled did I get out, dry off, and go to bed—where my mind continued to spin, caroming from one potential disaster to another. I could or could not still have a job as curator at The First Edition Society when Charles Henry got finished with us. The police might or might not be closing in on Trist's killer. I might or might not have a dinner date for Friday.

I needed to fill my mind with happy, peaceful images or I would never get one second's sleep, and so I inhaled deeply and exhaled slowly. I thought of Val. I thought of the seaside. I thought of Dinah's baby eyes following the china figurine as it twirled. I thought of Val again. At last, I fell asleep, and awoke rested and ready for my day at seventeen minutes past two in the morning.

For the next half hour, I stared at the ceiling, and then decided there was nothing else for it—I arose, made tea, and went back to reading Lady Fowling's notebooks.

Strange thoughts come to one's mind in the middle of the night. As I ran my hand over a marbled cover, I again had the sense I'd seen one of these exercise books before. Mrs. Woolgar thought they'd all been packed away, but a stray must've been left behind.

Where had I seen it? Closing my eyes, I cleared my mind and waited for the answer. Nothing came—nothing except the notion of putting my slippers on and having a nose round my office.

The light from my flat illuminated my way down the first set of stairs, where I held up outside the library and studied Lady Fowling's portrait in the soft glow.

"If you know something, you should just tell me, don't you think?" I asked.

Think for yourself, she responded. *You're good at that. You've had to be.*

How should I react to this—be pleased with her confidence in me or worried for my sanity talking to a painting? And also, shouldn't I look in the library? But without making a conscious decision, I continued to my office, switched on all the lamps, and blinked in the brightness.

"Why here?"

There was only one way to find out—a search. I sat down, moved my laptop to the floor, and began with two stacks of unread mystery magazines, holding each one by its binding and giving it a shake. Finding nothing hiding between the pages, I set to cleaning out the drawers.

That's when Bunter appeared at my door.

"Sorry to disturb you, cat, but I'm glad of the company."

He stretched—first, extending his front legs until they were almost flat on the floor and his bottom in the air, then reversing. Only when he'd finished did he saunter round the desk, sit down, and stare at the bottom drawer.

"I'm afraid I ate the last of the custard creams you saw in there," I told him, opening it as proof. But he might not have believed me—he stood on his hind legs, reached a paw in, and began an excavation, his claws catching on papers deep down. He shook them loose and continued, as if determined to reach to the bottom.

"Bunter, what is it? Not a spider, I hope, because if it is, I'll leave you to it and go make the tea."

He had sunk his foreleg up to his shoulder. It caught and he struggled to release it, tugging and making noises in his throat until at last his paw broke free and his prize went sailing through the air. A catnip mouse.

"When did you put that in there?" I asked, but Bunter paid no heed, and instead crept forward on his belly, stalking his prey, which had landed near the fireplace.

"Why ever have I saved all this?" I asked, pulling out a mountain of papers. I set the pile on my lap, and half of them slipped to the floor, and when I leaned over to retrieve them, I spied it at the bottom of the drawer.

A worn exercise notebook, the sort with the marbled cover. As I reached for it, the memory came back to me. I'd found it in the library on a Thursday, the day after the writers group had met. I hadn't seen anything out of place the night before, but upon inspection the next morning, Mrs. Woolgar's eagle eyes had spotted the library stepladder moved, and when I walked to the other side of the table, I'd spied the notebook on the floor and had snatched it up so she wouldn't have even more to complain about.

I had assumed one of the writers had left it, and so without a second look, I'd taken it downstairs and dropped it in my desk drawer, intending to ask them the following week. But it had become buried under draft proposals for literary salons and so forgotten. At that point, I had had no hint of Lady Fowling's cartonful of notebooks, and so it had never occurred to me it might be hers. But now, on closer inspection, I could see her name in spidery script in the corner—I hadn't noticed it before because a thick line had been drawn through it with a darker pen.

I opened the notebook and cried out, sending Bunter racing from my office.

"Who did this?" I hissed.

Not only the cover, but also the contents of the exercise book had been defaced. A heavier hand with a darker pen had scrawled comments in the margins, crossed out words in lists, and written over household notes as if the sheet had been clean. On one page, Lady Fowling's scrolly hand explained her love of St. Mary Mead and why Miss Marple's soft spirit and sharp mind represented a modern woman of the time. Across the top had been scratched: DON'T GO OUT AT NIGHT.

Who? Who shouldn't go out at night? Was this a reference to Trist's writing about Miss Marple and zombies? Or was it a warning?

In another entry, her ladyship had divided a page into two columns titled *Tommy and Tuppence versus Nick and Nora.* I knew next to nothing about Agatha Christie's married sleuths, but I'd seen the old films with William Powell and Myrna Loy. Lady Fowling had taken a lighthearted approach to the battle—she gave points to Nick and Nora for their witty banter and Nora for "those gorgeous evening gowns."

But I had trouble reading the light spidery script because across the page had been scrawled: SHOW SOME RESPECT.

In contrast to Lady Fowling's delicate cursive, the heavy hand and crude lettering radiated anger. An inky pen, it had left smudges, bleeding through, and making an imprint on the opposite page. My skin turned cold and clammy and I shivered in my thin nightshirt. Who would care if Tommy and Tuppence lost the vote to another sleuthing couple? I could think of only one person.

I switched off the lamps and took the notebook upstairs. It was going to be a long night.

Did I sleep? It didn't seem so, but I must've, because when my eyes popped open, sun streamed through the sitting room windows. I dressed in a hurry, downed a few gulps of tea, and walked round with a half slice of toast hanging out of my mouth as I dressed. Before I closed the door of my flat, I checked my bag—yes, I had everything I needed.

On my way downstairs, a text arrived from Pauline.

Must cancel this morning. Sorry. Pub.

Was she really at the pub or was she at the police station, "helping with their enquiries"?

Tugging on the hem of my jacket, I stepped inside Mrs. Woolgar's office. "Hello, good morning. No Pauline today, I'm afraid—she's helping her brother out at the pub."

Mrs. Woolgar stood behind her desk, reaching for a ledger on the shelf in the corner. She wore a long-sleeved, pumpkin-colored dress with a well-cut bodice and a wide scalloped collar that sported a brooch as big as the palm of my hand—topaz-colored rhinestones in a Celtic knot design. She pulled it off well.

"And how was your evening?" she asked.

Personally, dismal, and—as far as it concerned the enquiry— rather unnerving. "All right, yes, fine. I need to step out for a bit— can we put off our briefing?"

I had carefully thought this through—there was no need to share my fears until I'd learned what I could from the police. Then I would tell her all.

The secretary scrutinized me. I responded with a cheerful smile. "If that's all right with you," I added.

"Yes, of course. Mr. Rennie is coming round later."

"Is he? Should I stay?"

"No need, he won't be here until just before lunch."

"Is it about Charles Henry?"

Mrs. Woolgar nodded solemnly. "Yes, I believe it is, but he's shared no details."

* * *

Whatever news our solicitor, Duncan Rennie, had concerning Charles Henry Dill and his underhanded efforts to destroy The First Edition Society did not—for the moment—concern me. There would be time enough for that later.

The Minerva lay in almost a direct line on my journey to the police station—if I were to be suspected of snooping, that would be my defense. *I only wanted to see for myself you were all right,* I practiced as I turned off the High Street onto Northumberland Place.

The pub door stood ajar, and the sounds that emerged of glasses rattling and chairs scraping across the floor signaled someone was about. I stuck my head in. Pauline, alone, and wearing her cleaning coveralls and bandanna, paced behind the bar, muttering to herself and rubbing her forehead, her journey to and fro punctuated by abrupt stops to shift bottles or move glasses or pick up beer mats and put them down again.

"Hello?"

Pauline spun round, and the bar towel she held hit the front row of small tonic bottles and dragged them off the shelf. They crashed to the floor, and she froze, staring at the mess, wringing her hands, and shaking.

I ran to her, saying, "God, I'm sorry, Pauline. I didn't mean to startle you. Here, you stand back and let me do this."

"I canceled this morning," she said, her voice shaky.

"Yes, I know—it's all right. I only wanted to check on you." I steered her to a barstool, found a broom, and swept the broken glass and fizzing liquid under the counter. It would have to do for now. I remained on the serving side, leaned over the bar, and took Pauline's hands. They were cold, and she trembled. I looked into her red-rimmed eyes. "Tell me what's wrong."

It burst out of her. "She's been nicked!"

"Lulu?"

Pauline pulled her hands away. "Police have her for theft. Those places that had been broken into, but not broken into, because they had—"

"No sign of forced entry."

Pauline gulped. "Yeah."

"Were they your houses—for your cleaning business?"

"No, not mine. I don't know a thing about those break-ins. But Leonard does, I'm sure of it. My brother—he's thick as a brick, God love him. What will they do to him?"

"But the police know Lulu works for you—and you work at Middlebank."

Pauline panted, her eyes dark with fear. Slowly, she nodded. "They'll think I had something to do with what happened there, won't they?"

"Did Lulu get the key and code for Middlebank from you?"

"Are you asking did I hand them over?" Her voice rose, loud, shrill, and bordering on hysteria.

I locked my eyes on her, and she didn't look away. With as much confidence as I could muster, I said, "I am not accusing you, Pauline. But we need to sort this out."

She nodded, and her trembling subsided. "I've thought and thought," she said. "I'm quite careful with my customers' keys and such—it's my business and my reputation, after all. When I'm here, I lock my bag in the safe in the office." She pointed with her chin to the kitchen behind me. "But then there's the little princess swanning in and out of the place, never saying what she's up to. I caught her with the safe open. Had Leonard given her the combination, or had she stolen that, too? I thought she was after money, but now I see." Pauline's voice dropped to a wobbly whisper. "So, now it's not only theft—it's murder."

"Pauline, where does Lulu live?"

She straightened up and sniffed, regaining a sense of herself. "Grove Street. I know that, you see, because I always check on new employees. I didn't just take Leonard's word for her, you know. She had references, and I rang every one."

"Where on Grove Street?"

29

I need to see Sergeant Hopgood."

The woman behind the desk at the police station might've thought she could put me off with her world-weary sigh, but I had well-honed antennae for such theatrics, being only a few years out of rearing a teenager.

"I have vital evidence in the Trist Cummins murder enquiry," I added. "And it involves the woman being questioned in the string of break-ins."

That got her in gear. In two minutes, DC Pye escorted me through the locked lobby door and into the nether regions of the station. When he passed Interview #1, I paused.

"Aren't we going in here?"

"In use." He nodded to a small drop-down sign beside the door that read *In Use*.

"Is that where Lulu is?"

Kenny Pye's black eyebrows didn't have quite the same communication skills as Hopgood's, but when they knit together, I got the message and took a seat in Interview #2 next door.

He left, and I stared at the walls. They'd better be quick about it—adrenaline would keep me awake for only so long, rock-hard chair or no. But both officers appeared almost immediately and sat across from me.

Hopgood looked tired, alert, and annoyed, and I knew I'd better get to it.

"Lulu Ingleby is flatmates with Amanda Seabrook."

The sergeant scrutinized me as Pye opened a file folder he'd brought in.

"How do you know Lulu Ingleby?" Hopgood asked.

I explained, strongly emphasizing my belief that Pauline knew nothing about what was going on.

"Amanda Seabrook lives on Grove Street," the DS replied, "and Lulu Ingleby has given an address off the Old Fosse Road."

"No, not true. But she could've given Leonard's address."

"Ms. Lunn's brother—we're looking for him now."

"Here's what I think. Maybe when Amanda found out Lulu had broken into those other houses, she told Lulu about Middlebank. Maybe she told her there were valuables there in order to get Lulu's help breaking in."

I heard all the *maybes* coming out of my mouth and despaired. Would he think I'd gone round the bend?

"Why would Ms. Seabrook want to return to Middlebank on her own?" Pye asked.

"I don't know," I admitted. "But look at this." I took the exercise book out of my bag and laid it on the table.

"Lady Fowling kept notes on everything in her life," I explained. "Detective stories, recipes, diary entries from when Sir John was alive. I've only recently come across them—they were all packed away in a carton in the cellar. Except this one must've been left elsewhere—maybe in the library. And I believe Amanda found it. Someone's written over her ladyship's work all the way through—take a look."

Hopgood took a ballpoint pen out of his pocket and—pen nib sheathed—flipped open a page. Fingerprints. Why hadn't I thought of fingerprints?

"I'm sorry, I shouldn't've touched it. It never occurred to me it was evidence until after I'd seen what was inside."

"Not to worry, Ms. Burke," Hopgood murmured, turning another page or two. "It looks as if someone has done the fingerprinting work for us."

In the corner of one page, in what looked like the same black ink as the scrawls, was a perfect fingerprint. And that reminded me of something.

"Sergeant Hopgood, can you lift fingerprints with Sellotape and reapply them elsewhere?"

The eyebrows quivered. "Did you read that in a detective story?"

"Sort of—Amanda wrote about it for one of Val Moffatt's classes. One character was blackmailing another, who threatened to do that."

"How very imaginative. Just where did you come across this notebook, Ms. Burke?"

"It was on the floor of the library on a Thursday—the morning after the group met. The night before, I'd checked they'd put the room in order after they left, but we always have another look the next morning. That's when Mrs. Woolgar noticed the library ladder out of place and I saw this."

"Which Thursday morning?"

"The week before Trist was killed," I replied. Hopgood drummed his fingertips on the table, and I took advantage of the pause. "Amanda is strong. And quite possessive. I saw her push Peter almost to the ground when she thought he'd taken her satchel. And he's a sturdy fellow. Trist was tall, but as you said, weak. She could've carried him into Middlebank and up to the library."

Hopgood and Pye looked at each other out of the corners of their eyes.

"Since Trist died," I persisted, "she's changed a great deal. Without any discussion, she took over leadership of the group, and her writing has become more aggressive, more violent."

Still no reaction, and I faltered. It had made so much sense to me in the middle of the night.

"Am I joining up dots that don't even exist?" I asked.

"You've certainly given us reason to have another chat with Amanda Seabrook," Hopgood said. "Now, if you'll excuse us—"

"Lulu! Hang on, I have photos. That is, had." I dug in my bag for my phone. "I took photos that show Lulu and Amanda talking. Amanda told me she didn't recognize Lulu, but she lied."

"How is it you have these photos?" Hopgood asked.

"I . . . happened to see her when I . . . well, how else was I going to prove it to you?"

"It is not for you to prove or disprove—your suspicions would be enough for us."

They wouldn't be enough for Jane Marple—if she'd had the opportunity and an iPhone, she would've done the same thing.

"Will you show us?" DC Pye asked.

"I can't—Amanda deleted them." I could see a sharp gleam in Hopgood's eye, and so drove my point home. "Yes, destroying evidence." I related what happened and offered up my phone, adding, "Could you find them again, do you think?"

Hopgood deferred to Pye, who shrugged. "I can ask IT."

"No—wait!" I practically levitated when the thought hit me. "Val has them—he recognized Lulu because he'd seen her around Bath College during evening classes. I sent them to him, and he was going to find out if she was a student. Shall I ring him and ask?"

"No need," the sergeant replied. "Pye—don't we have Mr. Moffatt's number?"

I didn't see why they wouldn't let me phone him. It would give me a reason to enquire about our dinner date.

Kenny Pye stepped away from the table, and the DS and I sat quietly as I attempted to listen in on the phone conversation. "Mr. Moffatt? This is Detective Constable Pye, Avon and Somerset Police."

I hid a smile, thinking he could've identified himself another way—*Mr. Moffatt? It's your writing student Kenny Pye. I'm here with Detective Alehouse*...

I cut my eyes at Hopgood, who had his head bent as he studied details in the folder.

And in that moment, I saw what happened. What an odd feeling, the way thoughts—the clues and evidence—seemed to weave themselves together as of their own accord.

As Pye talked with Val, I said, "Sergeant, I think Amanda believed Trist had stolen that notebook from her."

Hopgood's head shot up.

"I think he knew she was getting back into Middlebank," I continued with confidence. "He might've followed her that night. I remember he said to me once that no one in the group should have an advantage over the others. He might've been talking about Amanda and the notebook and going back into the library. And so he confronted her and they argued out on Gravel Walk."

"That was quite an argument if she threw him against the railing post," Hopgood said, but in a thoughtful way, as if he, too, could see it.

Kenny Pye had ended his call and said, "All right, boss—he'll bring over his phone after his morning class ends, about twelve."

Hopgood stood with a smile. "Thank you, Ms. Burke. Now, I suggest you carry on with your own job, and let us do ours."

"But didn't I just—"

Didn't I just what—solve their murder for them? *What did you expect, Hayley—a medal?*

DC Pye escorted me to the lobby and watched me walk out. I contemplated sitting on Harry's low stone wall across from the station until Val arrived, but it was only ten now, and I'd had enough of wet bottoms for one week.

Instead, I took myself to Waitrose and had a Bath bun and a coffee and a morose stroll down the ready-meal aisle, remembering when Val and I had met here. I bought a sandwich for my lunch later and left.

But my feet dragged on the way back to Middlebank until they stopped moving altogether when I arrived in Queen Square. I took a bench and admired the cherry trees at the south entrance, putting on their brief autumn display, leaves catching fire in shades of orange and red. The square was a peaceful place known mostly for the tall obelisk in its center, which had been set there in 1738 by dandy and eighteenth-century fashionista Beau Nash. My former place of employment, the Jane Austen Centre, was only steps away. I had often come out to the square for my lunch and heard countless tour guides relate the history of the place. Perhaps it wouldn't be long before I'd be having my lunch here again after I got turfed out of The First Edition Society and Middlebank. Would the Centre take me back as assistant to the assistant curator?

With such depressing thoughts filling my head, I nonetheless put on a brave face for Mrs. Woolgar and Duncan Rennie when I arrived at Middlebank. I heard their voices in the secretary's office and found her behind the desk and Mr. Rennie sitting across from her. He rose when he saw me.

Our solicitor must be in the general vicinity of sixty years old. I had only ever seen him dressed as he was today—that is to say, impeccably. He wore a gray, pinstriped, three-piece suit with a smoky-blue handkerchief peeking out of a breast pocket. He had a shiny face and slicked-back brown to silver hair. His normal countenance—at least what I was accustomed to seeing—was a fretful look, as if business matters ate away at him constantly. Perhaps it was a hazard of his profession. But when he did offer a rare smile, all that worry fell away, and he gave off the air of a man who quite enjoyed the world.

He broke into a smile now, an impish grin. "Ms. Burke—we've got him."

My hand flew to my throat. "Charles Henry? Not—not for the murder, I suppose?"

Rennie's good spirits flagged slightly. "No, I'm terribly sorry about that, but still, we can put a stop to this latest trickery. He thought to break the Society's status as a charitable trust by saying that detective fiction shouldn't be considered a contribution to the arts. Well, as is his wont, he went about it in the most cack-handed way." The solicitor's face colored slightly. "Please forgive me."

It's a proper gentleman who apologizes for using a word that was more slang than offensive. "It's all right, Mr. Rennie, we all know what he's like."

"We do indeed," Mrs. Woolgar added.

"Suffice it to say," Rennie continued, "Lady Fowling had instructed that the governing documents be written in accordance with the law, and try as he might, Dill could find nothing untoward. The Society is solid, as he probably well knew. I believe he does these things only to make as much trouble as he can."

I nodded. "He's all mouth and no trousers."

The solicitor sputtered, and Mrs. Woolgar pushed her glasses farther up the bridge of her nose.

"Sergeant Hopgood said that," I offered, by way of excuse.

"Well, he was able to put the wind up the first curator, Ms. Merton, and so I'm delighted that you were not frightened off."

"Thank you, Mr. Rennie." My eyes pricked with tears. "Of course, without Mrs. Woolgar, I wouldn't've been able to hold up."

Mrs. Woolgar blushed, took off her glasses, and put them back on again. "We cannot see Lady Fowling's vision dimmed."

I scratched my nose so she wouldn't catch my smile—good on her, we weren't about to wallow in sentiment, were we?

"And so"—I wanted to be quite clear about this—"Charles Henry has told you he's backing off?"

"Not in so many words," Rennie said carefully, casting his eyes toward Mrs. Woolgar.

"It has to do with that other matter," the secretary said to me, her voice heavy with import.

This was no time for euphemisms. "You mean his affair with Maureen Frost?"

Before Mrs. Woolgar could object to such language, the buzzer sounded.

"Oh." The secretary stood. "That could be—"

"Don't bother, I'll go."

Maureen Frost stood on the front step with a commanding presence that had been missing from our other encounters—board meetings in the library. Now I could see her on the stage—how had I overlooked this? She had a deep burgundy scarf swept to one side, tied at the shoulder and tucked just under her steel-gray pageboy, and wore a black dress with a cinched waist and lipstick of a shade that perfectly matched the scarf. Behind her, wearing an oleaginous smile and his brown plaid suit, stood Charles Henry.

"Hello," I said warmly. "Do come in—both of you. I was just this minute having a chat with Mrs. Woolgar and Mr. Rennie."

"Thank you, Hayley," Ms. Frost said. As she walked by me, I half expected her to give the command "Come along" to her companion, but he followed without direction.

Mrs. Woolgar and Mr. Rennie emerged from the secretary's office, and we all stood in the entry. I felt unexpectedly lighthearted. "Shall I pop the kettle on?" I asked.

"No need, but thank you," Maureen replied. "We are on our way to lunch at the Gainsborough and only wanted to stop and tell the two of you—and you, too, Duncan, as you are here—that . . . well, Charles Henry?"

Dill gave Maureen a glance and she returned a warm look of encouragement. He nodded in reply, stepped forward, and put his hands behind his back as if about to recite a poem for a school award. "Mrs. Woolgar and Ms. Burke, I'm quite sorry if my actions have caused any concern on your part as to the stability of the Society. Old wounds, you know. Our pasts shape us more than we know or would like to admit, and I see now that events in my childhood may have colored the way I see what my aunt considered her greatest accomplishment. I do apologize and I withdraw any statements I made that could have in any way been interpreted as an accusation or a"—the word caught in his throat, until Maureen touched his arm and he coughed out—"threat."

Maureen then summed up Dill's pronouncement with, "Once I appealed to Charles Henry's better nature, he understood the distress he'd caused."

This was followed by a stunned silence in which I, for one, struggled with the thought of Dill having a better nature. Fortunately, Maureen saved us from responding by glancing at her watch and saying, "Lunch at one thirty."

Charles Henry stood at attention. "Yes, well—good afternoon to you all." He offered his arm to Maureen, and to us, a close-mouthed smile. I couldn't quite be sure it didn't have clenched teeth behind it.

The three of us stared at the door after they'd gone.

"Do you believe him?" I asked.

"A leopard doesn't change its spots," Mrs. Woolgar said.

"And yet," Mr. Rennie commented, "there's no point in worrying about his next attempt until it comes."

"Right, well," I said. "Thank you, Mr. Rennie, for delivering the good news. Now, if you'll excuse me."

I retreated to my office and took my sandwich from my bag, but came out only a moment later. Charles Henry had pushed the murder investigation to the back of my mind, but I needed to tell Mrs. Woolgar about Lulu and Amanda. I paused before I reached her door when I heard the solicitor say, "Are you sure you're all right, Glynis? You know you don't have to stay here."

"Yes, Duncan, thank you, I do know that," the secretary replied. "But I believe it's best for us—Ms. Burke and me—to remain. What would it look like to the world if the only employees of the Society turn tail and run over this incident? And surely the police are close to getting it sorted."

Mrs. Woolgar emerged from her office as she spoke, and we met face-to-face, both turning a bit pink.

"Oh, Ms. Burke," she said, averting her eyes. "Mr. Rennie and I are just going to lunch."

"Yes, lunch." My chicken and stuffing sandwich waited for me on my desk.

"Not the Gainsborough, I'm afraid," Rennie said, emerging from the office.

"Certainly not," Mrs. Woolgar replied. "It's the company that makes an enjoyable meal, not the price on the menu."

I watched as the solicitor helped her on with her coat, and I saw his hands rest ever so briefly on her shoulders. *My, my, Mrs. Woolgar—there's more to you than meets the eye.*

Rennie had opened the door, but the secretary hesitated.

"Ms. Burke, one of your writers stopped in."

"Oh—was it Harry?" Perhaps Harry had found a break in her busy day at the flower shop.

"No, one of the women," the secretary replied, and I had opened my mouth to explain that Harry was one of the women, when she added, "The one who cut off her long braid."

"Amanda?" I mouthed her name but wasn't sure any sound came out.

"Yes, that's it, Amanda. I explained you were out and she asked could she wait, and so I put her in the kitchenette rather than your office. Duncan and I were in the middle of the charitable-trust business. After about ten minutes, she looked in and said never mind, she wouldn't wait, and she left."

At the sound of Amanda's name, I had stopped breathing, but had enough time by the end of Mrs. Woolgar's explanation to start up again.

"Oh, good. Gone. Yes." I put my hand on my chest and felt my heart thumping.

"Should I have asked her to wait longer?"

"No! It's only that—" Really, what was the point of making them stay back from a lunch date to explain how far the enquiry had come? I would fill her in later. In an offhand manner I said, "Listen, as I'll be on my own here, perhaps I'll just set the alarm. Couldn't hurt, could it? Just so you remember to turn it off when you return."

That gave Mrs. Woolgar pause, but I didn't want to spoil their date, so I sent them on their way with a "Have a lovely afternoon—don't hurry back."

I shut the door, set the alarm, and called the police.

30

A manda was here, Sergeant, and not long ago."
  I stood in the middle of the front hall, my voice bouncing off the hard surfaces.

"I'll send someone round, Ms. Burke," Hopgood said.

"No, she's gone now. Mrs. Woolgar said she was waiting for me, but then decided to leave. Do you think she knows I found the notebook? Do you think she knows I suspect her of the murder? Has she heard that you've got Lulu? Is Lulu talking?"

"Ms. Burke, first of all, keep yourself safe."

"Yes, I'm all right. The doors are locked, the alarm is on."

"We are out looking for Ms. Seabrook now."

"You will let me know, won't you—when you find her?"

"Will do."

With that promise, we ended the call. I remained standing, as if glued to the flagstones of the front hall, wondering what it would be like when the police caught up with Amanda. I shook myself out of that daydream, went to my office, picked up my sandwich, and carried it into the kitchenette to make a cup of tea. But it seemed a bleak place to eat alone, and so I left the world behind me and took my lunch upstairs to my flat.

After I ate, I intended to get to work on . . . what? Writing the newsletter? Mapping out the salons? Beginning to read a new book from my piles of used paperback mysteries? The thought exhausted me—I had no energy, not even for books.

Instead, I stretched out on the sofa, thinking I could get quite accustomed to an afternoon nap. I closed my eyes and awoke what seemed like a minute later, disoriented, as afternoon light streamed through the sitting room windows. Four o'clock. I propped myself up on my elbows. I needed a cup of tea. Then a single word floated through my foggy brain.

Diorama.

Yes, there's an activity I could handle while I waited to hear from the police—find Dinah's diorama in the attic, give her a ring to tell her of my success, and ask a few questions about this fellow she met for a pint.

The attic door was unlocked, just as I'd left it the day before when Val had arrived with our Waitrose feast. Should I ring him to confirm our dinner date tomorrow? Shouldn't he ring me?

I pushed in the door and switched on the single overhead light. A tortoiseshell form scampered past and I followed him in.

"I say, Bunter, you wouldn't want to have a look at the gnawed furniture in the far back, would you? And if you find the responsible party, could you take care of things? If you know what I mean." He paused to shake a paw, and I noticed his prints in the thick dust and the police footprints that had almost vanished. I saw my own prints from yesterday—and then I saw a fresh set.

The prints had an intricate waffle design, like the soles of trainers—

so different from my black ballet flats. Their path led to the cartons that I had stacked in the center of the room—and that now lay open, their contents strewn about.

Bewildered, I crept closer, trying to make sense of what I saw. Who had done this? Not Bunter after mice. Were my stacks so precarious that the cartons had tumbled over of their own accord? I peered into the corners of the room to assess further damage, but saw none. *I should leave*—beyond that thought, my mind had become numb. Yes, leave—discretion is the better part of valor, after all. More to the point—ring the police.

I heard a noise behind me, and spun round to find Amanda pressed into the corner of the room.

She wore her red slicker over a skintight running outfit, and her blond shingle hairdo had cobwebs caught in it. She had her hands behind her back.

"Where's my notebook?" she demanded.

"How did you get in here?" I shot back, my voice strong, but my knees weak.

"Where's my notebook?"

Be reasonable, I thought. Perhaps that would get the wild look out of her eyes.

"Mrs. Woolgar said you'd left."

"Where's my notebook?"

"It isn't your notebook!"

Her eyes widened, and she advanced on me. That's when I saw what was in her hand—Dinah's old cricket bat.

"It *is* mine," she said. "You know what they say about possession and the law."

"Well, you don't have it now, do you? It's Lady Fowling's notebook—it always was and always will be. And she would never have condoned what you've done." As I spoke, I backed away slowly, threading my way through the mess of cartons.

"Lady Fowling—*pfft!* When I found it, the notebook became mine, not hers. It was stuck inside a copy of *The Secret Adversary* on one of the Christie shelves in the library. Tommy and Tuppence!"

"You came back to the library after everyone had gone."

She arched an eyebrow at me. "So what if I did?"

"You were a guest of the Society, and you took advantage—rummaging through the books on the shelves, taking what you wanted."

"Don't you see—the notebook was a sign, it was my talisman. It meant I could stop writing those same ten bloody pages over and over again. Then it went missing." Her eyes became glassy as she remembered. "Trist had seen me with it. And he had found out I was coming back into the library after we'd all left the pub. He thought he was such a wit when he claimed it was Lady Fowling's ghost moving furniture around."

I stepped over a heap of Dinah's school uniforms and old cooking utensils as I backed up and said, "He followed you here that night, and you killed him."

Amanda, in slow pursuit, shook her head. "That was his fault."

She pointed the bat at me, and I noted a good two feet of clearance between me and the weapon. I took another step away as she continued.

"He shouldn't've threatened me with telling everyone. I only gave him a bit of a shove. And then, there he was, dead." She gazed down at the floor as if she could see Trist's body. "Well, I couldn't leave him there on Gravel Walk, could I? So, you see, I did him a favor."

"If it was an accident, you could've phoned 999—they would've believed you."

"Would they? No, easier to bring him into Middlebank—and such luscious irony. Who's the body in the library now? What would his precious vampire-fighting Jane Marple say about that?" She became thoughtful, and I took the chance to glance at my position—I had put more distance between us but found myself farther back into the attic than I should be.

"Did you take his leather case?"

"I thought he had my notebook," Amanda replied defensively. "But all the time, it was you who had taken it."

She turned her attention and looked at me with fresh interest. I saw her hand grip the bat tighter.

"Did Lulu give you the security code and a copy of the key?" I asked.

Amanda laughed. "Greed makes a person easy to manipulate. I enticed her with the treasures of Middlebank—even though I knew there were none to her liking here. She was easily led. They all are—don't you see? It was nothing for me to take over the group after Trist. And I'm a much better leader—I'm sure they'd all agree."

"But you were blackmailing Lulu."

"Yes, poor sausage." Amanda laughed. "That worried her. I told her I'd collected drinking glasses in our flat that she'd touched and I'd hidden them away. I told her she'd be charged with murder if I transferred her dabs from those and put them all over Trist's leather case and then planted it somewhere. Out in the back garden here, probably—you really should trim that honeysuckle."

"All this for a notebook?"

"Does that seem trivial to you? Because . . . it isn't." She tapped the bat on her toe. "When I lost it, I lost my ability to write. I had been on the verge of a breakthrough—I could feel it. But then it was gone, and only wrong words came out. I thought Trist had taken it, but it was you—you stole it."

"I don't see how Lady Fowling's grocery lists and favorite Poirot books could make a difference in your writing. They are hers, not yours."

"Mine!" Amanda shrieked. "It was my connection to Christie and

to Tommy and Tuppence." A gleam appeared in her eyes. "But all right, perhaps the power is not in the exercise book itself, but in its first owner. So, if I can't have that notebook, give me another."

She actually held out a hand, as if I could pull an exercise book from thin air.

"No, Amanda, you cannot have another notebook. They don't belong to you."

She tilted her head, like a dog. Then the cricket bat came crashing down, obliterating a carton and sending a small wooden box flying through the air. It crashed into the wall, and my collection of matchbooks scattered across the floor. The cricket bat came down again, closer to me this time, and I leapt away, but it struck only the bedding carton and crushed only cardboard.

"Amanda, don't do this."

"Or what?"

"The police know everything."

Her laugh was full of derision. "They know nothing. You think I don't recognize that old trick?"

But the police did know everything. Apart from where Amanda was at this moment—and that was a problem. She stood between me and the door and had a large weapon. I, on the other hand, had nothing, unless I could pick up a heavy oak side chair and hurl it at her. If she was trying to frighten me, she was doing a good job. Was this to be my fate—beaten to death by an unhinged cricket-bat wielder in the attic?

"All right," I said, swallowing the fear that rose in my throat. "I suppose I could get you another of those exercise books. They're downstairs in my office." They were in my flat, but I certainly wouldn't let her follow me there.

"That's a lie. They aren't in your office—I looked. You really have terrible security here at Middlebank," she chided me, "and after Trist turned up dead in your library. When I told your secretary

I was leaving, she never even walked me out. She had no idea that all I did was open and close the front door, and then sneak up here. Last evening you told the group the notebooks had been in storage—but they aren't here either." She wiggled the bat at me with menace. "Where are they?"

I shuffled farther back and bumped into a table with no top that sat against the wall. Amanda drew the bat high into the air again and this time took aim at the carton marked BABY. In my mind I heard the strains of "Edelweiss" and saw the figurine and Dinah's eyes.

"Stop that this instant!" I screamed, and the sheer volume of my voice caused Amanda to freeze. I took my chance and made a break for it—circling round her and running an agility race as I hopped among the paraphernalia of my life. I had just reached the door when she recovered and I felt a whoosh as the cricket bat missed my head. I ducked, lost my balance, and hurtled forward through the door and across the landing toward the stairs. A strong hand grabbed my shoulder and held me back just long enough so that I slowed, fell to my knees, and wrapped my arms round the newel. But forward momentum caused me to swing out over the top step, and I caught a glimpse of where I had almost gone—down the steep attic stairs. I looked behind me. There was no one—except Amanda, cricket bat held high over her head, charging out of the attic, onto the landing, and straight at me.

Then a horn blared so loudly I thought it was going off against my ear. Only after my heart jumped into my throat did I recognize it as our alarm system. Had someone broken in? The noise caused Amanda to flinch mid-attack, and then, out of nowhere, a tiny gray form skittered across her path, followed close on by a tortoiseshell streak. She tripped, lurched forward, and—letting loose of her weapon—fell flat on her face next to me. The bat clattered down the stairs.

31

I screamed. *"Help! Upstairs! The attic!"* But the continued blast of the alarm swallowed my voice. I thought I heard shouts but couldn't make out the words.

Amanda stirred. I tried to stand, but my rush of adrenaline had dissipated and my legs wouldn't hold me. When I felt the vibration of feet, I stopped trying, and watched a swarm of uniformed officers beat their way up the stairs.

Most went directly to Amanda, but a female PC leaned over me. "You all right, love?" she shouted over the blast of the horn.

The alarm stopped, and the silence was deafening.

My ears were ringing, but I managed to say, "I'm not hurt."

I put my head against the rails and saw, at the bottom of the attic stairs, Sergeant Hopgood with the cricket bat at his feet. His eyebrows shot up when he saw me, and I managed a tiny wave as officers escorted a suddenly docile Amanda down to meet him. She stood, dazed and deflated, as the DS advised her of her rights, after which, two uniforms took her away. When the stairs cleared, I stood, and keeping a firm grip on the railing, made my way down to the next landing.

"Ms. Burke," Sergeant Hopgood said, "do you need medical attention?"

I shook my head. "I only need to sit down—and perhaps have a cup of tea." The door to my flat stood open. "Would you like to come through?"

Middlebank was, once again, awash in police—in uniform, in plain clothes, in those blue paper coveralls—they flowed in and out of my flat and up and down the stairs. I comforted myself with the thought that at least the medical examiner wasn't needed this time.

"Shall I put the kettle on?" I asked the sergeant.

"No, let me," the female PC said. "You have a sit-down."

"No, let me," Adele said as she came over to give me a hug and then a firm look. "You all right?"

I nodded. "How did you—"

"Val rang me. Glynis rang me. The police rang me. 'Where's Hayley?' You could star in your own picture books. Now sit."

I sat, the thought of Val bringing a smile to my lips. Then I remembered my circumstances. "How did you all get in?"

"Mrs. Woolgar arrived just after we broke the lock on the door," Hopgood said. "She was able to switch off the alarm, but I'm sorry to say you'll need the locksmith out again. She may have already given him a ring. If you'll excuse me for a moment, Ms. Burke, I need to have a word with my team before they search the attic."

"Yes, fine—wait! Sergeant, when they search, would you ask them to have a look round for a shoe box that has a diorama of a home inside—you know, a miniature model."

"Does this have to do with the enquiry?" he asked, eyebrows raised, but in a mild fashion.

"No, my daughter made it."

That seemed a good enough explanation for the detective sergeant. He nodded and stepped over to three waiting uniforms.

Adele made tea and set the kettle to boil again in anticipation of a second pot. She opened the biscuit tin, and before anyone else, brought me a mug and two chocolate digestives, and then began offering to the others. Her phone rang, and as she pulled it out of her pocket, she shook it at me. "Look," she said. "Phone. Pocket. A good combination."

"Yes, miss," I replied.

She grinned as she answered her call, but the grin disappeared in short order.

"Lenore!" she exclaimed. "How lovely to hear your voice!" Adele threw me a panicked look.

My mum? This didn't bode well.

"No, she's fine—"

I waved my arms wildly and shook my head, mouthing, *Don't tell her!*

"She hasn't had her phone with her all afternoon," Adele said smoothly. "I know, I told her the same thing. But I just happened to have stopped into Middlebank for a cup of tea, so let me hand you off to her."

Adele held her phone out to me at the same moment Kenny Pye stuck his head in the door and called out, "Sarge, she put up a fierce struggle when we got her downstairs and it took some doing to get her handcuffed and settled down."

I grabbed the phone and went off to the corner.

"Hi, Mum."

"I hope he wasn't talking about you," she replied.

I could play it no other way but straight with my mum, although I did stick with the highlights and not a blow-by-blow account. I wrapped up with, "So, you see, more of a kerfuffle than anything. And she's caught—that's the best part."

"The best part is that you are all right. You are, aren't you?"

"I am."

"And I'll see you on Saturday?"

"Of course you will."

"Good. I'll expect a full accounting."

We ended our call, and I sank onto the sofa and watched Adele make another pot of tea. That accomplished, she said, "Thought I'd look in on Glynis. I'll be back up."

Detective Sergeant Hopgood brought his tea over and sat beside me, and I recounted my day, and then turned the tables. "What about Lulu?"

"Lulu Ingleby," he said with a sigh. "She was with a gang down in Yeovil—they had a good racket, but she broke off, deciding she was the brains of the outfit and would make a go of it on her own. And so she moved here to Bath with great plans. She watched several streets until she narrowed her choice down to three houses—in areas that were mostly vacant during the day and where the cleaners came and went on their own. These homeowners were not Ms. Lunn's clients. Lulu would become friendly with the cleaner—and then would find a way to lift the key to make a copy, and take the code if necessary. After that, well, Bob's your uncle."

"Pauline caught Lulu with her hand in the safe at the Minerva," I said. "Pauline thought she had been after cash, but it was the key and code for Middlebank she wanted."

Hopgood nodded. "When she'd first arrived and was learning the city, she found a 'Flatmate Wanted' notice at the college, and that's how she met Ms. Seabrook. Latched on to Leonard Lunn after meeting him in the pub, and he got her on with Ms. Lunn's cleaning business. Ms. Seabrook got wind of what Lulu Ingleby really did for a living, and she fed her with tales of the treasures of Middlebank."

"Amanda talked her into lifting the key and code from Pauline. We must've been a great disappointment for Lulu," I said.

"She was spitting mad when she learned there was nothing here that suited her. 'Books?' she asked me. 'What good are a load of books?' And so, Amanda Seabrook kept Middlebank for herself."

"Lulu told you all this?"

"To avoid a charge of murder, yes."

"Amanda was blackmailing her," I said. "But, Sergeant, what about Pauline? Because Adele and I can't imagine that—"

"Is Ms. Babbage acquainted with Ms. Lunn?"

"Not as well as she'd like to be," I said. Hopgood's mustache twitched. "Are you charging her with something?"

"I don't do the charging, Ms. Burke—I gather evidence, question suspects, make a case—but at that point, I hand it over to my boss, and she's the one who decides the charges."

"You know, don't you, that Pauline had nothing to do with the break-in. Lulu took advantage of her."

Hopgood gave a single nod. "I can only say that this afternoon, Ms. Lunn's brother turned himself in to the station. He says he was not involved in the theft ring, but he admitted being aware of it, and would be happy to tell us everything. He swore his sister knew nothing. If he's believed, she might not face any charges."

"Leonard comes through," I murmured. "Good on him."

A commotion below—in the entry or on the library landing—put a sudden stop to activity in my flat. Kenny Pye stepped out, asked a question, and then said, "He's all right, let him up."

I heard footsteps on the stairs and Val came bursting in, holding on to the doorposts as if he had broken through enemy lines.

I leapt up, my head swam, and I plopped down, but like a jack-in-the-box, rebounded in time for Val to throw his arms round me.

We held each other so tightly I had trouble taking a breath, but I didn't care. There was no nuance to our embrace, no caressing, no whispered sweet nothings—only relief and joy. And I believe he felt the same. If only all these people would go away, this would be a perfect moment. But is there such a thing?

"Well, Mr. Moffatt," Sergeant Hopgood said cheerfully, "second time's the charm, wouldn't you say? Last week, when you called in Ms. Burke missing, she was safe in the cellar, but this time when you phoned us, she was indeed in danger."

"No danger," I said to Val, his face stricken. I was at once aware of our surroundings and turned shy. I dropped my hands from his shoulders, and he let my waist go, but not without a squeeze first.

"DC Pye rang to tell me it was over," he said. "I was all right until I rounded the corner and saw the ambulance parked outside."

"Ambulance?"

"Ms. Seabrook complained about her ribs," DC Pye said. "Thought she might've cracked one in that fall."

"I'll crack a rib for her," Val muttered, and I giggled. Entirely inappropriate to the occasion, I knew, but there you are.

"I wasn't in danger," I said. "I had Bunter to protect me."

"You were fair hurtling toward the attic stairs," Hopgood said. "I thought you'd end up at the bottom before we could get to you." His phone rang, and he stepped away.

I had been kept from tumbling down headfirst by that hand on my shoulder. I could feel it still—a strong grasp, but a delicate hand.

"I caught the newel just in time," I explained to Val.

He looked unconvinced—perhaps I'd explain another time.

"You can't possibly stay here now," he said.

"I can—Amanda's been taken off in handcuffs. Middlebank and

the Society are out of danger." I smiled. "And you really did save me this time, phoning the police."

"I had a good look at all those photos before I took my phone to the station. I saw Amanda and Lulu talking. I had to return to college for afternoon classes, but that's when I began ringing you. Calls, texts—no response. I didn't care if I looked the fool. I couldn't stand it any longer and let the police know. As soon as I finished my afternoon class, I rang Kenny—that is, DC Pye."

"Yes, it's Thursday—you have classes all day." My mind had already conjured up a vision of the evening ahead, but other forces were taking over. "You have another one starting soon."

Detective Constable Kenny Pye, close by, cut his dark eyes at us and then at his sergeant, who was engrossed in his notebook.

"Yes," Val said, "I have a class."

Adele reappeared at the front door, catching the last bit, and said to me, "You're booked this evening, regardless. We're having a girls' night in—Glynis is coming up."

"She is?" I was gobsmacked—Mrs. Woolgar had never set foot in my flat.

"Mr. Moffatt," Hopgood said, "about your statement."

Val stepped away for a brief exchange, and then returned to say, "That's me away."

"But," I said, "I'll see you tomorrow. Evening."

He didn't reply but narrowed his eyes as he studied me. Then, another swarm of police came in, and with a wave, he was gone.

"Well," I complained to Adele, "are we going out to dinner or aren't we?"

"I suppose you'd better ring him tomorrow and confirm."

"I don't see why—he's the one who asked me. And he was acting quite strange just then."

"Bloody hell," Adele said, laughing, "would you listen to yourself?" She gave me a soft nudge. "Come on, now—be an adult."

I was flushed and exhausted and at the edge of having my feelings hurt. "I tell you, sometimes I'm sick to death of being an adult."

"Pye," Hopgood snapped. "You're finished for the day. There'll be plenty more to do tomorrow. On your way."

"Right, boss. Thanks."

Hopgood nodded toward the departing figure of Kenny Pye. "He thinks I don't know he's a writer and that he's taking a course from Mr. Moffatt. What sort of a detective does he think I am?"

The police departed, but not before Sergeant Hopgood stopped in to deliver the diorama. It was a tad on the shabby side—one corner of the shoe box was slightly bent, and Dougal, the cottonball cat, had grown wizened. But at least it hadn't been creamed by a murderer wielding a cricket bat. I set it in pride of place on the coffee table, and Adele brought a subdued Mrs. Woolgar up to my flat. I gestured to the sofa, where she alit on the edge.

"We're all right now, aren't we?" I asked the secretary as Adele opened a bottle of wine. "The Society is, too."

Mrs. Woolgar's face—a knot of worry—eased slightly and she offered the smallest of smiles.

I rang Harry to give her the news of Amanda. I could tell she wanted to know every detail, but the wedding-flower order had yet to be finished. Next week, I promised her. Before we rang off, she said, "We cracked it, didn't we, Hayley?"

I thought of Pauline, and—giving Adele a quick glance—replied, "I'm sure there's still a great deal to be sorted."

Bunter emerged from his secure and secret location to join us. Settling near the front window, he watched the starlings gathering on the rooftop across the road as if nothing unusual had happened that afternoon and he hadn't just saved my life. *There's an extra catnip mouse in it for you, cat.*

Not even a glass of wine could make Mrs. Woolgar comfortable. The pizza arrived, and Adele and I wasted no time. I'd eaten two slices and was eyeing a third while the secretary remained perched on the sofa as if in a doctor's waiting room. She was still in her pumpkin-colored frock with rhinestone brooch, and I wondered if she stayed dressed up when she was alone in her flat. Now, there's a mystery to be solved.

"Are you sure you don't want a slice of pizza?" Adele asked her.

"No," she murmured, "thank you. I had quite a large lunch."

With her pencil-thin physique, I wondered what constituted "large." But I didn't believe she meant to be standoffish, it's only that she was in shock. At last, it came tumbling out.

"It's all my fault, Ms. Burke." She shook her head and frowned. "I let that woman in and left her unattended. I did not see her out as I should've. My attention was elsewhere—Mr. Rennie and I were going over the details of the charitable trust."

Over Mrs. Woolgar's bowed head, I caught Adele's eye and wiggled my eyebrows. Her reaction told me she'd had no idea something was . . . might be . . . going on between the secretary and the solicitor, and I was chuffed about my bit of in-house sleuthing.

But I would never want Mrs. Woolgar to feel guilty about being distracted by the attentions of Duncan Rennie—didn't we all deserve someone's attentions?—and so was severe in my disagreement.

"Not a bit of it," I said. "It isn't your fault at all. I should've told you about my suspicions yesterday. If you had had any inkling, you never would've let her over the threshold."

"I appreciate your allowance," Mrs. Woolgar replied.

"Would you like another glass of wine, Glynis?" Adele held the bottle out.

Mrs. Woolgar looked down into her empty glass. "Well, perhaps just a small one."

"Of course, we'll need to double our security efforts for the exhibition," I said casually. "The best of the collection out of the bank and here at Middlebank for all the world to see."

Mrs. Woolgar's head shot up and she gave me a sharp look. "I don't see how we could ever put rare books on display now. Why, Lady Fowling would never—"

I pressed my lips together to keep from smiling. There now, that's the secretary *in perpetuum* I knew best.

"Georgiana would be delighted with the exhibition," Adele said. "She'd probably want to throw a fancy dress ball the night before it opened. Everyone could dress as a character from one of the books—or maybe just in thirties clothes."

That wouldn't be difficult for Mrs. Woolgar, but what would I wear? My thoughts drifted to Lady Fowling's portrait on the stairs—and that dress.

"I tell you what," I said, shaking my head to clear away such thoughts. "There are several things I would've done differently during this enquiry. Asked more questions, avoided jumping to conclusions, taken a closer look at each person involved."

"You can't anticipate every possible outcome," Adele said to both of us, and then leaned over to me and added, "You'll do better next time."

"Next time?"

On Friday morning, I awoke at a proper time, even after half a bottle of wine, but was disinclined to dress in wool trousers and jacket—my curator clothes. Instead, I pulled on denims and a sweater and trainers and left my hair down. The evening before, I'd told Mrs. Woolgar that I would compare our catalog with the books on the shelves to make sure nothing was missing. She had tried to dissuade me—"let me take care of that"—but I felt the need to prove my worth, and a mundane task that would tax neither my brain nor my heart seemed appropriate.

I had wandered to the ground floor after a cup of tea and a slice of toast to search for the printed catalog in my office when the front door buzzed. I leapt up from my desk, my heartbeat setting a rapid rhythm as it drummed in my breast.

"I'll go," I said to Mrs. Woolgar as I passed her office. I threw the extra bolt lock off, but hesitated for a moment, my hand hovering over the latch.

Val stood on the doorstep, hands buried in the pockets of his duffel coat and a gray sky behind him.

"Hello," I offered.

"Good morning." His face gave nothing away, but I saw a sparkle in his eye. "I came to tell you that I've decided against dinner."

"Have you?" I asked in a pitiful, small voice.

"I'm taking you for a day out instead."

"Out?" I put my hands on my hips. "Out? I'll have you know I have a job—I am curator of The First Edition Society, and as such, I have a full day of work ahead of me." He took note of my outfit, down to the trainers and back up again. I crossed my arms. "And just where had you thought to take me if, in fact, I agreed to go?"

"Lyme Regis."

I dropped my arms. "The seaside?" I whispered, and bit my lip to hide a smile. "Why, it's almost the end of October—it'll be cold and windy at the seaside." And yet I could hear its siren song.

"I've blankets and waterproofs and wellies," Val replied. "I've a hamper filled with sandwiches and cakes from Waitrose."

He waited and watched.

"They have fossils at Lyme Regis," I said.

"So I'm told." His straight face wouldn't hold, and I saw the corners of his eyes crinkle. "And ice cream. What do you say?"

I took two steps out, meeting him nose to nose. I ran my finger down his smooth jawline and cupped his face in my hand.

Our lips brushed and caught and held for a moment. His hands slipped round my waist, and he pulled me closer. I turned my head away and called through Middlebank's open door.

"Mrs. Woolgar, I'm going out for the day."

KEEP READING FOR AN EXCERPT
FROM MARTY WINGATE'S NEXT
FIRST EDITION LIBRARY MYSTERY!

ona Atherton?" I breathed and glanced over to check the entry to the Assembly Rooms just as Dom had. "She's here?"

He nodded, his head bobbing up and down. "And so I'd better not stay, because . . . you know."

How well I did. Anyone with any sense would know to steer clear of Oona Atherton. But although Dom said goodbye and left, I didn't move.

I had erased Oona from my mind, but now all those memories came flooding back, and I saw myself once again her personal assistant and general dogsbody during the exhibition she'd mounted for the Jane Austen Centre five years ago. Held at the Charlotte, of course. She was brash and arrogant and had run roughshod over everyone—the word "demanding" didn't come close to describing her. I had ended many a day in tears—days that didn't end until nearly midnight.

The trouble was she worked miracles, mounting the most spectacular exhibitions. And, to be fair, she never asked more of the people under her than she was willing to give herself. If we were there adjusting lights and reconfiguring freestanding enclosed Perspex boxes of letters, lace sleeves, and quill pens, then Oona was there, too. That's what made it so hard to hate her—she stuck in and never let up on herself or anyone else.

Oona worked freelance, but her name had never occurred to me as I started planning our own exhibition—that's how completely I'd obliterated the memory of her.

But I had come a long way in five years. I had risen in my profession and built up confidence in my own abilities. *I* ran the First Edition Library and *I* would be in charge of the exhibition—the manager would work for me, not I her. And, after all, if it was a choice between pig's blood and Oona—well, better the devil you knew.

Keeping that thoght, I found myself making my way inexorably into the Assembly Rooms and then to the café where the doors stood open.

I did not go in, but instead ducked down behind the chest-high stand that displayed the menu, and, unobserved, peered over it into the room. The café—a wide open space—had a smattering of people at the tables, but I could've spotted Oona in the middle of a heaving crowd. I saw her now, sitting near the windows looking at her phone. She hadn't changed one whit—her thick brown hair scraped back into a low bun and wearing a tailored navy business suit and low heels. To those who did not know her, she may not look the tyrant, but even the sight of her made me break out in a cold sweat. And yet . . .

Throwing my shoulders back, I stepped into the room, and, as if she sensed a change in the energy field, Oona looked up and her face broke out in a wide smile.

"Hayley Burke," she called as she stood. "How the hell are you?"

Her voice echoed in the room and heads turned, but Oona took no notice. I scurried over.

"Oona, what a surprise," I replied in a low voice. We performed one of those awkward half-hug, air-kiss routines.

"Do you have a few minutes?" she asked. "Let's catch up. What can I get you—coffee? Tea?"

"Oh, no, let me. What would you like?"

I hardly had to ask—her usual order was tattooed on my brain.

At the counter, I said, "One Earl Grey, please—but not in a bag. If you don't have it loose, would you please tear the bag open and empty it into the pot? Make that two bags. With a slice of lemon, but only if you cut it fresh. And raw sugar. Do you have raw sugar? If not, Demerara will have to do. Also, one normal tea."

The woman behind the counter gave me a look that was oh so familiar.

The tray of tea things rattled as I carried them over, but Oona didn't seem to notice. That's an odd thing about her: she could spot a plate one-eighth of an inch out of alignment in a display of the Austen family's Wedgwood dinner set, but be oblivious to the feelings of people round her.

"Curator at the First Edition Society," Oona said as we sorted out cups, saucers, and teapots.

"Oh, how did you know—"

She nodded to her phone. "Looked you up this minute. I see you're starting off well—a series of literary salons. I always knew you had it in you to build a top-notch organization out of a well-meaning gesture."

"The Society is entirely Lady Fowling's creation," I said, "and it's only since she died that things have . . . slowed down."

"Regardless," Oona said, pouring her tea through a strainer, "you were obviously the right woman for the position."

"Well." I blushed. "And not only do we have the literary salons, but—" *Don't say it, Hayley. Yes, go on, tell her. No, don't.* "—we are now planning an exhibition."

I gulped my tea, the liquid searing my throat. Slowly, Oona took a spoonful of Demerara—no raw sugar available—tilted it over her cup, and watched the crystals sift into her Earl Grey like light brown snow.

"Is this exhibition about detective fiction—Christie, Sayers, Tey, Allingham, Marsh?" she asked.

"It's called *Lady Fowling: A Life in Words.* She was an amazing woman, Oona, and left behind a world-class collection of first editions from those authors and more."

"The exhibition is next year?"

"No, April."

"April?"

I could hear the scorn in her voice, but in for a penny, in for a pound.

"Yes, April. The Charlotte just became available, and I've booked it. I see no need to wait."

Oona took her time, lifting her cup and letting the steam drift round the contours of her face before she took a sip.

"You must have a crackerjack manager to be able to take the paraphernalia of Lady Fowling's life and showcase it for all of Bath—for all of Britain and the world—to see in such a short time."

I squirmed. "Yes, it is a short time, but I am confident it can be done. We're speaking with a local person for manager."

"So, you've filled the post?"

"We haven't quite reached an agreement yet." The silence at the table screamed in my ears, and to put myself out of my misery, I added, "So, how long have you been in Bath, Oona?"

"A few days—a week."

"On a job?"

"Holiday," she said. The fact that Oona continued to dress for work while on holiday did not surprise me at all. "I'm waiting for the tap on the shoulder from the British Library," she continued. "They have a position opening up this summer—it's only a matter of time before I hear."

Enough of this cat-and-mouse game—it was too stressful not knowing which role I played.

"As we haven't actually hired this local fellow, if you are at all interested, I'm sure the board would listen to your ideas on our exhibition. That is, if you didn't mind interrupting your holiday."

Only a twitch in her firmly-set mouth betrayed her nonchalance. "I suppose I could—that is, if you wanted to set something up."

"As it happens, we have a meeting this afternoon at four. If you arrive at half-past, they'll be ready for you."

"Done."